PERMANENT DEATH

Glenna Heckler-Todt

ISBN: 979-8-9987275-0-4

Cover design by: Jennah Bryant jennahbryant.com
Author photo by: Toni Dengel tdgraphicarts.com

For permissions, contact: glenna@glennahecklertodt.com Visit glennahecklertodt.com

Library of Congress Control Number: 2018675309
Printed in the United States of America

For Matthew, my Paul Child, without whom none of this could be possible—Ti Amo

For Madeleine, Katy, and Trinity, it's never too late to achieve your dreams

". . . I will bring out into the open things hidden since the world's first day."

—MATTHEW 13:35

"In the midst of chaos, there is also opportunity."

—SUN TZU

NOTE TO READERS

Dear Reader,

Being an independent author is difficult. Since *Permanent Death* is my first novel, there were aspects that were less than perfect which I wanted to correct. (That's not to say that this version is perfect either.) Therefore, this is an updated version from the original which was published May 6, 2025. The plot has not changed at all. This is not a new edition of the book. Rather, it is an update which corrects errors in consistency, grammar, and punctuation.

Thanks for reading!
Glenna Heckler-Todt
January 11, 2026

PERMANENT DEATH

CHAPTER 1

Emmy Sue

By all accounts it had been a spectacular dive. She would have received top scores had she been diving into a pool and not onto the concrete from the top of a Ferris wheel 100 feet in the air. I didn't see the finale of blood and bone as she splashed onto the street. I had turned my head and covered my eyes at the last second. In hindsight, I should have covered my ears as well. Nothing will ever erase from my mind the horrible splat of her body hitting the sidewalk mixed with the screams of horror from the crowd.

"I heard she was drunk."

"High as a kite is what I heard."

"You'd have to be one or the other to do a swan dive off a Ferris wheel in the middle of Spring Fling," said a third girl.

"Splat she went! Her brains were all over the street!" said a guy sitting nearby.

I felt sick. Obviously, none of them had been there, or they would not have been talking about Lori Landers's horrible death so cavalierly. It was more of the same that had been said all day. A senior girl, Lori Landers, had jumped off the top of the Ferris wheel last night during the opening evening of the town's annual spring carnival, The Spring Fling. All anyone seemed to care about was that the carnival was closed indefinitely and probably would not continue this year. To show my boredom and disinterest in their rumormongering, I turned my head and looked out the window, drowning out their whispers along with the droning voice of my English teacher, Mrs. Bitterroot.

I watched as a red-tailed hawk dipped its wings and swooped across the football field. It hovered, spying something my eyes couldn't see from my seat in the classroom. It stretched its wings, letting the mid-March wind flow over them as it soared above the field looking for its next meal. Then, as quickly as it had appeared, the hawk banked left and flew over the trees, far away from Middletown High School. I sighed, envying the hawk's freedom to fly away to whatever destination it chose.

"Miss Beckett, could you please share with the rest of class what is so important out on the football field that you can't turn your attention to our discussion of the requirements for a term paper which will account for fifty percent of your grade? Is Mr. Graham out there flexing his muscles or something?"

At the mention of the star quarterback's name, I became aware that Mrs. Bitterroot was talking to me. Everyone stopped whispering about the dead girl and began whispering about me. No one was paying attention to Bitterroot, yet she chose to call me out for looking out the window. Mrs. Bitterroot took pleasure in embarrassing me in front of my classmates, all college-track students; most of whom were popular and excelled in calculus and physics. I wrote short stories and worked on the yearbook. I had no interest in any of the football players and had no wish to be one of the popular, beautiful people everyone held in such esteem. So it infuriated me that Bitterroot would insinuate that *I* would be distracted by some jerk like Brent Graham.

"Well, I'm waiting," she said, pursing her lips, which were permanently puckered from years of cigarette smoking. "What's so important out there that you can't listen to what I am saying in here?"

How typical of her to assume that anything she had to say was important to me.

"If you really must know," I huffed, "a hawk."

"A hawk. Really? And why is a hawk so important?"

All eyes were on me. Did I dare tell the truth? What did I have to lose? Most people thought I was weird anyway. I took a deep breath and said, "He's free. Unlike me, he's free to fly away from this circle of hell to a place where no one knows him. To a place where he can do what he wants and no one will judge him. That's what I'm going to do. After graduation, I'm going far away from here and never coming back."

When I finished, no one spoke; they all stared at me. A few seconds later the final bell of the day rang, making everyone jump in their seats as if in delayed reaction to my honesty. I quickly gathered my books and hurried out of the classroom before Bitterroot had the chance to send me to the principal's office for giving a straight answer to her stupid question.

I walked as quickly as I could until I was in the girls' bathroom two floors away from Bitterroot's classroom. I put down my overstuffed book bag and pulled a Calvin Klein sweater and a lavender button-down Oxford out of it. Then I stripped off the black t-shirt I was wearing and put on the trendy designer clothes I had taken out of my bag. It was unseasonably warm for mid-March, and I didn't want to put the sweater on, but my Oxford was wrinkled from being balled up in my book bag all day. It was better to put the sweater on and sweat all the way home than to walk the streets in a wrinkled shirt. I re-tucked my Gloria Vanderbilt jeans into my black, high heeled boots, the one thing my mom and I had been able to agree on when back-to-school shopping last fall.

At five-eleven and one hundred and thirty pounds my jeans were too short and barely stayed up over my hips. I cinched my black studded belt tighter and pulled my sweater down to cover it. The belt matched the t-shirt I'd taken off and didn't fit the preppie image that the sweater and Oxford represented —the image that my mother had chosen for me. Pulling my long, red hair back into a ponytail, I heard my mother's voice in my head, "Emmy Sue, pull your hair back, so everyone can see your pretty face. And smile! You never smile! People will think you're unhappy." After I felt that my appearance would be satisfactory to the outside world, I exchanged books in my locker and headed out of the school, walking toward home.

My 1980 Pontiac Firebird was currently sitting behind my dad's garage waiting for him to get time to fix it. If I didn't put it in neutral at stoplights, it died and was hard to start back up. My dad was afraid it needed a new timing chain, which would probably mean that I'd permanently be out of a car. I held out little hope that I'd get my beloved car back before summer since my dad was fairly busy fixing other people's cars.

After the oil refinery closed, putting over half the town out of work, my dad began repairing cars out of our garage at home. Then one of our neighbors complained to the zoning board. My parents had a choice: my dad could look for work elsewhere and send me to college, but risk losing our house, or he could use my college money and open his own garage. They had tried to make me see their point-of-view, but my parents didn't understand that college was my only way out of this dead-end town. They told me that I could go to community college and then transfer to a four year university. Yet, the thought of waiting two or three more years to get away was an impossible idea for me to consider. I felt trapped and claustrophobic, like I was at the bottom of a well. The opening of the well was within my grasp. I only had a few more months of living in Middletown before I could go to college and be on my own. I could handle a few more months but a few more years? The thought of it drained all my strength and made me want to go to bed and never get up again. Thinking of staying in this town almost made what Lori Landers had done understandable. An impulse I might entertain if I was forced to stay here for the rest of my life. I scanned the sky for the hawk, but only saw a sparrow flitting between the trees.

I dug my sunglasses out of my book bag. It was a long walk home, but today there was no rush to be anywhere. I had the day off from my job at Middletown Public Library. I worked at MPL as many hours as I could because I was still determined to go away to Eastern Illinois University in the fall. I'd been granted a small amount of financial aid, and now I needed to make up the difference in tuition and pay for room and board. Last month my mom had taken me to visit the campus, and the head of the Journalism Department had promised me a work-study job in his office. I had already declared my double major as Journalism and Political Science. My dream was to write for *The Washington Post*. At night before I fell asleep, I'd think about Gloria Steinem and how she'd gone undercover as a Playboy Bunny or Nelly Bly and how she risked everything to become a patient in a mental hospital to expose the abuse mental patients suffered. Then I'd fantasize about the corruption and abuse I'd expose as a journalist.

As I turned onto State Street, I looked at my reflection in the window of Mankowitz's Clothier. I squared my shoulders and straightened my spine. From inside the store, Mr. Mankowitz waved at me. He lived down the street from us, and it had always amazed me that he drove his family two hours away every week to synagogue in Terre Haute, Indiana. I couldn't understand wasting every perfectly good Saturday on religion. I wasn't even sure God existed. Otherwise, why would He let the oil company put all these people out of work? I felt bad for Mr. Mankowitz. As if his life in Middletown wasn't hard enough being the only Jewish person in town, now he was probably going to lose his store. A discount department store had been built east of town, creating competition that Mr. Mankowitz couldn't keep up with. Why would anyone buy jeans from him when they could buy jeans for half the price at the big discount department store? At least that's what my mom had said to our next door neighbor, Mrs. Brown.

After the oil refinery closed, the town had no new revenue. Hundreds of people in a town of seven thousand were out of work, and their unemployment benefits were running out. The only other industries around were farming or working at Midwestern Mutual Insurance Company; neither of which were options to the people who had worked at the refinery. Farming requires a lot of start-up money and most of the farms had been owned by the same families for generations. The majority of the insurance company employees had college degrees of some kind while most of the refinery employees didn't. To create jobs and revenue, the town council voted to let a large, national discount store build a super center. But the plan backfired. Instead of revitalizing the economy, it was sucking it dry. The town square, which once had been bustling with activity, was now dotted with "closed" and "for lease" signs. Even an eighteen-year-old kid like me could figure the logic. You've got a town full of people who are out of work and on unemployment or welfare. You build a discount store. Where do you think the people are going to shop? At the small mom-and-pop store that sells the same thing for twice the price or at the cut rate place? I waved back at poor Mr. Mankowitz, standing alone at the cash register, and wondered how many more times I'd get the chance to see him in his store.

I walked past the newspaper office where my mom had tried to convince me to get a job. "Since that's what you want to do when you grow up," she'd said. But our hometown paper was more of a gossip rag than a real paper. Most of the paper was announcements of people bragging about their accomplishments or their kids' accomplishments, obituaries, and arrests.

I was thirsty, so I walked over to the closest thing Middletown had to a strip mall. Kreger's Grocery Store had been the original building on the site, and over the years, a sub shop, a dry cleaners, and a tanning salon had been built on, one at a time, giving the conglomeration of aluminum sided structures the appearance of Lego buildings that had been snapped together. Inside Kreger's, I picked up a bottle of Coke and a Reese's Cup and took them to the checkout counter.

"Hey there, Emmy Sue. How ya doin'?" the cashier asked, tilting her head in a sympathetic way. She was implying something, but I didn't know what.

"I'm fine, Judy."

"I heard," she said, lowering her voice to a whisper, "about the break up." Judy Walker was the sister of a friend of my mom's best friend.

I mimicked the angle of her head and smiled, "I guess the whole town knows then since you know." Walking away, I held my head high and my shoulders square, but inside there was only fury. Three weeks ago, I had painfully ended the year long relationship with a college guy when I found out that he had been cheating on me with a girl he'd sworn to me was "just a friend." It had only been a few days ago that I'd stopped constantly thinking about how he'd humiliated me and shredded my heart. Now, this imbecilic gossip had brought all those feelings back. I looked down at my boots, hoping I wouldn't cry.

When I raised my head again, I saw Nelson Kreger, Jr. walking toward me. His father owned the grocery store and three more like it in the surrounding towns. I made an abrupt turn and headed across the parking lot, but not before he flashed me a sly smile and gave me a wink. Nelson was a twenty-five year old lech. He was the kind of guy who would rape a girl and then say she liked it rough. At twenty-five, he was still dating high-school girls. His current squeeze was Maria Matthews, the Homecoming Queen and captain of the cheerleading squad. In any other community, their relationship would be at the least considered unhealthy and at the most illegal. In Middletown it was seen as a good match. My best friend Annie had told me that she'd seen Maria and her mom out shopping at Cheryl's Bridal. Maria had been looking at prom dresses, while her mom had been eyeing the wedding gowns. Somehow I didn't think it would get that far considering it was well known that Nelson's relationship with Maria didn't stop him from smiling at, winking at, or groping any girl who crossed his path.

The thought of Maria's mother willingly marrying Maria off to someone like Nelson turned my stomach. But, in a way, it was understandable. Maria's mother, Mrs. Matthews, had lived in Middletown all her life. She had never experienced the world outside the small realm in Middletown that she'd built for herself. Mrs. Matthews was still remembered for her days as Homecoming Queen and, in some circles, was still treated as if she had been crowned only yesterday. So to Mrs. Matthews, Nelson, who was rich, good looking, and privileged (much like her own husband), seemed like a perfect match for Maria.

Someone honked as they drove past me, and I snapped back to reality. I caught a glimpse of Mr. Tierney, the new English teacher and the yearbook sponsor. I gave him a vague wave as a chill ran down my spine. Thinking about Maria's situation made me ponder my breakup a few weeks earlier. Although it had been painful, I realized now that it had been a positive step toward the future I had envisioned for myself. I was looking forward to the anonymity of college and to the freedom of being who I felt I was deep inside. The person I had to keep restricted because I didn't fit into the expectations everyone else had for me. I had always been made to feel as if I must stay in my place and never try to struggle out of my allotted slot because if I did, I'd become an outsider.

I'd once read a book about the caste system in India. (That

fact alone confirmed that I am an outsider.) The book's main character was an Untouchable, someone whose profession was considered unclean. As he walked through a crowded marketplace, he had to shout "Unclean, unclean," so those around him would know not to touch him, lest they be soiled by his lot in life. That was how I felt most days, wandering the halls of Middletown High School. Now I realized that with my boyfriend gone he's one less person I have to deal with who had a preconceived notion of who I am and what my future should be. Suddenly, I was feeling more optimistic about the breakup.

As if to punctuate my thoughts about being an outsider, Julie Smith and Greg Lewis, two of my classmates from Bitterroot's class, cruised by me as I was turning into a residential neighborhood. Greg laid on the car horn as he leaned out the window and yelled, "Red-headed freak! Where's your black t-shirt now?" while simultaneously flipping me the bird.

I walked on as if I hadn't heard him, but I wanted to scream, "*Asshole!*" I looked over at the blue two-story house with the white picket fence that I was passing and saw the window curtains rustle closed. Someone had looked out the window to see exactly who the freak was.

I waved at the unseen person and said, "Hi. That's me. Red hair. I'm the freak." I wondered if my parents would find out before I walked the last ten blocks to my house.

At first glance, Middletown seemed like any other small town: tree lined streets, white picket fences, mom-and-pop stores, friendly smiles, nods, and waves as you passed through town. On the surface, everything seemed very Mayberry; the typical friendly small town like the one depicted in the 1960's television program *The Andy Griffith Show*. Anyone passing through town or visiting for a few days might mistake it for the same kind of rural community.

But behind the white picket fences and the storefront

windows, the neighbors peered out, looking to see if they could spot your weaknesses or weasel out your secrets. They looked for any flaw or abnormality they could magnify to show you how they were superior to you. Your neighbors' place in Middletown society was defined by your actions. If Mrs. Reynolds, whose husband kept a mistress across the river in St. Vincent, could look out her picture window and tick off a list of her neighbors' shortcomings, no matter how minuscule or mundane, she could still claim the moral high ground for herself. Thus, she retains her position as the most moral and righteous person in her neighborhood, securing, even if only in her own mind, her status within the community.

When city people fantasize about small town familiarity, they dream about going into a store where the owner calls them by name and chats about their family because he's an old friend. They don't dream about the realities of small town life, about how that same store owner is ripping them to shreds the moment the door closes behind them. Similarly, small town people dream of moving to the city where no one knows them. Where no one cares if they cut their grass on Sunday or buy beer every Tuesday. But they too omit the stark realities of crime and poverty that also go along with city living.

People in Middletown felt they were entitled to know their neighbors' business, and it was this entitlement to gossip and familiarity that got me in trouble every time I tried to be myself. It was this familiarity that was going to get me in trouble again today. I called it the Small Town Syndrome, like it was a social disease that Middletown suffered from.

From down the block, I saw that my mom's car was in the driveway. She was home early, which meant that she'd heard about something, but which something had she heard about? My outspokenness in Bitterroot's class, my backtalk to the cashier at the grocery store, or my classmates' verbal assault? Whatever it was, I knew I was in for a lecture about appearances, gossip, and fitting in, all symptoms of the Small

Town Syndrome. My mom was the secretary of the most powerful person in town, now that the refinery had closed. She was the executive secretary for the President of Midwestern Mutual. Position and appearances were everything to her. I tried to please her because it made my life easier; therefore, I was better behaved than I really felt I had it in me to be. It meant that I had to find other ways to rebel, like being a writer, wearing black t-shirts, and keeping my hair stringy when she wasn't around. However, I had to be careful; I couldn't fart in the hall without her knowing about it.

As I approached my house, I saw my mother's face in the kitchen window. She was watching for me. When I was in full view of the front of the house, she had come around to the front doorway, arms crossed, frown on her face. I squared my shoulders, took a deep breath, and readied my defenses. I reminded myself that if all went according to plan in a few more months I would be out of here. A few more months and I was never coming back.

CHAPTER 2

Sixteen Years Later

Memory is a funny thing. When you have distance, you forget what things were really like—you romanticize them and they become nostalgic. Imbued with emotion, nostalgia tricks you into thinking things were better than they really were. That those were the "good ol' days." If those were the good ol' days, then what is the present? If you weren't happy then (but now you think you were) and you're not happy now, then what does that mean?

I pondered these questions as I drove past the rusting, defunct oil holding tanks on the outskirts of Middletown. I wondered how much of the waste from those corroding relics was leaching into the town's water; the same water my children drank, bathed, and swam in. I thought about how the oil tanks were a metaphor for the town itself, decayed, eaten away from the inside.

I diverted my gaze back to the road and rubbed my head.

"How did I ever get back here?" I asked myself aloud.

"That's no secret, Emily," I answered in my head. "You know exactly how you got back here."

I had done what I did best, run away. I ran away from this town when I was eighteen because I felt stifled and trapped; now, I'd run away from Chicago, my home ever since I had graduated from college, because I was afraid and Middletown seemed like a safe alternative. Or at least, I saw it as a safe alternative for my husband, Jack, who had been a Vice cop in Chicago.

I hadn't been oblivious to the dangers of Jack's job, but it had never worried me much. He talked about his cases with me, but he also protected me from the danger he was in everyday, working undercover, making drug buys, and roughing up thugs for information. When I thought about the danger that went along with his job, I thought about it more in terms of a sexy sort of danger made attractive by the movies. It was the bravery, the fight for justice, that I thought about. But then the day came that every police officer's spouse dreads. The day the doorbell rings, and you open the door to the Precinct Chaplin and your husband's partner.

Jack and his partner, Sean Priest, had been making a drug buy when an informant blew their cover.

"Shots were fired. Jack killed the informant, but not before the dealer shot Jack," Sean explained. "I got the dealer after the fact."

"The E.R. doctor said the bullet missed his aorta, but his left lung collapsed. There's some damage involving his left shoulder where the bullet exited. He's in surgery now. He's in some danger, but the doctor expects him to make a full recovery," the chaplain, Fr. O'Sullivan, explained.

"He'll live?" I asked.

"Yes. The doctor expects him to come through surgery all right."

Knowing I needed to put on the brave face of the police officer's spouse, I squared my shoulders, held back my tears, and moved forward, just like I always did. But moving forward doesn't always mean you've dealt with whatever you're moving forward from. Sometimes, moving forward looks the same as running away—pushing all the emotions down, maintaining appearances, and moving forward as if nothing had happened when in reality you are, or rather I was, running away from reality and the fact that everything had changed.

After Jack recovered and returned to duty, I started having panic attacks. When he worked at night, I'd wake up in a cold sweat, fearing the worst. I'd make frantic calls and send texts to his cellphone, probably endangering his life, although he never said as much. I tried working with a counselor who specialized in support for police officers' spouses. I even tried medication, but nothing relieved my fear. We had two daughters who needed their father and I needed my soulmate. Jack had been the one person besides my grandmother who understood me. Jack let me be who I am. I didn't work without Jack.

Looking back now at that period of time after Jack was shot, I can see how my mother took advantage of my anxiety and subtly planted seeds of nostalgia for the safety of my childhood.

"Don't you want your children to grow up feeling the same security you did? Free to play in the yard or walk to a friend's house without being afraid that some sort of crime will be committed against them?" she had asked.

Her manipulation was quite effective, and while I tried my best to resist her attempts to influence me, I found myself thinking back to my childhood. For all the things I hated about Middletown, I had to admit that my childhood, for the most part, had been carefree. I had played all along my street with no fear of abduction or drive-by shootings. Although we lived in a good neighborhood in Chicago, I would never have considered letting my daughter Arabella, who's eight, walk down to the corner market by herself. At eight, I'd walked across town to the park pool to meet friends. I wouldn't let my other daughter, three-year-old Eleanor, play in our fenced in yard without Arabella or I watching her. As a child, I played for hours in the field behind our house without my mother so much as looking out the window. These memories of my small town childhood, memories that my mother helped conjure, made me do something I'd never imagined myself doing: longing to move back to Middletown.

But Chicago was Jack's home. His parents owned an Italian grocery store in Little Italy, and his two sisters each had apartments in the city. His career was also in Chicago. Jack and Priest had been rookies together, and together they'd worked their way to the vice squad in record time; they were the youngest vice cops in a decade. If he stayed on course, Jack would meet his goal of becoming a homicide detective within the next five years. Though I spoke fondly to him of Middletown, I couldn't ask him to give up all that he had worked so hard for to move to the middle of nowhere and to do who knows what, just so the sick feeling in the pit of my stomach would go away.

Then, a year ago, my mother called with the news that a sheriff's deputy was retiring, leaving an opening in the Sheriff's Department. When Jack got home that night, I presented the idea of moving to Middletown. After weeks of heated discussions, prayer, and inquiries, Jack agreed. He accepted the position with the Sheriff's Department, we sold our small brownstone in Chicago, and bought a huge Victorian in Middletown.

However, being nostalgic for a safer place and actually living in that place are two different things. Living in Chicago, I'd forgotten about things like the corroding oil refinery, the lack of variety in the grocery stores, and, most of all, the familiarity that the townspeople have with each other's lives. I'd gotten used to my anonymity. But now it was too late to admit that I'd made a decision out of fear and manipulation and that it was a big mistake. I especially couldn't admit it once Jack became Sheriff.

We had lived in Middletown for a year when Sheriff Griffin, the incumbent Sheriff who was seeking reelection, was diagnosed with colon cancer. When he found out, he withdrew from the election, but nominated Jack to run instead, highlighting Jack's experience as a Chicago police officer. My father got his friend, Judge Lawrence, to endorse Jack as well, making Jack a shoe-in. He won by a landslide against Brett Bradley, another deputy. Being elected Sheriff had made the move worthwhile for Jack.

Initially, I'd been happy to be living in Middletown again, but within the first month of being back, it started again. When I left for college, I was determined to be my own storyteller, to make my life what I wanted it to be, not what had been narrated for me by others. So I'd recreated myself. I gave myself the full freedom to be who I'd always been deep inside but had kept hidden to avoid conflict and ostracism. I was no longer Emmy Sue, the Beckett girl, whose dad had opened the garage after losing his job at the refinery and whose mother was the President of Midwestern Mutual's executive assistant. I was Emily Beckett, journalism student, writer, and political activist. However, my goals shifted a bit when I graduated from college and got a job at a large publishing house in Chicago as a proofreader. By that time, I was Emily Beckett, proofreader, budding novelist, and single woman on her own in the big city. Then I met Jack and got promoted. After I married Jack, I was Emily Romano, editor, wife, and eventually mother.

I'd been re-defining myself for so long and evolving my personality and goals that it hadn't occurred to me that the people who'd known me growing up would still be expecting me to be Emmy Sue. To them, I was frozen in time. To them, I was still the tall, thin, redheaded girl who didn't quite fit in but didn't make too many ripples in the pond about it. Most importantly, they still expected me to pound myself, a square peg, into that round hole because they thought I should. People weren't prepared for Emily Romano, the slightly chunky, Catholic wife and mother.

The initial shock came that first Sunday when we attended St. Michael's Roman Catholic Church. Since there were only a handful of Catholics in the area, a family of new faces stood out from the small crowd of regulars. I'd grown up Presbyterian and had converted to Catholicism right before Jack and I were married, so this was the first time that I'd ever set foot in St. Michael's.

The priest, Fr. Bob Lucas, was noticeably surprised to see a new family in the congregation. As soon as he saw us, he stepped down from the altar and asked us to introduce ourselves, an obvious breach of decorum for this small town congregation.

"I'm sorry. I don't mean to embarrass you. We so rarely get visitors."

"Well, Father, we're not visitors. We'll be here every Sunday from now on," I said, standing to meet his outstretched hand and introducing my family. "I grew up here although I was Protestant at the time, and we've recently moved back so . . ." I couldn't finish the sentence. As I looked around the congregation at the faces, hungry for some scrap of gossip they could take home with them, I froze.

Sensing that I was faltering, Jack stood next to me and said, ". . . so I could take a job with the Sheriff's Department." Father chatted with Jack for a few seconds more and then returned to his spot on the altar.

As soon as Mass ended and the last note from the organ sounded, we were swarmed with people welcoming us home. It was nice at first, but then I realized that we were being welcomed in a very left-handed way.

As I stepped into the center aisle to make my way out of the church, the middle-aged man behind me stepped into my path and said, "Welcome home. It's about time you came to your senses and realized that the big city's no place for a Middletown girl."

"Thanks?" I managed to reply.

I turned to grab Jack's hand but found him already engaged in conversation with an elderly farmer who'd been sitting in front of us.

"Emily," said a short, plump woman whom I slightly recognized but couldn't remember her name. "You always acted too big for your britches, but I can see you've grown up and gotten level-headed."

"Yeah," I replied, clutching Eleanor to me and wondering where Arabella was.

Then an elderly man came up behind the woman and said, "My grandfather went to Chicago in 'aught-nine', but soon found out that it's a dirty, crime-ridden place—as I'm sure your husband knows since he grew up there."

"Uh-huh."

Turning from them, I desperately looked for the door, but, instead, was confronted with a bitter, twisted-looking old woman who hissed at me, "Couldn't make it in the big city, huh. Had to come back here to your home where it's nice and safe."

Startled, I looked around for Jack, who was cornered on the other side of the pew, looking quite disturbed himself. I wondered if this woman was some agent of the devil. It was as if she'd looked right into my soul and fettered out my deepest fear—that I was a failure.

Sensing that we were being overwhelmed with "well-wishers," Father Bob made his way to us, "Okay, everyone, Emily and Jack are going to be regulars here, so you can say 'hello' some other time." Then leaning in close to me, he said, "It's good to have some new blood around here. I look forward to getting to know you both."

His genuine welcome was a relief, but for days afterward, the other comments rang in my head. The self-doubt that was beginning to nag me got louder and louder the more people I came in contact with. Everywhere I turned, I was met with the same kind of sentiments. Either I'd finally come to my senses and moved home, or I had failed to make it on my own and had returned to the cocoon of my youth. Any way they said it, the consensus was that I was a failure, and it seemed like everyone in town had made it their personal crusade to tell me so.

CHAPTER 3

I pushed the memories of our first months back in Middletown out of my consciousness as I pulled my minivan into the gravel parking lot behind a row of buildings that bordered the town square. I slipped into the parking spot marked "Reserved for Owner of COVER TO COVER BOOKS" and turned off the engine. As I walked around the back of my minivan, I read the bumper sticker on the tailgate: "My other car is a 1980 Pontiac Firebird." That bumper sticker made me chuckle every time I read it. Walking up the three steps to the back entrance of the store, I paused at putting my key in the lock. Instead, I popped the keys back into my bag and headed for the sidewalk leading to the building front.

I stopped in front of the corner store, *Cover to Cover Books*. My store. I liked peering in the front window and seeing row upon row of books outlining the perimeter of the store and the rich leather sofa and chairs which created an inviting space to sit and read. It was the kind of sophisticated bookstore that I loved to spend time in when I lived in Chicago. It made me proud that this was my store.

If those first few months back in Middletown hadn't been so difficult, I might not have opened the bookstore. It seemed as if everywhere I went someone had some kind of venomous comment for me. I felt lonely and isolated, which made me vulnerable to their poison. I couldn't share my feelings with

Jack after he'd given up everything he'd known to move down here. I had given up my job as senior editor at a publishing house in Chicago when we moved here, and I did not have a job. There were no jobs in Middletown that matched my education and skills. We had moved here knowing that, and Jack was encouraging me to write a book.

As the days wore on, I became more and more depressed. I put on a brave face when Jack was around or I was outside the house, but most days I busied myself with unpacking and settling in, becoming more lonely and isolated. It was summer and the girls spent a lot of time with my parents. My dad, though semi-retired, spent most days at the garage. He still owned it, but he'd hired someone else to manage the day-to-day activities. He still found time to be with the girls, and they loved going down to the garage where gramps would give them sodas and candy bars from the vending machines. They all enjoyed living nearby, and gram and gramps made up for lost time by spoiling the girls rotten. I was too busy wallowing in my depression and failure to care much about how spoiled the girls were getting. I was also relieved that the four of them got on so well and that my parents wanted to be with the girls. Like a lot of people, whatever failings they had as parents seemed to have been erased by grandparenthood.

Then one afternoon, Father Bob stopped by unannounced.

"Just thought I'd see how you're settling in."

Aside from my parents and a few family members, we hadn't had many visitors, so I took pleasure in showing Father around our house. Our small brownstone in Chicago had sold for almost twice what we had paid for it, and since property values were much less in Middletown, we'd been able to afford the old Victorian that I'd always admired as a child. We still had several thousand dollars left over that we were earmarking for the girls' education. I was itching to spend some of the money on furniture because the Victorian was three times larger than the brownstone, and we didn't have enough for every room.

"I always wondered what the inside of this house looked like," Father Bob said after I had given him the grand tour. "It has as much beauty and character on the inside as it does on the outside, which I suspect is also true of its new owner."

I blushed at his compliment and busied myself making coffee for us and telling him about our plans for the house.

"And what about you, Emily? What are your plans now that you've moved back home?"

I paused for a moment, thinking about how to answer his question, but found I had no plans and no words to tell him what I'd been feeling. So instead, I buried my face in my hands and began to sob.

"Oh, no! I wanted to know if you wanted to get involved in some of the ministries at church. I didn't mean anything by it," he said, patting my back, unsure how to comfort me.

I don't know if it was because he was my priest or because he was the first person who'd shown a positive interest in me since I'd returned, but I found myself confessing all of the feelings I had kept bottled up. I told him how I worried that I had made a big mistake and now I couldn't change it. I told him that people thought I was a failure and liked rubbing it in while others expected me to be the same person I'd been in high school.

"Emily, I have a confession to make as well. I didn't come here today to see your new house or to ask you to join a ministry. I've been hearing things around town—actually everywhere I go—the coffee shop, the tavern, the grocery store. I thought maybe you could use a friend," he said, smiling.

I nodded my head as I wiped my eyes and nose with a paper towel.

"You can't let it get to you. You're a curiosity now, but soon they will forget all about the small town girl who returned home from the big city," he continued.

"I've started to wonder if it's all true. Am I really a failure? I ran away from a place that I loved, tore my children away from their home and my husband away from his family and career because I was afraid. Not only am I the failure they say I am, but I'm also a coward. Otherwise, I would have stayed."

"But at what cost?"

I shrugged my shoulders.

"Look. A coward would have stayed away. You had to have had some idea what people would say, yet you came back anyway. That's not a coward's move. That is an act of bravery. I see you coming back here as a blessing. You and Jack have an aura of change about you. I can almost smell the change in the air. My heart tells me that God has something very special planned for you and that there is a reason He led you back here. Why else would you have consented to return to a place that so clearly makes you miserable?"

Again, I just shrugged.

"You know, Emily, the best way to stop gossips is to prove them wrong. Wasn't that why you left in the first place? To prove to the gossips that you were your own person, that you didn't need anyone to tell you who you were?" he asked.

And that's how my parish priest became one of my best friends. Jack was the only other person who saw me so clearly and understood me so completely.

So I spent the next few months thinking about how I could effect change in this small community. Having always been a big fan of self-help books, I longed to visit a bookstore and load up on "how-to change your life" type of books, but the nearest bookstore was over fifty miles away. That's when the idea hit me—a bookstore was just what this town needed. It had a public library; however, the collection was limited to the whims of the ancient head librarian. Middletown had never had a bookstore. It was something new, a change.

After more discussions similar to the ones we had had while trying to decide to move to Middletown, Jack agreed to let me use the leftover money from the sale of our brownstone to open Cover to Cover Books.

Stepping away from my storefront, I smiled at the memory of how my bookstore came into being. Then I walked into the shop next to mine, the Curl Up and Dye Beauty Salon. I'd chosen this location for my bookstore not only because it was an empty storefront on the town square or because it was a corner store on a busy intersection, but also because it was next to the busiest beauty salon in town. I reasoned that the salon would bring in a lot of extra foot traffic. Women looking for magazines or books to read while getting their hair done were likely to stop in. What I hadn't counted on was the salon's owner, Rhianna Reese or Annie as she had always been known to me.

Annie Reese, or Rhianna as she now wanted to be called by her full name, had been my best friend growing up. We had met in kindergarten and remained friends until we grew apart senior year of high school. We had been inseparable most of our childhood. When I went to college, she had visited me a few times, but we were both growing up and changing. Annie, tired of being pressured by her parents to perform academically, had passed up a scholarship to Northern Illinois University and instead had gone to beauty school. Then, she moved to another planet, Los Angeles. Eventually, our friendship had devolved into emails, Christmas cards, social media, and a few text messages now and then. As I became busy with my family and career, I had lost track of what was going on with Annie.

The name of the shop, Curl Up and Dye, had intrigued me,

and I was curious about the twisted mind that could come up with such a clever name. When I found the owner was Annie, or rather Rhianna, a feeling of peace came over me. For the first time in nearly a year, I felt I was on the right path. Rhianna had also felt suffocated by Middletown and felt she could not be herself here. Even though Rhianna and I had been best friends for most of childhood, I never had any idea that she was gay. For Rhianna, leaving Middletown had been a matter of life and death. If she had stayed, she would have killed herself because she couldn't be who she was or love who she wanted. In Los Angeles, she was able to live openly as a lesbian, find love, and a community of people who accepted her. Over the years, she was able to come out to her parents who surprised her by accepting her with open arms. She'd returned to Middletown for similar reasons. She had a son and wanted him to grow up in a safe environment. But moving back had cost her even more than my moving back had cost me. It had cost her her wife of ten years. If I felt the gossip about me moving back had been bad, it had been even worse for her when the town had found out she was a lesbian.

"As you know, I had dated boys in high school, and I had sex with them. I had to appear hetero. My wife and I wanted a child, but we couldn't afford in vitro or a sperm bank or even adoption. You think Chicago is expensive, L.A. is crazy. We both knew this guy and liked him a lot. He agreed to be my baby daddy, for lack of a better term. We slept together a couple of times before I got pregnant.

"At first things were really great. We were so happy to have Andy, but he was colicky and not a good sleeper. I was exhausted. But my wife couldn't handle it. Turned out she liked the idea of being a mother, but she didn't actually want to do the work. Since Andy was still an infant, we had not gotten the time to do the adoption paperwork to make her one of his legal parents. Sadly, that made it so much easier for her to walk away. Later, I found out that even though she'd been on board with how we went about getting Andy she couldn't get over the fact that I'd had sex with a man to do it. So we split. I couldn't afford to live in L.A. on my own and raise Andy, so I came back home. My parents were thrilled to have a grandson," Rhianna had explained.

Over the past year, Rhianna and I became close again. During the day whenever I wasn't in my own store, I hung around Rhianna's beauty shop, listening to the townsfolk gossip and clucking my tongue at their lowbrow ignorance. In my mind, their penchant for idle gossip drew the dividing line between them (the townsfolk) and me (the educated city person). I felt it was my duty to bring some culture and truth to this community, and I saw my bookstore as the best way to accomplish that task.

"Hi," I said as I walked in the door of Rhianna's beauty shop.

As always, Rhianna was there working away. She had a woman reclined into the sink, washing her hair. She opened her shop early, so she could be home with her son after school. In a farming community like Middletown, it wasn't difficult for her to find someone willing to come in for a six-thirty A.M. rinse. Morning had never been my forte. Most of the town has done nearly a day's work before I even opened an eye in the morning, so my store didn't open until a reasonable ten o'clock. My business hours also allowed me to drop my girls off at school in the morning which was important to me.

I usually had an hour or so to kill between the time I dropped Arabella off at school and Eleanor off at preschool and the time I opened the store. When I first became a business woman, I would diligently work away at bookkeeping or take inventory during this block of free time. But more and more, I'd been squandering that time at Rhianna's beauty shop. I had gotten into the habit of coming over to Rhianna's for a cup of coffee. Lately, my morning cups of coffee had also been accompanied by several cigarettes, a habit I'd given up before my first pregnancy. I wondered how much longer I could continue to smoke in secret before Jack found out and confronted me about it. Right now, satisfying my combined caffeine and nicotine addictions was all I cared about.

"So, how are tricks today, ladies?" I asked Rhianna and her nineteen-year-old assistant, Janney Dickens.

"Fine. I'm waiting for my eight-thirty to show," Janney said, bending down to pick up a stray curler from the floor.

I checked my watch. It was eight thirty-five.

"I hate it when the early appointments are late. I play catch up all day. Don't these people know I have to pick Andy up at school," Rhianna called from the sink.

"You know, I'd be happy to pick Andy up any day you can't make it," I offered. Andy and Arabella were in the same class.

"What? Are you going to close your store to go pick up my kid?"

"Well, when I say 'I would be happy to' I really mean, my mom would be happy to." My mom usually picked the kids up from school and either brought them to the store or kept them until Jack or I picked them up around dinner time.

"Yeah. I bet your mom would be thrilled to pick my kid up from school."

My mom wasn't a big fan of Rhianna's, nor was Jack. My mom didn't like her because she didn't know anyone who was gay, or at least no one she was aware of, and she didn't understand people who weren't like her. But I wasn't sure what Jack's problem was.

I rolled my eyes at her remark and asked, "Is there coffee in the back?"

"Help yourself."

As I passed the sink where Rhianna was now wrapping a towel around her customer's head, I saw that the woman was Mara Tierney, President of Midwestern Mutual Insurance Company, the wife of my high school English teacher, George Tierney, and my mother's boss. I didn't know Mara very well, but George came into my bookstore at least once a week. I liked him, but recently, I'd found myself cringing when I saw him coming because he liked to talk my ear off, which took me away from other customers and work I needed to do. But he was a customer, so I patiently listened to whatever he prattled on about, from teaching, to Mara, to whatever book I directed him to in an effort to divert his attention to something other than me. As I said "hello" to Mara, a woman no one particularly liked, I wondered how friendly, jovial George had gotten hooked up with her to begin with. I also wondered if she would tell my mom about this conversation. I mentally shrugged my shoulders and walked through the polka dotted curtain that served as a door to the backroom.

As I poured myself a cup of caffeinated sanity, I heard the bell on the door ring, and a new voice called out a greeting to Rhianna and Janney. I didn't recognize the voice, but the owner sounded like an elderly woman. Unable to make myself face whomever was out there, I plopped down into a large easy chair that Rhianna had stashed in the backroom of her shop. While the talk that I was a failure who'd returned to the roost had died down, especially since Jack had been elected sheriff and I'd opened my bookstore, it was still hard for me to mingle with the townsfolk in general. I could listen to them gossip to one another, but I never knew what to say and was always paranoid that whatever I did say would be altered and churned into the rumor mill.

I hugged my knees to my chest, lazily dragging on a cigarette that I'd just lit, and looked around at Rhianna's inventory. On one side of the room, there were shelves with rows and rows of perm kits and hair dye in every imaginable shade. There were extra curlers, combs, brushes, and hair clips as well. On the other side, were shelves filled with herbal remedies. Most of the remedies were part of a "wellness" program (read weight loss) called Herbal Vitality. Rhianna sold the herbal stuff on the side and had talked about expanding her business to include herbal remedies and aromatherapy. The majority of her clients clandestinely purchased her "other wares" because: a.) they didn't want others to know they were on a weight loss program, and b.) they wouldn't want it known around town that they believed in something as unconventional as herbal remedies. It was too New Age and L.A. for them.

Almost as if she had read my mind, Rhianna came through the curtain partition. She poured a cup of hot water for tea from an electric pot and a cup of coffee from the coffee pot, presumably for her customers. She eyed me for a moment, and then moved past me and took a bottle down from the shelf of herbal remedies. She handed the bottle to me.

"Saint John's Wort," I read.

"It will give you a little pick-me-up. Better than caffeine, anyway. If you ever decide you want to give up that nasty habit," she said waving the smoke from my cigarette away from her face, "I could probably find a remedy for that too."

I took a drag off my cigarette, rolling the lovely acrid taste around on my tongue. I sucked the smoke in, feeling my chest constrict a bit, rebelling against the poison I was willingly administering to my body. Then I released the smoke as I listened to the women in the front of the shop talk about some movie they'd all seen. A pungent odor wafted into the backroom stinging my nostrils.

Someone must be getting a permanent, I thought to myself, surprised that I could smell it over the cigarette smoke. I couldn't understand why perms were coming back in style. I felt a twinge of a headache starting and attributed it to the smell. *How do they work with that smell permeating the place*, I wondered. I could hear Janney, on the other side of the wall from me talking as she shampooed someone's hair.

"That guy that played her husband. He was totally hot," she said. "I read that he's gay, but I don't believe it. How could someone that good looking be gay?"

"Oh, believe me darlin', after living in L.A., I know that straight men get facials and use moisturizer too," Rhianna snorted. They all laughed for a few seconds, and then the unidentified elderly woman said, "I saw that movie, but I didn't like it. Too literary,"

I knew the movie they were talking about. The book was always better than the movie. I found it insufferable when Hollywood destroyed the essence of a novel by making everyone good looking and by tidying up their problems with a nice pretty bow. As a bibliophile, I hated it when good literature was turned into bad cinema.

"When George and I went to see it, we also saw Maria and you-know-who," Mara Tierney added. I had wondered how long it would take the conversation to turn to local gossip.

"They don't even have the decency to keep their affair secret. His wife was smart when she left him," said the elderly woman.

"It galls me how they think they can do whatever they want with no consequences," snapped Janney.

"Maria and Nelson were always like that in high school," replied Rhianna. "They thought because they had money it gave them the power to do whatever they wanted. She'd go to Chicago and get a five hundred dollar prom dress to make the rest of us feel inadequate in our Cheryl's Bridal dresses."

"Mm-hmm, the whole family acts like their poo-poo doesn't stink when we all know his brother got that girl pregnant, and they took her to Indianapolis for an abortion," said the elderly woman.

There was silence for about thirty seconds, and then I heard the whirl of the hair dryer starting.

"That guy in the movie; wasn't he the same guy who played Falcon on *Return to Tomorrow?*" the elderly woman asked. I couldn't hear the reply because now someone was at the sink running water, which drowned out their conversation. Every so often I'd hear Rhianna say, "yeah," or give a little chuckle.

I'm not sure how much time passed before the water was turned off, but I'd slowly smoked two cigarettes since it had begun.

As soon as the water was shut off, I heard Rhianna say, "Okay, Mara, time to rinse and take out the curlers."

I heard the dryer turn off and the hood hit the wall next to me as Rhianna lifted the dryer from Mara's head.

"Mara?" Rhianna asked. "MARA!"

Rhianna's desperate yell had me on my feet and standing in front of Mara within seconds. Mara's head was back, her eyes partially open, and her face was ashen.

"Oh my God," screeched the elderly woman, whom I now identified as Ruby Collins.

"What happened?" I asked the gawking women.

No one knew.

The women all stood there, frozen and staring.

"Call an ambulance! She's not breathing," I yelled. Looking at Rhianna, I yelled, "Help me put her on the floor!" Rhianna gave a violent shiver and then did as I had commanded.

I'd taken a CPR class about five years earlier and now prayed that I could remember how to perform it. As I touched the back of Mara's neck to tilt her head into position, the perm solution, which had dripped down the back of her neck, got on my hand, burning a row of open blisters on my palm that I'd gotten from gardening. "Someone get me a towel!"

Janney tossed me a towel from where she was crouched at her work station, and I wrapped it around my hand to protect it from the solution. As I performed CPR, I could tell that Mara was dead. Each time I blew a breath into her, there was no resistance. It was as if I were blowing up a balloon and then pressing the air out with the chest compressions. I don't know how long I breathed for her before the ambulance arrived. It felt like a long time, but probably had been about two or three minutes since the firehouse was three blocks away. After the paramedics had taken over, I took Rhianna into the backroom and asked her if she had a lawyer.

"Why?" she asked.

"She's dead."

Rhianna blinked at me in disbelief. "No, you're overreacting. She's not dead. Some people are allergic to the solution. It could have been a reaction to the strong smell," she rationalized.

"How many perms have you given her since she's been your client?"

"I don't know. A lot. About one every six weeks."

"Has she ever had a reaction like this before?"

"No."

I took her by the arms and looked her squarely in the eyes, "I'm the Sheriff's wife. I know a lawsuit when I see it! Call your lawyer—now!"

She shook her head and turned to make the telephone call. I pushed back the curtain at the back room door and saw the paramedics checking Mara's vital signs. As I looked over at the door, I saw the imposing figure of a man blocking the shop doorway. I couldn't see his face because the bright morning sun coming in behind him was blinding my eyes, but I'd recognize Jack anywhere.

I could see him surveying the room, and then his head stopped. Even though I couldn't see his eyes, I knew he was looking straight at me, wondering what I was doing there. He strode across the room toward me, and as he moved away from the natural light, I could begin to make out his face, the strong chin and high cheekbones that made him look more like a male model than a sheriff. I wanted to run to him and let him hold me in his arms, but his eyes were all business.

Jack was the kind of man whom people stopped and stared at. While I was a good looking woman, his presence and demeanor combined with his good looks to give him an aura that demanded attention. He never looked for attention and was even embarrassed by it. But at times like this, when he was the authority figure in the room, his sense of presence gave him a take-charge attitude that gained him respect from the right people and loathing from those who wanted the power that he had.

He was almost in front of me before I could make out the look on his face; it was a mix of wonder and concern.

"Are you okay?" he asked.

I nodded. The paramedics were taking Mara away, and Jack and I stood next to one another watching.

"So this is where you've been hiding yourself after you drop off the girls," he said.

"I'm not hiding—I'm having coffee," I replied. My hands and arms were tingling and my shoulder muscles screamed with exhaustion from giving Mara CPR.

"And smoking cigarettes," he added.

There was no denying it, especially when the smoke from my last cigarette still hung in the air, and my breath and clothing reeked of it. I began to feel nauseous. My hand with the blisters was numb and I shook it, trying to restore blood flow.

"What happened here?" Jack asked, ignoring my flailing hand.

I looked at him for a moment, trying to form my words, but

my mouth didn't seem to work. I felt really odd. Suddenly, my chest felt compressed; I could hardly breathe.

I could see Jack's lips moving but couldn't make out his words. I felt his arms around me lowering me to the floor. Then everything was black.

CHAPTER 4

I was underwater, drowning. I started choking as I gasped for breath.

"Breathe!"

I could see the surface but couldn't break through to where the air was.

"Breathe!"

I took a few gasping breaths and saw blurry shapes around me. Then it all went black again. Someone was holding something over my face and I struggled to breathe.

I'm being held under the water! I thought.

This cycle happened several more times. Then I blinked my eyes, and the fuzzy, yet familiar, outline of an old man came into my line of vision. He gently, but firmly said, "Emily. It's okay. You need to calm down. You have a tube in your throat."

I was confused. Why did I have a tube in my throat? I waved my arms around again, and again, they were restrained.

"Emily! I can't take the tube out until you relax. You're going to be okay."

I widened my eyes, hoping to convey my confusion to him. I wanted to ask him where I was and where Jack was, but I couldn't speak. I pleaded with my eyes, but he didn't seem to understand. There was some mumbled discussion and the sound of footsteps, and then Jack's face came into view.

"Every time we let go of her arms, she fights us. Can you get her to relax, Sheriff?"

"That's my Emily; she's a fighter," he said, tears glistening in his eyes.

What happened? I thought. *Why is Jack crying?* I wondered if something had happened to one of the girls.

He looked down at me as he stroked my forehead and said, "Emily, it's okay. I'm here. Relax so Dr. Thomas can take the tube out of your throat."

Seeing his face made me relax, so I did as he said and stopped struggling. The doctor pulled the tube out, and I gagged and gasped for air.

"What . . ." I tried to ask, but my throat was on fire and my chest ached. I tried to raise my hand to my throat, but one arm was a maze of tubes and Jack was gripping the other in his big hand. A thought made its way to me through the haze in my head: *I'm the one who's sick. It's me that Jack's crying about. I must be in the hospital.*

A woman loomed into view and placed something under my nose, and I felt a blast of oxygen flood my nasal cavities.

The old man, whom Jack had called Dr. Thomas, leaned over me, "Emily, do you remember me? I'm Dr. T. I stitched up your hand when you fell off your bike. You were about ten at the time."

I recognized him now, and I nodded.

"Emily, you've had a nasty encounter with some fentanyl. You stopped breathing, and you were given CPR. That's why your chest hurts. You were given several doses of narcan to revive you. When you got to the hospital, we put a tube in your throat so we could help you breathe," Dr. T explained.

I looked over at Jack and his face was crumpled with pain; tears were freely streaming down his cheeks. I could hardly believe what I was hearing. Was Dr. T saying that I had died?

Then I remembered a flicker of something and said, "Mara?" My throat was still too painful to say more than a word at a time.

"Shhh. Don't try to talk," Jack replied, trying to regain his composure. He smiled and said, "We'll talk later. You're going to be okay."

The hospital staff kept me in the emergency room for several hours observing me as I alternated between waking and sleeping. When I was finally moved to my own room, the sun was starting to set above the houses that sat across the street from my hospital window. Dr. T said that if I continued to improve I could probably go home the next morning.

Jack had stayed with me most of the time I was in the emergency room, leaving every once in a while to call into the station or to check on the girls, who were with my parents. He hadn't told me anything yet. Every time I tried to ask him about what happened he told me to rest. I remembered almost everything now, and I was positive that Mara was dead.

Jack confirmed my suspicions when we were finally alone in my hospital room.

"The fentanyl had to have been in the perm solution. I'm guessing that when Rhianna put the solution on Mara's hair it was absorbed through her scalp and went into her bloodstream. Depending on the dose, which must have been very strong, she would have stopped breathing in minutes, basically suffocating to death. Dr. Thomas said there was nothing you could have done for her. She was dead when Rhianna took the dryer hood off her head. It was fortunate that the paramedics were still parked outside when you . . ." his voice constricted, and he looked away from me, trying to maintain control of his emotions.

"So, I got some of the fentanyl when I tried to resuscitate her?"

"Yes," he said, clearing his throat. "Dr. T speculates that you absorbed the poison through the blisters on the palm of your hand when you put your hand on the back of her neck to perform CPR."

I raised my hand to look at the blisters, but my hand was bandaged.

"Why didn't the paramedics have a reaction?" I asked.

"Rubber gloves."

"And Rhianna?"

"Same. Rubber gloves."

We were silent for a minute, and then I asked the obvious question, "Who could have done this?"

"Well, we haven't formally charged Rhianna, but it was her shop, and she was the one giving the perm."

"What?!" I said, instantly regretting it as my raw throat burned and a sharp pain stabbed through my chest. I lowered my voice and continued, "That's ludicrous. What possible motive could she have for wanting to kill Mara Tierney? And why would she do it in a way that made her such an obvious suspect?"

"I don't know. That's what we're trying to figure out," Jack replied. "She did immediately call her lawyer even while the paramedics were still there."

"I told her to. She's a business owner and someone got injured in her shop. I thought she needed to take steps to protect herself from a lawsuit."

"It only makes her look guilty."

I heaved a slow, painful sigh. Despite my best efforts to help, I'd made a mess of things. "You know, Mara wasn't the most likable person in town. I'm sure she had enemies." As the president of Midwestern Mutual Insurance Company, Mara Tierney had made it a financial success by sacrificing the benefits of the policyholders and the company's own employees. Rumor had it that she was the cliché corporate battleaxe—heartless, contemptuous, and money-grubbing. And, she had been my mom's boss before my mom's retirement.

"Enemies who had access to Rhianna's beauty shop and who know about fentanyl?" he said, sounding a bit irritated. "Mara was in insurance, not organized crime."

"The only part of your description that fits Rhianna is that she had access to the shop. She isn't concerned about security. She keeps most of the cash in her smock and is always going out for lunch and such, leaving the door unlocked, so clients can come and go." He looked unmoved by my pleas for my friend. "What about product tampering? Maybe a disgruntled employee did something to the solution at the factory."

"That will definitely be an angle we will explore, but I doubt that's what it will be," he said, taking a deep breath. "Listen, you're going to be here overnight at the very least. This isn't going to go away before you get out of the hospital, so, please, lay back and relax. Can I get you something to eat?"

I understood that he was only being a good sheriff, doing what he's supposed to do. All the same, this woman was the closest I'd come to a friend in a long time, and I felt bad for making her look guilty.

"I'm glad you're okay. I was worried I was going to lose you," he said after a few minutes.

I smiled to let him know his apology was accepted.

He leaned over and kissed me. "What would you like to eat?" he asked.

"I'm not really hungry. My throat hurts too much to eat," I replied, shifting painfully in my hospital bed.

"I'm not surprised. . . . How about some ice cream?" he offered.

"Okay. Plain chocolate," I agreed. I wasn't the least bit hungry, but I knew he wanted to do something for me.

After he left to get the ice cream, I opened my hospital gown and saw an enormous bruise between my breasts. The gravity of the situation hit me like a safe falling from the sky onto a cartoon character—I was flattened by the realization. Tears filled my eyes as I thought about Arabella, Eleanor, and Jack standing around my grave. I imagined Little Elly not understanding where mommy had gone and why she wasn't coming back. I sat in my hospital bed sobbing and feeling stupid until I could hear Jack's footsteps in the hallway about fifteen minutes later.

When Jack returned with the ice cream, I felt like I needed to offer him something to show that I understood how close I'd come to leaving him forever.

"I'm not going to smoke anymore," I said, craving a cigarette as I made the promise.

"Good," he smiled, "then we don't need to have that conversation."

"I love you," I said.

"I know—me, too."

"If I'm staying here overnight, where are Bella and Elly?" I asked, picking at the ice cream he had brought me.

"With your parents. You can call them later."

Another thought came to mind and filled me with another kind of terror: How was my mother going to react to the news that I had been present at the death of her former boss? Suddenly, I hoped I could stay in the hospital indefinitely where I'd be protected.

"I heard you were spending time at that beauty shop next door to your bookstore, but I had hoped it wasn't true. Who knows what else THAT woman is into? Devil worship probably . . ." After my mother had shown the appropriate amount of concern for her only child's near death, she started the expected lecture.

"Mother . . ." I tried.

". . . I cannot imagine what people will say. My daughter was present at the killing of my former boss . . ."

"Mother . . ."

". . . People will think I had something to do with it."

"Mother!" I finally yelled into the phone.

"Emily Suzanne, you don't have to scream at me."

"Mother, I don't think anyone is going to blame you. I tried to save her life. Besides, Jack hasn't charged Rhianna with anything. It is all circumstantial."

"I'd heard she gave Althea Kent some *herbal* medicine for depression, and it turned out to be coyote."

"Peyote, Mother. And she didn't give Althea Kent peyote," I said, rolling my eyes at Jack. "Mom, can I talk to Bella and Elly? Wait, what did you tell them happened to me?"

"I said you weren't feeling well and that Jack had to take you to the doctor."

"They haven't been hanging around the kitchen listening to you gossip about this all afternoon have they?"

"Emily Suzanne, I do not gossip!"

Ignoring her incredulity at my remark, I asked again to speak to my girls. After a few moments, I heard them coming to the phone yelling, "Mommy, Mommy." Bella got to the phone first since she was the oldest. I'd never thought I was going to be able to get pregnant; I'd had endometriosis since I was a teenager, but after several painful procedures, I was able to conceive the good old-fashioned way. That's why we named her Arabella, "answered prayer." I had never intended to use nicknames with the girls since I'd always hated my nickname, Emmy Sue, but when Jack started calling Arabella, Bella, Italian for "beautiful," I gave in. Then when Eleanor came along, her name seemed too serious for a little girl with such a deep belly laugh, so it was only natural that she became Elly. But I drew the line at calling Bella "Belly," which was Elly's pet name for her big sister.

"Mommy, what's wrong with you?" Bella asked in her concerned, semi-adult voice.

"I'm fine, Bella; don't worry. But I have to stay here overnight because the doctor took some of my blood, and he has to wait until tomorrow to get the results. But I'll be home by the time you get home from school tomorrow. Okay?"

"Okay, Mommy. Don't worry; I'll take care of Elly."

"I know you will. You're such a big help to me, and I can think about feeling better knowing you're there to help your sister." I winked at Jack, and he squeezed my hand in return. "By the way, don't listen to any of gram's stories. She's got some funny ideas." At this Jack frowned, knowing no good could come of it.

"What kind of stories, Mommy?"

"Oh, never mind," I sighed. "Sleep well and I'll see you tomorrow. Put Elly on." I heard the shuffle of the phone.

"Mommy! I saw a butterfly and gram gave me cookies. I miss you. There was a mouse in the yard, but I'm not afraid of mice anymore. Belly kissed my head when I fell." Her three-year-old babble brought tears to my eyes. How I loved that sweet face. I loved both my girls equally, but a look from Elly could make me give her anything she wanted.

"Love you, Elly. Take care of gram and Bella," I said as a tear escaped from my eye. Then I heard the click of the phone as she ran off to something else that had caught her attention. I was a little disappointed as I hadn't gotten the chance to talk to my dad. Mom didn't say anything about him.

"Now, lay back and rest," Jack ordered, as he hung up the telephone next to the hospital bed and took the melting ice cream from my hand.

"I'm fine, Jack; please stop babying me."

"Emmy Sue, listen to your husband," said a deep voice from the hallway.

"Daddy!" I said, reaching for him. Jack moved away from my bed, knowing not to come between me and my dad.

My dad held me in a bear hug, lifting me a little from the bed. Overcome with emotion, I started to sob. I'd never seen my dad cry, but as I held him, I heard him clear his throat a few times. When we released each other from the hug, he turned his face away from me and wiped his nose with a hankie.

"Your mom said I could talk to you on the phone, but I wanted to make sure you were okay." Then clapping Jack on the back, he said, "I knew you were in good hands." Even though he never wanted to admit it, he liked Jack—a lot.

"Now, Missy, do I need to call the nurse to give you a sedative or are you going to do what your husband said?"

"*Okay*, I'll rest," I said as Jack used the automatic controls to recline my bed. I lay there with my eyes closed for a few moments, one on either side of me, holding my hands, but my mind was racing, trying to make sense of the day's events. That morning had been like any other: I had woken up, dressed and fed the girls, taken Bella and Elly to school, and then gone to the beauty shop—all normal. From there, everything was topsy-turvy, and I couldn't make sense of why it had happened.

I opened my eyes and saw both men staring down at me. "Have you been watching me all this time?"

"We want to make sure you're not going anywhere," Jack said.

"I'm not going anywhere," I said, looking longingly at my husband. Even though he was still my daddy, Dad knew and wasn't jealous of who the real love of my life was.

He kissed my forehead, and said, "I'll leave you two alone." Then looking pointedly at me, he said, "I'll see you tomorrow. Love you!"

"Love you too, Daddy."

As my dad turned to leave the room, Jack lowered the railing on the side of my bed and crawled in next to me. Finally, I felt safe and was able to let the day go.

CHAPTER 5

T he next morning while Jack was gone to the hospital cafeteria to find some breakfast, I was dozing in my hospital bed waiting for Dr. T to make his rounds in hopes that he would release me. I was awakened by someone tapping my shoulder and calling my name. When I opened my eyes, I saw Deputy Brett Bradley standing over me. I quickly sat up in bed.

"What are you doing here? Jack's in the cafeteria."

"I'm here to see you, Mrs. Romano," he stated matter-of-factly.

I pushed the button to incline the back of the bed with one hand and ran the other hand through my hair, trying to straighten it. I looked a mess, and I couldn't help but think that Bradley was taking pleasure in my obvious discomfort.

"What do you want?" I asked, annoyed.

"I need to take your statement about what you witnessed in regards to Mrs. Tierney's death," he said, placing a small handheld digital recorder on the tray that was swung across my bed.

"What did you do? Wait until Jack left the room, and then you came in here to ambush me?" I should have been more pleasant, but he'd woken me up.

Ignoring my accusations, he readied his notepad and pen and pressed 'record' on the digital recorder, "Could you tell me to the best of your recollection what happened that morning?"

I took a deep breath, trying to reign in my temper, and said, "I came into the beauty shop to have a cup of coffee before I opened my store. I didn't feel like talking, so I sat in the backroom. After about fifteen minutes or so, I heard Rhianna calling Mara's name. By the tone of her voice, I could tell something was wrong, so I went to investigate. When I came out of the backroom, I saw that Mara's head was back, her eyes were slightly closed, and her face was ashen. It didn't look like she was breathing. No one was doing anything, so I told them to call 911 and had Rhianna help me lower Mara to the floor. I began CPR. Then the paramedics came and took over."

"So how did you come about being exposed to the fentanyl? Was there something on her mouth? Or did you get it from her saliva? Was her mouth wet and moist?" he asked.

"What?" I asked, confused by his disturbing line of questioning. When he didn't elaborate, I went on, "The doctor thinks the fentanyl was in the perm solution, and when I put my hand on the back of her head to properly perform the procedure, I absorbed it through a row of blisters on my hand," which I held up to show him my bandaged hand.

"Let me ask you to clarify something you just said," he flipped back a page in his notepad and quoted, "'to properly perform the procedure'—do you think you properly performed the procedure? Don't you think if you had been more adept at performing CPR that Mara Tierney would be alive right now? Did you have any conflicts with Mara Tierney?"

I was confused again. Was he suggesting that I purposely let Mara die? He is a sheriff's deputy; he knows how fentanyl works.

Before I could answer, Jack's enraged voice came from the doorway, "Don't answer that Emily. Bradley, what the hell do you think you're doing?"

"I'm taking your wife's statement about what happened

yesterday."

"You did not have to come here and disturb her in the hospital. I was going to bring her to the department when she is released and have Sullivan take her statement—you know that. I told you that on the phone yesterday when you wanted to come down here and question her. You're bordering on insubordination here."

Most people—most smart people—back down from Jack when he confronts them, but Bradley wasn't giving an inch. He met Jack's level stare and evenly said, "I have what I need." He gathered the recorder and notepad and left, without once breaking eye contact with Jack.

After he'd gone, I said, "Well, why didn't you pull out your dicks and measure them to see who's got the biggest?—I'm bettin' he'd lose?"

With that, Jack shook his head and cracked a smile. Then getting serious again, he said, "I don't trust him. I don't know where he thought he was going with that line of questioning? It had no relevance to the simple statement of facts that he needed from you." Refocusing his attention, he said, "Don't let him play games with your head. You did everything you could to save Mara. It wasn't your fault she died."

"I know," I said, trying to keep myself from crying. Brett Bradley would not make me cry. "What's this?" I asked, noticing the bunch of red roses Jack was holding in his hand.

As if he'd forgotten they were there, he said, "Oh, these are for you—my beautiful wife." When he presented them to me, the bottom was crushed where he'd gripped them in anger. We both uneasily laughed at the crushed stems.

Just then, Dr. Thomas came in, creating the diversion we needed. After examining me, he released me from the hospital on the condition that I would rest for the next couple of days, which I had no intention of doing. Aside from my slightly scratchy throat and some soreness in my chest, I didn't feel as if I'd nearly died. Part of me wondered if my condition had been all that grave. At any rate, I couldn't let a few aches sidetrack me. I had a business to run, and I needed to get back to that as well as my children. I was also eager to find out how Rhianna was doing, and I wanted to pay my respects to Mara's husband, George. Now that I was on the mend, Jack wanted to get up to speed on the murder investigation, so he wasn't going to be around to make sure I followed the doctor's orders.

It was true that while making Midwestern Mutual a success, Mara had made enemies of half the people in town, but she could be courteous and sweet, especially if she wanted something from you. She had had her differences with Rhianna, as Mara had with a lot of other people. But Mara learned that if she wanted a good haircut, she had to be nice because Rhianna was the best stylist in town. I didn't see any reason why Rhianna would want to kill Mara or that Rhianna had it in her to kill; she was too much of an earth mother to have that kind of impulse. I'd known Rhianna most of my life. She wasn't a killer.

If Mara had made enemies in town, her husband, George, had been the opposite. He was one of the best-loved teachers at the high school. He had a very sophisticated and dry sense of humor that was often beyond his pupils' grasp. He'd been one of my favorite teachers when I'd been in school. Of course, that could also have been because he was so cute. Middletown was his first teaching job, and he was only six years older than his students at the time he was my teacher. After his first year of teaching, George and Mara had liked Middletown so much, they decided to make it their home. But that was right before the oil refinery had closed.

When the oil company announced that they were closing the refinery, George, fresh from college and still idealistic, tried to take the refinery management to task for the closing, leading pickets in front of the management offices. When that failed, he put in extra hours trying to find scholarships and other educational opportunities for students who suddenly saw their dreams of a college education go down the pipeline with their fathers' jobs. Mara, who'd just started working at Midwestern Mutual, convinced John Keene, the insurance company founder, to start a scholarship fund for Middletown High School students. George's willingness to help wasn't the only thing that made him stand out; he had a very different teaching style that made his classes fun. Students, especially boys, usually hated English literature, but he made it exciting and interesting. We often read the literature aloud as a class, and he'd assign a student dialogue that was often in direct contrast to that student's personality, which brought humor to even the most humorless piece of literature. By assigning papers to be written from the point-of-view of a character in a book, he invited creativity to paper writing that got the least likely students to read because they wanted to write the most outrageous papers.

When I returned to Middletown, I found George to be essentially the same person, but as a teacher, he'd become jaded. With the focus more and more on testing, George found that the creative assignments that had made his classes so engaging were frowned upon in an environment of teaching to the test. Disengaged students led to behavior problems in the classroom. With the rise of helicopter parenting and nothing is ever the child's fault, George and many of the other teachers were biding their time until retirement. Many teachers left the profession.

George and Mara had stayed because Mara had excelled at Midwestern Mutual and was made president of the local office after John Keene had died. In the meantime, George had seen himself losing his grip on his good sense of humor, and he no longer liked being a teacher. Mara was making more money than he was and had become so obsessed with her career that she wouldn't hear of leaving. In an effort to save his sanity, George had started writing mystery novels; none of which had been published. He'd write one novel, and as he was getting to the end, he'd lose interest and drop the whole project, only to come up with the spark for another novel and repeat the pattern. George had confided in me during one of his weekly trips to the bookstore that he felt he could finish a novel if he quit his job and devoted all of his time to writing, but Mara wouldn't hear of it. She said he'd be the laughingstock of the community for being a stay-at-home husband, especially since they didn't have any children, and that she'd be seen as an emasculating bitch—although that was how she was already described around town.

George told me that he looked forward to every evening when he could sit at his computer and lose himself in his latest novel. I asked to read some of his work, but he said each draft was too rough to share with anyone. One night, when we were alone in the store, I confided in him that he was the reason I loved literature so much and had gotten my Master's degree in English Literature. I told him how I even gave teaching a try but didn't have the passion for it that he had. To my surprise, he got tears in his eyes and left the store without saying another word. The next day, he left a bouquet of wildflowers at the front door of the store with a note apologizing for his abrupt behavior. We never spoke of it again, and I never mentioned the incident to anyone else.

After I was released from the hospital, we stopped by the Sheriff's Department, and I gave my statement of the events surrounding Mara's death. Then Jack drove me home. When he headed off to work, leaving me with strict orders to rest, I went upstairs, showered, put on a black sweater, black pants, and a brightly colored scarf, and headed over to George Tierney's house. I was anxious to talk to Rhianna, but first I wanted to pay my respects to George.

When I arrived, I knocked lightly on the door and then

stepped in. I looked down the hall and into the kitchen, searching for George but was surprised to see several women from the First Christian Church milling about the kitchen. I had not realized that George and Mara were churchgoers. When I peered into the living room, I recognized George's best friend, Joe Campbell, a science teacher and football coach at Middletown High School, and Joe's wife, Sandy, as well as several other teachers from the high school. There were a few people I didn't recognize but took to be relatives of either George's or Mara's. Joe stood up from where he was sitting on the couch and greeted me.

"Emily, how are you?" he asked

"I'm fine. Feeling fine," I offered.

"I heard about how brave you were. You're such a hero for the way you stepped in and tried to save Mara," Joe said with a catch in his throat. He took a deep breath, composed himself, and then went on, "This is such a tragedy. I can't believe something like this could happen here. But I guess that's what happens when you let someone like that Rhianna live in a decent town like this."

It seemed that in a day's time Rhianna had been tried and convicted in the court of public opinion for a crime she hadn't even been charged with. Given this town's love of gossip, I wasn't surprised.

"Well, I don't know . . ." I said, beginning to defend Rhianna, but before I could finish, I heard George calling my name.

"Emily!" he said as he descended the stairs. He looked as though he'd recently gotten out of the shower. I could smell the fresh aftershave that hung around him when he stopped in front of me. His close cropped hair, a vain attempt to hide the fact that he was balding, glistened with dampness. "Oh, Emily! What are you doing here? I can't believe they released you from the hospital already. You should be home in bed."

His sentiment and concern dumbfounded me. I guess I

shouldn't have been so shocked, considering that I did almost die. I didn't feel like someone who had been near death.

"I'm fine. I don't seem to have any ill side effects . . ." I stammered. I wasn't sure how to finish that sentence. I had been lucky and Mara hadn't been: *Why was that?*

George didn't seem to notice my distress because he plowed on, "I want to thank you for all you did for Mara. I heard you were the only one who tried to help her. That Rhianna just stood there and watched her die." George's words were full of fury, but I couldn't help feeling like I was in the middle of a bad made-for-TV movie, over-dramatized and over-acted. "To think," he went on, "that you befriended that woman and tried to make her feel welcome in this town, and she almost killed you in the process of killing Mara."

I didn't want to correct him, but he'd gotten it backwards —Rhianna had befriended *me* and welcomed *me* back into the community.

This was only the second time I'd seen George show his emotions, the first time being the night in my store when I praised him as a teacher. He was usually so placid that you wondered if he had a pulse. Now, his still handsome face was red and the veins on his neck were standing out. It was startling to see him like this. I took his hand and stroked it gently, trying to calm him. I wanted to refocus his attention on the reason I was here and away from Rhianna.

"George, I really didn't do much. I tried to help her, that's all . . ."

"You gave her CPR. You got that poison in you. You almost died, too."

By now all the church women who were washing and drying dishes in the kitchen were standing with their mouths agape, soaking up every word with their dish towels wagging along with their tongues. *How often do they get a ring-side seat to a real melodrama like this one*, I thought.

"Oh, Emmy, thank you! I don't know if I could have bared it if you'd died right alongside Mara because you were trying to save her." I bristled a bit at his use of my nickname, Emmy, which I considered to be a very intimate way to address me. Jack or my parents were usually the only people I permitted to call me Emmy. But when I was in school, I had been known as Emmy Sue. I also found it curious that my death would have been all about him. There was no mention of the loss my family, my children, would have felt. Surely, his grief was keeping him from thinking straight.

However, he must have been feeling rather emotional toward me because the next thing I knew he clutched me in a hug and began to sob. He squeezed me so tight that the bruise on my chest started to throb. My stomach was churning from all the adulation he was heaping on me. As I looked over his shoulder at the living room full of people wondering what to do next, I saw the fluffy, dyed-red hair of Ruby Collins, who'd also had a ring-side seat to Mara's death. I wondered if that was where he'd gotten his information about my heroics, as he put it. Ruby was so transfixed on the scene that at any moment I expected her to whip out a notepad and jot down what she overheard.

Then George loosened his grip on me, and I was thankful that the melodrama was nearly played out. What I didn't know was that it was only beginning to heat up. As George stepped away from embracing me, I saw that his face wasn't returning to its placid self but had become even more taut. His mouth was drawn in an ugly line across his face.

"I don't believe it," I heard Joe mutter.

Following Joe and George's gaze, I turned to see Rhianna walking up the front walk deftly carrying a chocolate cake that was so large she had to hold it with two hands. She was wearing a flowing black broomstick skirt and a purple tank top that seemed to add substance to her small thin frame. Her usual crystals hung around her neck, and her waist-length blonde hair was twisted into a bun. Except for the bun, she looked like a Stevie Nicks clone.

Before she could approach the front steps, George pushed me aside and was out on the walkway confronting her with Joe on his heels.

"I can't believe you have the nerve to show your face at this house after what you've done to me!" George yelled.

Stepping back from surprise at the force of his fury, Rhianna stammered, "I-I- wanted to come by and give you my condolences."

As I stepped out onto the front porch, I could hear the footsteps of every person in the house coming to any available window to get a first-hand view of the carnage.

"Give your condolences! And you're bringing cake. Did you put drugs in that, too?" George yelled.

"I didn't kill Mara! I don't know how the fentanyl got into that bottle," Rhianna answered, her cheeks pinking. She was clearly distressed by his anger. How could she have not predicted his reaction? I didn't believe that she had killed Mara, and I was ready to stand by her as a friend and say so. However, even I wasn't so blinded by my feelings for her not to understand that everyone else in town might not be ready to believe in her innocence.

"If this were three hundred years in the past, I'd burn you at the stake right now. These good Christian people would probably help me. Hell, they'd probably cheer me on," he shouted, taking a threatening step toward her.

That seems about right, I thought.

Rhianna gasped, covering her mouth with one hand. She had tears in her eyes.

George took another step toward her and she took another back. Worried at what would happen next, I hurried down the porch toward them. He took a final step forward. She stumbled backward, tripping over a section of raised concrete in the sidewalk. I lunged forward, trying to grab her before she fell, but George blocked my way. Losing her balance, she fell flat on her back and whacked her head on the walkway. Then, to add insult to injury, the cake she'd been straining to keep hold of, landed squarely on her face.

Since George was still standing in my way, I walked around him and knelt beside her, like I had done with Mara the day before, and gently lifted the cake from her face and wiped frosting away from her eyes, nose, and mouth. I could hear snickers coming from the house.

I glared up at George and said, "I suggest you back off before this gets any uglier."

George looked down at us with an evil sneer on his face. I looked over at Joe for help, but he seemed as stunned by George's behavior as Rhianna and I were.

"Or you could continue harassing Rhianna until my husband shows up with a deputy," I suggested.

George's shoulders slumped as if he were a balloon that had been deflated. Without another word, he turned and walked back into the house. After he'd gone, I helped Rhianna up. Joe was still standing in the yard like a deer caught in the headlights of an oncoming car.

"Joe," I said, forcing him to look into my eyes, "Go back in the house." Then I physically turned him on his heels and sent him back to the house, which was no easy task since he was about a foot taller than me and outweighed me by at least one hundred and fifty pounds.

After Joe and George were back in the house, I walked Rhianna home.

"I have never seen George act that way before," I said.

"It was stupid," she sobbed. "I don't know what I was trying to accomplish. I wanted him to know that I didn't kill her, but obviously, he thinks I did." She touched the back of her head and flinched.

"You need some ice. You'll probably have a goose egg." I paused for a moment and then said, "Well . . . I understand what you were trying to do. But do you realize what a risk you were taking going over there? Whatever you said could be used against you in court, and there was a house full of witnesses who could be called to testify about this incident?"

"It's not going to come to that, is it?" she asked.

"I wish I could say no, but I'm not sure."

"Jack doesn't think I did it, does he?"

"Jack wants to weigh all the facts before he makes any decisions," I said, realizing what a sticky situation I was in. "He takes his job very seriously, and the fact that you are my friend doesn't mean anything to him. He has to be objective and do what he sees is in line with the letter of the law. Besides, it would be the D.A. who would bring charges against anyone. Jack is simply investigating the matter."

She stopped walking for a second, trying to analyze the meaning of what I'd said. I hoped she'd realize that I was her friend, but I was Jack's wife first and foremost.

"I know," she said. "Even though my parents have been supportive, I've heard rumors that some of my extended family think that I'm unfit because I'm a lesbian. Someone called Child Protective Services on me last year."

I didn't know how to reply to her very valid concern, so I remained silent.

"I'm glad you're okay. I was really worried," she said. "I wanted to come and see you, but I was at the Sheriff's Department all night."

"Thanks, I know you wanted to be there," I replied.

We walked the rest of the way to her house in silence.

Strangely, Rhianna lived a few houses down the street from George and Mara. Not knowing what else to say, I reached over and took a finger of icing from her forehead. I licked my finger.

"Mmmmm. You may possibly be a killer, but you make damn good frosting!" I said.

She smiled at that.

CHAPTER 6

After we walked the short distance to Rhianna's modest Cape Cod, I determined that I had an hour before I had to pick up the girls. Bella got out of school a little after three, and my mom had picked up Elly from preschool at noon. Usually, I picked her up and brought her to the store for the afternoon where she napped on a small cot I kept in the storeroom. At two-thirty, a high school girl named Kylie Donaldson came in and worked in the store until it closed at eight. I would pick Bella up at school, work until four-thirty while the girls helped around the store or Bella did her homework, and then we would go home to make supper, leaving Kylie to close the store. Sometimes when Jack wasn't working the late patrol, I would come back to the store after supper and help her close up.

Since I had an hour before I had to act like a mother again, I told Rhianna to take a shower to get rid of the chocolate cake while I made coffee and got her some ice for her head. I sat at her kitchen table sipping my coffee as she showered. Rhianna's home was neat but modest and dated. Her choice of paint colors and window coverings told me that she had made efforts to update the home, but a total remodel was more than likely out of her budget. While she had painted her kitchen cabinets a muted green and updated the handles to a brushed silver to give them a more modern flair, the woodworking and soffits were clearly from the 1980's. The countertops were a worn formica and the linoleum was a faux tile with mauve centers. She had also hung a modern looking valance over the window at the kitchen sink and the appliances looked as if they had recently been updated as the refrigerator was stainless steel and the stove was black. They had probably been replaced as a selling point by the previous owners. Considering the remodeling we had been doing to our home, I felt humbled thinking about Rhianna's somewhat precarious circumstances. She was a single mother with her own business. She obviously was doing her best to give her son a home and all the things he wanted and needed, but she was more than likely stretching herself thin to do so.

About fifteen minutes later, Rhianna reappeared wearing a robe with her wet hair slicked down her back. We discussed whether or not the chocolate would come out of her clothes, and she went into the laundry room, which was directly off the kitchen, to soak them in the washing machine.

I picked up the zip-lock bag of ice I had put together for her and waited for her to come back into the kitchen. After a few minutes, I shouted to her, "This is the first time I've been to your house. It's really cute." I could hear the washing machine filling, and when she didn't answer, I figured she couldn't hear me. I waited for the water to shut off and said, "You've got a real sense of style. I envy how cozy, yet stylish you've decorated everything." I was beginning to feel like an idiot, standing in the middle of her kitchen holding a bag of ice. Finally, I decided to find out what was taking her so long.

When I entered the laundry room, I saw her bent over the washer with her head on her folded arms. I could see by the way her body was shaking that she was crying.

"Rhianna," I said quietly to her back.

"I'm okay," she said, trying to control her sobs. "I don't know how this happened." Her voice was constricted with emotion, and she could barely speak. "This looks so bad for me. What am I going to do?"

I went to her, unable to stand there and watch her cry. "I don't know what to tell you to do, but be honest about everything. Jack's told me about a lot of cases where people tell small lies about things they think aren't important, and it always comes back to make them look guilty."

She pulled away from me. "Do you think I'm lying about something?"

"No. I'm only trying to give you the best advice I can."

"Well, the last bit of advice you gave me made me look guilty."

"I'm sorry about that. At the time, I thought it was some kind of accident. There was no reason to think it was murder. Besides, it's easily explained. You're a business owner, and you were only trying to protect yourself and your business from a lawsuit. If a shelf of books fell over on someone in my store, whether they'd pulled it over, it had fallen, or someone else had pushed it over on them, I would immediately call my attorney as well."

"Yeah, but calling your attorney in that case isn't going to make people think you pushed the shelf over on the person."

"Well . . . in this town it depends on who the person is," I smirked. She smiled, which was the reaction I was looking for. "I'm your friend, and I'm going to do everything I can to help you."

"Good, then promise me something. . . If I go to jail, take care of Andy for me. My parents are in Europe for the next month. I haven't tried to contact them because I don't want to ruin their vacation. This might be nothing, and I'd hate for them to come home for no reason."

"Do you think that is wise?"

She looked at me sharply. I could tell there was a line she didn't want me to cross, but I was still trying to figure out where that line was. She wanted to be good enough friends that I could take guardianship of her son but not good enough to question her decisions. It was an odd place to be.

Trying again, I said, "Rhianna, your parents love you. I'm sure they would rather be here to support you than gallivanting around Europe while you and Andy needed their support."

"Emily, I haven't been completely honest with you."

"Yes?"

"Things between my parents and I are not as good as I have led you to believe that they are. They love Andy, and he's the only reason they have much of a relationship with me. They want to know their grandchild." She took a deep breath as if getting ready to jump into the deep end of the swimming pool. "The reason I didn't take those scholarships and ran off to California was not for whatever reason you might have heard or thought I did that. It was because I came out to my parents, and they couldn't accept it. They had tried to send me to counseling, but it was really a pastor trying to convince me that I was not really gay, just confused. I knew I had to get out of Middletown or kill myself. Since I didn't really want to die, I left."

"Rhianna, why didn't you ever tell me?" I asked. "I would have understood."

"Would you have? That was almost twenty years ago when you were small-town Emmy Sue, not Emily Suzanne who has lived in the big city and had a big city job," she said with a hint of sarcasm in her voice that took me aback.

"Well, you were Annie, my best friend, and not Rhianna, some California earth mother. I can't guarantee that I would have understood, but I would like to think that I would have tried. I loved you. I would have done anything for you."

"I loved you too," she said. However, the way she said it felt more meaningful than my "I loved you" with the implied "like a sister." Rhianna's felt like more than that.

She paused, collecting her thoughts, "When I had Andy and my partner left me, I needed help and my parents were willing to overlook my 'problems' to be in Andy's life. I could have done that from a distance, but I also wanted to come back for my sister."

Rhianna's sister, Reba, was ten years younger and married. Why would she want me to be Andy's guardian if Reba was able to care for him? I'd made too many assumptions already, so I waited to see if Rhianna would tell me why it was important to be here for Reba.

"Her husband is vile. He's abusive."

I looked down at my shoes, not sure what else to say, and noticed that I was still holding the bag of ice. I felt stupid, like I'd come out of the bathroom with my skirt tucked up in my pantyhose. Awkwardly, I started to offer the ice to her, but she brushed passed me back into the kitchen.

When I followed her, I saw her writing something. She turned and handed it to me. It was a note saying that if she couldn't care for Andy that I was to be his guardian. I wasn't sure how legal the document was, but I could see she was quite serious about me being Andy's guardian. I folded the paper and put it in my pocket to show her I was willing to go along with what I considered to be unfounded paranoia brought on by lack of sleep and an excess of chocolate cake.

I uneasily handed her the now half-melted bag of ice.

"Thank you," she said.

I looked at my watch. "We have just enough time for some coffee before the kids get out of school."

Despite the coffee, Rhianna was wiped out, so I offered to pick up Andy when I got Bella from school. As I waited for the children to be dismissed, I leaned against the trunk of a large tree in front of the school. A few of the other moms waved hello and asked how I was, but the majority of them stood off to the side in a gaggle, whispering and giving me sideways glances. To spite them, I began to stare them down. I figured they'd either be forced to disband under my glare, or one of them would be unnerved enough by my stares to muster the courage to come over and confront me. Before either objective could be reached, the bell rang and children began pouring from the school.

"Mommy!" Bella screamed as she ran at me, nearly knocking me over. I encircled her long, skinny body and picked her up. She wrapped her gangly legs around my waist and we hugged for a long time.

Bella is the image of her father. While Jack and I are both tall, I predict that someday Bella will outgrow my five feet eleven inches since she's already much taller than any of the other children in her class and, at eight, is often mistaken for ten or eleven. Her waist-length chestnut hair is a touch lighter than Jack's but has streaks of red that glisten in the sunlight, my small contribution. While her skin is lighter than Jack's as well, her facial structure is the same as his—square jaw and high, angular cheekbones. But the feature that makes her all Jack is her eyes, her penetrating and serious brown eyes. All her features combine to give her the look of an old soul, which she is.

"Mommy, what happened to you?"

"I wasn't feeling well, and Daddy thought I should go to the hospital to make sure everything was all right. I'm fine now. Nothing to worry about," I said, trying to give her a reassuring smile. I felt bad lying to her, but I wasn't sure if I wanted her to know how close she came to losing her mother. I gave her one last squeeze, and put her down as I saw her teacher, Jessy Becker, approaching with Andy.

"Emily, Rhianna called the office to say you were taking

Andy home. How are you doing?" Jessy asked carefully because of nearby prying ears.

"I'm fine, really. No lasting effects," I said, thinking of the gossip that would be generated from Rhianna's call to the office.

"I'm glad you're alright," she said. Then looking down at Bella and Andy, she said, "I'll see you guys Monday."

I loaded the kids into my minivan and headed across town to my mother's house to pick up Elly. When I got out of the minivan at my parents house, Elly came bursting out the door and jumped into my arms with complete confidence that I would catch her. If Bella was the image of her father, Elly was my photocopy. My mother was fond of comparing Elly's baby pictures with mine and testing to see if I could tell who was who. Elly has my red hair, although her hair is more of a strawberry blonde where mine is fire red. She also has my gray-blue eyes. She is tall like the rest of us and skinny, but she has my chipmunk cheeks and freckles. When we go to the beach, Jack and Arabella, the ones with the dark complexions, play in the surf, while Eleanor and I, sit under the umbrella so we don't burn.

At first, my mother was happy to see me, relieved that I was all right. But when she saw Andy in the back of the minivan, and I explained who he was, she clucked her tongue at me and took an affronted tone. She didn't say anything further about my involvement with Rhianna. To her credit, she may have been a hopeless gossip and could drive me crazy with her accusations, but at least she had the decency not to bad mouth a child's mother in front of him. She even went back in the house and got Andy a cookie, since she'd brought one out for Bella.

"Sorry, I didn't come to see you in the hospital," she said. "I've been so busy. Not only did I have your children, but I've been planning this funeral."

"You're planning Mara's funeral?"

"Why, yes. Until I retired, I took care of every detail of Mara Tierney's life. When George contacted me for help, I thought it was only fitting that I should manage the details of her death," she said, pretending that she felt put-upon, but I could tell she was enjoying the prestige of being asked to manage such an important event. I really wanted to believe that she cared about me more than managing Mara's funeral. Like Jack always says, *we prioritize the things we care about.*

"Thanks for taking care of the girls," I said, giving her a quick peck on the cheek. "I'll leave you to it." I got in my minivan and drove off. When I looked in the rearview mirror, she was already in the house.

As I drove Andy home, the girls chatted nonstop over one another, relaying all that had happened in the twenty-four hours since I'd last seen them. When I braked at the stop sign two blocks from Rhianna's house, I was shocked to see the sheriff's and the deputy sheriff's cruisers in front of her house. I could see Jack standing in the front yard, peering down the street and recognizing our minivan. I quickly turned down a side street, so Andy wouldn't see the sheriffs' cars in front of his house. The last thing the kid needed right now was to see his mom being handcuffed and taken away by the authorities.

"You know what, Andy?" I said, checking to make sure the slip of paper Rhianna had given me was still in my front pocket, "Your mommy was really tired. I'm going to take you to my house for a while and let your mommy sleep."

Bella and Elly simultaneously yelled, "Yea!" as Andy tentatively agreed.

When we got home, the kids raced up to the third floor playroom, and I headed straight for our home office to make the needed arrangements for taking temporary custody of Andy. I decided to order pizza for dinner, rationalizing that

I had been released from the hospital earlier that day and deserved to order dinner out. One of the pluses of living in this town was the awesome pizza. The local pizza parlor served the best pizza I've ever tasted. Even out of all the pizzas I had in Chicago, a city famous for its pizza, nothing compared to Dancing Dave's. There was something about the spices and the generous amount of mozzarella cheese that combined with just the right amount of sauce to create a gustatory delight. I had been eating pizza from Dave's for as long as I could remember and had never been disappointed with a single slice. But, as the old joke goes, pizza is like sex; even when it's bad, it's still pretty damn good.

Andy had been at our house for about an hour and a half when Jack came home. I had given the kids a snack and estimated that the pizza would arrive in about forty-five minutes. When he stepped into the office, he didn't say a word, but I saw him carrying a small suitcase with *Pokemon* on the side.

"Going somewhere?" I quipped.

"Don't you think you could have asked me first before you agreed to this? Do you know what kind of scrutiny this opens me up to? Besides, you were supposed to stay home in bed today."

"When I agreed, I never thought I'd actually have to follow through with my promise. But you've taken care of that! How could you have arrested her?" I asked, ignoring his rebuke that I didn't follow the doctor's orders.

"Emmy, don't do this to me. Don't make me feel guilty for doing my job." He was right, but at that moment, I perceived this as a great injustice. It wasn't fair to my husband; he wasn't the enemy. But I needed someone to turn my anger on, and he was the closest target.

"On what evidence did you arrest her?" I shot at him.

"The District Attorney felt that her relationship with

66

George was enough to arrest her, but hers were the only fingerprints on the bottle of perm solution. The lab results came back this morning. The perm solution was the source of the fentanyl poisoning."

"Whoa! I don't see how George and Rhianna being neighbors constitutes a relationship, and fingerprints are only circumstantial?"

"Well, the D.A. didn't see it that way."

"Robert Price wouldn't know a felony from a misdemeanor if *you* didn't tell him the difference," I said. Robert Price, the District Attorney, was a small whelp of a man whom I suspect had become an attorney so he'd finally have the power to push other people around.

"I agree, but I have to do what he says."

"Jack, this stinks to high heaven. All of this evidence seems too perfect. It's obvious someone is framing her. What motive did she have to kill Mara Tierney anyway?"

"Jealousy."

"What?"

"George Tierney is Andy's father," he said.

"*What?*" I couldn't believe what he was telling me. I felt a little dizzy, like the world had been turned on its head. "How is that possible? Andy is eight and Rhianna has only been back for four years."

"Rhianna had a big crush on George when she was in high school and made several passes at him, but he'd rebuffed her advances. Then about nine years ago, he and Mara were in Los Angeles on vacation when by chance they bumped into Rhianna at a restaurant where she was working. Later that night, George and Mara argued and George left their hotel in a huff. He found his way back to the restaurant where Rhianna worked, got drunk, and she took advantage of the situation to act on her unrequited crush."

I still couldn't believe what he was telling me. It didn't mesh at all with what she'd told me about Andy's conception. But I had to admit to myself that this seemed to be more of a reason to come back to town after all these years than her partner left her and her sister had married an abusive man. Of course, I wasn't going to share this with Jack.

"That still doesn't explain why she would kill Mara."

"She'd been stalking George," he said.

"Huh?" That didn't fit into Rhianna's character at all.

"When she found out she was pregnant, she'd written to George at the high school telling him so and demanding that he divorce Mara and marry her."

"This doesn't make any sense. She's a lesbian."

"Bisexual."

"Who told you this? Have you seen any of the letters?"

"George told me most of it, but Rhianna confirmed it when Bradley questioned her. George said he destroyed the letters."

"You let Brett Bradley question her?" I said. "Confirmed which part of the story?"

After Brett Bradley lost the election to Jack, he had tried to get a job with other law enforcement agencies in the area, but his reputation for abusive behavior and rage had followed him. He had been forced to stay in Middletown, and he took every chance he could find to make Jack's life difficult. Unfortunately, Robert Price was one of Bradley's biggest supporters.

"I didn't choose Brett Bradley to question her. Being second in command, he took over the investigation while I was at the hospital."

"She even admitted to stalking?" I persisted, ignoring his statement about Bradley.

"No, she denied the stalking, but she confirmed that George

is Andy's father and that she'd written to him at the high school."

"Maybe she wrote to him once, but if she had written to him regularly, there is no way he could keep that quiet. Those women in the high school office would have latched on to the frequency of the letters from Los Angeles and spread it around town that George had a 'pen pal.'"

"Yeah, you have a point." He slumped his shoulders a bit, and I could tell how tense he was. "But if the D.A. issues a warrant for her arrest, I have to arrest her."

Just then Andy appeared in the doorway. He looked at the suitcase Jack was still holding, and I wondered how much of our conversation he'd heard. I prayed that he hadn't heard the part about George Tierney being his father.

"You arrested my mom!" Obviously, he had heard that part.

"Sorry, buddy," Jack weakly replied, as if he didn't know what else to say.

Andy grabbed his suitcase from Jack, kicked him in the shin, and then screamed, "Now you can arrest me, too!"

"Jesus Christ!" Jack yelled as he bent to grab his shin.

"You're making friends right and left today," I said, running after Andy.

CHAPTER 7

S leep was nearly impossible that night. Not only was my head filled with questions that I had no answers for, but laying next to a man who was annoyed with me wasn't conducive to sleep either. Every time I tried to get comfortable, it seemed he was throwing an elbow into my side or a knee into my thigh. I woke up the next morning more exhausted than when I'd gone to bed.

On Saturdays, when Jack and I both worked, my parents took care of the girls. They were terrific about watching the girls whenever I needed them to. After living four hours away during the girls' early years, they were thrilled to be so close to them now. But this morning, my mother said she was too busy with the final details of the funeral to watch the 'children.' I was sure that the addition of Andy was the real reason for her refusal. It was asking a lot of her to watch him along with Bella and Elly. After several minutes of making me feel guilty, she finally relented and said she would watch them.

When my morning lecture from my mother ended, I got in my car and left her house, but I had no intention of driving straight to the bookstore. If I had been a more conscientious business owner, I would have gone to the store and busied myself with some task that needed done. But after such a restless night's sleep, playing the conscientious business owner felt like too much effort. I needed an infusion of caffeine and somewhere to think until I opened the store.

Since my usual early morning hideout, Curl Up and Dye Salon, was closed due to murder, I went to Wilma's Cafe.

Wilma's was next to the back gate of the now defunct oil refinery. In its hey-day, Wilma's had a prime location since this was the gate that the laborers had used to enter and leave work. As I entered the restaurant, a rush of memories washed over me. When my dad had worked at the refinery, he often brought me here for breakfast when he worked the night shift. We usually saw my maternal grandfather here as well, having a cup of coffee and chatting with his cronies.

My grandpa Jeffries had been the Circulation Manager at *The Daily Inquirer*. Always dressed in a gray flannel suit with a crisp white shirt, plain black tie, and dark gray fedora, he looked as if he'd stepped out of a black and white movie from the 1940's. After he died, Wilma had asked my grandma if she could have his hat to hang in her café, so it would always seem like he was around. I couldn't believe that it was still hanging on the coat rack. I was saddened to see that it was caked with layers of dust and grease that made a sort of dirty paste over the once rich felt. I wondered if Wilma's daughter, who now ran the café since her mother was long dead, even knew to whom it had belonged or why it was there.

I found a booth in the corner of the dark, smokey café and looked around. After the refinery closed down, the café had struggled for a while. Then a large fast food chain came in and tore down the town's other gathering place, an old train car called The Place, to put up a shiny new restaurant where the food tasted the same whether you were in Middletown, Illinois or New York, New York—greasy, bland, and processed. After The Place was torn down, people flocked back to Wilma's. Now, the town was divided into those who went to the fast food chain for breakfast and those who went to Wilma's. This was my first trip to either place since I'd returned, but I already knew to which camp I belonged.

Wilma's hadn't changed much since I was a kid—same horseshoe shaped counter with a smattering of booths around the perimeter of the room, same type of waitress (Flo wannabes), same high windows that let in little light through the grease-filmed glass, and, if I wasn't mistaken, even the same curtains hung at the windows. It felt safe and familiar here, the perfect place to sort out my thoughts. Besides, the second-hand smoke was helping allay my nicotine withdrawal.

As I sat in a booth with my knees hugged to my chest, staring at the cup of coffee in front of me and longing for my flavored creamer, I held an unlit cigarette between my lips. I had promised Jack that I wouldn't smoke anymore, but I'd never promised that I wouldn't put a cigarette in my mouth. It was all semantics. Speaking of semantics, I could hear a few not so soft whispers of which I was the subject. I caught a few phrases like, "too good for the rest of us," "highfalutin," "asking for trouble." I could feel those who weren't talking about me, looking at me, while pretending not to look. The whispers hurt my pride, but I understood why the simple farmers and retired people who patronized Wilma's might not have much use for someone who owned a bookstore. Besides, who was I kidding—I *was* highfalutin as far as these small town folk were concerned.

While I sat there pretending to be deaf and blind, I saw three women leave their seats at the counter and walk toward me. They were: Mrs. Carl Carlson, Miss Eileen Jefferson, and Olive Shaffer. Mrs. Carlson and Miss Jefferson were the engine of the gossip machine in town. Their information wasn't so much correct as it was colorful. I'd gone to school with Olive and had a bad history with her that I was ashamed of as an adult. Olive's mother had been mentally ill and, as such, hadn't always looked after some of Olive's most basic needs, for example providing simple hygiene products like soap and shampoo. Therefore, Olive's hair had often been oily and she had always smelled. Because of her oily appearance, I had dubbed her Olive Oil. I had said it flippantly one day when she'd pushed me too far during gym class. She had always been highly competitive and would have done well in sports if anyone had nurtured her in that direction. She had yelled at me during a volleyball game for missing a spike, and I'd screamed back, "Shut that decaying hole you call a mouth, Olive Oil." Unfortunately, the name stuck.

I looked up, as a trio of Emmy Sue's met my ears. The two older women had sat down across from me, and Olive was pushing against me as she scooted in next to me. Olive had always been a muscular girl with massive quadriceps that looked as though she could crack a walnut between her thighs. Nothing had changed in that regard, but she seemed to have grown into the look. Now, she had the powerful appearance of a sprinter. Florence Griffith Joyner sprung to mind, and I wondered if Olive ran. Her plain brown hair was cut in soft layers around her face. She'd grown into a lovely looking woman, regardless of her upbringing, or perhaps because of it.

"Miss Jefferson, Mrs. Carlson ... Olive." I said.

"You goin' to smoke that thing?" Olive said, gesturing at my cigarette, which I had laid on the table as they approached. I regarded it for a moment and then handed it over to her. To my disgust, she lit it up and took a long drag. I'd been wallowing the tip of it in my mouth for the past half hour, and the filer was soggy with my saliva, but that didn't seem to faze her.

Mrs. Carlson, the ringleader, spoke first. "So Emmy Sue, is it true?"

"It's just Emily now," I corrected, "and is what true?"

"That when the Sheriff searched that lezbo's house they found an altar for devil worshiping?"

"First of all, Mrs. Carlson, if you're going to refer to Rhianna in those derogatory terms, then you can go back to your own table."

73

"Sorry," she simpered.

"And, no!" I said. "The Sheriff did not find an altar for devil worshiping. Where'd you hear that?"

Mrs. Carlson raised one of her bushy gray eyebrows and shrugged her hunched shoulders.

"So, your husband's got her locked up now, huh?" Miss Jefferson asked, a wide smile crossing her wrinkled, puckered mouth, the mouth of someone who'd smoked all her life. (Yet another reason to quit, I thought.)

"Yes."

"It's been goin' 'round for a while that she had something over George Tierney. People seen them fightin' 'round town. Actin' like no one could hear them," Mrs. Carlson said.

"Hmmm," I murmured. I was getting the impression that if this meeting went well I could be making three strong allies. If it went badly, I'd be mud all over town. I didn't care about having my name bandied about some more, but I could use them later for information if I had to. I had to stay calm, which was going to be hard since Olive was now blowing the smoke from my own cigarette in my face. I guess she still held a grudge; I deserved the bad treatment.

"She wanted money," Miss Jefferson added.

"No, Eileen, I heard she wanted him," Mrs. Carlson corrected.

"What did he want?" I asked, amused by the obvious irony here. First, Mrs. Carlson referred to Rhianna as a "lezbo" and then didn't bat an eye at saying she wanted George. I shouldn't have been surprised; verisimilitude has never been a key element of gossip.

"Far 'z I could tell, he wanted to be left alone," Mrs. Carlson replied.

"Used to be a real nice guy, but after he started writin', he holed himself up in the house and didn't want to do nuthin' but sit at his computer," Miss Jefferson added.

Olive didn't say anything. She just sat there continuing to blow smoke in my face.

"He writes porno books," Miss Jefferson said.

Now, as I said before, I knew George was writing mystery novels. "Erotica," I corrected.

"Huh?" asked Miss Jefferson.

"Erotica—that's the term for that genre of literature. Besides, he told me he was writing a mystery novel."

"Well, you'd know," Miss Jefferson sneered.

"So what's your husband have to say about all of this?" asked Mrs. Carlson.

Now, the real reason they had sat down here was revealing itself. They were looking for information from the sheriff's wife. Suddenly, I noticed that the only other noises in the café besides our conversation were the sounds of forks scraping plates as the other patrons ate or spoons tinkled against coffee cups as others stirred their coffees.

"It's official police business. My husband doesn't usually divulge confidential information to anyone, especially me." I said. Obviously, this was a lie; Jack always used me as a sounding board, going over the details of his cases. That's why his anger about my involvement with Rhianna and Andy stung so much. It was too close to home.

"Uh-huh," grunted Mrs. Carlson.

"I hear you got strapped with taking care of her bastard kid," shot Miss Jefferson, still a little sore about being corrected regarding the accurate literary term for erotica. I had to control my temper and play this cool, but I couldn't stand for someone to malign an innocent child who had no control over how he came into this world.

"With all due respect, Miss Jefferson, I'll ask you not to call

Andy a bastard. We cannot blame or label a small child for the choices his mother has made," I said as sweetly as possible. But she still bristled at, yet again, being corrected. I thought I'd blown the whole thing, when Mrs. Carlson spoke up.

"She's right, Eileen. No need to speak ill of the child. Not his fault," she said.

Olive blew the last of my cigarette in my face and then dropped the butt in my half-full coffee cup.

"Well, it's been nice talkin' to ya. We've gotta get outta here. Leave you to your breakfast," Mrs. Carlson said, looking at my now cold cup of coffee with the cigarette floating in it.

The three of them got up from my booth and left the café. It hadn't been an enlightening exchange but interesting all the same. Now that they'd left, everyone else turned back to their conversations, looking at me sideways trying to see how I would react to my visit from the tittle-tattle trio. I fished another cigarette out of my pocket and asked the waitress for a new cup of coffee, trying to look as unaffected as possible.

After I left the cafe, I still had an hour before I had to play shopkeeper, so I stopped by the Sheriff's Office.

"Hello, Mrs. Romano. The Sheriff's on patrol," said Dan Sullivan, the deputy behind the dispatcher/reception desk. Since Middletown was such a small community, the other deputies took turns filling in as dispatcher and taking care of citizens who walked in off the street.

"Sully," I said, using the nickname he had been known by since he was a small boy, "I've known you since we were in the first grade. Drop the Mrs. Romano and go back to calling me Emily; it's too weird for you to call me 'Mrs' anything."

"But you're the sheriff's wife," he said, blushing.

"Yes, but I'm not the sheriff's property. So I'll keep calling you Sully and you keep calling me Emily. Okay." I'd always liked Sully; he was a good ol' boy with a heart of gold in that he liked fast cars, wore plaid shirts (flannel in the winter and cotton in the summer) and jeans when not at work, and had simple tastes. Plus, he was a sweetie with the cutest dimples, earnest blue eyes, and sandy blonde hair. He was smart, too, but he'd never let you know it on purpose.

Then with a mischievous look in his eye, he asked, "Can I call you Fire?" Nicknames are a staple of small town life. Some people were called Bubba, Butch, or Bud; I was Fire, a nickname Sully, himself, had given me when we'd met as six-year-olds at Arlington School. Upon seeing me the first day of school, he had said my hair was the color of fire. I was lucky; Fire was better than Pancake Pam (because her chest was flat as a . . .) or Backseat Brenda, which were the nicknames of two girls I had gone to high school with. Only one other person had tried to call me that since I'd come back to Middletown—Ernie Oakhurst. Ernie had been a buddy of mine in high school. Two days back in town and I heard someone in the grocery store yelling "Fire! Hey, Fire" at me. I turned to see Ernie leaning out from behind the Butcher's counter, completely oblivious to the near panic he had caused shoppers within earshot. I had given him such a dirty look that he seemed surprised he hadn't been petrified on the spot.

"Not if you want to live," I said with that flare of spitfire that had made the nickname stick. Getting back to my original mission, I said, "I'm not here to see the sheriff. I want to see Rhianna Reese."

"Oh, okay. Well . . . I need to see your driver's license," he said, also getting back to business.

Shortly, I was sitting in a visiting area talking to Rhianna on one of those phones like in the movies. Deep circles outlined her eyes, and she looked like she hadn't slept all night. The orange jail jumpsuit made her look pale and emphasized the dark circles.

"How you holding up?" I asked her.

"I'm okay. Everyone's been real nice, especially the sheriff. I guess that's one of the perks of being arrested in a small town," she said as if she were forcing herself to keep the conversation light. "How's Andy?"

"He's okay, considering."

"Thank you so much for everything," she said. "Please don't bring him here. I don't want him to see me here. I'll call him at your house. They've been good about letting me make phone calls. I don't think they're used to having a woman murder suspect as a prisoner."

"I'm glad I can help. I'll tell Andy you'll call him," I said, trying to gather my thoughts. "Rhianna, I want to help you. Jack told me about George being Andy's father."

"Yeah, who would have guessed that George would turn out to be such a jerk? It wasn't all Mara either."

"George told Jack that you'd been stalking him."

"That's not true!"

"I didn't believe it when he told me, but the D.A. certainly does. With Andy being George's son, the D.A. thinks that gives you a motive for wanting to kill Mara. Rumor has it that you wanted her out of the way, so you could have George all to yourself."

"That's not true either!" she screeched. I saw the deputy sitting in the corner of the visiting room getting antsy.

"Calm down. It's not me you have to convince of your innocence. I believe you. I'm only telling you what's going on, so you know what you have to defend yourself against. I can't speak for Jack, but I know him; he's not one to believe idle gossip. He's a good police officer and he works with solid, provable facts. I can't say the same for the D.A. or Brett Bradley." I paused, letting everything that I had said sink in. She nodded her head, understanding what I was telling her.

"What about the fentanyl?"

"I have no idea where it came from or how it got in the perm solution."

"Is your lawyer from around here?"

"No. He's a guy that I knew from L.A. who's living in Chicago now."

"You better have him talk to someone local, someone who can keep him in the loop with gossip and the social waters."

"I know exactly the person," she said, smiling at me.

"Rhianna, I can't. I've already taken a big chance helping you with Andy without asking Jack first. You're my friend, but if I help your lawyer, it may cost me more than I'm willing to give."

"Okay, you've helped so much already, and I understand how it looks for the sheriff's wife to be taking in the child of someone accused of murder. I'll find someone. Maybe Janney can help."

"Speaking of Janney, what should we do about the shop? Can she still come in and do hair if you're not there?"

"No, she's in training. She doesn't have a license and can't cut hair unless a licensed professional is present. The Illinois Department of Financial and Professional Regulation would shut me down, and I'd be in worse trouble. Poor Janney. I don't know what she's going to do." Rhianna had been helping Janney since Janney's mother had died of breast cancer the year before. Janney had won a scholarship to college, but had turned it down so she could stay in Middletown and take care of her little brother, who was now sixteen.

"Do you have money?" I asked.

"Not a lot. I'm probably going to have to put up my house and the shop as bond," she said, heaving a sigh that I knew was keeping tears at bay.

"Don't worry. We'll think of something. What about your family?"

"Like I said, my parents are in Europe, and my sister's husband has already been here to tell me not to ask for money or help and that they are drawing up papers to take Andy."

"Rhi, don't you think your parents would want to know that you're in trouble? Wouldn't they want to help?"

She just shrugged her shoulders. There was more there, but I didn't want to push.

"Well, don't worry. I'll have to see an actual court order before I'll even let them within ten feet of him."

She'd been trying to keep her composure, but my resolve to protect her child proved to be too much for her, and she dissolved into tears. At that moment, the deputy came over. "Time's up. Sorry," he said.

"Rhianna, don't worry. You focus on getting out of here, and I'll focus on taking care of Andy."

She nodded her head, still unable to compose herself as the deputy led her away.

My head felt heavy and thick with everything that had happened. I was so distracted as I left the Sheriff's Office that I didn't notice Jack pulling into the parking lot as I was pulling out. It wasn't until I was several blocks away that I realized he was following me, sirens blaring. I pulled over and got out of my car.

"Really, Jack, is that necessary?"

"Being the Sheriff has its benefits," he said, walking toward me. My God, the sight of him in his uniform turned me on. His shirt was crisp and taut, but not tight, across his chest, and his trousers hugged his muscular behind—and all the other areas —just the right amount.

"You like to play with the siren."

"You're the only thing I like to play with," he said as he swept his Smoky from his head and grabbed me, holding me tight against him as he kissed me deeply, right there on Fifteenth Street. Apparently, he had forgiven me.

"Why, Sheriff," I said in my best Southern drawl, "is that your nightstick or are you happy to see me?"

My encounter with Jack made me feel like I was walking on feathers for most of the day. It seemed like he'd forgiven me for taking in Andy without asking him first. Now, I could go on with the rest of my day without that hanging over my head.

The store was busy, which surprised but didn't shock me. However, I was disappointed to find out that most people were patronizing the store more out of curiosity about me and the murder case than out of a dire need for good literature. Being right next door to the scene of the crime also brought people in. There was a steady stream of people walking slowly passed Rhianna's shop, rubbernecking as they went by. Some even outright stopped and peered in the window as if Mara's corpse was still lying on the floor for all to see.

Whatever the reason was, I was pleased to have the extra business, especially since I'd been closed for two days because of my hospitalization. I selfishly took the opportunity to educate everyone I could on the benefits of reading something besides Danielle Steele and Harlequin Romances. I begrudgingly sold books that I considered fluff and not worth the paper they were printed on because my distributor told me that I couldn't have a bookstore and not sell what he swore were staples. But I refused to sell bodice-ripper romances. I was sure my ban on bodice-rippers was hurting my business, but there were some standards I wouldn't bend on. Whenever a customer asked for one of these "fluff" books, I always tried to redirect him or her to something more substantial yet still entertaining. Sometimes I was successful and the customer would come back to thank me and buy more, and sometimes I was revealed for the bibliophilic snob that I am. But, it's my store, and that's my prerogative.

During a lull around two o'clock in the afternoon, Kylie sidled up to me and pointed out the window to where an elderly man was sitting on a park bench across the street. The town square was bordered by four streets and rows of brick and stone buildings on all four sides with the courthouse on a patch of lawn in the middle.

"He's been sitting there all day. It gives me the creeps," she said.

The man was Hairy Harry, an indigent who lived in town. During the day, he sat on park benches around town, watching people go about their daily routine. At night, he prowled the streets. I never knew how he'd gotten the nickname "Hairy" Harry; looking at him now, I could see the sun glistening off his bald head. In fact, I couldn't remember him ever having had hair. He had been around since I was a kid. Some people said he was shell-shocked in Korea and had never spoken since. I had never heard him speak or heard anyone say he talked to them. He went to our church every Sunday, but I never saw him sing or respond during the Mass.

"He's harmless, Kylie. He's probably like everyone else and wants to see if there's going to be any more action in our little corner of town." She didn't look convinced, so I added, "If he keeps it up, I'll have Jack tell him to move," which seemed to relieve her.

CHAPTER 8

Whatever remnant of afterglow I had from my brief encounter with Jack that morning was gone when I walked in the door at home that night. The bustle of the day had started eroding it, but when I picked the kids up from my mother's, she made a big fuss about how tired all the extra responsibility (i.e. Andy) was making her. She claimed she didn't take the kids to the library that day for story time like she usually did because she was so tired. I thought it was more likely she didn't want anyone to see her with Andy. Her pettiness infuriated me.

When I got home, I found that Jack had eaten the roast beef I was going to use for dinner and had left his dishes and the mayonnaise on the counter. It was the third time he'd come home for lunch this week and eaten what I was going to prepare for dinner or had left food out on the counter to rot. It really wasn't like him to leave dirty dishes around and food out. I was starting to see it as some kind of subtle hostility. The thing that made it so strange was that he didn't usually come home for lunch. I hadn't said anything because at first I thought it was a unique situation, but this was the last straw. I'd had enough and decided to confront him. I called his cell.

"Jack, on your way home, stop by *Dancing Dave's* and pick up some sandwiches since you ate the roast beef I was going to make for supper tonight," I said, throwing the spoiled mayonnaise in the trash.

"Emmy, I haven't been home since I left at six o'clock this morning. I didn't eat the roast beef."

Puzzled, I said, "This is the third time this week I've come home and food's been eaten, plates left out, and newspapers are strewn all over the couch," I said, peeking into the family room.

"It's not me, Em."

With a sigh of relief, I said, "I'm sorry, Jack. It's been a long couple of days. I should have known you wouldn't do something that inconsiderate." Even though I was now concerned because someone was breaking into our house during the day, the queasiness in my stomach that I felt when I thought my husband was being passively-aggressively hostile, resolved itself. Jack was not passive-aggressive by nature. This situation was starting to make me feel like my marriage was on slippery ground. Or even slipperier ground than it had been over the last few days.

"Who do you think it is then?"

"Oh, I think I know, and I'm going to get to the bottom of this."

"Are you okay?"

"Yeah. It's nothing to worry about. Will you still get the sandwiches?"

"Yes, I'll be home in about half an hour."

After I hung up the phone, I walked next door to my neighbor's house. Kelly Jackson was a nurse who worked the night shift at Mercy Memorial Hospital. Her husband, Butch, worked on his dad's farm outside of town. He wanted to live in the country, but she preferred it in town. They saw very little of each other, and I often wondered why they bothered to stay married. Force of habit, I figured. Since she worked nights, she was home most days and usually knew what was going on in the neighborhood.

"Hey, Emily. What's up? How you doin'?" she asked, greeting me with a concerned look. "Come on in."

"No thanks. I can't stay. The kids are home alone. I ran over to ask you if you've seen anyone around our house during the day this week."

"Just your dad. He was here today. I saw him weeding your garden," she answered. "Anything wrong?"

"No. It's a family thing. Thanks for your help. Let's get together for coffee some morning," I called over my shoulder as I jogged back home.

Now the question was: Why was my dad coming over when I wasn't home? Suddenly, little things that had been bothering me over the last few weeks clicked into place. Like the previous Tuesday when I came home and found our bed all messed up when I was sure I'd made it that morning. And how the garden miraculously stayed weed free when neither Jack nor I had weeded it. Was he also going through our drawers and looking at everything around the house? His invasion of my privacy made me feel naked and vulnerable. My parents came over for Sunday dinner every week, a tradition we'd borrowed from Jack's parents, so I planned to take him aside the next day and get some answers.

◆ ◆ ◆

What happened that night was the accelerant for the bomb that went off a few days later. It was a series of unfortunate events that set Jack and me on a collision course that I wasn't sure our marriage would survive. In hindsight, I can take full responsibility for the hurt and indignation that he felt and that led to our eventual blow up.

When Jack came in the house an hour later, and not the half an hour that he had promised, I was ready to jump down his throat because the kids were hungry and whining. But before I had the chance, he tossed his cellphone onto the table where I was sitting. One look at his face told me he was furious.

"What the hell?" I asked.

"Why don't you open my phone and find out," he said through gritted teeth.

I punched in the passcode to his phone and saw that a video was queued up. I hit play and I watched confused for a few seconds as I saw two strangers sitting in the visitors room at the jail. Then the video jumped, and I was watching Rhianna and me talking on the telephones in the jail. I watched and listened as the video replayed me telling Rhianna about how Jack had shared information with me regarding the murder investigation and heard myself malign the D.A. and Brett Bradley's professional abilities.

I could only cover my face and groan.

"Yeah! Emily, how much more of an idiot can you be! I'd think you of all people would know better. At the very least, anyone who has ever seen a cop show on television knows that the conversations in the visitors' room are recorded."

I had nothing to offer. An 'I'm sorry' would only have seemed lame and disingenuous, and he was right. I should have known better.

"Right after I got off the phone with you, I got a call on the radio to come back to the station. Price reamed me five ways to Sunday for this. And you can guess who provided him with the video. Do me a favor, Emily, and stay out of this investigation. I don't need this kind of help," he bellowed.

I couldn't look at him, but out of the corner of my eye, I saw him leave the room. I heard him stomp up the stairs and slam our bedroom door.

Later that night after a quiet and uncomfortable dinner,

Rhianna called to talk to Andy. It was the first time he'd talked to his mom since she'd been taken into custody the day before, and he was relieved and excited to talk to her. I answered the phone when she called.

"He's doing fine," I told her after we'd exchanged pleasantries. "In fact, he's starting to squabble with the girls."

"Oh, sorry. I hope he's behaving himself," she replied.

"No, Rhianna, I meant that as a sign that he's settling in, getting used to us. He feels at home, so he can drop the politeness and be himself."

"Andy's usually always polite," she shot back.

"Listen, Rhianna, I'm not trying to say your kid's a brat. I'm only saying he's getting comfortable here, and he's being a normal kid. Your emotions are raw right now, so don't start reading into everything people say to you; it won't do you any good at this point."

"Sorry. My lawyer was just here and everything's still right on the surface. I'm really trying to hold it together, so I can talk to Andy without worrying him."

"How about a joke?"

"Okay."

I thought for a moment and then said, "What do you call a dead blonde in a closet?"

"I don't know."

"Last year's hide and seek winner."

"Hey," she said laughing. "As a blonde, I take offense to that."

I had accomplished my goal, so I called Andy to the phone.

After Andy took the phone from me, Jack appeared in the kitchen, having heard my end of the conversation.

"Have you learned nothing from the video?" he asked. "All telephone conversations are recorded!"

"I was only trying to make her laugh . . . Oh, never mind," I said, throwing up my hands and walking away.

No sooner had Andy hung up the phone and was sent off to get ready for bed, than the doorbell rang. When I opened the door, I was met with a tall, blonde stranger. He introduced himself as Rhianna's lawyer, Mark Jennings. Despite his expensive suit, he looked more like a surfer dude than a lawyer. I stepped out onto the porch to talk to him, hoping Jack wouldn't happen along.

"Listen, Mr. Jennings. I already told Rhianna that I can't help you. I'm not sure if you're aware of it, but my husband is the sheriff."

"Yes, ma'am, I know who your husband is. But I need an 'in' here, someone who can help me understand the town and its politics."

My own advice once again came back to bite me in the ass. "Well, I'm not that person. I've already gone out on a limb, taking guardianship of her son. I can't . . ." But before I could finish the sentence, Jack stepped out onto the porch, still in uniform, but rumpled.

"Mr. Jennings, it is highly inappropriate for a defense attorney to be asking the sheriff's wife for help in defending a murder suspect. I suggest that you get back in your car and go looking for help somewhere else before I'm forced to call Judge Lawrence at home and tell him you're harassing my wife for information." Without another word, Mr. Jennings walked back to his car and drove off.

"Jack, I had that under control," I said, turning to confront him only to find that he had silently sulked back inside the house, leaving me alone on the porch talking to myself.

As I closed the door, I heard a scuffle of children in the family room. I arrived in the family room doorway in time to hear Arabella say, "Give it back or I'll tell my daddy, and he'll put you in jail right along with your mother!"

We tried to use time-outs with the kids, instead of corporal punishment, but at this moment, I felt a strong desire to give my oldest a ringing slap to the mouth. With great effort I refrained from following my impulses and instead yelled, "Arabella Maria Theresa Romano, you get upstairs to your room and go to bed before I do something we will both regret."

I turned to Andy to smooth over his hurt feelings because he was now sitting on the floor in a heap, weeping. "Shhh. Don't cry, sweetie," I crooned to him. "Bella didn't mean what she said. I'm certain she was sorry the moment the words left her mouth," especially since I'd been right there to hear them, I thought. All children can be cruel, but when I witnessed it in my own children, it never failed to shock and sadden me.

"Is my mommy going to die in the electric chair?" he asked.

"No, sweetie, she didn't do anything wrong, and her lawyer, and Sheriff Romano, and I are going to do everything we can to find out what really happened and who is responsible." He seemed to settle down a bit after that, so I helped him up to bed and tucked him in with a story, a back-rub, and a kiss: the royal treatment, as the girls called it.

"Mommy, I'm sorry." Arabella called out to me as I passed her room on my way back downstairs. I went in to talk about what she had said.

"It's not me you need to apologize to. It's Andy. This is a good lesson for you to learn, Arabella. You have to think about what you are saying before you say it. Because once it leaves your mouth, you can never take it back. And saying you're sorry can never erase the hurt you've caused." It was dark in the room, but I could feel the tears on her cheeks when she leaned against my bare arm, looking for a hug of forgiveness. "Bella, you're such a sweet and considerate girl, always trying to mother everyone. It hurts and disappoints me that you'd say something so unkind to someone so vulnerable."

"He made me mad. He's been bugging me all day."

"I understand. We get irritated with people sometimes, especially when we have to spend a lot of time with them. Please try to remember that he needs extra patience and love right now." She nodded, understanding what I meant. "You can apologize tomorrow because he's sleeping now." We kissed and hugged.

As I got up from the bed to leave, she asked, "Why did Daddy put his mom in jail?"

I took a long, slow breath and knew I couldn't avoid telling her the truth any longer. I had tried very hard to keep her in the dark about what had happened. I never should have underestimated her; Arabella has always been a perceptive little girl.

"Well," I said, lowering myself back onto her bed, stalling for time to think. I wanted to be honest with her but not tell her too much. How do you explain a fentanyl overdose to a kid? "You know when I was in the hospital the other day?"

"Yes."

"It was because I got some poison in me that made me very sick. I got that poison from a woman in Ms. Reese's beauty shop. This other woman, Mrs. Tierney, she got the poison in her first, and it made her stop breathing, so I tried to help her breathe with CPR. You remember what that is don't you?"

She nodded her head.

"When I did the CPR, I got the poison on my hand," I said, showing her where the now healed blisters had been, "and I had to go to the hospital and get some medicine. Anyway, Daddy's boss thinks Ms. Reese gave the woman the poison on purpose, so he told Daddy to put her in jail. But Daddy's boss has made a mistake because Andy's mom didn't do it."

"What happened to the other woman? The one you had to give CPR?"

I paused for a moment. I couldn't lie, but I didn't want to alarm her either. "She died. I wasn't able to save her."

"Why?"

"She had too much poison in her. She was too sick."

Arabella studied my face for a long time and then gave me a big hug that seemed to say everything that I knew she was thinking.

I said goodnight to her again, and I left the room to find Jack eavesdropping in the hallway. Not expecting him to be there, I jumped when I saw him.

"Jesus, you're doing a lot of sneaking around tonight."

"Do you think you should have told her that?" he hissed at me.

"What was I going to do, lie to her when she asked me pointblank?"

"At least, you could have discussed it with me first. But you seem to be making all the decisions for both of us lately," he whispered through clenched teeth.

For the second time that night, he had rendered me speechless.

"Oh, and as far as thinking about what you say before you say it, you should practice what you preach, *Mom*," he continued.

"You know, Jack, maybe you should . . ." But instead of saying something I couldn't take back, I flicked my thumb under my two top teeth. It had the same effect. He turned away from me and stomped down the stairs in anger.

CHAPTER 9

I t was another sleepless night. Jack came to bed several hours after I did. I suspected that he fell asleep on the couch, woke up well after midnight, and then came to bed. When he did come to bed, I endured another night of him sticking out his elbows and knees at me. The exhaustion, anger, and disappointment that we both felt left us ill-prepared for the challenging day we had ahead of us.

Right from the start of Sunday morning my patience was slowly eroded, until I was a frazzled mess. I hadn't thought about church when I'd told Rhianna that I'd take Andy. (Obviously, I hadn't thought about a lot of things when I agreed to take care of him.) I wasn't sure what his mother had told him about religion, but when I woke him up that morning to get him ready for church, he seemed almost terrified. His face looked pale and his eyes were wide.

"It's okay, Andy. We're not going to make you get baptized. You're too young to stay by yourself. This family goes to church on Sunday. Since you're staying with us, you will go, too," I explained.

Things went progressively downhill from there. Jack and I had a strict dress code when it came to church; however, when I looked through the clothes Rhianna had packed for him, there wasn't anything that we would consider passable for church attire. Finally, I settled for a pair of nicely pressed khaki shorts and a red polo shirt and left him to dress on his own, while I moved on to Bella and Elly.

A few minutes later, I heard Jack talking to him in the hallway.

"Andy, we don't wear shorts to church. We wear our best clothes to go to the house of God."

When I stepped into the hall, Andy was standing in Jack's shadow with his lower lip trembling, struggling not to cry.

"Jack," I said, going to Andy's side, "this *is* his Sunday best."

Jack stared at me blankly for a moment and then pulled at his tie as if it were choking him, and said, "Oh. . . Come on, buddy. Let's get some cereal." As he gently ushered Andy downstairs, he shot me a look over his shoulder that let me know he'd put another tally mark by my name on his mental shit-list. I wanted to crawl back in bed and pull the covers over my head until tomorrow.

As soon as we entered the church narthex, I wanted to kick myself for being so obtuse. It had never occurred to me what sort of reception we'd get for bringing 'a murderer's son' into the house of God. We would have been greeted with more warmth and less talk if we'd been covered in oozing pustules.

When we got home after church, I was more than happy to retreat to the kitchen where I could block everything else out and concentrate on preparing the meal. Most Sundays Jack would help or he'd make the meal himself, but today he kept his distance. I wish I could call Sunday dinner off, but I definitely did not want to deal with the fall out from that decision. My parents usually came over between eleven-thirty and twelve, depending on if they'd gone to church or not. Still Presbyterian, they didn't go to the same church as we did.

When they arrived at twelve-fifteen, I pulled my dad into the kitchen while my mother was still doling out hugs and kisses. I was surprised to see her give Andy a squeeze.

But before I could confront him, he pressed twenty dollars in my hand and said, "Here. This is for the food I ate."

"Dad, I don't want your money," I said, trying to give it back to him. "Why are you coming over here during the day? If you want to see me, all you have to do is come to the store."

He pushed the money back at me and said, "Your mother is driving me crazy. She wants to control what I do all day. I can't just putter or take a nap. She's right in my ear. Nag, nag, nag. And she's starving me to death with all that low fat shit." He took a deep breath, and then said, "I cannot spend another minute of my life listening to her talk about Mara Tierney. Twenty years was enough."

I pressed the money back into his palm and said, "If you need to get away, why don't you come to the store? You could read the paper, and I wouldn't bother you."

"She'd find me there," he said, sticking the money in the pocket of my jacket.

"And she can't find you here?" I asked, removing the money and putting it in the breast pocket of his shirt.

"Hasn't so far," he said, grinning, while he removed the money.

As he lifted the lid of a nearby cookie jar and dropped the money inside, I tried to gently explain to him why his coming over had created problems. That he had eaten food I'd set aside for dinner and that he made messes that I blamed on Jack.

"I'm sorry. I won't come over any more," he replied.

"No," I said, smiling in surrender that he'd won our little back-and-forth with the twenty dollars, "if you need to get away, you can come over here. I'll label whatever it is we're having for supper, so you don't eat it by mistake. And if you'd clean up after yourself, I'd appreciate it."

My dad and I had a mutual understanding—we indulged one another. He could rarely say no to me and I had the same fault with regard to him. Unfortunately, my mother often felt on the outside and worried we were conspiring against her. It was the classic mother-daughter-father triangle, intensified since I was an only child.

"Thanks for weeding the garden," I said, standing on my tiptoes to kiss him because at six feet two inches, his lips were out of my reach. The few times my family and Jack's family have been together the pairing has been almost comical. We make them look like dwarves. At six-five, Jack is the tallest in his family, since their average height is five-five. It's a mystery where Jack got his height from. Even my mother, at five feet eight inches, is taller than both of Jack's parents and his two sisters. When Jack and I started dating, it felt awkward to bend down to hug his father.

"Well, isn't this cozy," my mother said, oozing sarcasm, as she barged through the kitchen door. My dad gave me another squeeze and then slid past my mother to join Jack and the kids in the family room.

I was putting the finishing touches on veal parmesan, spaghetti, and a roasted red pepper and egg frittata. I'd spent hours in Jack's Nana Peppina's kitchen watching her cook and learning her recipes. Peppers and eggs was one of her specialties that I could never make to my own satisfaction, but I still loved to prepare it. Eating it put me right back in her kitchen, hearing her stories about growing up in Chicago in the 1920's, and learning her little tricks, like putting a pinch of sugar in the sugo or meat sauce. But it was the down-home cooking that I'd learned in my grandmother's kitchen that had served as a basis for everything I learned from Nana. From the time that I was old enough to stand on a chair and hold a spoon to stir, I had cooked with my grandma. Jack still swears that it was her fried chicken that cinched his desire to marry me.

As I was dishing out the spaghetti and sauce (or "gravy" as my mother-in-law would call it) into separate bowls, my mother said, "Now, remember, your dad likes his spaghetti and sauce together."

"Well, he can mix them together on his plate," I snapped. I tried to have the meal prepared when my parents arrived, or my mother drove me crazy with little micromanaging suggestions.

As we were all finishing up our food, my mother pushed herself away from the table, her food all gone except for a crust of bread and a pile of sauce, and said, "Do we always have to have Italian? Why don't you all come to our house next week for a good, home-cooked meal?" As if the meal I'd served her had come from a box and didn't take two hours to prepare. "These rich cheeses and such can't be good for your father's cholesterol."

"Oh, and the fried chicken and hamburgers you make are so low in fat?" I said.

Seeing a storm on the horizon, my dad got to his feet and asked, "Who wants to go to Dairy Queen?" Of course a hail of "yeas" erupted, and Jack, my dad, and the kids made a quick escape.

As soon as the screen door banged behind them, I was on the attack.

"Mother, I'm an adult. I have a husband, two healthy, happy kids, I own my own house, I own a business, and I remember to pay my taxes and set my clocks forward and back every year. When are you going to stop second guessing everything I do and trying to make me look and feel like an incompetent fool?"

"Why, Emily, I have no idea what you're talking about?"

"Oh, come on, Mother, I'm not buying that whole innocent act that you're so good at playing. *'I never do anything wrong. Everyone always picks on me,'*" I said, mimicking her like a petulant child.

"Maybe if you acted more responsibly . . ."

"More responsibly?! Really, mother. All the things I just listed take responsibility. I'm one of the most responsible people I know."

"Taking in a child of such a person. That boy has a family who could take care of him."

"Well, this is new. So you've been angry with me not only because Rhianna is who she is but because I took in Andy?"

"At least he'd have a chance at a decent upbringing if his family raised him."

"Did you ever think that maybe he is getting a decent upbringing and that maybe there are circumstances at play here that you know nothing about?"

"I've heard the talk. That Rhianna was always adept at telling lies. Saying her brother-in-law tried to rape her and such," she said, rolling her eyes. This surprised me because it wasn't something that Rhianna had divulged to me. "Nothing was ever proven."

"Was it even investigated?" I asked.

"Why would it need to be investigated? It was all fabrication by a rebellious, bad seed. Her brother-in-law, Calvin Haslop, is an upstanding citizen of the community, if not a little over zealous. He owns Haslop Insurance Company."

"I guess that makes him above reproach?"

"Yes, it does."

"Mother, people abuse their power all of the time. Even the President of the United States."

"How is that child going to influence your children? Did you ever consider that?" she said pointing a knobby finger at me.

"What are you getting at? Andy is a very sweet, well-mannered child. I have no problem with him being around the girls."

"Well his mother's a . . ." She got a sour look on her face as if the words she was trying to say left a bad taste in her mouth.

"What, Mother? A lesbian? That doesn't mean she has some disease that's going to rub off on the girls. We're not all going to turn into lesbians because we know one."

"You know it's going around town that you're her lover."

"Now, Mother, you can't think that's true?" I said, rolling my eyes so hard I thought they were going to permanently stay that way.

I couldn't help but think what a cliche this all was. People othering Rhianna and her son because Rhianna is different from them. Of course, they couldn't believe that a gay person could have straight friends. To most of them, being LGBTQ was probably a lifestyle choice and not who someone was born to be.

"You two were awfully close as kids. The way you've been acting I wouldn't be surprised at anything!"

I could see that her key aim was to hurt and humiliate me, so she could regain control over my behavior. I wasn't going to let that happen. That's why we bumped heads all the time: She wanted to control me and turn me into who she was, while I wanted to be myself. To head off her intentions, I called her on it.

"Mother, you have to stop trying to control me. I'm me, not you."

"I don't try to control anyone," she said, her blue eyes widening with disbelief. Her dyed platinum blond hair was so stiff with hairspray that it moved as one unit as she shook her head in protest.

"Please! Do you know dad comes over here during the day so that he can have some peace and quiet, without you nagging him all the time and trying to control what he does every moment of the day?"

"I know he comes over here. He parks right in your

driveway. Like I'm so stupid that I couldn't find him if I wanted to."

"Then let the man have some peace, so he can relax in his own home."

"You're always on his side. You both always gang up on me."

"That's right mother; you're the victim here. *'Nobody likes me, everybody hates me, I think I'll go eat worms,'*" I said, quoting something she used to say to me as a kid when we'd argue, and I'd accuse her of being unfair. Okay, I was being childish. Some old patterns never changed.

"You know, Emily, I've always resented how you ran off to college and never came home. Always making your father and me feel guilty, saying you were working to pay your tuition. Do you know how many times your dad told me how bad he felt that he couldn't pay for your education?!"

I stepped backward. Had I really made my dad feel that way? Had I been that ungrateful? Then I realized that this was another one of her tactics. She was using guilt to turn the argument back on me.

"That's right! Emily's an ungrateful child." I retorted. "She goes off to get an education, instead of staying here at home so I can harass her and run her life!"

"Well, I can see you don't want me here. I'm going home."

"What about dad?"

"He likes it here so much; he can stay here then," she said, grabbing her clutch purse that matched her navy blue pants suit and navy pumps and stomped out the door.

I felt a rush of relief when I heard the squealing of her car's tires as she sped away. We had squabbled with one another practically since I could talk, but this was different. Today, we laid all our cards on the table, and instead of folding when we saw this was a bad hand, we had gone all in and played it out. Unfortunately, we both lost. The relief I felt over finally getting some of these issues off my chest was gone almost as soon as I felt it, and it was replaced with sadness and guilt. Since no one was home to witness it, I began sobbing like a baby and had a good cry until I heard Jack and my dad pull into the driveway with the kids about an hour later.

"Well, was it big?" my dad asked as soon as he stepped into the house and saw me sitting with tear-stained cheeks at the dining room table which was still cluttered with dirty dinner dishes.

"Oh, yeah," I replied. "Everything that has been building up between us for years came out. By the way, she said if you liked it here so much, you could stay here."

"Oh," he said, contemplating the ramifications of that statement, and then added, in the authoritarian voice that I always associated with my childhood, "Well, I'm sleeping in my own bed tonight, and if that woman thinks she can stop me, she's got another thing coming."

I could hear the familiar "eek, eek" of the swing set and knew the kids were out back playing. Jack came in carrying a sleeping Elly. He looked at me and then at the uncleared table and then back at me with my red, swollen face and eyes. A look passed between us that asked and gave forgiveness for the anger we were holding, and without a word, we were both absolved. Turning to my dad, Jack handed him Elly and asked him to take her to bed. Then Jack came around the table, pulled me to my feet, and held me in one of his bear hugs. We'd had so little contact in the last few days that I liquefied into tears again.

"She'll never forgive me," I sniffed.

"She will. You needed to do it. Her behavior was uncalled for. I almost went after her when she insulted your cooking. You work so hard to prepare a fabulous meal for them and she's never happy. She's jealous and doesn't like to be outshined by her daughter."

"I agree," said my dad as he reentered the dining room. "Jack's right. You should have stood up to her a long time ago. Maybe I should take my own advice. I'm going home," he said, coming over and kissing me on the forehead and giving Jack's arm a squeeze. Then he walked out the door. My parents lived across town, but I figured he needed the walk to decide what he was going to say to her. It was a beautiful day anyway.

"I'll clean this mess up. Why don't you go take a nap," Jack suggested. I did feel wiped out.

"Okay. My stomach hurts, too."

"Probably indigestion from all that pent up anger," he said, smiling.

CHAPTER 10

That night Jack and I had a brief discussion about how my actions were making it difficult for him to gain credibility with key people who were bent on making his professional life hell—the D.A. and Bradley. I agreed to think things through before I acted, and he agreed to forgive me. What had happened between us over the last few days was more complicated than that, but we were both emotionally spent from everything and needed a short, simple solution to our problems.

In the past, whenever adversity had crossed our path, we'd clung together like ballast in a hurricane, using the adversity to make us stronger and bring us closer. We'd never faced something that put us on opposite sides of the fence. My argument with my mother gave us something against which we could unite. Jack loved my mother, but he'd had his differences with her as well. Like a good husband, he always came down on my side of the battle line. My current argument with my mother had one positive outcome—Jack and I were on the same side again, which brought peace to our house, if only for a few hours. That night we fell into each other's arms like two people who had been on a hunger strike falling on a steak dinner.

We made love for the first time since I'd accidentally been overdosed. Because of all that had happened in the last week, our emotions were on the surface and all our feelings went into our lovemaking, which made it sweeter and more intense. When Jack saw the still prominent bruise in the center of my chest, his eyes filled with tears. In return, I took a finger and circled the scar directly below his left collarbone, remembering the fear I'd felt when the precinct chaplain and Jack's partner showed up on our doorstep to tell me Jack had been shot. I began to cry, too.

Afterward, as he held me in his arms, he said, "I understand now."

I raised my head from his chest and looked into his eyes. I noticed for the first time how tired he looked. His dark eyes seemed unusually sunken and darker than normal.

"I understand what you must have been feeling when I was shot and how hard it must have been for you to watch me go off to my job afterward, knowing the same thing could happen all over again. Knowing that the next time, I might not be so lucky."

I kissed him and laid my head back down on his chest.

"I'm glad we came back here. I can see now that this is where we're supposed to be. I like being Sheriff. My job is much more varied than if I'd become a homicide detective. I have the chance to affect change for an entire community, not just one small segment of it."

I still didn't say anything; I just held him tighter. Eventually, his breathing got deeper and I knew he was asleep. I lay there listening to my husband's deep, even breathing, thinking about what a mess I'd been for the past two years. I couldn't understand why this man still loved me. Jack had always seemed larger than life to me, and even after ten years of marriage, I still questioned why he loved *me*.

To this small town girl whose life had progressed like stair steps (high school, college, career, marriage, children), Jack's life seemed like an action-adventure movie. When I met him, I was twenty-two, a fresh college graduate, and he was twenty-seven. It seemed to me that he'd already lived a lifetime in those twenty-seven years. After graduating from high school, Jack had spent eight years in the Marine Corps, most of it in the Marine Security Forces providing security to embassies. While in the Marines, he'd gotten a college degree online. After his eight years in the Marines were up, he decided that he'd traveled the world enough and went home to Chicago, instead of reenlisting. His high school pal, Sean Priest, had gone to the police academy and was now a seasoned Chicago police officer. Jack decided to go to the academy as well, and they became partners when Jack graduated.

That's how I met Jack. I was being mugged at gunpoint when Priest and he happened along on a routine patrol of my street. I was unlocking the entrance door to my apartment building when a man put a gun in my ribs and ordered me to turn around. The street to my apartment from the L stop was dark, and there was no outside light at the doorway, so I had been using a large Mag-lite flashlight to light my way when I came home from work at night. When I turned around as the man had ordered, I pointed the light directly into his eyes, blinding him long enough to use the heavy flashlight to whack the gun out of his hand. By then, my fight or flight instincts had kicked in, and instead of doing the sensible thing and running away as fast as I could, I began hitting him about the arms and torso with the flashlight, screaming "NO!" as I did so.

It was my screams and the strobe-like effect of the flashlight as I hit the offender that drew Jack and Priest's attention as they cruised by on an intersecting street. After they pulled me off the mugger and assessed that he'd chosen the wrong woman to mug, Priest proceeded to lecture me about how crazy my actions were. But Jack just stood back and watched me. I thought he figured I was some sort of head case, but on our first date, he told me he admired how I'd fought back.

"During my short time as a cop," he told me, "I've seen so many women victimized. It's not their fault that they fall victim to crime, but so many of them are afraid to fight back. Afraid to be embarrassed or to offend someone, so they get taken advantage of."

"If you talked to anyone in my hometown, they'd tell you I was more of a rule breaker than a rule maker," I replied.

"Don't get me wrong," he shot back. "What you did was totally nuts. The guy had a gun."

At the time, I laughed at his kidding admonishment, but I soon learned that he was pointing out a difference between us that would remain constant in our relationship—he was prudent and went by the book, while I wasn't—and didn't.

I lifted my head from his chest and looked up at his peaceful face. I silently thanked God that Jack loved me despite all my crazy flaws, and then I rolled away from him and got out of bed. I felt content, but I couldn't sleep, so I put on my robe and went downstairs to the computer.

Obviously, I knew what fentanyl was and that narcan was the antagonist used to save someone's life. But I really didn't know what fentanyl did to the body. I learned that fentanyl suppresses respiration to the point where the lungs become almost paralyzed, making it nearly impossible to draw a breath. The pupils become like pinpoints and the victim loses consciousness almost immediately. Due to the lack of oxygen, their lips and fingernails turn purple. People suffering from severe overdose will often regain consciousness if narcan is administered in time. However, they often fall back into overdose, requiring several doses of narcan and breathing support to reverse the effects, if possible. I thought about my experience, what little memory I had of it, and the feeling that I was trying to surface from being underwater. Those must have been the times that the narcan had been administered, and I was fighting to regain consciousness.

I had to stop reading. I felt like a dam had burst in my brain and a river of thoughts were crashing on to my consciousness all at once. I realized how lucky I had been that the paramedics were on site and I could receive the narcan so quickly. I also realized that Mara, obviously, had not been so lucky. I was unsure how long she had been under the dryer, but within a few minutes she must have overdosed and asphyxiated before anyone even realized anything was wrong.

I grabbed a nearby notebook and started writing all of this down, wanting to make sense of it. I wanted Jack's input, but I didn't want him to think I was meddling again after the wonderful night we'd had.

After I'd poured my thoughts onto paper, my greatest talent, I closed the notebook and made my way back upstairs. I grabbed my rosary from the nightstand and sat down on the window seat in our bedroom. Our bedroom was the room in the house containing the round turret that is characteristic of Victorian houses. We'd made that cozy alcove into a window seat, and I often sat there and read. Now, I was doing what I usually did when I couldn't sleep: I said *Hail Marys* until I drifted off.

I laced the rosary loosely around my fingers, and then I released my hair from the ponytail I'd been wearing it in. Jack was fond of comparing my mass of red curls to a lion's mane because he said it reflected who I was: beautiful, but dangerous. He said I looked harmless enough, but like a lion, I should never be underestimated. I had a fierce heart that made me passionate and ready to fight in an instant, but also made me loyal and strong. I liked the analogy, so I'd never pointed out to him that it was the male lions that had the mane. I'd grown to like the color of my hair now that I was an adult and knew what lengths other women went to in an attempt to duplicate the color. However, as a whole, I saw my hair as an annoyance. I kept it long because Jack liked it that way, and I looked better with long hair. It was so curly and bushy that I'd often start the day with it cascading around my shoulders, but before ten in the morning, I'd end up twisting it into a bun or pulling it into a ponytail.

Now, as I sat in the window seat hugging my knees, I let it fall around my bare shoulders to keep them warm. I rested my chin on my knees and stared out the window, lightly fingering my rosary as I kept track of my prayers. The night was clear and a full moon was waxing, so the outside was quite illuminated. Sheer curtains hung at the windows, giving the outside a misty quality as I gazed out the window. My alarm clock read two-thirty. I was dreading the next day, knowing I was going to be very tired.

As I sat there, my eyes rested on a figure standing in the shadow of a large blue spruce tree in our neighbor's front yard. I stood up, but didn't part the curtains. I couldn't see where the figure was looking or who it was, but I could see that it was definitely a person. I could see it shifting its weight from one foot to another, and then I saw the smolder of a cigarette. There was no light in the room behind me, so I didn't think the person could see me looking out the window. I hated to do it, but I had to wake Jack. If someone in the neighborhood got robbed and I later confessed that I'd seen someone hanging around in the middle of the night, he'd be angry.

"Jack," I said, quietly, and then I remembered that the window was open, so I went to his side of the bed and shook him gently, "Jack, there's someone outside."

Before I had touched him, he showed no signs of being awake, but when I said someone was outside, he was on his feet so fast I staggered backwards with surprise. He went straight to the closet to retrieve his gun from the small lockbox he kept it in when he was at home.

"Where?"

"Across the street standing next to the Jensens' blue spruce."

Jack's honed instincts took over. He held his gun stiff-armed and pointed to the floor as he crept down the hall to the backstairs that led to the kitchen. I assumed he was going out the back door because if he went out the front, he'd be spotted right away. My heart was pounding in my ears as I went back to the window. I couldn't tell if anyone was still there. I couldn't see the ember of the cigarette or see any movement, but that didn't mean there wasn't anyone there.

After what seemed like several minutes, I saw Jack steal across the street. He stooped and picked something up, probably the cigarette butt, and then dropped it again. He went down the side of the Jensens' house and out of my view. After a minute or so more, I saw the Jensen house light up. Before long, Jack was crossing the street in a casual, but purposeful manner, only stopping to pick up whatever he'd looked at before. Now that I could see he was safe, I went down to the kitchen to meet him.

"I didn't see anyone, but I scared the piss out of Roy Jensen," he chuckled. I realized that Jack must have been a sight sneaking around in the dead of night barefoot, only wearing boxer shorts, and carrying his SIG Sauer.

"Sorry I got you out of bed for nothing," I said.

"Don't be. There was someone there," he said, holding up a still smoldering cigarette butt. I shivered as a sudden chill ran down my spine.

"Who do you think it was?"

"I don't know, but I wouldn't worry. It could have been anyone," but he didn't succeed in convincing me that he wasn't worried about it. "Go back to bed, and I'll be up in a minute."

Upstairs in bed, I heard the quiet murmur of his voice on the phone. He was probably calling for an extra patrol to go around the neighborhood looking for prowlers. Then I heard him checking all the door and window locks. When he finally came to bed, he sank into the mattress next to me and said, "Oooo, we're going to be tired tomorrow; it's three o'clock. Have you even slept?"

"No. I guess I'm wired." I replied.

"Well," he said rolling towards me, "let's see if we can do something about that."

Even if he didn't catch the prowler, at least it led to sex. I chalked it up to excess adrenaline that his cop body needed to work off. Whatever it was, it didn't matter because the second best thing to make-up sex is unexpected-middle-of-the-night sex.

Finally, I was able to sleep.

CHAPTER 11

Unfortunately, I wasn't able to sleep in because Rhianna's arraignment was early that morning. Since Rhianna had been arrested on a Friday, she had to stay in jail all weekend before she could be arraigned. Jack wanted to wait until Monday to arrest her for that reason, but the District Attorney insisted he bring her in on Friday. The D.A. thought she was a flight risk, which didn't bode well for her being granted bail.

Court got started early, so I was able to attend the hearing before opening the store that morning. I needed to find some daytime help. When I spoke to Rhianna's lawyer a few minutes before the proceedings started, I was relieved to discover that he seemed to know what he was doing.

I sat in the front row of the gallery behind Rhianna. She didn't seem to have any family support, so I took on that role. Her parents were still in Europe, but her sister and brother-in-law were sitting behind the D.A. I took that as a sign of where they stood on the question of Rhianna's guilt or innocence. If what my mother said was true about Rhianna making accusations against her brother-in-law, it made sense that they wouldn't be jumping to come to her defense. I was mildly surprised that George hadn't shown up at the arraignment but thought maybe he couldn't bring himself to face Rhianna again so soon.

As I looked around the gallery at the other spectators

(because that is what they were, spectators), I could easily pick out the reporters because they sat together in the second row, cordially chatting with one another, pad and pen or cellphone in hand. There were five of them in all. As the gallery began to fill up, I was glad that I had gotten there early, or I may not have found a seat. Rhianna's arrest was the hot topic in town, and everyone who was available that morning was packing into the courtroom to witness the proceedings. As I craned my neck to take inventory and see if there was anyone I knew, I recognized Ruby Collins and Mrs. Carlson sitting together in the back row. They separated their talking heads long enough to give me a little wave. I was sure they were talking about me, but what they could find of interest to say, I didn't know.

Jack was there, too, but he was sitting off to the side reserved for law enforcement. I caught his eye from across the room and gave him a wink. He shot me a quick smile, and then made his face blank again. We'd been married for ten years, and he still gave me butterflies.

The bailiff brought Rhianna in and my heart sank when I saw she was wearing the standard inmate's orange jumpsuit. I was hoping she would be given the dignity to wear her own clothes. I was thankful that she wasn't handcuffed. I wanted to tell her she had my support, but before I could say anything to her, the judge entered the room. I blanked out during most of the legal mumbo jumbo, but was brought back to reality when Judge Lawrence, my father's friend, read the charges.

"Rhianna Reese, you are charged with the first degree murder of Mara Tierney and with the attempted murder of Emily Romano. How do you plead?"

"Not guilty, your honor," she said loud and clear.

Had I heard that right? She was being charged with attempting to murder me. Jack had never mentioned that the D.A. had also charged her with attempted murder as well.

"Your honor, on the matter of bail," Mr. Jennings continued, but before he could finish, Robert Price, the D.A., barreled ahead.

"The State feels that bail should be denied. The defendant has ties in California and could easily flee prosecution."

"Your Honor, Ms. Reese has a young son to care for and has lived in *this* community most of her life," Mr. Jennings rebutted.

"All the more reason to deny bail, your Honor," the D.A. replied. "She could take her son and flee. She has a family that is more than willing to take the boy in. They are in the courtroom today and could testify to that fact." So that's why Rhianna's sister and brother-in-law were there; they were hoping the judge would turn Andy over to them.

I couldn't let that happen. I had promised her that I wouldn't let them have Andy. I felt responsible for her being in this courtroom, so I had to follow through on my promise. My chest was tightening. I had to do something.

"Your Honor, Ms. Reese is estranged from her sister and her parents are out of the country. She does not want her son to be with them. She has given guardianship to Mrs. Emily Romano," Mr. Jennings argued.

"Sheriff Romano's wife? The same Emily Romano that the defendant is accused of attempting to murder?" the judge asked, looking at Jack. Jack met the judge's eye but didn't acknowledge the question since it hadn't been asked of him. I felt a surge of guilt for bringing the judge's scrutiny upon Jack, but I was still convinced that I'd done the right thing.

"Yes," Mr. Jennings replied.

"This is a case of first degree murder. We have very few of them around these parts. I'd hate to be the judge to have a defendant skip bail on him." Judge Lawrence sighed as if he didn't want to say the next words.

I was desperate. I had to act. Before I even realized what I was doing, I was on my feet.

"What if I retained custody of Andy?" I blurted out. I heard a collective gasp from the people in the courtroom gallery, bewildered at this breach of procedure, and knew they were staring at me. I could feel my cheeks pinking from the attention. I glanced at Jack who was staring at me, wide-eyed as if he couldn't believe what he was seeing.

"Mrs. Romano, you may be the sheriff's wife, but I must ask you to refrain from interrupting or you'll be shown out," the judge said, gently rebuking me.

I quickly sat back down.

However, Mr. Jennings was right with me and picked up where I had left off, "Your Honor, if Mrs. Romano retained custody of Andy Reese, Ms. Reese would be compelled to stay and stand trial. She'd rather go to jail than flee and leave her son behind. Who better to keep him than the sheriff and his wife where they can make sure that Ms. Reese doesn't skip town?"

I dared not look at Jack; I could almost feel his eyes burning into my skin from across the room. My big mouth was getting me into trouble again.

The judge thought it over for a few minutes and then gave his ruling, "Rhianna Reese shall be released on $200,000 bond under the condition that custody of her son is retained by Sheriff and Mrs. Romano and all visitations between Ms. Reese and her son be supervised by the sheriff or Mrs. Romano." That had done it. With the bang of the judge's gavel, my coffin was nailed shut.

"Your Honor, I must object. It is improper for the sheriff to take such a personal interest in a murder suspect. Besides, the defendant is charged with . . ."

"Mr. Price, that bang you just heard—that was me making my ruling. Court's adjourned."

Knowing Jack would be waiting for me, I wished I could have snuck out the prisoners' exit.

"Come in here," he said between his closed teeth, grabbing me by the arm as I walked up to him in the hall. He led me into a small room that was used for attorney-client consultations. When we were out of earshot, he continued, "Didn't anything that I said to you last night sink in? I thought I made it clear that what you do in this town affects my career. How do you think this makes me look? It is a direct conflict of interest for me to be involved with a murder suspect like this."

I couldn't blame him for being furious. I had put him in a compromising position, and Jack was always a stickler about propriety where his job was concerned. No matter how well placed his anger was, it still hurt.

"Jack, don't you see? This way she can get out on bail and work on being acquitted, and the judge's ruling makes it harder for her sister to take Andy away from her."

"Emily, how is that our concern?"

"I made a promise to her, Jack, and I intend to keep that promise."

"But, Emily, what about me? What about our family? Did you ever think that maybe she did it and in the process she almost killed you, too?" he said, the volume of his voice rising with each sentence.

"She didn't do it, Jack."

"She certainly had motive, and all the evidence points to her."

"So what? So what if George is Andy's father, and she wanted child support? So what if she administered the perm solution that killed Mara? That doesn't prove she put the fentanyl in the solution. And why kill Mara to get to George? Why not kill George if she was going to kill someone?"

"Did you ever think that you don't know everything? Rhianna has a lover here in town, and Mara knew who Rhianna's lover is. Her lover is not 'out,' and Mara was going to out her if Rhianna didn't drop the child support case. Now, I call that motive," he yelled.

This news made me think a bit, but I was still positive Rhianna hadn't killed Mara.

"Jack," I said more softly because I realized that we were both shouting and could be heard in the hallway. "I realize that I've put you in a bad spot, and I'm sorry that I didn't think of you first. But this is the right thing to do, and I'm not sorry that I did it. She needs my help. Andy needs my help."

"Do you *ever* think of me first, or is it all about you and the promises you make to other people? Do you realize that I'm an elected official?!" he yelled.

Now, I was angry. Before, I was only hurt because he was so angry at me and refused to support me for the first time in our marriage. Now, what he was implying made my blood boil, sending me on the attack.

"Jack Romano, you are not going to stand there and tell me that this is about politics! Are you saying that I should start acting like a politician's wife and not do anything that isn't politically correct? Or are you implying that Rhianna's arrest and possible conviction could help you get reelected?"

Ignoring my accusations, he continued, "She's got some sort of spell over you, and I'm not going to take a backseat to this woman for whom you feel some kind of misplaced obligation to. Or is it more than that?" he asked, turning the tables back on me.

There had been many times in our marriage when I'd lashed out and said reckless things that I was later sorry for. But Jack had always been level-headed, keeping his emotions and his responses in check. This was the first time that he'd ever directed such irrational anger at me, and I was stunned. When I was hurt, I became defensive and all reason went out the window, as evidenced by my recent wrangle with my mother.

"Jack, surely you don't listen to idle gossip. Because it sounds an awful lot like you're accusing me of having an affair with Rhianna. Because if you are, you better think about what your next words are going to be. It was bad enough when you implied that I needed to act like a politician's wife, but this! I have never cheated on you, and I'm not going to start now. Rhianna is my oldest friend. We have a long history together that goes back to childhood. That's all! You don't want me involved in this? Then why don't you stop acting like a jealous husband and start doing your job!"

"I have the late shift tonight," he shot back. "I won't be home when you get there. Kiss my daughters and tell them I love them." With that, he left me standing there wondering if our marriage would ever be the same and if it would survive this trial. It was the first time he'd left for work without kissing me good-bye.

A few minutes later as I was walking across the courthouse lawn toward my bookstore, shaking with anger and struggling to keep from crying, I saw Sully leading Rhianna to his cruiser. She had to go back to the jail until she arranged for bail. I caught up with them and asked Sully if I could speak to Rhianna for a moment.

"Jack told me that Mara knew who your lover was and was going to out the person if you didn't drop the child support case against George."

"Did he tell you her name?" Rhianna asked.

"No. He more or less let the information slip while he was shouting at me."

"Yeah, it's true."

"Will you tell me her name?"

"Leave her out of this," she pleaded.

"I will. You can trust me."

"I can't betray her like that, even if your intentions are good." She thought for a moment and then said, "All I will say is that you know her. Now, it's up to you to figure it out."

I know half the town, so her hint didn't really narrow it down for me.

Before I could say anything else, Sully was at our side saying he had to get her back to the jail.

When Sully's cruiser was out of sight, I turned to walk back across the street to my store. I saw Jack, sitting in his cruiser, obviously having witnessed the exchange between Rhianna and me, shake his head at me, and then he peeled out of his parking spot, speeding away.

When I finally got across the street to my store, Janney, Rhianna's assistant, was waiting for me. She looked tired. Her long, brown hair was stringy, and her clothes were rumpled as if she'd slept in them. I showed her inside and motioned for her to sit on the leather sofa by the newspaper stand. She took me up on my offer for a cup of coffee, and I went off to the storeroom to brew a pot.

When I came back several minutes later with two cups of coffee, I found her crying.

"I don't know what I'm going to do. How long do you think this is going to go on?" she asked. I wasn't sure what she was referring to, so I didn't say anything. "Rhianna was helping me get my beautician's license. Now I don't have any income. How long is she going to be in jail?"

"She was arraigned today, and as soon as she posts bail, she will be out of jail, but not out of trouble."

"When do you think she can reopen the shop?"

"I'm not sure. It's still closed because the Sheriff's Office is still collecting evidence. Besides that, the Department of Financial and Professional Regulation has closed it down pending further investigation." I suspected it had been closed under pressure from Robert Price. "What about another shop? Can you finish your training somewhere else?"

"I've tried that. It cost money—Rhianna was helping me pay for the training as well as giving me a salary for helping around the shop. We had a deal worked out. She'd pay for my tuition to beauty school and pay me to help around the shop until I finished school. In exchange, I promised to work in her shop for the next five years and give her forty percent of what I made, instead of the usual ten percent that stylists pay for their chair at a shop." She paused for a moment, and then added, "Besides that, no one will hire me—not even to sweep the floor. They are all treating me like I'm poison. I can't pay the rent. My landlord thinks I'm cute. He said we could make a deal. I've even thought about . . ." She couldn't finish the sentence. It didn't matter; I knew what she'd thought about.

"Listen. Don't do anything like *that*. How much do you need? Will five hundred hold you for a while?"

"I can't take your money," she said, hiccuping from her sobs.

"I'm not giving it to you. You'll work it off. The shelves need dusting; I've got a big shipment coming in on Friday that I'll need help with, and I might need a new babysitter. I've ostracized mine," I said, thinking about my mom.

I wrote her a check and sent her off to cash it and go run some errands for me. I wondered what Jack would think of me helping Rhianna's assistant but decided for now that it didn't matter what Jack Romano thought. Besides, I'd written the check from the bookstore account, so it was none of his business.

CHAPTER 12

G ossip killed. Or at least that's the way it looked from my point-of-view. Whoever Rhianna's lover was, she was obviously a person of some prominence or at least someone for whom being outed as a lesbian would be volatile to her life here in Middletown. There was a female pastor at the local United Methodist Church. Even though the UMC had accepted LGBTQ+ people as ministers, it was creating a schism and some United Methodist Churches were leaving the sect and joining with the Global Methodist Church. Knowing how conservative most of the townspeople are, I could imagine that even the rumor of the minister being gay could cost the woman her job. I couldn't imagine Rhianna getting involved with someone who was religious. Besides, this was all speculation. I couldn't start scrutinizing every woman I knew looking for clues that she is a lesbian. What would those clues be anyway? That the woman drives a Subaru?

Pushing these silly thoughts aside, whoever this woman was, it was obvious that Rhianna was willing to risk her life by being found guilty for murder, a murder she probably didn't commit, to protect the woman she loved. I realized that things were starting to look bad for Rhianna. The most damning evidence was that she was the person who administered the perm with the fentanyl, unwittingly or not. Then the realization that Andy was George's son, that she wanted him to pay child support, and, finally, depending on who you talked to, that she wanted George as well. And now there were the ramifications of Mara knowing who Rhianna's lover was and what would have happened if Mara had told. Whoever was framing Rhianna was doing a good job of establishing motive.

The more I thought about the circumstances the more upset I got. I considered Rhianna my best friend, and as such, I'd told her a lot about my life and my marriage, but she had obviously not reciprocated. I was starting to realize that our relationship had been one-sided since she had never confided in me about any of the things I was now learning about her. Even going back to our childhood, I can see now that our relationship lacked the intimacy of friends who shared everything. Maybe she was worried about what I would think of her. However, the thing that confused me the most was that if Mara was such a miserable bitch, why did George stay married to her? And, if Mara cared so much that George had an illegitimate child, why didn't she cut him loose? From what I had gathered, it was a loveless marriage. Could it have been money? George liked his comfy life and the vacations that Mara's salary afforded them; something he'd never be able to afford on a meager teacher's salary. Although with life insurance, that would be a different matter. With Mara out of the way and with her life insurance, which I assumed was a substantial amount given her position as President of Midwestern Mutual, he could devote his life to writing and traveling. But how would he have gotten the drugs into the perm solution without anyone noticing?

Now I was reaching for answers. I wanted to talk to Jack about this, but I was sure he didn't want to hear anything I had to say about the case. I realized he felt like I was betraying him, and he probably didn't trust me at the moment. I couldn't blame him. I had put my friendship with Rhianna and my need to help Andy before our marriage. On two or three occasions now, my actions had put him in a very awkward situation as my husband and as sheriff. He had a right to be angry and hurt. I had run headlong into things without thinking of him or our family. But I wasn't sure I wanted to talk this over with him anyway because all of the evidence was so damning. He was an excellent investigator, but I was positive he was wrong. It wasn't like him to be so wrong. I couldn't figure out if he was dead set on pinning Mara's murder on Rhianna because I had almost been killed as well or if it was political pressure from the D.A. It also wasn't like him to be so emotional about a case. He had learned a long time ago when he was dealing with child prostitutes as part of his job in Vice that he had to disconnect his personal feelings from his job because feelings get cops killed. I prayed that I could figure out what was going on inside his head so that I could regain his trust, and we could work together on the case, if our marriage lasted that long.

These were the thoughts that were whirling around in my brain as I rocked Elly for her nap in a rocking chair that I kept in the storeroom. My dad had dropped her off earlier, leading me to believe that my mother wasn't ready to make up with me yet.

"Mommy, sing about God's gifts," Elly asked. I liked to sing a prayer to the girls called *Surely the Presence*, but Elly thought it was *Surely the Presents*.

"Okay, Elly," I replied and began singing:

"Surely the presence of the Lord is in this place,

I can feel His mighty power and His grace.

I hear the brush of angel's wings;

I see glory on each face.

Surely the presence of the Lord is in this place."

That was the sacred balm I needed. I felt a little better, and she was asleep. It never took much to put her to sleep in the afternoons because she was always worn out from preschool. I laid her on the cot and went out into the store.

I hadn't heard anyone come in, so I was surprised to see

Father Bob browsing through the popular fiction section.

"I love those James Patterson books," he said without looking up at me. "Give me Alex Cross over Mike Hammer any day."

Since his initial visit to our house when we first moved back to Middletown, Father Bob Lucas had become more than my parish priest, he was my dear friend—our dear friend. He was different from any priest that I'd ever known. He drove a turquoise 1972 Chevy pick-up truck that he'd inherited from his father, a farmer. He was a die-hard Bruce Springsteen fan, and he was known to go to Gary's Bar on nights the Bears were playing, especially if they were playing the Packers. Some of the older parishioners were put off by what they considered his un-priestly behavior and his more liberal views on the Church. Considering that the last priest had been so old that he'd known God when He was a boy, Bob, being only forty-five, was practically a teenager in the older parishioners' eyes. Jack and I liked him because he was ever mindful that he was a human doing God's work and not God himself.

"You have a beautiful voice," he said, coming across the store to hug me. He must have been in the store for a few minutes. Father Bob was a big, barrel-chested man who never gave anyone a light hug; he gave these wonderful bear hugs that could make even the surliest church member turn into a smiling fool. If he liked you, he never shook your hand; he always encircled you with all of his warmth and love. "Larry Grant had told me that you did and that we should get you to sing in the choir."

"I'd make trouble for Mr. Jones," I said. Mr. Jones was the choir director and felt that the slower you played the more reverent you were being. At Christmas, I told Jack that I'd never heard *Oh Come, Oh Come Emmanuel* played as a funeral dirge before.

"Sounds like you've been making trouble for other people,

too," he said, getting to the reason why he was here. "Jack came to see me, Emily. He's very upset and worried."

I dropped onto the sofa and let out a long sigh that sounded like air being pushed out of fireplace bellows. "Yeah, I've made quite a mess of things. Jack's not speaking to me. My mother's not speaking to me. I'm not very popular right now, except with the gossips."

"Emily, don't be so hard on yourself. You're a good Christian. Taking that boy in—I wouldn't expect anything less from you, and frankly, neither would Jack. But you also need to remember the other commitments in your life." He sat down next to me and patted my hand. "Don't worry. Jack will forgive you, if he hasn't already. His coming to me is a good sign. He seemed more upset with himself than he was with you. But I wouldn't count on him saying so—at least, not right away." He paused for a moment, letting that information sink in. "You know, Emily, he's been on an emotional roller coaster the last few days. He thought you were going to die, and if you had, he would have blamed himself."

"Why? He didn't give me an overdose of fentanyl."

"He would have felt he'd failed you."

"How?"

"In not reviving you."

"What? Bob, please stop being so cryptic. I have no idea what you're talking about."

"Emily, he was the one who performed CPR on you and gave you the initial doses of narcan. He wouldn't let the paramedics touch you. Deputy Kaiser said he kept saying that he wasn't going to let you leave him. He only let the paramedics work on you because he ran out of narcan."

I covered my face and began to sob. I was such an idiot; Jack loved me so much, and here I was throwing that love away over my misplaced sense of duty to a friend.

"I'm such a bad person. I didn't know, Father. He never told me—no one told me."

"Emily, stop. You're not a bad person," he said, putting his arm around me and pulling me into his chest. "Jack's mostly angry with himself. He's torn between you, whom he loves and admires, and his job that he loves and wants to do well. But when it comes to it, he'll pick you every time, Emily. There's no contest as there shouldn't be." I reached for the box of tissues that I'd put on the coffee table when Janney had sat crying in the same spot I was sitting in now. "Don't worry. You'll both get through this and be the better for it." His confidence in us was reassuring.

He got up to leave, brushing his salt-and-pepper hair from his eyes, then turned and said, "You know Emily, one of the reasons you never seem to be able to please your mother is because you're an extremely brave person. You've done things in your life that she's never attempted to do. You moved away from home, started your own business, tried to save the life of a dying woman, and most importantly, you have the courage to stand beside a friend whom everyone else is against."

Earlier I had prayed that I wanted to know what Jack was thinking and here was God's regular messenger to me, Father Bob. He was not only telling me what my husband was thinking but also how to mend things with my mother. I stared out the window of the store, pondering what he'd told me. He was right, of course, and I felt relieved. As Father Bob gave a wave and walked out of the store, my eyes focused on what I was really staring at: Hairy Harry, who was sitting across from my store, as he had been for the past week. I jumped off the couch and called Father back to the store.

"What can you tell me about Hairy Harry?" I asked. Father Bob began to turn around and look toward where Harry was sitting across the street; he must have seen Harry sitting there as well. "No, don't look."

We turned slightly away from the window and proceeded to pretend that we were in deep discussion about a book.

"He's been sitting in front of the store ever since Mara Tierney died. What is he up to? Should I be worried? I see him at church, so my instincts tell me he's harmless. But why all of the sudden is my store of interest to him?"

"You're right. He's harmless. I can't tell you much," he said. "At least, I can't reveal to you all that I know because I learned about it during the sacrament of reconciliation."

"So he can speak?"

"Yes, he's what you call a selective mute. Is that the right term? Anyway, he chooses not to speak."

"I heard when I was a kid that he was in Korea and something awful happened to him there. When he came home, he wasn't the same, so his wife left him and he hasn't spoken since."

"Well, that story's true. I can tell you he was one of the Chosin Few. You know who they are, don't you?"

"My husband's a Marine; of course, I know who they are. They were a group of Marines cut off from any reinforcements as they were battling the Chinese. The Marines fought their way out of the Chosin Reservoir after several days, carrying their dead and wounded with them because they never leave anyone behind," I explained. "No wonder he had problems. That must have been a horrific ordeal."

"Yes. All I can tell you is that he is harmless, and I'm sure he has a reason for sitting out there. If I were you, I'd feel more at ease with him there. If anything, I'd say for some reason he's looking to protect you or someone who works here." For the second time that afternoon, Father had given me comfort and relief.

Father Bob's visit had made me feel more at ease about my fight with Jack, and I was desperate to talk to him and make things right. I wanted to be reassured that everything was okay between us; I wanted to hold him. But most of all, I wanted to tell him how incredible I thought he was and that I needed his love. Father had also made me feel better about Harry, and I was sure now that he wasn't stalking me; however, I was more curious than ever about his reasons for being outside of Cover to Cover.

The rest of the day was uneventful. Andy and Bella had made up. I helped the kids with their homework when they came to the store after school. I made dinner when we got home, and everyone got along until bedtime. Even though my soul felt at ease, my stomach felt like it was in knots. After flipping through the channels and not being able to find anything to numb my brain, I went to bed. I was exhausted from the lack of sleep the night before and from the emotion of the day, so I slept soundly until early morning.

CHAPTER 13

The next morning I awoke in terrible pain. I was awake for about an hour before my alarm went off. As it blared in my ear, I laid in bed curled in the fetal position in too much pain to move. Jack, who'd been on the night shift after our argument, had only been asleep for about half an hour when the constant, obnoxious beeping woke him up.

"Emily, turn off your alarm clock," he growled.

"I can't,"

He let out a low grumble to tell me I was being childish and leaned over me to bat the alarm off with his hand. As he rolled back across me, he glanced at my face and saw tears on my cheeks.

"Listen, Emmy, I said some things yesterday I wish I could take back now. I've been tired and really angry with you."

"It's not that," I sighed, trying to keep the overwhelming pain at bay. "I'm hurt."

"What do you mean 'you're hurt'?" He said, surveying my face for clues. "You're pale; what's going on?"

"I have a horrible pain in my side."

"Where? Show me?"

"I can't . . . I can't move . . . it hurts too much."

"Come on," he said gently, coaxing me to do what he asked.

I took a deep breath and rolled onto my back, moaning as I

did so. I still couldn't uncurl my legs, so I kept my knees bent. I pointed to my lower left side to the right of my pelvic bone. I saw a look flash across his face that I couldn't quite place, and then he recovered himself.

"It's too low to be your appendix."

"Wrong side, too."

He paused for a moment, as if looking for the right words, and then asked, "Em, are you pregnant? Could you be pregnant?"

"Maybe," I said. He was thinking the same thing I'd been thinking for the past hour—I was having a miscarriage. "I'm late, but I've been stressed and upset, too—not to mention overdosed."

"How long have you been in pain?"

"About an hour."

"Since I came to bed and you didn't say anything?"

"Yes—I was being stubborn."

"You can be such an ass sometimes, Emily."

I nodded my head in agreement. He was right. What kind of an idiot would lay in pain for an hour because she's not speaking to her husband?

"I have to take you to the hospital."

"What about the kids?"

"I'll call your mom; she can be here in ten minutes. Can you hang on that long?"

"Yeah, I think so."

As he dialed my parents' number, he slipped on some jeans, a polo shirt, and a pair of running shoes. I couldn't help thinking how hot he looked at that moment, and I decided that it couldn't be very serious if I still had the strength and presence of mind to find my husband attractive.

Jack carried me downstairs, and I thanked God that my no longer svelte body wasn't too heavy for him to carry. As he carried me out the front door, we saw Rhianna coming up the walk. It was still early, but she must have been anxious to spend time with Andy now that she was out on bail.

"What is it? What's wrong?" she asked, running up the walk when she saw us.

"Em's sick. I have to take her to the ER. Her mom's on the way."

"Don't wait. I'm here. I'm sure Mrs. Beckett will be here any minute."

I could see Jack mulling it over for a second because I'd promised the Judge that all of Rhianna's visits with Andy would be supervised, so she wouldn't jump bail. But in the end, his concern for me outweighed his need to enforce the law.

"Okay, the kids are still asleep." He said, giving her a look that said, *I'm trusting you.*

We raced to the hospital in his cruiser with the siren blaring. I thought Jack was overreacting, considering that the hospital was five minutes across town. When we arrived, I felt an appreciation for small town hospitals—no waiting. Before I knew it, I was in a gown, had given the nurse my history, and was lying on the examining table with my feet in the stirrups waiting for the doctor to see me.

Suddenly, the examining room door swung open, and I was face-to-face, so to speak, with Brad Johnson, an old boyfriend from high school. Instinctively, I sat up, ignoring the pain, and pulled the drape that had been laid across my knees down to my ankles.

"Brad! I had no idea when the nurse said, 'Dr. Johnson will be right with you,' that she meant Brad Johnson. I didn't know you were a doctor."

"Yep. Now, lay down and let me see what's wrong."

"NO! You can't . . . I mean I won't. . . NO WAY!" I shouted.

"Emmy, I'm a doctor and . . ." he said, clearing his throat and letting a sheepish smile cross his lips, "it's not like I haven't seen it all before."

I shot Jack a look and saw that he was smiling, almost laughing. "I'm glad you find my utter embarrassment so funny," I said, laying back on the examining table with a great moan, defeated. "I hate small towns."

"For some of the situations you've put me in recently this is pretty equal justice," Jack said chuckling—that was until Brad began probing my abdomen, and I cried out in pain.

"I'm going to get the ultrasound machine," Brad said. "The nurse should have brought it in by now."

"What do you think it is?" I asked.

"I can't say with certainty yet, so I don't want to make any guesses."

"Please tell me?"

"Could be a cyst or a recurrence of endometriosis. It says in your chart that you could be pregnant—could be an ectopic pregnancy. That's why I want to do an ultrasound and have the nurse come in and draw some blood."

After he left the room, I turned to Jack, tears once again leaking down my face, "Jack, I'm sorry."

"I know. Let's not talk about that now. We've both been acting like idiots."

"No. I'm sorry about the baby. I know it's going to be ectopic. I have the reproductive history."

"It's not your fault. Nothing for you to apologize for," he said leaning over to kiss me and taking me in his arms. As we pulled apart, I saw Brad and the nurse come in.

"Christ," I muttered under my breath. "Olive. Hi. I didn't realize you were a nurse." She scowled at me, letting me know that neither my friendliness nor my pain was going to carry any favors with her. "Well, the gang's all here." I announced. "Why don't we get Samantha Marshal in here, and this little class reunion from hell will be complete." Samantha Marshal had been the captain of the cheerleading team.

"Listen, Olive," I asked her, "Could you take the blood out of my hand? I have really bad veins."

"Nope," she said as a small smile crossed her lips. She was relishing the thought of having control over me and possibly causing me even more agony. I was getting payback for all of my sins at once.

I turned my attention to the ultrasound, but Jack was blocking half the screen from my view. I looked back at Olive, resenting that I had to share this emotionally and physically painful moment with her. She was finished drawing my blood, and I hadn't even noticed.

"Wow, Olive, I didn't even feel that."

"I guess I'm not as dumb as you thought I was," she said. Before I could respond, she had left the room.

"Emily," Brad said, drawing my attention back to the ultrasound. "Emily, I'm sorry. It's ectopic. There's nothing I can do to save the pregnancy. We'll take you upstairs and do a laparoscopy. You might be able to go home tonight."

Fearing the worst and hearing it confirmed were two different things. I was devastated and a desperate cry escaped from the brave exterior I'd been trying to hold together.

Brad leaned over me and took my hand. For an instant, he became the sweet boy I'd gone to third base with back in high school. He was talking as my friend, not my doctor.

"Emily, Jack tells me you've had fertility problems in the past. If I don't remove the embryo from your fallopian tube, it will rupture and could cause infection, or you could even bleed to death. Your fallopian tube would be destroyed, and you may never get pregnant again." He paused, composing himself, and I could see that this was hard for him, too. "We do this, and you may be able to have more children. I have no choice."

I nodded. He cupped my cheek with his hand, and then straightened up. "I'll do this myself. I'll call upstairs and get everything set up."

After he left the room, Jack scooped me up into his arms, and we consoled one another.

"Jack, why didn't you tell me?" I asked between sobs, "Why didn't you tell me you were the one who saved my life?"

"I don't know," he said into my shoulder. "It didn't seem right." Then he pulled away from me, looking into my eyes, and said, "Out of all the dangerous situations I've been in from the Marines to Vice, giving you CPR was the scariest moment of my life. If you had died, I don't know what I would have done. I need you!"

"Thank you," I replied. "I need you every bit as much as you need me. *Ti amo*, Giovanni."

"Let's not ever let our relationship get to this point again," he said. Then he picked me up off the examining table and held me on his lap like one of our daughters until the nurses came in to prep me for surgery.

Despite the nurses' objections, I was able to go home that night. Since only a small incision was made in the abdominal wall with the laparoscope, there was very little blood and little chance of infection. I agreed to go to Brad's office at the end of the week for a follow-up exam. I ignored the nurses' clucking tongues at releasing someone at ten o'clock at night and went home. I'd seen too much of that hospital this week, and I wanted to go home and be with the girls. It must have been scary for them to wake up and find us both gone. I knew my mother would try to protect them from the truth but for this to happen twice in one week could really frighten them.

Jack had called ahead to tell my mother that we were coming home and to have the bedroom ready for me. I felt crampy, but other than that I wasn't in much pain. However, I was willing to accept Jack's coddling. I welcomed it. As we drove up to the house, I saw my mother and Rhianna hugging on the front step. *Now isn't that cozy*, I thought. The woman my mother admonished me for being friends with was now in her embrace. Even when we were kids, my mom didn't much like Rhianna. I gave a small grunt of disapproval, and Jack patted me on the leg.

When we'd come to a stop, Rhianna opened my door and asked, "How are you?"

"I'm okay," I said, giving her a small but strained smile.

"I'll come by tomorrow and help you get the kids ready for school."

"That would be a good idea," Jack said, coming up behind Rhianna. "Let's get you inside."

"See you tomorrow," she said, giving my arm a squeeze, and she headed off down the sidewalk toward her house.

Jack helped me out of the car and picked me up in his strong arms where I was safe from any harm.

"Oh, Jack, surely she can walk," my mother called from the porch.

"I don't care. This woman's been through a lot lately, and I'm not about to make her walk into the house when I'm strong enough to carry her." I kissed his neck as I buried my face there.

"I love you," I whispered.

As Jack carried me up the steps of the house, my mother opened the front door for him and said, "You know that

Rhianna is misunderstood."

Neither Jack nor I replied as he started up the stairs with my mother on his heels.

"She's so nice," my mother said, again trying to engage one of us in conversation.

As she pushed past Jack, almost shoving us both into the wall so she could get ahead of us and open our bedroom door, she said, "She's so accomplished; did you know she can draw?"

When we got to our room, Jack sat me on the edge of the bed. He'd run home during the day to get me some clothing since I'd gone to the hospital in my nightgown and robe. I was wearing a long, knit sundress, the roomy kind that I loved because they hid the evidence that I'd never lost the last fifteen pounds I'd gained when I was pregnant with Elly. Jack said he liked the extra weight on me, that I'd always been too thin.

"You want to change your clothes?" he asked.

"No. I'm going to sleep in this. I don't have the strength to change."

"Don't you want to take off your bra, dear? I'm sure you'll be more comfortable," my mother said from behind Jack.

"I'm not wearing a bra, Mother."

"You didn't wear a bra home from the hospital? What will people think?"

"Mother, I just lost a baby. I don't give a fuck what people think."

"You couldn't have been that far along. You didn't even know you were pregnant. It's not like it was a real baby."

I inhaled sharply as if she had slapped me.

"Sue Anne," Jack said gently, "we really appreciate you coming over today and helping out with the kids."

"Well, it was really no trouble . . . especially with Rhianna's help."

"I'm glad," Jack said, tilting his head in a way that only I would recognize as a sign that he was about to choke my mother. "Listen, we're both very tired as I'm sure you are, too. Why don't you go home now, and we'll call you in the morning." He sounded calm and diplomatic, but when his voice got soft was when you needed to get out of his way. He was more likely to whisper than shout when he was angry, and it was more unnerving than being screamed at. That was another reason why our argument the day before had hurt so much. It wasn't like him to yell. "I'll walk you to the door," he continued, and with that, he ushered her out of the room and down the stairs.

When he reappeared a few minutes later, he said, "You know, when I think she could rise to the occasion and give you the benefit of the doubt, she disappoints me."

"This is like when I was a kid. She was everybody's friend but mine. She always understood everyone else's problems better than she understood mine. Then she doesn't understand when I'm angry. Why wasn't she ever my friend?"

"The thing that really gets me is the way she minimizes our loss. It didn't happen to her, so it's like it didn't even happen," he said, throwing a pillow across the room, hitting the wall.

"Let's stop talking about this. We're both tired and wound tight," I said trying to dissipate the anger we were both feeling. "You've got to be exhausted. How much sleep have you had in the past twenty-four hours?"

"Are you hungry? Can I get you anything?" he asked, dodging my question.

"I'd love a bowl of chocolate ice cream." Chocolate ice cream was my cure-all. I always craved it when I was sick.

"Chocolate ice cream, coming right up."

◆ ◆ ◆

When he brought the ice cream back up, I must have been asleep. The next morning I found a bowl of melted ice cream on my bedside table and Jack curled around me. Untangling myself from his gangly arms and legs, I quietly grabbed some clothes. When I came out of the bathroom after showering and dressing, he was still sleeping like a rock. I was sore and took some over the counter pain reliever. Other than that, I felt pretty good, so I'd decided to go to work. Jack would be against it, but I wasn't going to wake him to ask. I called his office when I got downstairs and was told that he wasn't on until that afternoon, so I let him sleep.

Rhianna and I got the children off to school without waking Jack up, and she dropped me off at the newspaper office. I wanted to put an ad in the paper for help in the store. Inside the newspaper office, I was greeted by Miss Bette. Miss Bette was the managing editor of the newspaper and two days older than dirt. She'd been an old lady when my grandfather had worked as the newspaper's circulation manager. I'd been to the newspaper office several times in the past year for advertising purposes, but I'd never run into her before.

"Well, Emmy Sue, I can't believe I haven't run into you before now."

"Hello, Miss Bette. How are you?"

"Hangin' in there, girl. Hangin' in there."

"I thought you had retired," I said. She wrote a goings and doings column, but I didn't know she still worked in the office.

"Yup. They'll never get rid of me. One day I'll be sittin' here, and I'll just burst into flames and crumble into dust like a phoenix. Then I'll rise from the ashes and be a twenty-five year old blonde with perky boobs and a tight ass," she cackled, slapping her knee. "I like to answer the phones and see what's goin' on. I still give story ideas and edit copy."

"Well, that's fantastic. I'm sure it keeps you young."

"Young? Hell, do I look young?" She cackled again, like the old crone that she resembled with her long white hair in a disordered ponytail hanging down her back and her wrinkled, saggy skin. I'm sure she'd never used sunscreen in her life, and her skin was as brown as Colombian coffee.

"What can I do ya for today?"

I told her I needed a help wanted ad but wasn't sure how to word it. What I really needed was a clone. I wanted someone with a college degree, who didn't want much money, and would be as devoted to the store as I was. She said she'd write it up for me, and despite my better judgment, I agreed.

As I turned to leave the office, she said, "You know, Emily, your granddaddy'd be proud of you. I remember when you were a little thing. You'd come to the office here and sit at his chair," she said motioning to the desk chair by the window, "and bang on the typewriter. You write?"

"Some," I said.

"Thought so. You have the look."

I wasn't sure what look she was talking about, but I felt complimented all the same. Miss Bette wasn't known for handing out kind words.

"I still miss Granddad," I said. I was about Arabella's age when he died.

"He was the kind of man you miss for the rest of your life," she said with a gleam in her eye that made me more than a little curious. "I'll write up the ad, Kid, and charge your account."

"Thanks," I said. As I was walking out the door, I remembered something I wanted to ask her. "Miss Bette, do you know where Mara Tierney went to college?"

"Not off the top of my head, but I'm sure it was in her obit. Want me to look it up?"

"Yes, please. Call me later when you've had a chance to look for it." I thanked her. I'd been wondering about who Mara's outside acquaintances were and if any of them could have wanted her dead. It was a long shot, but I also knew that she wasn't a very likable person. Probably most people she came in contact with had wanted her dead at one time or another. I thought college was the best place to start.

As I pondered this, I walked into the flower shop that was right down the block from the newspaper office. There was someone whom I was sure had plotted *my* demise at sometime in her life; someone to whom I wanted to make it up to now. I chose a greeting card with a blue butterfly on the front sitting on a yellow buttercup, and in the blank interior, I wrote:

Dear Olive,

I was an awful, spoiled child who had no idea what life must have been like for you. Several years have gone by since, and I realize now that you were humiliated many times because of my horrible words. I can't hope that you'd forgive me, but I wanted to tell you how truly sorry I am for any hurt that I caused you. I hope that someday I may call you my friend. Until then, please accept these flowers. One dozen is to say I am sorry, and the other is to say thank you for the excellent care you gave me in the hospital.

Humbly yours,

Emily

I ordered two dozen yellow roses to be sent to her at the hospital. It was expensive, but I didn't care how much it cost; I owed her. I was only relieving my own conscience, but I meant what I wrote. People did things when they were kids that they'd like to take back but never got the chance to. This was my chance to make up for the harm I'd done. All I could do was hope she'd accept my apology and forgive me. If not, at least I'd taken responsibility for what I'd done.

CHAPTER 14

After ordering Olive's flowers, I crossed the busy intersection at State and Main streets and opened the door to my store, which was on that corner. I felt tired and crampy, but I was resolute; I had to keep the store open today. It had been closed too often in the past week, and I was going to lose customers, let alone money. I was sitting in one of the overstuffed leather chairs resting for a few minutes before I opened up when I heard someone rattling the door. I looked at my watch; it was exactly ten o'clock. So I hauled myself up and went to the door.

On the other side was a woman I didn't know. Not that I knew every customer who came in the store, but I usually recognized them from around town. This stranger looked like a suburban soccer mom with her khaki pants, light blue twin sweater set, and loafers. Her hair was a plain, dark brown, cut into a bob around her chin. She was very thin and looked clean and nice. She wasn't especially pretty, but her brown eyes and her face emanated a light that made me feel warm and welcome, which led me to believe that despite her appearance, she wasn't quite what I was making her out to be.

"Sorry," she said when I opened the door, "I thought you were open."

"It's okay. It's opening time."

She stepped inside the store, and I walked over to the cash register and sat on a stool behind the counter. She followed me, and as if she'd read my mind, she stuck out her hand and said, "Hi. I'm Madeleine Burn."

"I'm Emily Romano."

"Yes, I know. I've been in here before, but I don't think you were here."

"Where are you from? I don't remember ever seeing you before."

"I'm originally from Chicago, but I've lived here for about five years. Nelson Kreger is my ex-husband."

So this was the woman whom Ruby Collins had praised for leaving her philandering husband.

"Oh, yes. I know who you are now. I'm originally from here, but my husband and I lived in Chicago for ten years before we moved back. Where in Chicago did you live?"

"Western suburbs mostly. Naperville. But in college I lived in Wrigleyville."

"We lived mostly in Lincoln Park. But my in-laws live in Little Italy." I gave a little sigh at the thought of our life in the city and how much I missed it. "Well, if you're not married to Nelson anymore, why are you still here?" I asked. "I'd flee back to the city as soon as I could if I were you."

"I'm not much of a city person and believe it or not—I like this little town."

"Now, *that* I do find hard to believe. But I guess if you didn't grow up here, you might have a different perspective on it." Just then I saw Jack's cruiser pull up in front of the store. "Oh, no. I've had it now," I said.

Madeleine gave me a curious look, but before I could explain, Jack was walking into the store.

"You are in a load of trouble," he said, playfully shaking a finger at me.

"Madeleine Burn, this is my husband, Sheriff Jack Romano.

Jack, this is Madeleine Burn."

"Yes," said Madeleine. "We've met. Your husband is a very kind man."

"Yes," I said. "I'm very lucky." Now it was my turn to be curious.

She turned and shook Jack's hand and said, "It's very nice to see you under happier circumstances, Sheriff."

"You, too, Ms. Burn." Then turning to me, he said, "Emmy, you know you're supposed to be at home in bed."

"I had a . . . surgical procedure yesterday," I explained to Madeleine. "I'm fine, Jack, and I can't afford to have the store closed one more day. I promise; I will sit myself on this stool all day and won't lift a finger except to ring up a customer."

"I can see that there is no persuading you to do otherwise, so I'll drop it and see you tonight. Tell Kylie I'll come back tonight and help her close up and take the deposit over to the bank."

"All right. I'll grant you that wish."

Looking at Madeleine, he said, "I didn't think I said that in such a way that I was leaving her a choice. But that's how it is with stubborn mules." He gave us both that heart-melting smile of his and headed out the door.

As he walked to his car, I shouted, "I learned from the biggest donkey I know, *Giovanni*."

Madeleine laughed at our marital repartee. "Giovanni?" She asked.

"That's his given name, but the only person who calls him that is his mother. Giovanni is the Italian version of John, and his dad was a big fan of JFK's, so he called his son Jack."

For a moment, there was an uncomfortable silence. I'd gotten the feeling that Jack had met her in an official capacity, but I wasn't going to question her about her personal life. Turns out I didn't need to.

"Your husband was very helpful to me when I was evicting Nelson from our home," she offered. "Nelson can be quite a son-of-a-bitch." Her use of profanity surprised me; she seemed too classy to swear.

"Yeah. He has quite a reputation. I have two cousins who worked for him, Jemma and Jenny Stone." Madeleine's face colored, and she lowered her head, looking at the counter. "Oh, yeah. How could I be such a clod?!" I exclaimed. It was then that I remembered that Madeleine had caught my cousins, identical twins, frolicking after hours with Nelson in his office. Jemma had told me the whole story when she'd come looking for a job at my store.

"It's okay. I don't blame them. They were young and Nelson can be quite persuasive and charming. Let's say that was the proverbial last straw."

"Well, if it's any consolation, Jemma was quite detailed in her story, right down to the *littlest* detail. I'm very sorry. How miserable that must have been for you," I said, holding my two index fingers up about an inch apart.

"Yes, a lot of his arrogant behavior is a compensation for some other *shortcoming*," she said, making us both laugh. The laughing hurt, and Madeleine noticed me holding my side but didn't say anything. "Well, the reason I came in here today wasn't to buy books or to discuss my ex's teeny, tiny penis. Actually, your husband sent me. He told me you might be looking for someone to help out around here, and I need something to do. I got a nice alimony, and I got the house in the divorce. But he got all of our friends and any connections I had in the Garden Club and at the Country Club if you get what I'm saying."

"Ever since you divorced, he's made it impossible for you to socialize with the same people that you did before. You're social poison, so to speak."

"Yep."

"Well, I can't pay you much."

"That's fine. I don't want a lot of money. I don't need money; I need a meaningful way to pass my days if I'm going to continue to live here."

"Great! When can you start?"

"Right now. It looks like you need it," she said. "Your husband was right; you should be home in bed. You're very pale."

"I'm a redhead."

She didn't get my little joke. After I called Miss Bette to cancel the ad for a store clerk, Madeleine ordered me to sit down on the couch and made me hot tea in the storeroom microwave. There were very few customers, so we were able to get to know one another.

She told me how she'd met Nelson while she was finishing her Master's Degree in English Literature at the University of Illinois at Chicago (which must have been why Jack thought she'd be perfect for the store—cheap help, but knowledgeable) and Nelson was getting his MBA at Northwestern. Although arrogant, Nelson was also very smart, which was a dangerous combination. Nelson spent the first six months of their relationship love bombing her with expensive gifts and a lot of attention. He'd been charming and persuasive, and she'd fallen madly in love with him. When he'd asked her to marry him, she easily said yes. Both of her parents had died two years before she'd met him, and she and her sister were estranged for reasons she did not disclose. At the time, she was very alone in the world and vulnerable, so when Nelson came along, she thought she'd found her savior. In reality, she'd found a demon disguised as Cary Grant.

Everything was fine until after they were married and living back in Middletown. Then he seemed to change. He was angry a lot and yelled. She never seemed to do anything right, no matter how hard she tried. Sometimes he hit her. Then she started hearing rumors of infidelity. Chiefly, he was still hung up on the cheerleader he'd dated in high school, the aforementioned Maria Matthews, who was also married to someone else.

I told Madeleine that was one of the curses of small town life. People never seemed to get over their high school loves, and it was quite common for those who didn't marry their sweethearts to carry on affairs with them for years afterward. I couldn't figure out if it was boredom or lack of variety in their lives, but small town people seemed to be more preoccupied with sex than city people although I doubted Candace Bushnell, author of *Sex and the City,* would agree with me.

It turned out that it wasn't only Maria he was sleeping with. He was sleeping with any woman who would consent (and possibly some who didn't) and then would come home and refuse to touch her. She'd begun to feel ugly, inept, and worthless, until about a year ago when she realized one day that she didn't have anyone but herself to rely on. If she was going to have a life, she was going to have to make her own way in the world. It was only a few days after she'd had this revelation that she'd found Nelson with Jemma and Jenny. The next day she'd gone to Chicago to hire the best divorce lawyer she could afford—a real barracuda. He'd gotten her a fabulous settlement because Madeleine had known so much about Nelson's business. For example, he planned to sell to a large grocery conglomerate after he took control of the family business when his father retired. If his father ever got wind of it, Mr. Kreger would leave the business to Nelson's cousin Monty instead.

"In the world of divorce law, they don't call it blackmail; they call it community property and shared assets," she joked.

But a few months ago when the divorce was final, she couldn't get him to remove his belongings from the house, so she had them moved out. That's where Jack came in. Nelson had shown up drunk and had knocked her around a bit before she could get away from him long enough to call the police. After Jack arrested Nelson, Robert Price, a personal friend of Nelson's father, had pressured Madeleine to drop the charges, so the whole mess was never in the newspaper. After Nelson was taken away, Madeleine had been pretty upset. Jack had sat with her for a while, having a cup of coffee. It was then that he'd urged her to contact me; he thought we'd make good friends and that she could be a big help to me around the store. Talking to her, I could see why Jack thought we'd hit it off.

After Madeleine finished her story, I told mine. I told her about how we'd moved back here and why, about me starting this business, and about me getting involved with Rhianna and her problems. Finally, I told her about the pregnancy, and I cried. I cried for my lost baby, for my argument with my mother, and for all the trouble I'd brought to my marriage. She sat and listened; she wiped my tears, and I could tell that we were going to be good friends.

A few hours later, I was sitting on my perch behind the cash register when the phone rang.

"Cover to Cover Books, Emily speaking." I answered.

"Here's the thing, Kid. When I looked up her obit, there wasn't any education listed," Miss Bette said, launching right into her story, dispensing with the conventional pleasantries, such as 'hello.' "Usually, the deceased's family puts in so-and-so was a 1964 graduate of Who Cares U, but there was none of that, so I called over to the insurance company to find out when she was made President. Then, I looked up the announcement that ran. It said she graduated from Northwestern University with an MBA."

"Wow, Miss Bette, I didn't think it would take that much research to find out such a little tidbit of information. Sorry about that."

"Whatta you mean, Kid? That's the most fun I've had in six years. I never get to do real research anymore. If this town moved any slower, they'd send in the CDC to find out what killed everyone. Know what they'd find?"

"No, what?"

"They'd all killed each other with gossip and sex," she cackled and then hung up without saying goodbye.

It seemed odd to me that George hadn't put anything about Mara's education in her obituary. Miss Bette was right. Prominent obituaries were usually mini-resumes, and as President of Midwestern Mutual, Mara was a prominent person in town. I thought it was curious that she had attended Northwestern; I'd only had a handful of conversations with her, and she knew I had lived in Chicago but not once had she mentioned it. When people don't know one another very well, they search for a commonality, such as living in the same city, as a conversation starter. Then they rely on that commonality like a crutch and talk about it whenever they find themselves in a social situation together. If Chicago was your common frame of reference, there were statements like, "What about those Bears?" or "What's everyone around here whining about? They call this wind; they should feel the wind coming off Lake Michigan." But she'd never mentioned it. Maybe she hated Chicago and didn't like to talk about it. No, that was too abhorrent a thought to even entertain.

"Madeleine," I called across the room to where she was dusting a display of Margaret Atwood books. "When did Nelson go to Northwestern?"

"Well," she said, replacing a copy of *The Handmaid's Tale* on the table and walking over to me, "he went there twice. First for undergrad and then for his MBA. That's when I met him about seven years ago. Why?"

"You say you moved his stuff out. You wouldn't have inadvertently kept anything, such as yearbooks, by any chance?"

"Maybe. I could look," she replied.

"I'd be interested in his undergrad years."

"Okay, I'll see what I can do."

Then from the door, I heard, "Emmy PooPoo."

It was my Uncle Matt followed by my Aunt Kate, two of my favorite relatives.

"Emmy PooPoo," Madeleine mouthed, laughing.

"Not a word," I said in a threatening whisper. "Uncle Matt, I thought I told you not to call me that in public. It's bad enough that you call me that in front of the girls." I went around the counter and hugged and kissed them both.

Aunt Kate held me in her arms for a few seconds and said, "Your momma called me yesterday and told me about the baby. I'm sorry." Aunt Kate was one of my dad's seven older sisters; he was the youngest of eleven.

"Is that why you're here?" I asked harshly and was immediately sorry for my tone.

"No," she replied.

"Here as a peacemaker?"

"Yep. Your momma's real upset about that fight you two had and she doesn't know how to make it right."

I turned away from her, rubbing my forehead. I caught sight of Madeleine and took that chance to divert Aunt Kate's attention.

"Aunt Kate and Uncle Matt, this is my new assistant, Madeleine Burn. Madeleine, this is Kate and Matt Ellison."

They shook hands and made small talk, which gave me time

to figure out how I was going to nicely tell my favorite aunt to butt out. Kate and Matt had two daughters with whom I'd been close to as a child but didn't see much of now that we were adults. I had hoped to rectify our lack of contact now that I was living in Middletown again; however, all three of us had children who kept our lives busy. Matt and Kate lived about fifty miles away in a town even smaller than Middletown. They had been like another set of parents to me. I'd gone to their house during summer vacations for a few weeks at a time, and we had often seen one another on weekends. Besides being my dad's sister and brother-in-law, they were also my parents' best friends.

When I wasn't paying attention, my Uncle Matt had asked Madeleine about a book he was looking for, and she guided him along the bookshelves to the back of the store. What a well-oiled machine they were.

"Pretty slick," I said to my Aunt Kate, who was now standing in front of me waiting for my attention. "Uncle Matt takes care of Madeleine while you try to talk me into making up with my mother."

"Never underestimate the value of proper training," she joked. She then turned serious and continued, "I know your momma can make herself a burr in your side, but she's your mother, and it's not right to fight with her."

"She started it. She started it almost the day I was born."

"She wants so much for you."

"Aunt Kate, what could she possibly want for me that I don't already have?" I asked, motioning around the room, indicating my family and my business.

"She wants to have more in common with you. She feels left out of your life."

"She excludes herself."

"It seems that way because she doesn't express herself well, but she loves you, and she doesn't know how to make a connection with you anymore."

"Aunt Kate, not once last night when I came home from the hospital did she acknowledge my loss. She acted like it never happened."

"She doesn't know what to say, so she doesn't say anything." She paused for a moment, and then she said, "Don't make the same mistake."

"I'll try for you."

"No!" she said sharply, pointing her finger at me. "If you won't do it for you and your mother then don't do it at all. She's not perfect, but neither are you, Emily Suzanne."

"You're right."

"Fine. Now, let's get you home. You look like crap."

"I can't. This is Madeleine's first day, and she doesn't know where anything is."

"We promised Jack."

"You talked to Jack?"

"He pulled your uncle over on the way here."

"Uncle Matt, did Jack give you another speeding ticket?" Jack pulled Uncle Matt over whenever he saw him in town because he knew it made him mad.

"Naw, he just harassed me some. I told him I was going to turn him in for police brutality and profiling."

As we were all laughing at Uncle Matt's joke, Kylie walked in the door. Aunt Kate said I didn't have any excuse now, and after I introduced Kylie to Madeleine and gave my employees a few instructions, I let my aunt and uncle take me home. Aunt Kate made supper while Uncle Matt helped the kids with their homework, so I could rest. I offered to let them stay the night, but they refused. One of their grandkids had a school play the next day that they wanted to attend.

I went to bed right after the kids but woke up when Jack slipped into bed next to me at two-thirty. He had patrol until one, but if he had any paperwork to do, that delayed him from getting home. He'd been going to work when he stopped by the store the day before and that was a little after ten in the morning. He'd been putting in a lot of hours because he had paperwork to catch up on since he'd been away from the office two days this week and had a murder investigation to oversee.

"How was your day?" I asked as he threw the covers over himself.

"I'm sorry; I didn't mean to wake you," he whispered.

"No. I'm glad you did. I've missed you," I said, turning to my side and kissing him. "So, *how was your day?*"

"Drunk driver," he sighed. Jack hated drunk drivers; he considered them almost as loathsome as child molesters. "We caught him weaving down Route Fifty. I'm glad we caught him before he killed someone. I had to take him to the hospital for a blood-alcohol test. I saw your friend Olive. She asked how you were."

"You're kidding? Did she seem friendly or happy?"

"No, she very seriously asked if you were healing all right. The ER was abuzz with the rumor that she had a hot relationship. Someone had sent her two dozen roses."

"Well, good for Olive," I said, deciding to keep my anonymity. If it helped her reputation for people to think she had a lover, I wasn't going to let it out that I was the flower sender.

"Actually, I'm glad you're awake. The autopsy results came back on Mara Tierney."

"Well?" I asked, turning to face him.

"Definitely a fentanyl overdose," he said. "Depending on

151

body weight, two milligrams of fentanyl can kill someone. The solution that was applied to Mara's scalp had three times the amount needed to kill an adult. The medical examiner believes whoever put the drugs into the solution didn't have any experience with fentanyl; they wanted to make sure they got the job done."

"Whoa," I said, falling back on the bed. "Someone really wanted her dead."

"The bottle contained mostly water, fentanyl, and alcohol. It certainly never would have curled her hair."

"Where would someone get that much fentanyl?"

Jack looked at me for a moment, and then said, "Emily, don't be naive. I could go over to the park and buy two pills that look like that rainbow candy. One of those pills has enough fentanyl in it to not only kill me but everyone in this house."

My eyes widened in surprise.

"Another interesting finding was that Mara had psoriasis on her scalp. The sores brought on by the psoriasis absorbed the drugs more quickly than if the skin hadn't been broken. With all the blood vessels in the scalp and around the brain, the fentanyl sped through her system. Because of those blisters on your hand, the fentanyl entered your system more easily than if your skin had been unbroken."

We laid there silent for a few moments, and then I turned and looked at him, "Why would someone with psoriasis be getting permanents? Surely, it would burn."

"That's a good question," he said.

"An even better question is: Why would Mara get her hair done by the woman who had an illegitimate child with her husband?"

"Another valid question," he admitted.

"It makes me wonder if she was there for some other purpose besides getting her hair done," I said. I rolled to my back, thinking to myself. "Hey, Jack," I said after a few minutes. He must have fallen asleep while I was thinking because when I said his name, he jerked awake.

"What," he mumbled into his pillow.

"Did you know that George didn't put any information about Mara's education in her obit?"

"No," he grunted.

"Don't you think that's odd?"

"No," he grunted again.

"Okay. Go back to sleep."

"Mmmfrmh," he murmured. I wasn't sure if he was cussing or saying okay, but I didn't dare ask. He was always grumpy when you woke him shortly after he'd fallen asleep.

I slept fitfully that night because questions kept swirling around in my brain and mixing with my dreams. I woke up with a start at one point, dreaming that my hair was falling out.

CHAPTER 15

The next day the weather was beautiful. The end of the school year was only a handful of weeks away, and the kids were excited about the prospects of summer. The warm weather brought their excitement to a new level of hyperactivity. Some of their excitement rubbed off on me, and I felt energetic and hopeful for the first time in weeks. That morning at breakfast, we talked about trips to the pool, picnics, and camping. I wasn't sure if it was the weather, the kids, or that I was going to the bookstore to spend the day with a woman whom I had a feeling would become my dear friend. I felt good and was happy. I felt so good that I called my mother and made an appointment to have breakfast with her the next morning after I took the kids to school. She didn't say so, but she sounded relieved that I was making the first move. She even offered to keep Elly all afternoon.

Unfortunately, my happy feelings didn't last long. The day started like any other day—send the kids off to school, open the store, blah, blah, blah—but around noon, things got strange.

True to her word, Madeleine brought in some of Nelson's yearbooks that she'd found in the attic. Of course, Nelson had been in a frat, so his books were covered with signatures and raunchy notes. I scoured the three books she'd brought in and could find no trace of Mara Tierney. Of course, she'd been there getting her Master's and graduate students usually aren't as involved in campus life as undergrads. I wasn't deterred from my course, not yet at least. I decided that I'd have to call Northwestern to find out what I wanted to know. I left Madeleine making a new window display, highlighting the latest vacation and diet books, all essentials for summer, while I went to the storeroom to make some phone calls in private.

Mara's full name had been in her obituary, Mara Mary Michaels Tierney. It was hard not to remember all of those M's. After making several calls, I was finally connected with the Registrar's office, but there I hit a roadblock.

"I'm sorry; I can't look for any records without a social security number," the woman at the Registrar's office told me.

"Well this applicant read some crazy article about identity theft and said she won't give me her social security number until after I hire her, and she has to fill out a W-2," I fabricated.

"Sorry. No soc., no info.," she said, unsympathetically.

After I hung up the telephone, I sat at my desk for a few minutes tapping a pencil on the ink blotter, trying to figure out how to get Mara's social security number. A light flicked on in my dark and cavernous brain, and I picked up the phone and dialed.

"*Daily Inquirer*," croaked the voice on the other end.

"Miss Bette, ready for some more fun?

"Sure, Kid, whaddaya got?"

I explained the situation to her. She said it would be difficult but not impossible, and she'd call me back soon with the information I needed.

As the call ended, Madeleine stuck her head in the door to tell me there was a man in the store who wanted to see me. When I emerged from the storeroom, I was met with Phillip Reese, Rhianna's father.

"Emily," he said as I approached him.

"Mr. Reese, how was your trip to Europe?" I asked.

"Europe?" he said. "What in the hell are you talking about?"

"Rhianna said you were in Europe, which is why you couldn't take Andy and why you weren't at her arraignment."

Mr. Reese, a serious looking man, stared at me like you would a slow-witted dog, impatiently but with pity. The few times I had encountered him over the years I had never once seen him smile. When I looked into his eyes, I knew I was looking at a person who had never felt any real joy in his life. Today, he was dressed in a dark gray suit with a white shirt and black tie; he looked more like he was going to a funeral than coming to a bookstore to talk to his daughter's oldest friend. His double breasted suit jacket hung off his rotund midsection, giving him a shape resembling a bell.

"Emily, you always were a gullible girl, especially where Annie was concerned," he said using Rhianna's name from childhood.

I glanced over at Madeleine who was standing near the cash register. There were two women near the mystery section who had been discussing a book but now were looking deeply uncomfortable.

"Mr. Reese, I'm not sure what you mean."

"Emily, Anne is not who you think she is. She never has been. You followed her around like a puppy when you both were young. I thought when you came back to town that things would be different because you're a grown woman now. But here you are: Your business is right next to hers—"

"—I didn't know," I started.

"—and you're right back to following her around, believing everything she says."

"Mr. Reese, I am confused. Rhianna said you were in Europe and that you and your wife were supportive of her and Andy. Supportive of her. . ."

". . . her deviant lifestyle?"

156

"No! I have to insist that you not use such bigoted terms when you're in my place of business."

"You stupid woman! Don't you lecture me!"

I never saw Madeleine move from her spot, but without looking, I now felt her standing next to me and slightly behind, a non-verbal "I've got your back" kind of gesture.

"You need to leave," I said, calmly but firmly.

"Listen, I didn't come here to debate with you. You know what I want," he said.

"No, I don't."

"I want my grandson."

"I can't help you with that. Rhianna left Andy in my care, and I cannot go against the promise that I made to her," I replied. I couldn't believe he had the gall to come to my place of business, insult me and his own daughter, and then demand that I hand over Andy as if he was a dog I was holding hostage.

"Surely, you can't side with an unfit mother like my daughter over giving a boy a decent, Christian upbringing?" he asked, his face beginning to redden.

"If you are so disapproving of Rhianna's life and how she's raising Andy, then why have you acted so supportive?"

"My wife and I knew that one day something like this would happen. We wanted to be nearby for Andy so that we could make sure no harm would come to him from his mother and her choices."

I noticed that when he referred to Mrs. Reese, it was as "his wife" and not as Rhianna's mother. Not once had he referred to Rhianna as his daughter. He was treating her like a stranger. I felt compelled to defend her.

"Rhianna's doing a fabulous job with Andy. He's well-mannered, kind, and happy." I replied. "Obviously, between the two of us," I said, indicating with my index finger that

I meant him and me, "I am the only one who cares about Rhianna, her wishes, and the safety of Andy, especially if he is going to be around your son-in-law."

"What are you talking about?" he asked, a defensive tone creeping into his voice.

"Oh, you know what I'm talking about. Do you really want me to say it out loud so that everyone in the store can hear?" I asked, looking at the other three faces in the room.

"She made that all up. Nothing was ever proven," he said. Clearly angry now, he was shaking his head in an emphatic manner that made his jowls wobble.

I had said my piece. I was not going to argue with him any further, so I stood in front of him, defiantly, with my arms crossed.

"I'll get a lawyer," he retorted.

"Then get a lawyer. Now, as a business owner, I reserve the right to refuse service to anyone I please, and I'm exercising that right. Mr. Reese, there's the door."

He turned on his heels and left the store, only to run headlong into George Tierney. I couldn't hear what they were saying, but I could tell from Mr. Reese's face that word had gotten out who Andy's father really was. Or maybe the Reeses had known all along. George had a curious smile on his face even though Mr. Reese began shaking a finger in George's face. Spittle was flying from Mr. Reese's mouth as he shouted at George. After the behavior I'd witnessed from George at his house when Rhianna had come by to pay her respects, I was beginning to fear for Mr. Reese's safety. But George remained calm and stood there with a goofy grin on his face, which seemed to enrage Mr. Reese even more. Finally, Mr. Reese threw up his hands in what appeared to be disgust and stalked off.

"Jesus, he's a caustic old bastard," George said as he entered the store, wiping his face with his shirt sleeve.

"The thing that really burns me up is that he thinks he's so pious," I replied.

We stood there for a moment, both of us trying to make sense of our interactions with Phillip Reese. Finally, I said, "How are you doing, George?"

"Fine, fine," he said cheerfully. "I came in to see what's going on."

"With what?"

"With the investigation," he said matter-of-factly.

"I don't know why you're asking me," I said. I was puzzled as to why he'd think I could tell him about official Sheriff's Office business. "You should call Deputy Bradley or Sheriff Romano about that."

"Well, you being the Sheriff's wife, I thought you'd have the inside scoop."

"Jack doesn't discuss his cases with me. That's law enforcement business, not family business." I was getting better and better at that white lie the more I told it.

"I feel so out of the loop. Who are their prime suspects?"

"*Well, George,* I can only guess, but I don't think they are looking for any suspects since they've charged Rhianna with the murder." Why was he asking about suspects when he knew someone had been charged?

"Oh, yeah, yeah. Right, right. Well, I'm not good at this legal stuff, and I never watch TV, so . . ." He was shifting his weight from foot-to-foot so much that he was almost bouncing. I wondered if he had to pee. He picked up a book from a display next to the cash register, flipped through it, and then snapped it shut and put it back.

"Are you okay?" He seemed high, but his eyes weren't glassy or dilated.

"Great, great," he said, almost chipper, and then as an afterthought, he solemnly added, "considering."

His behavior must have seemed odd to Madeleine as well because she came over to me and asked, raising her eyebrows and darting her eyes toward George, "You need anything, Emily?"

"No," I answered. "I'm fine right now."

"We're neighbors," she said to George. "I'm Madeleine Burn, used to be Kreger. My house is kitty-corner and behind yours."

"Oh, yeah," he answered, and for the first time since he had appeared in front of the store, he became serious and sullen— emotions that were more in keeping with his role as a recent widower.

"Madeleine, this is George Tierney," I said.

"Yes, we are definitely neighbors. I've seen you in your backyard." At this, George jerked his head up and squinted at Madeleine as if she'd insulted him.

To divert his attention, I asked him, "George, I was wondering. Why didn't you put any information about where Mara had gone to college in her obituary?"

"Don't know. Never thought of it. Happened so suddenly and all. Why?"

"That's understandable," I replied, but I wasn't convinced. "Her obituary was rather short for someone in her position."

Then he looked at both of us and smiled that goofy, strange smile he had had when he came in the store. He knocked his fist on the cash register as if knocking on a door and said, "Well, if you hear anything, let me know. I'm anxious to find out what the autopsy results are. Nice meeting you."

As he walked out the door, I turned to Madeleine and said, "That was weird. What's next?"

To see if anything or anyone else strange was coming my

way, I walked out onto the sidewalk in front of the store and looked both ways. Then I shaded my eyes with one hand and looked out into the town square. There was Harry, sitting on the same bench he'd been on since Mara's murder. I waved a big wave to him. As I turned to go back into the store, I saw him slightly raise his hand in response.

When I came back inside, Madeleine motioned me over to the counter and whispered, "You know, Emmy, I never read the *Daily Inquirer,* so I didn't know what George Tierney looked like. I didn't know he was my neighbor until now." She stopped and looked around the store to make sure the customers were still out of earshot. "I see him sneaking across the backyards of his neighbors late at night and going to a house that is about four down from his."

"No way!" I shouted, drawing everyone's attention. Then lowering my voice, I asked, "Which way does he go? Toward Tulip or toward Ash?"

"Ash."

"I knew it!" I said in a strained whisper. "Rhianna's house. How often do you see him doing this?"

"Well, before Nelson moved out, I had insomnia and I'd be awake two or three times a week. We have a big three story Victorian like yours, and on the third floor I have a library . . ."

"Oh, very nice. We have a playroom."

"Anyway, I'd go up there and read. Almost every night I was awake, I'd see him sneak by at about one o'clock. He'd always set off the motion light at the backdoor to Rhianna's house. He'd walk right in." Then she laughed, embarrassed, and said, "After I saw him do it a few times, I started watching for him. There was only one time when I watched for him that he didn't sneak over to her house."

"What about now? Have you seen him lately?"

"No, but I sleep like a log now that Nelson is no longer

sharing my bed."

"Madeleine, will you do me a favor and look for him tonight?"

"Yeah," she said, giving a thrilled giggle. Then more seriously she added, "But you know he seemed concerned when I said I was his neighbor and that I'd seen him in his backyard."

"Yeah, he did react strangely, but his entire demeanor was strange. Besides, he had no way of knowing you meant in the middle of the night."

"You're right. Now I'm the one acting paranoid."

"Double, double, toil and trouble. Fires burn and cauldron bubble," I said, rubbing my hands together quoting *Macbeth*.

"You're devious," she said. "I'd never guess that about you."

"And I'd never guess that you spied on your neighbors."

As we stood there laughing, Janney came in. "What's so funny?"

"Oh, it would take too much to explain it. Suffice it to say, we've had our share of strange visitors."

"Mmm," she said, still wondering what was going on. "What do you have in mind for me today?"

"Well, first I'd like to talk to you about what happened the day Mara died," I replied.

CHAPTER 16

A t first, Janney didn't want to talk about Mara's murder. Then after I reminded her that she'd have to testify in court about what happened and that it might be good to keep the events fresh in her mind, she agreed to go over the details with me. The two customers who had been in the shop when Mr. Reese came in and then for my conversation with George were now gone. Janney and I went into the storeroom to talk, leaving Madeleine out front, unpacking boxes of books. Janney told me she'd gotten to the shop around seven o'clock that morning, and when she arrived, Rhianna was giving an elderly woman, whom Janney didn't know, a rinse. Janney said she went about preparing for her first few appointments of the day, and then Rhianna asked her to mix the dye for Ruby Collins.

After I arrived at the beauty parlor that day, Ruby Collins had come in for Janney to cut and dye her hair. But Janney told me that Ruby wasn't supposed to be her customer; Mara Tierney was. At the last minute, Rhianna switched customers with her, giving her Ruby and Rhianna taking Mara.

"Why did she switch appointments with you?"

"Mara always gave me a hard time, and I was not looking forward to spending the next hour and a half with her," Janney answered.

So, I thought to myself, *Rhianna didn't usually do Mara's hair as I had previously thought. Last Thursday was out of the ordinary.*

"Why did she give you a hard time?" I asked.

"That's just how she is . . . was. She was hard to please. She'd look for mistakes or reasons to be dissatisfied. I always thought she was cheap and wanted a free perm."

"What did she complain about?"

"She'd say the perm solution leaked out of the batting and ruined her designer blouse and such. I told her to wear old clothes to get her hair done, but she wouldn't do it. She always wanted to look like a million dollars."

My mind flashed on an image of Mara lying on the cold tile floor of the beauty shop with her green silk blouse cut open. Shaking off the image, I asked, "Did you know she had psoriasis on her scalp?"

"Yes."

"Wouldn't the perm solution make her scalp burn because of the psoriasis?"

"I would think so, but she never complained about that—just everything else."

"Was George in the shop that morning?"

"Yes, he left right before you came in."

"Did Mara and George ever talk privately with Rhianna? Or ask her personal questions at any time since you started working for Rhianna?"

"You mean about Andy?"

"So you knew?"

"Yeah. Rhianna had told me a long time ago that George was Andy's father. They never discussed him, not that I ever knew of. Rhianna did say that George bothered her some."

"Bothered her, how?"

"He followed her one night to a bar out in The Patch and

started a fight with her." The Patch was the local nickname for the next town over. Bruceville was the name of the town, but everyone called it The Patch because it was a cluster of five houses, a bar, and a gas station on a "patch" of dirt.

"About Andy?"

"Yes."

"What about Andy," I asked in an exasperated tone. It was like pulling teeth getting any details out of her.

"I don't know. She told me about it the morning after it happened. It was real casual. Kind of like how she had a crappy night because George showed up and started bugging her about Andy. She wasn't specific, and I didn't ask any questions."

"Weren't you curious?"

"Sure, but I don't like people prying into my business, so I don't pry into theirs," she said pointedly.

Ignoring her comment, I decided to go back to the switched appointments and asked, "Who got out the perm solution that was used on Mara?"

"Rhianna did."

"But hadn't you already gotten a kit out to use?"

"Yes, but she got her own."

"How come?"

"Force of habit I guess."

Oh, God, I was screaming inside my head in frustration. No wonder cops have to be taught the art of interrogation. Either Janney was being extremely closed mouth, or I stunk as an investigator. Just then the phone rang. I went over to my desk in the storeroom and answered it.

"*Cover to Cover Books.*"

"Hey, Kid, I got it."

"Hold on a sec." I covered the receiver and told Janney to go help Madeleine unpack the shipment that I had received that morning of summer reading books for the high schoolers and that we could talk more later. After Janney left the storeroom, I told Miss Bette to give me the numbers.

"How'd you get these?"

"A good reporter never reveals her source," she said, giving her familiar cackle and hanging up.

Once I had the social security number, I called Northwestern back and was shocked at what I found out. No one with that social security number had ever attended Northwestern. When I questioned the woman at the Registrar's office about the validity of their records, she got perturbed and suggested that it was I who had made the mistake. Since I didn't doubt Miss Bette's ability to get the right numbers, I was left with the conclusion that Mara Tierney, or someone else, had lied about where she'd gone to school.

I got out a notebook and jotted a few notes and questions. Then I gathered my things and decided to leave for the day. It was almost time to get Bella and Andy from school, and I wanted to talk to Rhianna before I got the kids.

When I walked out of the backroom, I saw Ruby Collins talking to Janney. When Ruby saw me, she enthusiastically greeted me.

"Oh, Emily, I'm so glad you're alright. And I'm so sorry to hear about your baby," Ruby gushed. I wondered how she knew about my ectopic pregnancy, but knowing how efficient the gossip network was, I shouldn't have been shocked that even confidential medical procedures weren't kept secret in this town. Maybe Olive had spread the news; she certainly had no obligation to be kind to me. My cheeks colored as Janney gave me a puzzled look.

"Thank you," I replied.

"I was trying to convince Janney here to keep a secret for me," she said, conspiratorially taking me by the elbow and walking me a few steps away from the others. "You see, no one knows that I dye my hair."

Muffling a giggle, I tried to look shocked. I doubted that anyone would mistake the bold, brassy red that Ruby routinely had her hair dyed as natural. Even a man who hadn't a clue about women's grooming would have known it wasn't her natural color. Besides it being such an unnatural red, the color clashed with her skin tone, bringing out a green undertone in her skin that made her look sallow. All of this, coupled with her propensity for wearing fuchsia and brick reds, which would look awful on even a natural redhead, made her look like a fashion-challenged circus clown. She'd once gotten angry with me because I refused to cut a lock of my hair for her to use as a guide: "For the day when I have to dye my hair to maintain my natural color," she had said.

"How does this concern Janney?" I asked.

"Well, she's going to have to testify at Rhianna's trial, and I don't want her saying on the witness stand that she was dying my hair."

"Surely you wouldn't want Janney to perjure herself?"

"Well . . . no, but if she said she was only cutting my hair that wouldn't be a lie because she did cut my hair that day. You saw her."

"Yes, but if she's asked specifically what she was doing that day, she'd have to say that she prepared the dye for your hair. If she lied, she could go to jail." I was blowing things out of proportion, but I was enjoying goading her.

"Even for a little white lie like this?"

"I'm afraid so, Mrs. Collins."

She thought about it for a moment and then turned away from me, walking back over to Janney, "Well, you think about it, dear. I'd hate to have to take my business elsewhere." With that threat, she said goodbye and went on her way.

"See what I was talking about?" I said to Janney, referring to all the strange visitors we'd had that day.

"If that is only a sample of what you experienced earlier, I don't even want to know about what happened before I came in," she said, rolling her eyes and returning to unpacking the summer reading books.

Within a few days of her release on bail, Rhianna and I had fallen into a comfortable routine. She'd walk over to the school. I'd meet her there, and then we'd take the children to my house. She usually stayed at the house until she put Andy to bed that night. Jack seemed tired of running into her whenever he came home, but he didn't say anything about it.

I didn't know how she spent her days. She wasn't sharing much with me about her legal defense or about anything else. But her silence on her personal life wasn't any different than the rest of our relationship. I started to realize more than ever how one-sided our friendship was. Even though I shouldn't have let Mr. Reese's words get to me, his accusation that I was gullible and "followed Rhianna around like a puppy" were obsessively running on replay in my mind. My pride had been hurt when Janney had told me she had known for a long time that George was Andy's father. The events surrounding Mara's death had made me do a lot of thinking about my friendship with Rhianna. I came to realize that I had imbued our current relationship with the feelings from our childhood friendship. When I came back to town, I had leaned on that friendship to get comfortable in town again. No matter what Mr. Reese said, I knew who she was. However, I was realizing that she hadn't held our friendship in the same level of esteem that I did. Before Mara's death, Rhianna had not needed me. The tables were turned now. She needed my defense of her and she needed me to care for Andy, which also begged the question: Why did she choose me to be Andy's guardian if she had not valued our friendship in the same way?

I suspected that there wasn't much happening on the legal front regarding Rhianna's case. The police investigation was coming to an end now that the autopsy report was back. All of the physical evidence had been collected. Now, it was a waiting game until the trial, which had been set for July sixth. Her lawyer had gone back to Chicago to review the evidence and prepare her defense. I don't think she talked about it too much because her case looked pretty hopeless. Her fingerprints had been the only ones on the bottle of perm solution, and she had administered the fatal overdose via that perm solution to Mara's head. She had a history with the victim, giving her motive. Most prosecutors would consider that an airtight case, as I was sure the overly confident Robert Price did. The deck was stacked against her, and it was friendship that kept me on her side, even if that friendship wasn't equally returned.

Despite her lie about her parents being in Europe and her father's statement that Rhianna wasn't who I thought she was, I felt like I knew who she was as a person. As a result, I was adamant she was not guilty. But I was starting to wonder if my conviction regarding her innocence was more about my inability to believe that anyone I knew could commit such a crime? In reality, it was neither. It was pride. I was too proud to admit that I could be fooled like that by someone so close to me. I prided myself in knowing people and could usually tell in the first minute what someone was like. I often disliked people on the first meeting whom other people trusted until proven untrustworthy. I couldn't admit that I didn't recognize someone's murderous traits whether the murderer turned out to be Rhianna or someone else.

When I pulled up to the school, Rhianna was sitting under a tree in the schoolyard. When she saw me, she came over and got into my minivan. We exchanged pleasantries, and then I got to the meat of what I really wanted to know.

"Why did you tell me your parents were in Europe when they weren't? And they clearly are not on your side or accept that you're a lesbian. Or is it bi-sexual? I really don't care about the label. What I care about is being lied to."

A sad expression replaced her pleasant smile. She didn't even attempt to deny anything that I said.

"I guess I wanted you to think I had it better than I really do. My parents and I have a cordial relationship because they help me with Andy and are kind to him. As far as I can tell, they don't say negative things about me to him. But outside of our interactions about Andy, we don't have a relationship." She thought for a moment and then said, "It was easier to lie than to admit the truth. I'm sorry I lied to you."

In that brief moment, I could see my friend Annie that I had grown up with. Not Rhianna. I trusted what Annie told me. Rhianna, I was still trying to figure out.

"Thank you," I said. "I appreciate you admitting that you lied and telling me the truth now."

We were quiet for a few minutes, and then I told her I'd talked to Janney about the day Mara died and that Janney was concerned about Rhianna. Rhianna seemed to think that Janney was mainly concerned because Rhianna was her meal ticket.

"She sees you as more than a meal ticket," I said in Janney's defense.

"She's a sweet kid. She's been through a lot," she said, referring to Janney's mother's death.

"You know, we've never talked about that day."

"What's to talk about? Mara walked in for a permanent and left permanently dead."

Her punny retort about Mara's death unnerved me, but I went on, "What did you do that morning before Mara came in?"

She looked at me sideways as if she resented me asking her about this. But when she saw that I wasn't going to drop it, she told me she gave Althea Kent a rinse and set. Althea Kent must have been the elderly client whom Janney had not recognized. I told her that I was confused about her relationship with George and Mara because George didn't want anything to do with Andy, and Mara hated Rhianna because she wanted child support. Plus, Mara had this bit of information about Rhianna's lover that she was holding over Rhianna's head.

"Yet, when I was in the shop that morning, you, Mara, Janney, and Ruby all seemed to be having a friendly conversation. I don't understand how you could be so pleasant to people with whom you have such an acrimonious relationship," I asked.

"It was business. Mara was the head of the largest company in town. She could have put me out of business by bad mouthing the service she received at my shop. So I was nice even if it killed me."

Or her, I thought. Then I asked her, "So you didn't have an argument or anything with her that morning before I got there?"

"No, *I* didn't," Rhianna replied.

"What do you mean *you* didn't."

"Janney argued with her."

"What about?"

"The usual—her mother. Well, the argument wasn't about her mother, but that's what all the animosity was about."

"What animosity? Remember, I haven't lived here that long."

"Janney's mother worked at Midwestern Mutual, and when she got sick and started to miss work because of chemo, Mara fired her. Janelle, Janney's mother, was unable to pay for insurance after she was fired because of the cancer and had to stop chemo since she couldn't pay for it. She died because she stopped treatment. The cancer spread. It was horrible. It went to her brain, and in the end, she didn't even recognize Janney and her brother."

"That's so awful. I can't imagine being an eighteen-year-old kid trying to deal with the loss of my mother and take care of a sixteen year old brother, too. How could something like that happen? How could someone be so heartless as to fire a person who so desperately needed the money and the benefits?"

"That was Mara. She was promoted to president because she was so good at cutting costs, which usually meant cutting benefits. The whole town is full of stories like Janelle's. That's what gets me about my situation. There are a lot more people in this town who had better reasons to kill her than child support. I wish I knew how those drugs got into that bottle," she said, hanging her head into her hands. I looked past her to where a group of mothers were standing on the sidewalk, giving us sideways glances. It hadn't occurred to me until now that our meeting at school and all the time Rhianna was spending at my house was probably perpetuating the rumor that I was the secret girlfriend who was not out of the closet.

I focused my attention back on Rhianna and asked, "What did Mara and Janney fight about?"

"You know, Janney gave up a scholarship to the University of Illinois to take care of her brother after her mom died. After funeral expenses, all of her mother's life insurance went to pay medical bills. Janney was going to study chemical engineering and find a cure for cancer. That was her dream. Anyway, you know how caustic Mara was; every time she saw Janney, she picked at that wound. It started with a comment from Mara about what a shame it was that Janney had to be a beautician, and that she could have done so much more with her life. It was probably a cut at me as well, but I've been dealing with

Mara for a while and have gotten used to her crap. So that's what set Janney off and she went after Mara."

"What do you mean 'went after her'?"

"She wanted to attack her. Janney started toward her, and I put my body between them. I could barely separate them."

"What did George and your customer, Althea Kent, do?"

"George wasn't in the shop. He'd just left. Althea didn't do anything to help. She hates Mara, too, but I don't know why.

"It seems so out of character for Janney. She never mentioned the argument when I talked to her."

"She's a good kid. She probably didn't mention the fight because she was embarrassed that she'd lowered herself to Mara's level. Janney's proud. It's been difficult for her to accept my help. I wanted to help her because I understood what it's like to see the life you dreamed that you'd have evaporate before you."

"How, after all that had happened, were you all having such a friendly conversation when I came in. Acting like nothing had happened."

"Mara had inflicted pain and mayhem, so she was happy. Janney was only doing what I was doing, putting on a friendly air for Ruby Collins, who is one of the worst gossips in town."

"Yes, that I know."

I wanted to ask her about switching customers with Janney, but the kids came running out of the school, and we went to greet them.

While I was hugging Bella and asking her about her day, I saw Jessy Becker walking Andy over by the hand to Rhianna.

"Is Andy okay?" I asked Bella.

"Some boys were picking on him today."

"Oh no!" I said, leading her to the car and making sure she got buckled into her booster seat. Then I went around the front of the car and got in on the driver's side. I saw Jessy squat down on Andy's level and give him a hug. Then she stood up and gave Rhianna a hug, a rather long hug. I saw Rhianna subtly pull away and look around to see if anyone saw them.

I wondered what that was all about. Then Rhianna turned and led Andy to the car.

After she got in, I asked, "Is Andy okay?"

"Let's not talk about it right now."

I didn't press, but she never did tell me what happened.

CHAPTER 17

That night I stayed up late mulling over the day's events. There were still so many questions I wanted answers to but didn't know how to go about getting them without doing some real investigative work. I wanted to dig around for myself; I was itching to, but if I was caught, I would upset Jack again. We'd only recently healed that wound. But sooner, rather than later, I'd find the cosmos or maybe the townspeople were sucking me into the investigation, and I would have no choice but to get involved.

Case in point: I finally turned off the light and drifted off to sleep around twelve-thirty. At one o'clock, the ringing telephone jolted me awake. My heart began to race. Late night phone calls only meant bad news.

"Hello!" I answered frantically.

"Emmy," someone whispered on the other end.

"Yes?"

"Emmy, it's Madeleine. Is your husband there?"

"No, he's working. Why? Are you in trouble? Is it Nelson?"

"No. It's George. I've already called the Sheriff's Office. Someone should be here soon enough, or maybe I should say the authorities should be at Rhianna's soon enough."

"What?" I said, jumping out of bed.

"There's a fight over at Rhianna's."

"What's happening?"

"I was watching for George, like you asked me to."

"Madeleine," I interrupted her. "Are you in your house?"

"Yes," she whispered.

"Then why are you whispering?" I asked.

"Oh," she shouted into the receiver, overcompensating for whispering. She went on to tell me she'd seen George about forty-five minutes previously crossing the backyards walking toward Rhianna's house. When he got to Rhianna's, he wasn't able to walk in as usual because the screen door was locked. After several minutes of him rattling the door, Rhianna came out onto the screened-in-porch. Although Madeleine couldn't hear what they were saying, she could tell that Rhianna wanted him to leave because she was pointing toward his house.

He did leave but came back a few minutes later with a crowbar and tried to pry the door off its hinges. She said Rhianna came back out and yelled at him some more, but when he didn't stop, she disappeared inside the house. Madeleine assumed she'd gone in to call the police, but a few minutes later a balding man with a big belly and skinny legs showed up and tried to take the crowbar away from George. Then George swung the crowbar at the man and nearly hit him with it.

"I thought George was going to kill him, whoever he is, so that's when I called the police."

"The other man is Joe Campbell, George's best friend," I explained. "How did you see all of this?"

"I'm using binoculars," she giggled. "I feel a bit like Mrs. Kravitz from *Bewitched*."

Then law enforcement showed up, which included my husband, and Madeleine gave me a blow-by-blow of the action. She was impressed by how easily Jack stripped the crowbar from George's hands and had him on the ground, cuffing him.

"That man's got muscles," she said in such a way that I could almost imagine the smile on her face.

"Yes, you should see him naked," I bragged.

Then the action heated up a bit, and we squelched our girl talk. George had tried to run away from Jack, in handcuffs no less. But Jack caught up with him in a few steps.

"Now, there's a deputy there giving George a field sobriety test," she said.

"What's he look like?"

"Tall, dark hair. Now he is slamming George against the squad car door."

"That's Brett Bradley; police brutality is his specialty."

"Oh, it looks like things are breaking up now. Jack's letting George go," she explained, bewildered.

"If no one wanted to file charges, and he passed a field sobriety, Jack probably doesn't have anything to hold him on. Maybe disturbing the peace, but Jack's not big on handing out nuisance violations."

"Bradley doesn't look happy. His face is all red, and he's arguing with Jack."

"He'd do anything to contradict Jack and try to make his life difficult."

"Joe's hugging Rhianna and taking her into her house."

"What? Only last week Joe acted like he wanted to rip her head off."

"Looks like everyone's gone now."

"This is all so strange. Why was George going over to Rhianna's, especially after he practically attacked her in his front yard the week before. Maybe he wasn't satisfied and was going over to confront her again, and she called Joe for help. But that doesn't explain why Joe was being so friendly to her. She could have called the police herself. Uhhgg," I yelled in

177

exasperation. "I'll see you tomorrow."

I was sitting in the window seat still clutching my phone in my hand when I saw Jack's cruiser pull into our driveway. I went downstairs to meet him.

He took one look at the phone in my hand and said, "Looks like you've been talking to Ethel."

"Ethel?"

"You're the redhead, so that means you must be Lucy, which would make Madeleine Ethel," he said referring to the hapless friends from *I Love Lucy*. "I saw her standing in her third floor window, holding binoculars up to her face, and talking on the phone. I figured she must be talking to you."

"What was going on over there?"

"I'm not sure. We couldn't get a straight answer out of anyone. Rhianna said George was trying to break into her house, but she didn't want to call us, so she called Joe. When George saw Joe, he went berserk. No one wanted to press charges, and I wasn't going to bring a nuisance charge against him, so we let them all go."

"Madeleine said you had to pull Bradley off George."

"George was acting very strangely, like he was high. Frankly, he never would have been able to hit Joe with that crowbar because his depth perception was way off. Bradley insisted on giving him a field sobriety, but before he could start administering it to George, George called Bradley a pig. Very original," he said, rolling his eyes. "Bradley went off."

"I'm telling you, Jack. It's only a matter of time before Bradley hurts someone."

"I know. But the D.A. has a real hard-on for him."

I told him that George was in the store the day before acting in a similar way, and that he'd been asking about the investigation and who the suspects were. Jack found that as odd as I did.

Jack said he was going to jot down some notes for his report tomorrow and that I should go on to bed. I said goodnight and went up upstairs but knew I wouldn't be able to sleep with all the questions whirling in my brain. The main question was: Why a group of people who publicly hated one another were secretly so chummy?

Either I put myself to sleep with all the internal questioning I was doing, or Jack stayed downstairs longer than he thought he would because I never felt him come to bed that night. When I got up the next morning, he was already awake and dressed. I was having trouble getting myself moving from lack of sleep. I had a breakfast appointment with my mother, which was going to take more emotional effort than I thought I had.

When I wandered down to the kitchen in search of much needed coffee, the other love of my life, I found Jack making the girls and Andy breakfast. He'd promised to take them to school, which was a rare treat and always made the girls' day when he could arrange it. I was concerned that he hadn't had much sleep, but he said he had a lot on his mind. *That seems to be going around*, I thought.

Since Jack was taking the kids to school that morning, I was able to meet my mother earlier than I'd thought. As I sat in my booth at Wilma's waiting for her to arrive, I inhaled as much secondhand smoke as I could and resisted the urge to put an unlit cigarette in my mouth. When my mother came in, I saw her lightly touch my grandfather's hat like a Catholic dipping her hand in holy water before entering church. She made eye contact with me, and I stiffened my spine and screwed on a smile.

"Good morning, Mother."

"Morning, Emmy Sue," she replied. She seemed to be putting on an air of coldness, protecting herself from whatever verbal assault I had planned for her.

"Your emissary came to see me." I was being flippant, which wasn't the right way to start this meeting. I had to remind myself that I was here to make peace.

"What?"

"Aunt Kate."

"Oh."

"Look, Mom, I was annoyed the other day, and you stepped on the wrong nerve."

"It seems like I always do that. I don't know what to say to you anymore, Emmy Sue. You treat me like I'm stupid."

"I do not!" I shot back. "And if I do, it's because you *act* stupid."

"Well, I don't have the education you do. I never had that opportunity handed to me."

"If I remember right, it wasn't handed to me either," I said, remembering how I worked two jobs to make the tuition.

"You always have to throw that up in my face don't you!" she shot back. "It wasn't your father's fault the oil refinery closed."

This was not going well. We both glared into our coffee cups. I needed to take a different approach if this was going to work.

"Listen, I don't think you're stupid. It seems to me like you put on this airhead act. And I understand that it wasn't Dad's fault he had to use the money for my education," I said, trying to figure out exactly what to say. "You didn't have the opportunity to go to college like I did. And I'm thankful that you and Dad made that happen for me." She was still staring at the table. "Mom, you are a very smart person with some wonderful talents of your own. You couldn't have been the executive assistant of the president of a company if you weren't smart."

"Oh, stop it, Emily. You're not going to smooth this over by sucking up to me." My mother never called me Emily unless she was very angry with me.

"I wasn't trying to suck up to you. What is it that you want from me, Mother?"

"Respect. You've never respected me."

"Have you ever respected me?"

"I respect you!"

"Really. So whenever you insult my cooking, criticize my parenting methods, or doubt the choice I made for a spouse, you're respecting me?"

"I don't know what you're talking about."

"'Do we always have to have Italian?' 'I never let you talk to me that way.' 'I still can't believe you married a police officer.'" I quoted. "You don't remember saying any of those things?"

"I don't understand you, Emily. That's all I meant."

"What do you mean, you don't 'understand me.'"

"Your life is so different from mine."

"Ah, now we're getting to the real issue here. You don't approve of my life. Is that it?"

"No. I just . . ." her voice caught, and I was afraid she was going to cry. I had asked her here to make up, not to humiliate her in public.

Finally, I said, "Mom, I'm not you. Even though I chose a different life than you, doesn't mean I don't love you or that you raised me wrong or that I'm rejecting you in some way. Just the opposite. It means that you raised me to be a confident person who believes in her own abilities."

"Well, you must have gotten that from someone else. You couldn't have gotten it from me."

"Why do you always do that? You're the one putting you

181

down, not me. Look at all the things you've done with your life."

"What have I done? I've lived in this town all my life. Same thing, day-in, day-out."

"I find living in this town a chore. Yet, you've made a successful life here and you like it. I find that amazing. You and Daddy have made the garage successful. Where do you think I got my entrepreneurial spirit? You're also a talented cook and seamstress. People in Chicago looking for folk art would pay big bucks for the work you do. Look at your marriage. You've made it work for forty-five years now. You had a successful career. All of those things are wonderful accomplishments, and I envy every one of them."

"Don't tell me you envy my 'career,'" she said, making air quotes with her fingers. "They're nothing compared to . . ."

"Compared to what? Compared to getting a Master's degree? Compared to living in Chicago? Compared to owning a bookstore? It's all relative. You could do all of those things. It's never too late to try. And besides, while you're envying all of my 'accomplishments,' you should be patting yourself on the back because who do you think made it possible for me to do all of those things? Who gave me the freedom to spread my wings and fly?" I could see her cheeks pinking with embarrassment. "Look at some of the people we know whose children never left home. How many of them stayed because they wanted to and how many stayed because they were never given the confidence and freedom to do otherwise?"

"Is that why you never came home to see us? Because you wanted to be free?"

"What?" I asked.

"Until you moved back here, it was like pulling teeth to get you to come home for a visit, and when you did visit, you only stayed for a few days. Did you hate us that much?"

"Mother! I didn't hate you. It was the town I hated. I hated how everyone talked about everyone else. I hated having my life examined by everyone I came in contact with. I wanted to live my life on my terms and not have to worry about what the gossips were going to say about me. If Jack hadn't been shot, I never would have moved back here," I said, and then realizing that I was still leaving my parents out of the equation, I added, "But I'm glad I did move back because now I can be near you and Daddy again, and you both can be with the girls and get to know them."

She still didn't look at me, but she reached her hand across the table and squeezed mine. "Emmy. I'm sorry about your baby. I can't imagine how hard that must have been for you. I didn't mean to. . . I've never experienced that kind of loss, so I didn't know what to say. I'm sorry I didn't say so sooner."

"Thank you, Mom. I'm okay. Hopefully, we can have more children if we want to later." We were both silent for a moment, and then I said, "Let's make a deal. I'll stop being so condescending and grow up a bit if you promise to stop second guessing everything I do."

"Deal."

We fell into an awkward silence. Then I said, "Mom, tell me about Mara Tierney."

"What do you want to know about her?"

"Anything. What was she really like?"

"People thought she was a b-i-t-c-h, but she wasn't really. Could she be demanding? Yes, but she was the boss. Could she be controlling? Sure, but she wanted things done right." She got a faraway look in her eye, and then said, "She taught me to stand-up for myself."

"What?" I said, incredulously. "When did you ever need help standing up for yourself?"

"Emmy Sue, you didn't know me as a girl. You only know me

as your mom."

"Fair enough," I said. "Did she ever talk about George?"

"Not really. She liked to keep work and home separate. Mara was a very private person. Appearances meant a lot to her. Not just how she looked, but what people thought about her and George as a couple. The last few years right before I retired I got the feeling that she wasn't happy in her marriage."

"What makes you say that?"

"She had several out of office appointments that I later learned were with lawyers and accountants."

"How did you find that out?"

She smirked at me. I knew she wasn't going to tell me. "All-in-all she was not a bad boss. We got along pretty well and I respected her and she respected me. People expect women who work together to be best friends. We weren't friends. She was my boss and I was her secretary. It was business, not personal."

In my mind that translated to cold, but if it worked for them, who was I to judge?

"Thanks for sharing that with me, Mom."

She smiled warmly.

We ate our breakfast, and she caught me up on all the family news that I had missed out on when we weren't talking. It seems my cousin Jemma was getting married. When we left the restaurant, we both knew that we had a new relationship ahead of us. I was hopeful that it would be a relationship in which we began to enjoy one another as adults, instead of an envious mother of a disrespectful and condescending daughter.

CHAPTER 18

After I said goodbye to my mom at the restaurant, I drove over to George Tierney's house, determined to get to the bottom of what had gone on at Rhianna's the night before. I was surprised when George opened the door looking bright-eyed and alert. It was nine o'clock, still early for someone who'd been up late the night before and had been under the influence of. . . something.

He welcomed me into the house with a smile. When I crossed the threshold, I was shocked at what I saw there. The house was no longer the ordered, neat home that I'd seen the day I had come to give my condolences. The smell of cigarette smoke permeated the house as if he'd just snuffed out a butt. I didn't even know he smoked. Books, papers, and clothes were scattered all over the floors and furniture. In the kitchen, the trash was overflowing and the counter was littered with dirty dishes and discarded cans of soup and pasta sauce. He offered me some coffee, picking up a mug from the counter. He dumped old coffee and several cigarette butts out of the mug and into the sink, and then ground the remains of the cigarettes in the garbage disposal, washing them down the sink. He rinsed the mug with water and filled it with coffee. I reluctantly took it, repulsed that he hadn't even used soap; after all, I was a guest. He made no apology for the mess but, instead, launched into questions about the investigation.

"The sheriff told me the autopsy findings. Do you have any

idea where she got a hold of fentanyl?"

"No," I lied. He might have been playing dumb, but I hadn't known where to buy fentanyl either.

"Hasn't the prosecutor told you about these things?" I asked.

"No. I don't talk to him. He gives me the willies. Besides, I figure he knows what he's doing. So how's her kid?" he asked, again catching me off guard. I was starting to wonder if I had ever really known George because the teacher I'd known in high school was nothing like the man sitting before me today. Could his callousness and odd behavior really be the result of years in a loveless marriage and a thankless job or was this who he'd been all along?

"You mean, *Andy*? *Your son*? He's fine."

George slowly closed his eyes and squeezed them closed while he took a deep breath. "She says he's mine, but she's such a liar. It's hard to know the truth."

"Well, there's one way to find out. You could do a DNA test. Did you ever think of that?" I said.

Ignoring my question, he asked, "You going to give him to her parents when she's convicted?"

"No. I haven't discussed that with Rhianna, and I don't think she'll be convicted."

"Why not?" he exclaimed. "She killed Mara. She ruined my life!"

"I'm not sure she did it," I calmly replied.

"Who else could have done it?" he asked. I wasn't certain, but his distress didn't seem believable to me. His voice was raised, but his color was pallid and the animation in his face didn't match the strenuous tone of his voice. *Could he be play-acting for my benefit?* I wondered.

"Her guilt or innocence is not for me to decide," I answered. This was not going the way I wanted it to. I wanted to regain control of the conversation, so I got right to it, "George, why were you over at her house last night?"

"How'd you know about that?" he asked, a sly tone creeping into his voice.

"Jack."

"I thought he didn't talk to you about police business," he said, repeating the lie I'd told him the day before.

I raised my eyebrow and waited for him to answer. I wasn't going to let him regain control of the conversation.

"I'd been drinking last night, and I went over to confront her."

"Jack said you weren't drunk."

"So?"

"George, yesterday when you came into the store, you were acting very strange, as if you'd been smoking pot or something."

"Can't you see that I'm devastated? Aren't I allowed to act a little strange?" he asked. But again, his indignation didn't ring true to me.

"George, I know that you're having an affair with Rhianna, and that last night isn't the first time you've snuck over to her house in the middle of the night," I said, going for the jugular.

He jerked his head up and said, "I knew she'd seen me!" Madeleine had been right about his reaction yesterday to her saying she'd seen him in his backyard. "I love her," he admitted, rubbing his head vigorously, which I thought was a bad idea considering how little hair he had. "We've been having an affair since she was in high school."

"But she's a lesbian, and she has another lover."

"Bisexual," he corrected. It seemed like I'd had this conversation before. "I don't care. I want her and now she's abandoned me. She doesn't want to see me anymore. How could she do this to me?" I felt like he was trying to sell me on how much he was grieving and how hurt he had been, but I wasn't buying it.

"George, if you loved Rhianna so much, why didn't you divorce Mara and marry her?"

"Mara wouldn't divorce me because of Midwestern Mutual. The members of the board of directors are very traditional, and she was afraid if she was divorced they'd replace her as president. The only reason they agreed to make a woman president was because she didn't have children, which was why she didn't want me to take responsibility for Andy. Even if she'd had a stepchild, they would have thought her family responsibilities were more important. With a child, they would have thought her place was in the home, not as the head of an insurance company."

Based on what my mom had said about Mara caring about appearances, I could see some of what he was saying could be true. It is also believable that the board members would have traditional values.

Switching gears, I asked, "Does Andy know you're his father?"

"I don't think so. Rhianna said she didn't want to tell him if I couldn't be fully in his life. She thought it would only be painful and confusing for him. These women have taken everything from me, even my son." His behavior was confusing me. When I walked in, he was casual to the point of callousness about Rhianna being accused of his wife's murder; now, he was nearly sobbing, expecting me to feel sorry for him.

"Why didn't you leave Mara even if she wouldn't give you a divorce?"

"She said she'd tell the school board about my affairs with former students."

"Oh, God." My stomach was churning with disgust. I had

admired this man. Now, he was sitting in front of me telling me he'd slept with students, and he wanted my sympathy for how his life had turned out. "So, you knew that Mara had never gone to Northwestern and that's why you didn't put any educational information in her obit," I said.

"Mara never even finished college because she married me instead. When we moved to Middletown, Midwestern Mutual was just getting off the ground, and John Keene, the owner, never bothered to ask for transcripts. Mara impressed Keene, and he'd taken a liking to her, which is how she became president when he died a few years ago. The fact that she had never gone to college was my bit of dirt on her," he said smiling.

Shaking my head in disbelief, I asked him why he'd attacked Joe.

"Mara and Joe were having an affair. Two days after Mara died, Joe's wife received a letter, signed by Mara, revealing that they'd been having an affair. Joe's wife threw him out. He's living in a trailer behind the football field." He giggled strangely and said, "I wrote the letter and signed Mara's name. Even if I hated her, she was still my wife and he was my best friend. That's not something you do. It's unethical."

He was one to talk about ethics, I thought. Then I said, "I'm still confused about why Joe and Rhianna are all the sudden like old chums, and why you attacked her the day she came to your house to offer her condolences if you're so in love with her?"

He cocked his head a bit and began to laugh. "Yeah, Rhianna was really mad about the cake. I figured I had to do something to keep people from thinking anything suspicious was going on between us. As for Joe and why he's so friendly with Rhianna now: I don't know. Maybe he's happy she killed the miserable bitch. I know I am. I might have done it sooner or later if Rhianna hadn't taken care of it for me."

I'd had enough; I wanted to get as far away from George Tierney as I could.

"When will the funeral be?" I asked, knowing my mother had been working on the arrangements but that no date had been set. She had been waiting on Mara's body to be released by the Medical Examiner's Office. The least I could do was attend the funeral and pay my last respects.

"There won't be a funeral. She's already in the ground. They turned her body over to me on Monday morning, and she was in the ground in a pine box by Monday afternoon."

"Does my mother know?" I asked, imagining how furious she would be not only because she had done all of that planning, but she had also admired Mara. "And her family let you get away with that?"

"Mara didn't have any family who cared about her. Her parents are dead, and her two brothers couldn't have cared less when I called to tell them she was dead. In fact, one of them asked me how I could have lived with her for so many years. Good riddance. I think that describes the general attitude of everyone involved."

I couldn't get away from George's house fast enough. I would have never guessed what a raving loony George Tierney was. Not only was I more confused than ever, but I was also saddened to see what George was really like. How could her own family not care that she was dead? Why would Rhianna want to be mixed up with someone like George Tierney? All I could imagine was that he must have been some kind of god in bed. But even the most talented lover needs to be likable. Of course, my mistake was in thinking that everyone had the same standards that I did. Perhaps an earth shaking orgasm was all some women needed.

I also couldn't believe how freely George had talked about his dislike for Mara. How stupid was it of him to tell the sheriff's wife that he had thought about killing his own wife? He must not have thought it incriminated him in any way. Even though it seemed physically improbable that George planted the tainted bottle of perm solution in the beauty shop, it wasn't impossible. His statements about Mara alone were enough for him to be a suspect.

All of these questions made my head ache. I needed more coffee since I couldn't have a cigarette. When I got to the store, I made a pot. I hadn't touched the cup George had given me. While I waited for it to brew, I stood in the middle of the store staring out into the town square. Harry was sitting on his bench, and I wondered if he sat there all the time or if he went home at night. I went into the backroom, poured two cups of fresh-brewed magic, and headed across the street.

Harry didn't move or acknowledge my presence in any way when I sat down next to him. I handed him a cup, which he took after I held it out for several seconds.

"I didn't know if you liked cream or sugar. You seem like a black coffee kind of guy to me," I said. He didn't sip the coffee or even make a noise but just sat there staring straight ahead. He smelled of *Old English* aftershave. It was a familiar and comforting scent. Now that I was close to him, there was no mistaking his military background. His short-sleeved plaid shirt and khaki pants had crisp creases ironed into them, and his black shoes had a high polish on them. His white hair was cut into a high-and-tight, the distinctive Marine Corps cut, similar to Jack's. If you didn't know Harry was a person, you might have mistaken him for a statue because he sat straight back with his hands on his knees as if he were sitting at attention. As I sat next to him, his clear blue eyes focused straight ahead as if they were boring a hole into the front of my store.

"We haven't been introduced. I'm Emily Romano." I didn't offer him my hand because I didn't think he'd take it. "I'm sorry, but I don't know your last name. I hope you won't think I'm being disrespectful if I call you Harry."

He didn't respond.

We sat in silence for a few moments. I watched cars pass by, waving at the few people whom I knew and getting strange stares in return.

Finally, I turned to him and said, "Harry, this town is full of strange and deceitful people. Seems like everyone's got something on someone else. Personally, you and I may be the only normal people living in this town, with the exception of my husband, who by the virtue of not being from here is exonerated from any wrongdoing. The way I see it, all these other people," I said pointing all around me, "they are more of a threat to me than you are. I want you to know that you're welcome in my store any time you want. You don't have to buy anything. You can come in and read the paper or just sit on my comfortable leather sofa."

He still didn't respond in any way. I sat back again, looking up at the sky and the big pillowy clouds floating by. It was a beautiful day, warm, sunny, friendly. I looked at my watch; it was ten.

"Harry, I've got to open up now. I hope to see you soon. Enjoy your coffee."

As I walked across the street, I saw Harry in the reflection of my store window. He raised the mug to his lips and took a drink. I smiled to myself, letting all the bitterness and cynicism that George had poisoned me with melt away. I'd done a good deed, and I was going to take pleasure in it.

When I unlocked the front door to the store, Madeleine was inside, waiting to hear about my encounter with George. She'd seen me pull up to his house this morning and wanted all the dirt.

"Well, Mrs. Kravitz," I teased, referencing the nosy neighbor from the television show *Bewitched*, "is this your new pastime now? I ask you to spy on someone once and now you're obsessed."

"Stop teasing me and tell me what happened."

"Well, either I've just witnessed an Academy Award winning performance or George Tierney is a lunatic—actually it could be both."

I told her all about the neat little circle of betrayal that George, Mara, Rhianna, and Joe had created for themselves, and I also told her about my conversations with Rhianna and Janney. I was amazed at the chaos and mess this group of people had made of their lives. Then I realized that there was a sort of order, a delicate balance, that they had created. Each person relied on the others to keep certain secrets, to keep the chaos in balance. In relying on the others, they had created a network of people whom as individuals were untrustworthy, but as a whole, they had to be trusted to keep their network in order. They were all links in a chain of lies. However, if one person in this link failed to keep his or her end of the blackmail bargain—if one of them told the secret he or she was holding —the entire order could be thrown out of balance and actual chaos would ensue. Was that what was happening now?

"So, let me get this straight," Madeleine said when I'd finished my summation. "Everyone who was in the beauty shop that morning hated Mara and couldn't have cared less if she was dead?"

"Everyone except me and maybe Ruby Collins, but who knows about her?"

"There was a struggle, during which anyone could have switched the perm solutions."

I told her to wait a minute, and I ran in the back to get my notebook.

"You have a notebook? Don't try to tell me you're not

investigating this murder," she teased. "Jack'll be angry if he finds out."

"Rhianna's fingerprints were the only ones on the bottle," I said, ignoring her. "It doesn't sound like enough of a struggle to divert anyone's attention for more than a few seconds. Not enough time to wipe fingerprints from the bottle."

"That's a good point, but I don't think we can rule anything out at this point."

"*We?*" I asked.

"Could someone have broken in and put the bottle there the night before?"

"That seems unlikely. Yes, it's possible, but she has rows and rows of perm kits, hair dye, and such. I don't think someone could have switched the solution in one kit without it being obvious that something had been tampered with. From what I could see, it was random which kit was chosen from the shelf. Besides that, Janney was supposed to do the perm. It was at the last minute that Rhianna switched the customers around," I said.

We determined that whoever was in the beauty shop that morning was a suspect, but then we narrowed it down to anyone who was present during the scuffle since that seemed the most likely time for someone to switch the regular perm bottle with the tainted one. Therefore, we didn't consider Ruby Collins or me suspects. Then we decided to go over each suspect individually. In my notebook, I made a chart to record suspects, motives, and means. For Rhianna, the prime suspect, we decided to go with the D.A.'s version of motive, child support. As for means, according to Jack it was simple to get fentanyl on the streets, and of course, she had access to everything in the shop.

For George, we decided that his hatred for his wife was enough motive as anything else. As for means, he could have obtained the drugs as easily as anyone else. It would not have been difficult for him to find out what type of perm kit Rhianna used in the shop and to purchase one and replace it during the scuffle. Althea Kent stumped us a bit. We didn't know who she was or what her reasons would be for wanting to kill Mara. I'd heard her name around town but drew a blank when I tried to recall her face. We decided that she could have some unknown motive and left it at that. For means, same as George

"It seems that the scuffle between Janney and Mara was key to getting the tainted perm solution in place. Do you think two people were working together?"

"That would mean that no matter how the perm solution got switched that Janney was in on it. She could have purposely started the fight with Mara to cause a distraction."

"Janney?" I questioned in return.

As if summoned by the mention of her name, Janney walked past the window and into the store. I fumbled with my notebook a bit but got it closed before she got close enough to read what I was writing.

"Hi. What are you two up to?" she asked, eyeing my notebook.

"Oh, just making a list of things to do around here. I thought that if you don't find it too demeaning you could give the store a good dusting. You'd be surprised how dusty the tops of these bookcases get," I said.

Then, as if I were a director who'd yelled action, Madeleine got up off the couch and headed to the backroom to get a box of books, Janney stowed her things behind the counter and began dusting, and two customers walked in the door. Reluctantly, I put my notebook away and closed my mental door on all the chaos in my brain and got to work.

Later that day after Janney had gone home and Madeleine

had gone to get us some lunch, I was in the backroom putting Elly down for her nap. After I had tucked her in and headed back into the store, Harry was sitting on the sofa reading the paper. The coffee mug I'd given him earlier was on the counter, empty, but washed and sparkling clean.

CHAPTER 19

I had gone over and over in my mind the conversations I had with Janney, Rhianna, and George. Around noon, I started to get angry. The information I'd learned from my tête-à-tête with George had simmered in my brain all day like a rich sauce and had made my anger so concentrated that if it had been a sauce, a teaspoon full would have covered a pot of pasta. By three o'clock that afternoon, I was feeling betrayed, misled, used, and foolish. I'd been such a champion for Rhianna. I'd believed in her when no one else would, and she had kept important information about her relationship with her parents, who Andy's father was, and her on-going affair with George from me as repayment for my loyalty. Deep down I knew my anger was a reaction to my hurt pride. I didn't want to be wrong, but I especially didn't want to admit that our friendship had meant more to me than it did to Rhianna. Had I really been that needy?

Although what I'd learned about George had horrified me, I was easier on myself about being fooled by him than I was about Rhianna. After all, I'd been an impressionable teenager when I'd first met George and all of my feelings about him were based on that initial relationship. However, I found myself obsessively racking my brain for memories that may have been some clue into his behavior, something that might have triggered that uneasy feeling I sometimes got about people. I couldn't come up with anything. Like most of the girls in his literature classes, I had had a crush on him. He had been very good looking, but it was his knowledge of literature that had made him so appealing to me. It wasn't until I went to college that I discovered that his expertise was minimal compared to all there was to know and learn about analyzing literature. I couldn't help but wonder if George had made a pass at me at some point, and I had been too naive to notice.

Trying to straighten out the facts about Rhianna and her lovers was like trying to untangle a basket of yarn; it was difficult if not nearly impossible. Who was this mystery lover of Rhianna's that no one could know about? Whose reputation would be so harmed if it was uncovered that she was gay? A married woman perhaps? Someone in a position of authority? Who would bigoted people feel threatened by if they found out someone they thought was straight was gay? A minister. But I had already examined that pathway. It had to be someone in authority or . . . Then it hit me. It was someone who works with children.

Finally, I decided that I couldn't simmer anymore. My sauce of a brain was overcooked. I knew what I had to do. I called my mom and asked her to pick Elly up from the store and then Bella and Andy from school. I told Madeleine and Janney I had an errand to run, and I'd be back to help Kylie close that night.

I jumped into my minivan, sped across town, and parked a few blocks down from the elementary school where I could see the cars picking up children. I waited until all the cars were gone, including my mother's, pulled around to the back of the school, and parked in the teacher's parking lot. I jogged into the school, not sure why I was in such a hurry. Perhaps my anger was driving me to act as if everything was so frantic.

As I entered the school, I was hit with the odor of Elmer's paste and sweaty kids. Walking up the stairs to the main floor of the school brought a wash of memories from my own days in those hallways. The wooden floors squeaked in a familiar way as I walked to the classroom that had belonged to Mrs.

Mitchell, my first grade teacher. Now it belonged to Jessy Becker, Bella and Andy's second grade teacher—and Rhianna's lover.

Jessy, who was sitting at her desk, jumped in her seat when I stepped into her room, closing the door behind me.

"Emily! You scared me!" she exclaimed. I must have appeared as frazzled as I felt because she looked me up and down, and then asked, "What's wrong?"

"Jessy," I said, walking across the room and planting myself on top of the student's desk next to hers, "I want answers and I want them now."

Without missing a beat, she replied, "I wondered how long it would take you to come to me. How long have you known?"

"Known about what? Known about you and Rhianna or about Rhianna and George, or about Mara and Joe? Anyone else I need to list?"

She only shrugged.

"Jessy, I'm angry. I haven't been this angry since I found out my high school boyfriend had been screwing someone else behind my back. I'm angry now for the same reason I was angry then: I don't like being deceived and made a fool of. Back then, everyone knew he was cheating on me, but no one had the decency to tell me. Now, it seems like everyone knew that Rhianna was seeing George, but no one clued me in. Of course, I'm no one important," I yelled. "I'm only the fucking woman who has put her own reputation and her husband's career on the line to defend Rhianna and to take care of her son!"

"You might want to keep your voice down. There are other teachers still in the building."

"Listen," I continued undaunted. "I'm no stranger to deceit. I just don't like to be a victim of it, especially when I have so much at stake. All I want are some facts. This whole arrangement confuses me, and I'm starting to lose sight of what is real. I thought Rhianna was having an affair with you; now, I find out she's been having an affair with George since she was in *high school*."

"I can sum it up like this," she said. "Rhianna's not a lesbian."

"Bisexual," I corrected, having that conversation déjà vu again.

"She's not that either. I mean, you want to talk about being confused. It's all George's doing. He's been preying on young, confused girls his entire teaching career."

"That's the second time I've heard that today, and the first time was from George himself, and I still don't believe it."

"Believe it! He's been having sex parties and student affairs ever since he got here."

"George? Mild-mannered George. Pallid, pulseless George? Even if I could comprehend it, I don't understand how he kept it quiet all these years in this small town of all places."

"George is a smart guy, smarter than he leads on. Blackmail, pure and simple, is how he's gotten away with it. In this town, you have to work hard to keep your secrets hidden. Because if these vipers find out your secrets, then they own you."

I sat there dumbfounded as she told me about how George would never move on a girl until he had some kind of dirt he could use against her. If he couldn't find dirt, he'd create it. With some girls, he made them believe that he'd caught them cheating and would mount so much evidence against them that they had no choice but to submit or have their academic record sullied. This approach was especially useful with the brightest students who were bound for big name universities. Sometimes he'd get them involved in illegal activities or make them believe they'd been involved in something illegal, and sometimes he used dirty pictures and videos to keep them silent. With other girls, he would promise a scholarship from Midwestern Mutual to get them to cooperate with his sexual advances.

"Why would Mara go along with all of this, especially the scholarships? George had his own piece of dirt on her, but why would she go along for all those years?"

"You might want to ask yourself if maybe Mara wasn't always so miserable and vindictive or if she became that way over the years—always watching her back, wondering what her husband was going to do next or make *her* do. Maybe she was forced to do things she found morally reprehensible—not only unethical things, but also sexual things. After a while, you might stop fighting against them and figure you're in so deep that you're trapped. This is your life. Mara Tierney is the biggest victim of all in this twisted mess," she explained.

"All of this doesn't explain why George is responsible for Rhianna's sexual confusion."

"Sure it does. First of all, the people in this town have such one track minds that if they thought Rhianna was a lesbian, then they would automatically dismiss any rumors that they heard about her having a relationship with George," Jessy replied. I thought back to Mrs. Carlson and how she didn't seem to have a problem seeing Rhianna as a lesbian and insinuating that Rhianna and George also had a relationship. In my mind, this explanation was full of holes.

"The second reason is that Rhianna came back here because George promised her something, but when she got here, she found herself stuck in the same psychotic game that she ran away from and with almost the same players."

"If she's not really a lesbian, then why do you continue a relationship with her?"

"Are you listening to me? She's stuck in the same game with the *same* players," she said, emphatically. So Jessy had also been talking about herself when she was explaining Mara's motives for staying married to George.

"So your relationship with Rhianna is based on circumstances more than love?" I didn't like how Jessy was inferring that sexuality was a choice. There were too many labels flying around: lesbian, straight, bisexual, murder...

"Love? You've got to be kidding me?"

"What's George got on you?" I asked.

"Do you think I'm going to tell the sheriff's wife?"

"You're already telling her a lot. Why is that?"

"George is losing control. He's controlled all of us with blackmail for years. Now that blackmail has little value because it looks like it is all going to come unraveled with the investigation of Mara's murder. I don't know if Rhianna killed her or not, but whoever did, certainly did us all a favor. Things are going to come out whether we like it or not. Now we have to brace ourselves for the storm ahead. Some of us will weather the storm and make a clean start. Some of us will choose a different path or have that path chosen for us," she explained so casually as if she had already resigned herself to the fact that she was going to be ruined when all of this was made public. Under which category did she consider herself? Her explanation verified my theory that the balance of order had been thrown out of whack with Mara's murder and the chaos was beginning.

"What about Rhianna? She hasn't spilled her guts about all she knows regarding her relationship with George and Mara. Why?" I wondered aloud.

"Because George could take something from her that is more valuable than her own life."

"Andy."

She nodded her head.

"Which is why she chose the sheriff's wife to be his guardian?"

Again, she just nodded her head.

As I turned to go, Jessy called out to me, "Emily. Witch's Flying Ointment."

"What's that?" I asked.

"That's all I'm going to say. You figure it out. You're the smart one."

Now what did she mean by that? I'm the smart one. Had I been that much of a condescending goody-goody in high school? As far as the gossips were concerned, I had made myself out to be better than I really was, putting on airs and acting superior. Some of that I was guilty of, but I still felt I was being misrepresented.

Pushing my narcissistic thoughts out of my head, I thought about Witch's Flying Ointment as I headed back to my minivan. What did Witch's Flying Ointment have to do with Mara's murder?

As I sat behind the wheel of my minivan trying to figure out if I was on to something or being led down a cold trail, I started to feel exhausted and wanted to do nothing but go home and crawl under the covers. But I had children to take care of, and I'd promised to close the store that night. What I was really dreading was going home and facing Rhianna. I was still angry and was almost convinced that she'd killed Mara. I didn't have the strength to face her and pretend like nothing was wrong.

It was four o'clock in the afternoon. I still had a little time before my mom would want to get home to make my dad supper. I drove in the direction of the bookstore, not really knowing where I was going. I parked my minivan in the lot behind my store and walked down the alley toward State Street. When I got to the street, I crossed it and walked into the newspaper office. Miss Bette was sitting behind the counter talking to a young man, who, next to her, looked like a teenager, but was probably in his late twenties. They both turned their attention to me as I walked over to where they were sitting. Ignoring the young man she was talking to, I leaned so far across the counter that I was almost in her face.

In a low voice, I asked her, "Miss Bette, you know that matter I talked to you about yesterday?" The young man eyed me. I looked a wreck; my clothes were rumpled, my face was glossy with half-a-day's stale make-up and sweat, and my hair was more down than up. I gave the curious kid a short "Hi," and he excused himself from the counter.

"What's up, Kid?"

"That person—do you know anything about her spouse?"

"Some."

"Anything unsavory?"

"Just rumor."

"No facts?"

"No."

"Sexual?"

"Yes."

"How long ago?"

"Years."

"Has it been going on for years or was it years ago that the rumors were circulating?"

"There's been talk for years. About five years ago, the talk suddenly increased, but nothing official," Miss Bette clarified.

Knowing Miss Bette had her ear to the ground and knew all of the town gossip, I asked her, "Do people think I'm nosy?"

She thought for a moment, and then said, "Not nosy. Curious, intelligent. . ." and then choosing her words carefully, she added, "aloof."

"Aloof?" That last word stung. Aloof was a polite way to

say that I was a snob. I couldn't believe people thought I was a snob. It's true that I was trying to bring some good taste and education back to this broken-down town, but I wouldn't say those were the intentions of a snob.

As I turned to go, Miss Bette grabbed my arm and said, "Kid, don't get yourself into trouble. These people . . . they may seem harmless, but they have nothing to lose now, if you understand what I mean. Don't be afraid to ask that sexy husband of yours for help."

I thanked her and headed back to the bookstore. When I got to the store, I was happy to see five customers browsing the shelves. Things had been slow after the initial surge of rubberneckers from Mara's death. Now that I had two new employees to support, I needed all the business I could get. I said hello to Kylie, who was helping a middle-age woman find some books on yoga. I told Kylie I was going to the back to work on the week's book order. But when I got to the back, I plunked myself down in my desk chair and stared at the wall. After a few minutes of indiscernible brain activity, I called home.

My mom answered, and I felt a giant weight lift from my shoulders when she said that Rhianna wasn't there. I told her I'd be home in a few minutes, and then I told Kylie I wasn't feeling well, so I was going home. Kylie told me that Madeleine had said I wasn't acting like myself and that she'd come in and help Kylie close. *Great*, I thought, *now everyone thinks I'm losing my mind.* I'd have to call Madeleine later and fill her in, but I wasn't sure I was up to rehashing the afternoon's events. Besides, if Miss Bette was right about George and his circle of friends, Madeleine might have already put herself in harm's way. I didn't need to add to the danger by telling her every detail that I knew.

When I got home, my mom, God bless her, had made dinner: fried chicken, mashed potatoes with chicken gravy, and buttered corn—my favorite comfort food. She said my dad was taking her out, so she thought she'd give me a hand and make dinner for us. When she saw me, she said she was glad she had. I dropped my purse and book bag on the floor where I was standing and went over to her and buried my face in her neck, like I did when I was a child. She didn't pry, she didn't judge, and she didn't criticize; she just held me and rubbed my back. An outsider never would have known that only this morning we had made up from years of acrimony. This morning felt like so long ago that her comfort felt natural. I guessed every now and then I did still need my mom.

Composing myself, I sat down in a kitchen chair watching her as she finished dinner.

"Mom, when we were kids, did I follow Rhianna around like a puppy?"

"Why would you ask that?"

"Mr. Reese came into the store the other day. It was not a happy conversation. He called me gullible and said I followed Rhianna like a puppy," I explained.

Mom put down the tongs she was using to turn the chicken and said, "Emily, when you were a kid, you saw the best in everyone. If you saw someone hurting, you wanted to fix them. If they seemed broken, you wanted to be their friend. Sometimes, that wonderful quality made you trust the wrong people. That's why I never liked Annie. . . Rhianna. I saw something in her that you didn't." She was quiet for a moment and then said, "It's a wonderful quality, and I still see it in you to some extent. But I also see that life has given you the wisdom to understand that not everyone is as they first seem. You still want to fix everyone. How do you think you got into this mess in the first place?" she asked, non-judgmentally.

"You make a fair point," I had to admit.

"One thing that you have going for you is that people underestimate you, which is a dangerous thing to do."

"I love you, Mom."

"You too," she said, turning back to the chicken.

CHAPTER 20

L ate that night, I sat on our side porch, pouring over my high school yearbooks and smoking several cigarettes. As I savored every drag of each cigarette, I was well aware that I was breaking a promise to my husband, and I hoped he'd understand if he caught me. I leafed through the books, looking for some clue, something that would make it all fall into place. I had George for three classes in high school, and I had participated on the yearbook staff, which he supervised. All of my experiences with him in high school were incongruous with the information I was now discovering.

Had he hit on me in high school and I'd either been too naïve or too obtuse to notice? I had to admit that I was usually one of the last people to know when something was going on at school. I was too busy with my college boyfriend and my books to take too much notice of the high school activities around me. I certainly hadn't been an "insider." The typical high school trials and tribulations all seemed so petty and immature compared to my world. *Maybe I was aloof*, I thought to myself.

I put aside the yearbook, opened to a picture of the yearbook staff on a trip to the regional conference of high school yearbook staffs. It was a picture of me, Rhianna, Jessy, Brad Johnson, Angie Wilkes, Sam Free, and Jeff Robins sitting in front of a big statue of an Indian at some roadside picnic area.

I'm sure George was the one taking the picture. As I looked at the photo, I pulled the wool shawl I was wearing tight around my white cotton nightgown. Monday was Memorial Day, so the days were fairly warm, but the nights were still damp and cool. I was sitting cross-legged on our glider loveseat. I tilted my head back and closed my eyes. I drew in each smoke filled breath, savoring the taste of the tobacco. If I was going to betray my husband's trust, I might as well enjoy it. My love affair with the cigarette was much like Gollum's love for the ring of power in Tolkein's trilogy. Cigarettes spoke to me. They made me feel sexy and sultry. I was more productive and thought better when I smoked. But like the Ring of Power, cigarettes were slowly stealing my life. I both loved and hated cigarettes, just as Gollum both loved and hated the ring. My dad had smoked since he was a teenager, but now was experiencing symptoms of COPD. My family's concern for my health was valid. But cigarettes were a seductive bitch.

In the middle of savoring my fifth cigarette, I heard Jack's Corfam-sheathed feet walking toward me on the porch. Without saying a word, he plucked the cigarette from between my lips and sat down next to me on the glider, crushing my Precious under his heel. Without opening my eyes or saying a word, I laid my torso across his lap. He responded by caressing my hair.

Finally, he said as if I was one of our daughters whom he had caught in the act of being naughty, "Emily, I trust you have a good reason for breaking your promise to me."

"I do," I said, still keeping my eyes closed. If I looked at him, I'd crumble into dust. He had that power over me. "Let's just say it was a choice between drink and cigarettes, and I chose to remain in full control of my mental capacities while my spouse was not home. Now that you're home, I can stop abusing my lungs and start abusing my liver."

"Do you want to talk about it?"

"No. Not yet," I said, raising my head to meet his lips. Whispering into his mouth, I explained, "I have to talk to someone tomorrow, and then I'll be ready." As much as he hated my cigarette smoking, he never pulled away when I offered him a kiss even though my breath reeked of tobacco.

"Let's go upstairs," he said, and for the second time in recent days, he carried me into our house and upstairs to bed.

The next morning dawned bright and beautiful; the world was swimming in sun and everything looked clean and pure. The lawn glistened with dew, and the flowers looked vibrant. As I squinted my eyes against the sun, my mood was so black that I stood at the open window and prayed for rain. I should have felt cheerful, but instead, I resented the morning and wanted to stay in bed where I didn't have to face the world and all that I had to confront that day. What was even more trying was that my dear, sweet, intelligent husband was acting so male. Jack is a complex man with many moods and ways of expressing them, but when it came to sex, he acted like every other man on the planet: He was happy when he was getting it and not happy when he wasn't. This morning he was happy. Although his happiness made my head pound like I had a hangover, I took advantage of it. Kissing his ear and enticing him with the promise of more sex, I asked him if he'd take the kids to breakfast and then to the park since it was Saturday and his day off.

Smiling, he replied, "Sure, but why."

"Because I want to talk to Rhianna alone."

"Is she the person you said last night whom you needed to talk to?"

"Yes."

He studied my face for a moment, and then said, "I trust you. I'm happy to take care of the kids. We'll stop by the bookstore later and say hi. Maybe we can even persuade you to go for ice cream."

"That sounds like something to look forward to. Remember, I have that follow-up appointment with Brad Johnson, so I won't be in until right before noon."

"Right," he said, taking my face in his hands and kissing me.

After taking a longer than usual shower and dressing in a loose butter-yellow empire-waist sundress, I went down to the kitchen to find Jack rounding up the kids, and Rhianna sitting at the table eating eggs. Jack had made some coffee and some eggs for me as well. I plastered a cheerful expression on my face and said goodbye as Jack and the kids walked out the door, escaping whatever debacle that was sure to result from my impending conversation with Rhianna.

I poured myself some coffee, offering Rhianna some, too, but she already had hot tea. Then I sat down to my plate of eggs. Unfortunately, I couldn't touch them. My stomach was in knots. I wasn't sure how to start what I had to say, so I decided to launch into it. No matter what, it wasn't going to be pretty.

"Rhianna, we need to talk about what you want to do with Andy if you're convicted."

She banged her tea cup on her plate as she lowered it to the table, and said, "What? What do you mean?"

"I love Andy," I paused. This was harder than I thought. "But surely, you want Andy to be with family if . . ."

"You think I'm guilty!"

My hands were shaking and my voice quivered when I spoke. "You know what I think? You haven't been honest with me. Why did you really come back to Middletown?"

"I told you already," she said, lowering her voice to a hurt whimper and covering my hand with hers.

I jerked my hand away. "That's bullshit," I said, as I stood up, knocking my chair over. I hadn't intended to knock my chair over, and I was sorry I had because it made me look furious and out of control. I bent over and righted it. "You didn't come here for your sister. Your sister won't even speak to you. Your parents are not as accepting as you said. Now tell me the real reason!"

"All right!" she yelled. "I came here to be with George. He'd promised me something and I believed him. So I came back to be with George."

"What did he promise you?"

"It's not important. He didn't follow through, so it's not important."

"Tell me! What did he promise you?!"

"He said he'd marry me!" she screamed back.

I leaned against the counter trying to steady myself and calm down. "George told me you wouldn't marry *him*."

She looked at me. Apparently, he hadn't told her I'd been to see him. "Mara wouldn't divorce him, so it doesn't matter who refused who."

"Mara's out of the way now, so what's stopping you?"

"That's really none of your business. Actually, none of this is your business," she said.

"Well, actually it is. You made it my business when you asked me to take care of Andy," I said, mocking her tone. "I've put my reputation and my husband's career on the line to take care of Andy. I stood up for you when no one else would. I've been a true friend to you, and you've shit all over me." She didn't reply. She knew I had her dead to rights, and there was nothing she could say. She took a step toward me, but I recoiled, almost sitting on top of the counter. I slid away from the counter and moved out of her reach. "What about Jessy?"

"You've talked to Jessy, too?"

"Yes."

"So you know I'm nothing to her then?"

I didn't answer. I wanted to see how far she'd go with this on her own; maybe if I gave her enough rope, she'd hang herself.

"I'm just a plaything to her. She doesn't love me anymore than George loves me."

"If George doesn't love you, then why did you come back here?"

"I don't know anymore." She looked at me with tears in her eyes and said, "I feel like a pawn in a game I can't control or understand."

I wanted to say, "*Welcome to my world, Babe*," but I stayed silent instead.

Softening, she said, "Thank you for taking care of Andy. I'll find someone else to take him."

"Andy's no trouble. We love having him, but let me remind you that you can't find anyone else to take Andy. Your bail is dependent on me retaining custody of him. I'm pretty sure if someone else takes him you have to go back to jail."

She stood and stared at me. My level of involvement in the situation had finally gotten through to her, and it was sinking in that her freedom relied on my willingness to cooperate with the Judge's conditions to her bail. Without saying anything else, she turned and left.

I gathered our plates from the table and scraped the eggs into the trash. I was sorry that I hadn't eaten Jack's eggs, but they wouldn't have stayed down if I had. I filled a large travel mug with coffee and creamer. I went to the closet I used as a pantry and felt along the inside top of the molding for a pack of cigarettes I kept hidden there. Instead of the cigarettes, I pulled down a package of gum with a note taped to it. The note read:

Roses are red,

Violets are blue,

Cigarettes will kill you,

But gum you can chew.

I want to grow old with you.

Have a stick of gum.

I love you,

Jack

I threw the gum into my purse and grabbed my book bag and keys. I needed to leave for my follow-up appointment with Brad, but my Precious was calling to me, and I needed to satisfy it. I went out to the detached garage and pressed the door opener. While I was waiting for the door to open, I crouched on the ground near the corner and pulled at a loose brick near the foundation. When it didn't move, I got down on my hands and knees to examine it further. There was fresh mortar around the brick. Jack had found my other secret hiding place and closed it up. I envisioned my cigarettes walled up behind the brick and mortar like Fortunato in Poe's *The Cask of Amontillado.*

"Damn, damn, damn," I said as I got into the minivan and backed onto the street. As I paused at the corner stop sign, a row of chirping birds sitting on the electrical lines caught my eye. I imagined myself taking Jack's gun and blowing their warbling little heads off. I was aware that I was acting like a crazed addict, but I didn't care. I needed a smoke. I was going to have to stop before I went to Brad's office. Driving up State Street, I hit a red light at State and Main, right next to my store. Harry was sitting on his bench, and I tooted my horn at him and waved.

The light turned green, and I moved forward and waited for the oncoming traffic to clear so that I could make a left and go down the street to the package liquor store where the cigarettes were cheap. As I was beginning to make my turn, I saw a car speeding perpendicularly toward me.

The impact was right behind my door. I remember hearing screaming, which must have been me, and I remember spinning and coffee flying through the air. I was wearing my seatbelt, but I banged my temple against the door window. Thinking back, I remember Harry pulling me across the front seat of the minivan. I thought he was talking to me, telling me it was going to be okay or maybe that I needed to get out. Then there was a loud noise, a lot of heat, and everything went black.

CHAPTER 21

"**I** don't care how many times you come to this hospital; they are not going to name it after you," a woman's voice said. I knew the voice, but couldn't place it. As I blinked against the pain in my head and the bright lights all around me, I began to focus on the face. It was Olive.

"Why am I here? My head hurts."

"You've got a concussion, Emily. You were in a car accident," said a man's voice. He stooped over me so that I could see him. It was Dr. T. "You know, if you wanted to be my girlfriend, all you had to do was ask."

"I thought I was poisoned."

"That was a couple of weeks ago, Emily," he said.

"Are my kids okay?"

"They weren't with you. You were alone. Remember?"

I had a vague sense of a car and faces, but I couldn't piece together what had happened.

"Who hit me?"

"Jessy Becker," he replied.

"Is she okay?"

"No, Emily. Jessy's dead."

"What? I don't understand," I said, struggling to sit up.

"Be quiet now, Emily," Olive said, gently pressing me back down onto the gurney. "You need to rest. We've called your husband, and he should be here soon."

I felt as if I was falling, and then everything went black again.

When I woke up again, I was alone and afraid.

"Jack! Jack!"

The curtain around my bed was yanked aside, and Jack rushed over to me with Robert Price on his heels.

"Emily, I'm here."

"Well, you seem to be accident prone these days," Price said cheerfully.

Jack turned and glared at him.

"Jack, what happened to me? I remember Dr. T saying there had been a car accident and that Jessy Becker was killed."

"Yes. It was serious, Emily. The minivan blew up. Harry saved your life."

"Yes, it seems the old bum isn't worthless," Price added.

"Shut up," I said to him, not caring who he was. Then, looking at Jack, I asked, "Why is he here?"

"What do you remember about the accident?" Jack asked.

"I was turning left onto Main Street to go buy cig . . .", and then I caught myself.

"Yes, you were going to buy cigarettes," Jack said, shaking his head at me. "Go on."

"I was waiting for the traffic to clear, and as I was beginning to make my turn, a car came speeding toward me and hit the side of the van."

"Anything else?"

"I remember Harry pulling me out of the car and a loud noise. I must have lost consciousness after that."

"See, I told you she didn't know anything," Jack said to Price.

"You still haven't told me why he's here," I said.

"This may be a criminal investigation, Mrs. Romano," Price explained. "Jessy Becker didn't die from the car crash. She may have been dead before impact. Right now it looks like she died from cardiac arrest and for a woman her age that seems highly suspicious."

I stared at them. Cardiac arrest? I had just seen her the day before, and she seemed fine.

"You rest now, Emily. I'm going to walk Mr. Price out, and then I'll be right back," Jack said, but I wouldn't let go of his hand. "I promise you; I'll be right back."

Jack stayed with me in the hospital that night. Dr. T said I could go home the next morning, but they wanted to observe me overnight. I told him I'd been observed enough over the past few weeks, and I wanted to go home. I'd been poked with needles so much from my three recent visits to the emergency room that I thought the bruises on my inner arms were going to be permanent. Even though I had no control over the accident, I was embarrassed that this was my third trip to the hospital in such a short timespan. It was ridiculous.

Jack slept in my hospital bed with me; his long body curled around me as if he were trying to make sure I didn't go anywhere. In the middle of the night, I woke up from the pain pounding in my head. When I looked around the room, there was Harry sitting in a chair at the foot of my bed. He was holding my purse and book bag in his lap; apparently, he'd not only saved me but also my belongings. We looked at each other for a while until I eventually fell back to sleep. The next morning he was gone. I wasn't sure if he'd really been there or if I'd dreamt it, but my purse and bag were sitting in the chair at the foot of my bed.

Before I was released that morning, Brad Johnson came to examine me during his rounds, so I didn't have to reschedule the follow-up appointment I had been going to the previous morning. He said I was healing fine but cautioned me to be careful. Like everyone else, he said I'd seen too much of the inside of the hospital lately. I couldn't have agreed more.

After I was released from the hospital, I went home and spent the next three days in bed. Madeleine, Janney, and Kylie ran the store while I recuperated. By day two, my head had stopped pounding, but I stayed in bed, hiding from the world. Jack was content to let me linger in bed because then he could be certain I was staying out of trouble. My mom and dad took care of the girls and waited on me hand and foot.

The only time I left the house during those three days was to go to church on Sunday. As we entered the church, several people put out their hands and asked how I was doing, which was one of the reasons I'd been hiding at home. I wasn't ready to face the townspeople's questions about the car accident because I still didn't understand exactly what had happened. I tried to be polite, smiling and saying I was fine, but in return, I got several sour looks. What did they expect from me? Maybe I should have apologized for not dying in the crash.

During the sign of peace, I politely shook the hands around me, saying "Peace be with you." As I shook the hands of the people behind me, I caught a glimpse of Harry standing in the back by the door. Without a word to Jack, I walked up the aisle to where Harry stood, threw my arms around his neck, and said, "Peace be with you." In return, he hugged me tightly and patted my back. Instead of walking back to my seat alone, I grabbed Harry's hand and led him to the pew where Jack, the girls, and Andy were watching, along with the rest of the congregation. A stunned silence fell over the church. No one had ever offered Harry the sign of peace, not that he would have accepted it. Several people jumped, startled, when Father Bob continued with the Eucharistic prayer. After that, Harry sat with us every Sunday.

On day three of my self-imposed seclusion, I began to feel like I was taking advantage of everyone's goodwill, so I got myself dressed and called Madeleine for a ride to work. We only had one car since Jack had a police cruiser to drive to work. I needed to go looking for a new minivan before Jack sunk all our money into a Humvee to keep me safe.

Around noon, Jack stopped by the store.

"I've rearrested Rhianna. Jessy Becker died from a fentanyl overdose."

After taking several missteps in trying to investigate this increasingly complicated web of murder and lies, Jack and I decided to join forces, and we made a date to talk that night when he got home from work. I opened a bottle of wine early in the evening after telling Andy that his mom had been rearrested. It was one of the toughest things I've ever had to do. When I told him, he was inconsolable. Who could blame him? His mom was all he had, and now it was looking like she was going to prison for the rest of her life. I was relieved that the death penalty in Illinois had been repealed. I couldn't imagine what the trauma of having your mother put to death would do to a child. After Andy sobbed for an hour, I was on the verge of calling our pediatrician when he fell asleep from exhaustion. By the time Jack got home around eight-thirty, the kids were all in bed, and I had a good buzz on. I was badly craving a cigarette but didn't dare light up. He had tolerated my lapse twice now; he may not be so generous a third time.

During the three days after the accident, I wasn't interested in anything but staying in bed and hiding, so we hadn't had the talk I promised him after I confronted Rhianna on Saturday. Now, we both had information to share. I told Jack about my conversations with Rhianna, George, and Jessy and about the sex, the blackmail, and the scholarships. He found my information intriguing, and he understood why I had been so agitated the night before the accident. Jack also felt that everything I learned made things look bad for Rhianna. Despite the alarming information that I'd uncovered, there wasn't anything that would constructively contribute to the investigation or at least Rhianna's defense. I agreed. All it amounted to was gossip. Besides, I couldn't be sure that any of the people I'd talked to were telling me the truth. Even if they were telling the truth, it was all hearsay. No one had ever filed a complaint against George. I didn't know if George was currently abusing any of his students, and though twisted, all the people whom I had spoken to were all adults and free to practice whatever type of consensual sex they chose. Even if the sex wasn't consensual because of the blackmail involved, neither Rhianna nor Jessy had made any legal complaints against George.

"Don't you think the accusations Rhianna and Jessy made against George are enough to reopen the investigation and take a look at him as a suspect?" I asked.

"Personally, yes I think so, but two things are working against me. First, the hard physical evidence that only Rhianna's fingerprints were on the bottle of permanent solution, Rhianna administered the the solution to Mara's hair, and Rhianna had means to poison the solution and motive to do so. Second," he continued to categorically explain, "Robert Price is convinced that Rhianna is guilty. He refuses to even hear evidence pointing to other suspects. Since the state is prosecuting Rhianna, I would have to have some kind of hard, physical evidence to take to Price to persuade him that it is worthwhile to reopen the investigation. Accusations made by people George is blackmailing doesn't do it. Maybe if one of these people came forward with a complaint or with evidence that George was planning his wife's murder, then I'd have something to work with."

"But George told me that if Rhianna hadn't killed Mara he might have."

"George making a statement like 'I might have killed my wife' and someone coming to us with tangible evidence, such as he had talked to them several times and in detail about killing her or hiring someone to kill her, are completely different things."

I sighed in frustration. I had underestimated the role small town politics was playing in this murder investigation. Now, Jack's argument about him being an elected official made more sense to me. If good hard police facts were what it was going to take to convict someone of Mara's murder, and now Jessy's, that is exactly what Jack had.

"Jessy Becker was given an overdose of fentanyl and then put behind the wheel of her car, probably to make the wreck either look like an accident or suicide. She must have kept the car on a straight path for several blocks. She either lost consciousness right at the end or actually died, while the smoothness of the street and the speed of the car kept it moving in a straight line. The thing that has me puzzled is how the car maintained speed after she lost consciousness. Her foot would have either lessened pressure on the gas pedal or fallen off altogether."

We both were thoughtful for a moment, and then he said, "A theory I have been playing around with is whoever poisoned her actually was in the car with her steering the wheel and pushing the gas pedal, and then they jumped out as the car approached the intersection. But no one has come forward to say they witnessed any such thing happening. We've swabbed the steering wheel and the dash for DNA."

I thought about it for a moment, and then said, "That street dead ends into the Nature Conservatory, which butts up to the town cemetery. Unless there was a funeral, there probably wouldn't be anyone around at eight-thirty in the morning." The Nature Conservatory didn't amount to much more than a grove of trees bordered by a stream on one side and the Embarras River on the other. During the day, neighborhood kids played in the stream, and at night, teenagers used it as a make out spot.

"That's right. It's probably secluded enough to put her in the car without being seen but close enough to side streets to allow for a quick and undetected getaway. But that's several blocks from where she hit you."

"Did the medical examiner say if she was alive at impact?"

"She would have survived the car crash. She was seat belted in and had no other injuries that would have killed her. In fact, with your concussion, you were more severely injured. She was definitely dead when bystanders pulled her from the car because one of them immediately determined that she had no pulse and started CPR. Her heart had probably stopped seconds before impact, and she must have been conscious up to that point. How else would the car maintain its straightforward path if she hadn't been steering it?" He thought about it for a minute, and then said, "The M.E. said that even if the people at the crash scene had known she'd overdosed, she would have died anyway."

"Large dose?"

"Yes, about the same that you and Mara received; therefore, it would have been fast acting. None of the bystanders recognized the signs of an overdose and none of them certainly didn't have any narcan on them."

Switching the focus of the discussion, I started to ask Jack some questions that had been bothering me for days, "Why did the van blow up?"

"The point of impact was between the driver's side door and the opening to the gas tank. The gas tank ruptured, causing a gas leak that was ignited by sparks from Jessy's engine. It's a good thing you had a full tank of gas, or the van might have exploded on impact from the accumulation of gas fumes in the tank."

"Thank God I was alone. If Elly had been with me . . ." I didn't have to finish my thought because we both knew what would have happened. She would have been sitting at the point of impact. "Why did Jessy hit *me*?"

"Emily, it seems to have been a fluke. Whoever put her behind the wheel intended for it to look like an accident. You just happened to be the person she hit."

"You don't believe in flukes and neither do I."

"It's easier to say it was a fluke than to try to figure out the divine ramifications of it all," he said. We sat in silence for a few minutes drinking our respective poisons.

This time it was Jack who broke the silence. "Rhianna wants you to come see her tomorrow."

"Did she seem sorry?"

"No," he said. "Hopeless. Undone."

"I don't understand why Price thinks Rhianna killed Jessy. Just because she died of a fentanyl overdose like Mara did? That doesn't mean the same person killed them both or even that Jessy was murdered. How do we know that? Maybe she was a drug user.

"Also, the timing isn't right for Rhianna to have killed Jessy. She was with me until fifteen minutes before the accident. That doesn't give her enough time to find Jessy, administer the overdose, assuming that she had the drugs with her, have them take effect, and put Jessy in the car. If Rhianna was involved, she would have to have an accomplice."

"I've been thinking the same thing, but it has been my

experience that if more than one person is involved in a crime, as long as you have one of them, you have both. The one in custody either rolls over on the other person, or the other person will slip up on his own," he explained. Then seeing the forlorn look on my face, he added, "If she is innocent, there's nothing we can do for her at this point. It's up to her lawyer to prove reasonable doubt. Even if she is guilty, if he can give the jury enough to doubt, they may acquit anyway. That's the double edged sword of our justice system. It's something as a cop you learn to accept early, or your entire career will seem pointless as you arrest criminals who are continually set free."

"Jack, when you stayed with me that night in the hospital, did you see Harry in my room?"

"You saw him, too? I thought I was dreaming. I wonder how he got in at that time of night?"

"He probably snuck in through the E.R. The people in this town treat him as if he's invisible. I'm sure it isn't that hard for him to go anywhere he wants to go unnoticed."

"He sure is a strange old coot, but I owe him a big thank you for saving your life."

"He's my guardian angel. Father Bob told me that Harry is watching over me. That's why he was sitting on the bench across from my store and why I invited him to come into the store whenever he wanted. I couldn't stand to see him sitting in the baking sun everyday. I didn't want to be the cause of him getting melanoma."

We were both sick of the conversation, so we decided to not waste anymore of this late spring evening on talk of murder and betrayal. I was happy that we had turned the conversation to lighter subjects. I was pretty drunk, and it was increasingly difficult for me to hold up my end. Jack rubbed my feet, and we talked about Bella and Elly and our plans for the summer. We were planning a trip to Bethany Beach, Delaware that summer. We were all looking forward to it like children anticipating

Christmas. We've gone there almost every summer since Arabella was born. We were excited about the trip because Elly would be old enough to enjoy the water, and we wouldn't have to stop her from eating handfuls of sand as we'd had to do in the past.

Going to see Rhianna the next morning was even harder than the day I confronted her in my kitchen. I had almost lost all faith that she was innocent. I wondered how I was going to sit in front of her and act hopeful and supportive, but she took care of that. She must have known how I felt.

"Don't say anything. I don't want to hear what you have to say," she said as soon as she sat down on her side of the glass. She looked awful. Her eyes were sunken and her skin was a sickly yellow. "I know you don't believe in me anymore. I don't believe in myself. I'm sorry that you did so much for me, and I wasn't as good a friend to you as you were to me. I want you to know I didn't kill Mara, and I certainly didn't kill Jessy. I loved Jessy." She paused for a moment. I started to say something, but she held her hand up and glared at me. "Since I'm back in jail and my bond has been revoked, you are no longer obligated to keep Andy. I've called my sister Reba, and she's going to come and get him. Turns out she has decided to leave her husband. My parents are livid because they think she should stay married, no matter the circumstances. She's moving far away and taking Andy with her. If I ever get out of here, I'll join them and try to start my life over *again*. I'll call Andy tonight and tell him myself."

Before I could respond, she got up and walked back to the guard, who escorted her back to the cellblock. I was both stunned and relieved. I would be sorry to see Andy go since he was a sweet child. I felt sorry that he didn't have a stable home life. On the other hand, I was also looking forward to the prospect of getting my family back to normal.

Two days later, Andy was gone. Reba had grown into a nice, grounded young woman. She said she had a teaching job and a cute little apartment although she wouldn't tell me where. I suspected that she didn't want her husband to find out where she had gone. She also said that she intended to spend the summer helping Andy be a kid, which sounded wonderful to me. The girls had picked out a teddy bear to give to him as a remembrance of them. When they gave it to him, he acted all macho, as if boys didn't need teddy bears. At the same time he clutched the bear to his chest as if it were keeping his heart inside where it belonged. I gave him a slip of paper with our address and telephone number and told him we'd always be happy to hear from him and to call us if he needed anything. The most surprising thing was the way he clung to Jack's neck when he said goodbye. He'd always acted angry and tough around Jack because Jack had arrested his mom, but at some level, Jack must have gotten to him. Or maybe it was simply that Jack was the only man Andy had ever been close to.

School ended a week after Andy left. At first the girls were sad that they no longer had a live-in playmate, but when school was over, I did everything I could to keep their minds off Andy. As children do, within a few days, they'd almost forgotten he had ever been a part of our family. The wound that took Bella even longer to get over was the loss of her teacher, Miss Becker. She was upset that Jessy was dead, but she also had feelings about how Jessy died that she wasn't sure how to reconcile. Jack and I listened when she wanted to talk about it and responded as best we could. We also knew it was something that would take time to heal.

Bella and Elly must have felt as Jack did: that I'd tried too often lately to leave them. They wanted to spend every moment they could with me. Whenever I wanted to leave the house without them, they hung on my legs, begging to go with me. They spent a lot of time in the store those first few weeks after school was over. They were well-behaved and helped out with small chores. I was surprised at how well a three-year-old could dust bookshelves. Elly dusted the low ones that we adults broke our backs bending over to do. She was thrilled to have such an important task.

Summertime made me appreciate living in a small town. There was a newsstand/soda fountain on the other end of the block, Aleene's. It was one of those old fashioned places where they still mixed the vanilla and cherry sodas from scratch, just soda and flavored syrup, and the ice cream was homemade. You could get floats, milk shakes, and malts, and the soda jerk, Old Man Crowley, made everything to order. Most afternoons, I'd let Bella and Elly walk down for a treat. Sometimes we left Kylie and Janney minding the store while Madeleine and I took the girls to the pool. Madeleine still had a membership to the country club where they had a wonderful kiddie pool. She'd take us there, basking in the angry stares of Middletown's self-described elite.

One morning at the beginning of June, the girls and I were alone in the store with Harry. Although he never spoke to them, or any of us, they seemed to have a kind of understanding among them. Elly had an uncanny knack of knowing exactly what Harry wanted when he used the few signs that he did use to communicate. Or maybe he was eager to please and indulged her by pretending that she got him what he wanted.

On this morning, Bella was reading a picture book to Elly as she sat placidly listening from Harry's lap. It was a sweet little story about a grandfather taking a walk in the woods, showing his grandson all the wonders of nature and how God was in all that they saw.

I was standing nearby, organizing the magazine rack, when Elly looked up at me and quietly said, "Mr. Harry's crying."

Bella and I both looked at Harry as tears gently rolled down his craggy cheeks. At first I wasn't sure what to do, but I quickly recovered. I pulled five dollars out of my pocket and told Bella to take Elly down to the soda fountain for a lemon shake-up.

After they left, I sat down on the coffee table in front of Harry and took his hands in mine. "Harry . . . I don't know anything about your life. I don't know what happened to you in Korea, or why your wife left you, or what happened to your family. I do know that whatever happened to you has been painful and has caused you a lot of sorrow. I could never understand unless it had happened to me. I also know that whatever burden you've been carrying around inside you for all these years that you've carried it long enough. Harry, you need to put that burden down."

He didn't look at me or pull his hands away, so I went on, "God has forgiven you for whatever it is that you think you've done wrong. Now, it's time for you to forgive yourself."

Then to my surprise, he leaned forward and put his arms around me. I held him tight and told him I loved him.

CHAPTER 22

L   ike Al Pacino's Michael Corleone in The Godfather, Part
        III, when I thought I was out, they pulled me right back
        in. Someone wanted me involved in this investigation,
and I was going to be involved come hell or high water, as
my grandma was fond of saying. But it was the unlikeliest of
people who sought me out and pulled me back into the chaos.

In the middle of June, the thought that was foremost in my
mind was the impending shipment of the current bestseller,
My Boyfriend, the Sulky Vampire. I hoped this well-hyped book
would bring me more business. Things had tapered off after
the initial curiosity over Mara's murder. Then, it picked up a
bit again after the car accident. Now, most people have gotten
back to their lives or at least moved on to the current scandal.
It had recently been discovered that the prom queen was
pregnant. I was worried about my profit margin and wondered
if I was going to have to create a scandal for myself to bring
people back into the store. As I was admonishing myself for
even thinking about bringing trouble to my doorstep again, my
good friend and personal Nurse Ratchet walked in, bringing
with her all the chaos I would ever want or need.

Harry was sitting in his usual spot on the leather sofa,
doing the *New York Times* Sunday crossword puzzle. He had
been working on it since Monday—it was now Thursday. I
was relieved that genius wasn't the cause of his eccentricities.
I'd attempted the *Times* Sunday crossword many times, but

could never finish it within a week without cheating. He'd brought the puzzle to me once and pointed out a number he was stumped by. When I suggested looking up the synonyms of one answer in the dictionary, he'd forcefully held up a hand and hadn't asked me for help since. I guess he was above cheating. I was sitting behind the cash register doing some paperwork when Olive pushed a book in front of my face.

"Here. I thought you could do something with this," Olive said, opening the book to a place where a newspaper clipping was marking the page. At first, I was confused. I scanned the pages of the book. It was an Agatha Christie mystery, *And Then There Were None*. Then she pointed to the newspaper article. The headline read: *NATIONAL HONOR SOCIETY STUDENT FALLS TO HER DEATH: Suicide suspected.*

The article, which was dated four years prior, reported that Anita Kent, a high school student at MHS, climbed out onto the roof of the high school one Friday night and had fallen to her death. She was found the next morning when the janitor came to prepare the gym for a wrestling match. The coroner had ruled it a suicide, but the sheriff at the time had been baffled by how she'd gotten access to the roof. There weren't any outside ladders and none of the doors or windows had been jimmied. Everything was locked up tight. She didn't have drugs or alcohol in her system either.

From the condition of the article, I could tell that Olive had had it since it first appeared in the newspaper. Obviously, she'd found this young woman's death suspicious enough to keep for future reference.

"She's not the only one," Olive said when I looked up at her after skimming the article.

"Can I keep this?"

"Yes. Put it to good use. It might help your friend," she said, and then she snapped her book closed and marched out of the shop.

The part I thought was odd, besides Olive coming to me with this information, was that she seemed to feel the need to put up a front for why she was there. Why didn't she just hand the article to me or better yet, why not mail it to me anonymously or mail it to Jack? Maybe my flowers had melted some of the coldness she felt toward me.

I was still puzzling over the article when Madeleine came into the store with Bella and Elly in tow. She'd taken them to the country club for a swim, and now they were begging me to walk them down the block for an ice cream. Madeleine was due to begin her shift at the bookstore. As I relented to the girls' pleas, knowing I was spoiling their dinner, I pointed out the newspaper article to Madeleine and told her I'd be back in about twenty minutes.

As we were approaching the door to Aleene's, Elly grabbed my hand and pointed into the store.

"There's daddy," she squealed.

As I followed where she was pointing, I was surprised to see Jack at the soda fountain in the middle of the afternoon. It was unlike him to goof off while on duty, much less indulge in an ice cream. Jack ran ten miles at least three times a week and rarely indulged in something as fat-laden as ice cream. I was the one with the more, shall we say, flexible eating habits. The one who started a healthy eating kick only to polish off a pint of *Ben and Jerry's Chunky Monkey* after everyone else had gone to bed. I tried to squeeze exercise into my schedule but sleep usually won over. It was no wonder I'd never shed the last fifteen pounds I'd gained during my pregnancy with Elly. The only way I kept from gaining more weight was that I didn't take much time to eat while at the bookstore. Since Madeleine had started working for me, now even that trick was gone. She was fond of bringing in baked goods or going over to Dancing Dave's for lunch, but she also exercised religiously and could afford the snacks and slices of pizza.

I looked at the back of Jack, standing at the counter paying for his shake with his smoky and sunglasses firmly in place. I couldn't suppress the mischievousness that was coursing through my veins. I put my finger to my lips and whispered for the girls to wait there. I tiptoed into the shop, drawing stares from the handful of customers enjoying a mid-afternoon treat.

With one swift motion, I slapped Jack on the ass and said, "Hey Baby, you're going to lose those washboard abs if you keep indulging in milk shakes."

Then the person whom I had thought was Jack turned around and whipped his sunglasses off his face. It was Brett Bradley. My eyes went wide as I slapped both hands over my mouth. I felt my cheeks burning bright red and could hear the other customers snickering.

"I'm so sorry. From behind you looked like . . ."

"I don't care who you thought I was. I can't believe you have the audacity to disrespect an officer of the law in such a way. I could book you for sexual assault and for assaulting an officer. Really, Mrs. Romano, as if you haven't embarrassed your husband enough—to think you'd treat him in such a way in public," he said, grabbing his shake from the counter, glaring at the other patrons, who could barely keep their composure.

His implication that I was an embarrassment to Jack stung, but for once I decided to play it smart and keep my mouth shut. I wouldn't put it past him to drag me off to jail just for the bother of it. When I didn't offer any more apology or explanation, he replaced his sunglasses on his face and stalked out of the shop.

"Well," I said to the other patrons after he'd gone, "I guess he can't take a joke."

Everyone busted out laughing and laughed all the while we were ordering our ice cream. Old Man Crowley told me he hadn't laughed that hard for years and gave us our ice cream on the house. I could have kicked myself for even entertaining the earlier thought of causing a scandal for the purpose of bringing business into the bookstore. Be careful what you wish for. That was the moral of this story.

When I told Madeleine the story a few minutes later, and after she stopped laughing, she told me she'd had a similar incident with Bradley.

"I didn't smack him on the ass, but I was in the grocery store and saw him from the back. As I was about to go up to him and say 'Hello, Jack,' he turned around and I could see it wasn't your husband."

"Well, I should have known that Jack would never be so rude as to keep his cover and sunglasses on inside."

That night when I got home, my cheeks still burned with embarrassment every time I thought of my run-in with Bradley, but that encounter was pushed out of my mind as I searched the house for the notebook that I'd been putting my theories and clues about Mara's murder in. I hadn't touched it since the car accident, and now I couldn't find it anywhere. It wasn't at the store because I looked there before I came home. I couldn't remember where I'd left it and was worried about all the information that I'd written in it.

When Jack came home at two o'clock in the morning, I was still searching the office and was frantic that I couldn't find it.

"You say you carried it around in your book bag wherever you went?" he asked.

"Yes."

"Emmy, it's simple. It must have fallen out of your book bag during the accident and burned up in the fire."

I thought about his hypothesis for a moment and then agreed. "I feel silly for obsessing over it."

"I can understand why. You wrote down a lot of assumptions that could be harmful if put in the wrong hands."

His comment sparked my memory, and he followed me into the kitchen as I retrieved my bag. "In my hysteria, I almost forgot this," I said, handing him the newspaper article.

"Where'd you get this?" he asked after he'd read it.

I told him about Olive's covert visit to the bookstore earlier that day and how she'd said there were others.

"Other what?"

"I'm not sure. Maybe she meant other suicides. She also said 'it might help your friend.' I suppose she meant Rhianna."

"Hmm, this is worth some research," he said, running his hand over his high and tight haircut. I loved the velvety feel of the back of his head when he had a fresh cut. He saw me watching him and in one quick motion, much like the one he'd used with George some weeks ago, he swung his arm around me, encircling my waist, and pulled me into him. I put my hand on the back of his velvety neck and kissed him. After a while, we were just standing in the kitchen holding each other, breathing in and out together. I locked my hands at the small of his back and rested my head over his heart, listening to its healthy lub-dub beat.

The serenity of the moment was broken when Jack's chest began to violently shake. I stepped away from him and looked into his face, expecting tears, only to be met with a big open mouthed smile as he held his head back laughing so hard there was no sound. Finally, he caught his breath and regained his composure enough to say, "I would have loved to have seen Bradley's face when you smacked his ass."

My cheeks stung again as they filled with color and I solemnly said, "How'd you find out."

He waved his hand in front of him and said between chuckles, "Doesn't matter. Word gets around."

Then I thought about Bradley's insult to me, which Jack obviously hadn't heard about or I doubted he'd be standing there laughing. I began to laugh too, assured that I wasn't an embarrassment to Jack after all.

The prospects that the newspaper article presented both excited and sickened me. The thought that it would lead to more information that could help Rhianna was exciting to me. However, the possibility that several teenagers had died by suicide over the past few years and no one in the community had taken steps to find out what was leading them to this decision made my stomach hurt. Jack quickly came to a stand still in researching the Anita Kent case or finding any more like it, even though Olive had said there were more. I wish she'd been clearer about what she meant by "more."

But Olive's vague hint wasn't the only thing holding up Jack's investigation. Anita Kent's suicide had happened four years ago, and the department's records had only been computerized for five years, a drawback of being a small town sheriff succeeding a much older sheriff who didn't believe in computerization. The lack of computerized records made looking for older, similar cases difficult. Jack had my old friend Sully manually looking for similar cases, but it was slow going, especially since it wasn't top priority.

After about a week, I decided to take matters into my own hands. Rhianna's trial was a week and a half away, so we didn't have much time. I knew the person who could help me— the Phoenix—Miss Bette. I called her at home because I didn't want anyone at the paper to overhear our conversation. Plus, I didn't want to ruin my mental image of her natural habitat by going over to her house. I pictured her living in a dusty house full of books. I wouldn't be able to stand it if her house was full of doilies and not a book to be seen.

When I called her, I was taken aback that she was reluctant

to look into the deaths.

"Kid, you sure you're in the right business? You have a nose for trouble. Ever consider newspaper work?"

"Yes, but don't get me off track," I said. "Why don't you want to look into this?"

"Well, your source was right; there have been others. It's something that's been whispered about for years."

"Any whispers about why these kids would kill themselves or who would help them along the way?"

"No one doubts that they were suicides or accidents. Most of the talk blames drugs. Every time a girl dies, because they've all been girls, they say drugs or pregnancy or being ditched by her boyfriend. People mostly blame the school and the parents."

"They've all been girls?" I replied. "How many?"

"At least five, but maybe upwards of ten."

"You still haven't told me why you don't want to look into this."

"This is one pot I don't want to stir. Too much emotion. Too much danger."

"Since when did a journalist ever run away from danger and emotion? I thought that's what you newspaper people lived for." I was goading her and she knew it.

"I'm not going to get myself into trouble just 'cause you call me chicken, Kid."

"The only reason this means so much to me is that Rhianna's trial is coming up soon, and these suicides could have something to do with Mara Tierney's death."

"You still believe in her, do ya, Kid?"

"I don't want to have been wrong about Rhianna. There must have been something there that I liked. I don't want to have been fooled because I'm no fool."

"Uh-huh. Let me see what I can find out, but if I get into a jam, it's your ass, Kid."

There was one thing that was bothering me more than anything else about Anita Kent's case; it was her name. I'd heard that name somewhere before. I wish I had my notebook. I felt lost without it. Finally, I picked up the phone again and called Madeleine at home.

"Hey, Ethel, does the name Anita Kent mean anything to you?"

"Ethel? Is that you Emmy? Are you drunk?"

"No, I'm not drunk. Jack calls us Lucy and Ethel. So, does the name Anita Kent mean anything to you?"

"Well, how come I have to be Ethel?"

"Madeleine! I'm the redhead, so I have to be Lucy. Now, would you answer my question?"

"No, I don't know who Anita Kent is, but Althea Kent was the other person in the beauty shop the day Janney had her spat with Mara."

"That's right! Thank you! There was something about Althea Kent too that I'd heard, but I don't remember what it was. I wonder if Althea and Anita are related."

"I don't know, but since they have the same last name and Middletown isn't exactly a metropolis, I'd think it would be pretty safe to assume that they were," she speculated.

After we hung up, I paced around the kitchen trying to figure out if Althea and Anita were related and what I'd heard about Althea. There was one person I knew who could tell me what I needed to know. I dialed my parents' number and as soon my mom answered, I realized I'd woken her up. I looked at the clock and saw that it was ten. I should have known better than to call after nine, their usual bedtime. I apologized and tried to beg off the phone call, but she said since I'd already woken them up, I might as well tell her what I called for.

"The Kents own the dairy farm right outside of town. Remember, Althea is the one that I said Rhianna sold the herbal medicine to. What did you call it? Pay-ol-ee?"

"Peyote," I corrected. "I still don't think it was peyote."

"That's what killed Anita."

"What? Peyote? I thought Anita died by suicide."

"No. The Kents used to be Catholic."

"What? You're talking in circles, Mom. What do you mean they 'used to be Catholic'?"

"Father what's-his-name wouldn't let them have a service for Anita because the Coroner said it was suicide."

"Father Bob?"

"No, the one before him. Thomas or Timothy. Something like that."

"So why didn't the Kents think it was suicide when the Coroner did?"

"Althea had brought this herbal stuff from Rhianna because she was feeling down. Rhianna told her to rub it on her temples and it would perk her up. Well, it made her high was what it did. She only used it once, but when she went to throw it away, the bottle was gone and a week later, Anita was dead."

All of this speculation seemed far-fetched to me, but I thanked my mom for the information and decided I'd call Mrs. Kent the next day.

When I looked up the Kents' number in the phonebook the next morning, I saw that they were still running the dairy. I decided to drive out instead of calling. She couldn't hang up on me if I showed up in person.

I was the only person in the dairy store, so I put on a show of looking around a bit. There was a thin, frail looking elderly woman behind the counter, but I wasn't sure if that was Althea or not. She had left the shop that day before I had arrived, so I didn't have a face to put with the name. My parents had gotten milk here when I was a kid, but that was nearly thirty years ago and nothing looked familiar to me now.

Finally, the woman behind the counter spoke, "What do you want, Emily?"

"How do you know my name?"

"There aren't that many women in town with fire red hair, aside from that awful dye job Ruby Collins keeps trying to pass off as her own. Besides, I've seen you in your shop before when I was going to the beauty parlor."

So this was Mrs. Kent, I thought. "What makes you think I want something?"

She jutted out her hip and put a hand on it, "All we sell are dairy products. People generally come in for what they want, get it, and leave. They don't browse."

"Okay. So I do want something, but I'm not sure you're going to like it."

"What do you want to know about? Mara Tierney or Anita?" She was a smart old bat. Either that or someone had told her I was asking questions around town.

"Actually, I'd like to know about both."

"Good because they have to do with one another. Anita's death was ruled a suicide, but that kid never would have killed herself. She had a scholarship to U of I. She was going to be a large animal vet and come back here and help her brother run the farm. Anyway, because they said it was a suicide, Mara Tierney wouldn't let any death benefits be paid from her life insurance policy."

How was that Mara's fault? I thought. Insurance companies always based the payment of insurance funds on the death certificate. If it said suicide, they wouldn't pay. "Why do you think Anita's death was an accident?"

"I don't think it was an accident either. Someone gave her that drug and put her up on that roof."

"What drug?"

"The one Rhianna gave me for migraines," she said. This part was a little different from the story my mom had told me, but things got twisted through the rumor mill.

"How would that have caused her death?"

"The stuff made me loopy. My heart pounded and my head was all light and foggy. Felt like I was going to take off."

"Do you remember what it was called?"

"Bella-something."

Bella-something sounded familiar to me, but I couldn't place it. Then I asked her, "Why do you think Anita took it?"

"She told me she did. I asked her to give it back, but she said she'd given it to a friend." She looked at the floor, and then said, "She never would have crawled out onto the roof in her right mind. She had Virgo."

"Vertigo?"

"Yes. She hated heights. She wouldn't even go up in the hayloft of the barn."

"Mrs. Kent, how do you think Anita got out on that roof or even into the school?"

"That's enough questions. You either need to buy something or get out."

Her sudden change perplexed me, but I cooperated. I bought a bottle of skim milk and left.

CHAPTER 23

As I drove to my bookstore, I had another feeling that I was missing something. I was sure that there was more to Althea Kent's story. Why was she keeping something from me? But the thing that bothered me most about my visit to the Kent Dairy was that my mom was right. Rhianna had sold some kind of psychotropic drug to Althea Kent—herbal or otherwise. It was looking like the rumors that Rhianna was a drug dealer of some kind might be right. What drug was called bella-something? The only Bella I was knowledgeable about was my Arabella.

When I arrived at the store, I logged onto the computer and typed into my web browser "drug bella something" and the search returned: Belladonna.

Belladonna, also known as night shade, has some of the same medicinal properties as aconite. It is applied locally to lessen irritability and pain and is used as a lotion, plaster, or liniment to relieve neuralgia, gout, rheumatism, and sciatica. Interestingly, small doses can help allay cardiac palpitations; however, a large dose can cause cardiac arrest and delirium.

Aconite. I wondered what that was. The name didn't conjure any memories for me. As I continued to read, the dots started connecting themselves.

Belladonna, along with aconite, is the key ingredient in Witch's Flying Ointment. When applied to the soles of the feet and palms of the hands, it is quickly absorbed into the system. The delirium caused by the belladonna combines with the heart palpitations brought on by the aconite to create the sensation of flying.

Witch's Flying Ointment was the last thing Jessy Becker had said to me the day before she was killed. Rhianna must have given Althea Kent Witch's Flying Ointment. That's why she felt high when she used it. It would make sense that Anita would be able to climb onto the roof without suffering the effects of vertigo and why she would have jumped off: She must have thought she could fly. But that still didn't explain why she was in the school late at night and how she got there to begin with. Obviously, she was with someone who had a key.

"I suppose it wouldn't be hard for a student to lift a master key from an inattentive or unscrupulous janitor," I speculated to Madeleine later that morning as I gave her a full report on the information I had found from both Mrs. Kent and the Internet.

"You're probably right," she said, sipping her Earl Grey tea. How I had become friends with someone who didn't like coffee was beyond me. We were sitting on the sofa enjoying a quiet moment with no customers. Business had picked up in the last day or so, but I couldn't decide if it was the bestseller or my fiasco with Brett Bradley that brought people into the store. I reached for a lemon poppy seed muffin from the plate on the coffee table. Madeleine had learned that I rarely ate breakfast, another one of my poor dietary habits. So, when she worked in the mornings, she had taken to bringing in something for breakfast, a light breakfast casserole, fruit salad, or simply muffins. The funny thing was I'd lost five pounds since she'd started doing this. I guessed there was something to the saying that breakfast was the most important meal of the day.

As I leaned back into the sofa, taking a bite of my muffin, a good-looking woman walked past the store window. She was wearing a floral print sundress, large, dark sunglasses, and a floppy straw hat, reminiscent of the hat Scarlett O'Hara wore in the barbecue scene at Twelve Oaks in *Gone with the Wind*. The woman went to the corner and stood looking in every direction.

"Isn't that Maria Matthews?" I asked Madeleine. But before Madeleine could answer, the woman was on the move again. "I can't believe she'd have the nerve to come in here," I said, which she did after giving another furtive glance over her shoulder.

She stopped short at seeing the two of us on the sofa and gave us a light, wispy "Hi" as she removed her sunglasses.

"What's wrong, Maria? Don't want anyone to know you can read?" I asked.

"Well, actually, ever since *she's* started working here, Nelson has suggested to everyone at the country club that they shouldn't patronize your store," Maria explained.

"Nelson's on the membership committee," Madeleine said to me out of the side of her mouth.

"You can tell Nelson that I wouldn't want a bunch of self-absorbed, snobs coming into my store anyway."

"People in glass houses . . ." she retorted as if we were two grade schoolers name-calling on the playground.

As I started to stand up, Madeleine put out an arm to stop me. Instead, she got to her feet and said, "If you're not here to buy books, then why did you risk being black-balled at the country club to come in here?"

"Well, I came in here to ask you a favor," Maria said.

Madeleine turned and looked at me, wide-eyed with

disbelief. I raised my eyebrows to her in response.

"What is it?" Madeleine asked.

"Well, I know you're a member and all, but your presence at the country club really makes Nelson uncomfortable. And you bring guests, who really don't fit in with our crowd," she said, eyeing me as if I were too stupid to figure out she meant me and my children. "Well, it brings down the status of the whole club and makes people not want to renew their membership. I thought it was high time someone took action before everything was ruined."

I felt my hackles start to rise and my face prickle with anger. Without missing a beat, Madeleine put her arm around Maria's shoulders and slowly walked her to the door as she said, "You know, Maria, if it had been anyone but you who'd come in here insulting my best friend and acting like they owned the universe, I probably would have decked them. But seeing as how it was you, the woman who's been sleeping with my husband for the past sixteen years, I'll make an exception. You know why?"

Maria shook her head, clearly afraid of what Madeleine might do next.

"Maria, I've figured out over the years that you aren't very smart. Because if you were smart, you'd have figured out by now that Nelson's only after you for your money. You know he doesn't really have any money of his own. That's why he married me. I have money. Who do you think pays for Nelson's country club membership? And who do you wonder will pay for it next year since we're divorced now?" Madeleine reached out and opened the door to the outside.

Continuing her speech, Madeleine said, "You know, I've actually begun to feel sorry for you because I've also realized that you've never had any good sex. Because if you had, you certainly wouldn't still be banging my pencil-dicked ex-husband who couldn't find a clitoris if Masters and Johnson themselves drew him a map." Without another word, Madeleine gave Maria a gentle shove out onto the sidewalk and closed the door to the store behind her.

I jumped to my feet and clapped my hands, "Brava, Brava!" I was impressed at how Madeleine had told her off in such a classy way. I probably would have reverted to profanity and violence. But instead of taking a much deserved bow, Madeleine stood with her back to the window, tears running down her cheeks.

"Is she gone?" she asked.

"Yes."

She put out her arms to me like a child who had fallen on the playground, so I went to her and held her as tight as I thought she could stand. After a minute, she wiped her eyes, and we went back to sit on the couch.

"I have to tell you something. I'm very rich," she said, hanging her head in shame as if she'd just told me her deepest, dirtiest secret.

"Yeah, so."

"No, you don't understand. I'm very wealthy. I could buy and sell Oprah."

"Madeleine . . .," I was dumbfounded as to why she thought this was bad news. "What's wrong with that?"

"I feel bad taking money from you when I don't need it."

"It's only minimum wage."

"What I said about Nelson marrying me for my money was true. It's why I have this money that is upsetting me." I didn't say anything. I patiently waited for her to tell me her story when she was ready.

She took a deep breath and said, "My mother's father started one of the advertising agencies in Chicago, so it was really my mother who had money although my father came from a family with some money as well." She paused, taking another deep breath. "I told you before that I have a younger sister, whom I haven't spoken to in almost seven years. Genevieve, Vievy, got into drugs—meth—and was arrested on a prostitution charge when my parents cut her off because she was spending all her money on drugs. After that, my parents changed their will, leaving everything to me.

"I tried to help Vievy. We used to be close before the drugs. But she blamed me for being the perfect older sister, and finally, I realized, like my parents had, that all the money I gave her went to support her drug addiction." Madeleine doubled over her arms, rocking and hugging herself. I just rubbed her back and waited. After a few moments, she regained control and continued. "One night in a drugged-up frenzy, she broke into my parents house with some of her friends looking for money. When my dad confronted her, she killed him—my mom, too. Shot them both in the face with the rifle my dad used for deer hunting."

By now, I was sobbing as hard as she was. It was an unbelievable story. I could hardly comprehend how she remained so positive and cheerful after all that she'd been through: her parents' brutal murder, her sister's drug abuse and incarceration, and now a divorce. It was hard to believe that this well-dressed, well-mannered woman sitting next to me had been touched by such pain and brutality.

She wiped her face with her hands and put an unconvincing smile on her face, "So that's why Nelson married me; I have money. Nelson's father keeps a tight rein on his trust fund, which is smart, because Nelson spends money like it was water. But when he found out that I wouldn't use my money to improve his lifestyle, he began openly cheating on me with Maria, among others, and degrading me, even hitting me, whenever he felt the urge. The smartest thing I ever did was make him sign a prenuptial agreement.

"See, I feel very guilty about having this money because of the way I came to have it. If my parents had both lived to ninety and I'd inherited my share with my sister, I'd have no problem using it to better my lifestyle, but to me, it has their blood all over it. So I only use it when I need to, like when I divorced Nelson. I don't get alimony like I said I do, and I bought the house from him; I didn't get it in the settlement. I live off what I make here."

"Well that's the cheapest way of asking for a raise that I've ever witnessed," I said, hoping she wouldn't mind me joking at such a serious moment. But she laughed, used to my habit of reverting to humor whenever the subject got too serious. It was kind of like a tic.

We had developed a quick, close friendship in the short time she had been working for me, but now I felt an affection for her well up inside of me only equal to the feelings I'd had for Jack or the girls, for my own family. I hoped she wouldn't think I was being melodramatic or too forward, but I said what I felt in my heart. I cupped her cheek with my hand and said, "Madeleine, I'm your family now. My family is your family. I know that we can never replace your loved ones, but as long as I have a home and a business, you always have a place to call your own."

She hugged me, squeaking out a constricted, "Thank you."

Then I held her out at arms length, and said, "With one exception—you can't sleep with my husband."

"Well forget the whole thing then," she said, laughing through her tears.

Throughout the day, I found myself playing out in my head the scene of Madeleine's sister murdering her parents, which led to flashbacks of Mara slumped in the dryer chair and me trying to revive her. I began thinking about Jessy Becker and wondered what would happen if someone used too much belladonna or too much aconite when making Witch's

Flying Ointment. Could someone be accidentally or not so accidentally poisoned if the wrong proportions were used? *Why not?* What would happen if you mixed the potion with a little fentanyl to make you fly extra high? I picked up the phone, eager to share the events of the day with Jack, but I got his cellphone's voicemail. I called the dispatcher, and she told me Jack was in court. Damn, I thought to myself. I wouldn't be able to share the information I'd learned from Mrs. Kent or from the Internet with him until later that night. Just then the phone rang.

It was my mom. She and my dad wanted to take the girls to a nearby drive-in movie theater to see a Disney double feature of *Freaky Friday* and *Flubber* and then have them spend the night afterward. My parents planned to take my dad's truck and have the girls lay in the bed with their sleeping bags while they watched the movie like I used to do when I was their age. It sounded like a fun evening; just the thing I needed after the heavy emotions I'd been feeling all day. But I also saw it as a chance to be by myself and sort out my thoughts. After I made arrangements with my mom to get the girls' things, I asked to speak to my dad. I suddenly had an idea of how I could make the time go by more quickly until I could share all of this new information with Jack. It was also the best way to clear my head.

"Yello."

"Dad, can you get my car out of the garage?" I asked as sweetly as I could. My dad stored my 1980 Pontiac Firebird for me and kept it running. In his free time, my Uncle Matt and he liked to restore classic cars. Begrudgingly, I had to admit that a 1980 Firebird was now considered a classic. Of course, it had been bordering on a classic when I drove it in high school.

"You're not going to hot rod are you? You've got a bad reputation lately with cars."

"Why, Daddy, you know I'd never hot rod."

"Keep it under seventy," he said. "I'll bring it over when we come to get the girls' stuff."

When I hung up the phone, I felt pounds lighter.

CHAPTER 24

A few hours later, I was going eighty miles an hour down a country blacktop. Driving fast might not have made me think better, but it made me feel better. The wind was whipping my hair around like Medusa's head full of snakes and Van Halen was blasting from the speakers. As I was coming over a rise, I met a Sheriff's Department cruiser. The lights went on as the driver made a U-turn in the middle of the deserted country road. Sirens blaring behind me, I pulled onto the shoulder of the road, praying that it wasn't my husband, but also that it wasn't Bradley. As the cruiser pulled up behind me, I saw that it was my old friend Sully.

I got out and met him between our two cars.

"Emily, you were going mighty fast."

"You going to give me a ticket, Deputy?" I asked, shamelessly, but harmlessly flirting. Sully was so sweet, and we'd known each other since the first grade. I couldn't help myself. It was the nature of our relationship.

"Nah. I knew it was you anyway. No one else in the county has a 1980 Firebird—or at least one that looks this nice. I can't tell you how many times I've stopped your dad out here."

"Where do you think I got my lead foot?"

Smiling he said, "This is such a sweet ride. You never would let me drive it."

"Nope. It beat that jalopy of yours," I said, maligning his

baby, a 1970 GTO, which he still drove, and despite how I was teasing him, he kept it in mint condition. Classic muscle cars were a prerequisite for small town adolescents. He didn't try to defend himself; he just flashed me those dimples.

"So, what are you doing out here?" he asked.

"Blowing off steam."

"How come?"

"I've got some theories about those deaths that Jack's got you looking into. I'm trying to percolate them into something coherent by driving fast and feeling the wind in my hair," I explained, sitting down on the hood of his cruiser. "Did you find anything yet?"

"So far, only one other possible victim that fits the same particulars. Tammy Black. She fell off or jumped off the Embarras Bridge several years ago," he explained, leaning against the cruiser next to where I was sitting. "Truthfully though, I haven't had much time to devote to it. I think Bradley knows that Jack's looking for evidence that will let him reopen the Tierney case. Since Bradley is the D.A.'s lap dog, he keeps finding reasons to keep me away from the files."

"He won't give an inch, will he?"

"He still resents not being elected sheriff. Actually, I don't think he resents not being elected as much as he resents being beaten by an outsider. Besides, he's got his nose so far up Robert Price's ass I bet he could tell Price if he has polyps."

"Yuk, Sully," I said, punching him in the arm. We were quiet for a moment, looking out across the corn fields.

"Not quite knee high yet," he said.

"Well, there is still a week until the Fourth of July," I said. 'Knee high by the Fourth of July' was an old farmer's saying to tell if a corn crop was going to be successful or not. After a minute, I asked, "Sully, why didn't you ever ask me out in high school?"

He looked at me and then looked at the pavement in front of him. His cheeks were red, and it wasn't from sunburn. I playfully nudged his arm with my leg, prodding him to answer. Finally, he said, "You were out of my league."

"You've got to be kidding. I wasn't out of anyone's league. I wasn't even popular."

"No, you were beyond popular. You were untouchable."

"Untouchable?"

"You were so cool. You told dirty jokes and drove a fast car and were gorgeous. Are gorgeous," he said, casting me a sideways look. "Way too sophisticated for a hick like me. It made sense that you had a college boyfriend."

"A college boyfriend who treated me badly and cheated on me."

"I'm sorry to hear that."

"You know, I always had a crush on you. I would have gone out with you if you'd asked."

He didn't say anything; he just gave me one of his heartbreakingly sweet smiles.

"Mary Ten, this is Dispatch, what's your twenty?" his radio crackled, breaking up our remembrances of what-might-have-been.

"Oh, shit. I called in that I was pulling over a speeder. They probably think you've got me hog-tied."

"Thanks for the talk," I said, jumping back into the Firebird, my head and heart both lighter than they'd been in weeks.

"Slow down!" he yelled after me as I burned rubber and flew down the road.

I was still high from my drive—and from my conversation with Sully—when I got home. Even though I was a happily married woman, it made me feel good that someone out there still considered me a catch, and possibly, was pining for me a little bit. As I sat at the table eating a sandwich and enjoying the solitude, I sorted through the mail. Mixed in with a pile of circulars was a thick letter addressed to me, written in shaky handwriting. The handwriting of a ninety-year-old, I guessed. I ripped the envelope open to find several photocopied newspaper clippings accompanied by a sticky note, which read: *Kid, there are seven in all. Hope this helps. Stay out of trouble!*

The note wasn't signed, but I knew who it was from.

I cleaned up the rubbish from my supper, and then lay on the couch and scanned the articles:

KIM BEAKMAN, MIDWESTERN MUTUAL SCHOLARSHIP WINNER, DIES IN ONE-CAR COLLISION. She was seen driving erratically and then hit a concrete abutment on a highway underpass.

NATIONAL HONOR SOCIETY STUDENT FALLS TO HER DEATH. This was the article about Anita Kent's death.

JULIE CONNERS, MHS STUDENT, COMMITS SUICIDE. Coroner found that the girl was pregnant.

TAMMY BLACK, 17, KILLED IN FALL FROM EMBARRAS BRIDGE. Drugs were suspected, although the article said none were found during the autopsy.

MHS HOMECOMING QUEEN, ALICE WALKER, DIES

AFTER FALL FROM HAYLOFT. Her death was ruled a farming accident even though she fell in the middle of the night.

BITSY BYERS, CHEERLEADER, DIES UNDER UNUSUAL CIRCUMSTANCES. She told her parents she was going for a walk and was found two days later floating in a creek. Eventually, her death was ruled a suicide.

LORI LANDERS JUMPS TO HER DEATH FROM FERRIS WHEEL.

This one I remembered. I was there when it happened. It was spring of my senior year, during the annual Spring Fling. She was sitting at the top of the Ferris wheel when it stopped to let some people on at the bottom. She inexplicably stood up and did a swan dive from her seat. I still wake up in the middle of the night with the splat of her body on the pavement echoing in my ears.

I leaned back on the couch and closed my eyes. It was so much to take in. Were these all really accidents and suicides or could someone in this small town have been getting away with multiple murders for over sixteen years? Could I add Mara Tierney and Jessy Becker to this list? The question that pressed the most upon my mind was: Is Rhianna responsible or at the very least a co-conspirator in these murders? I told myself that I could take comfort in the fact that she *wasn't* a drug dealer since all the ingredients in Witch's Flying Ointment were legal.

During my internal questioning, I must have fallen asleep. The next thing I knew I was being awakened by a gentle kiss.

"Hi," I said sleepily to Jack as he sat on the edge of the couch.

"Are the girls asleep already? It's only eight o'clock."

"They aren't even here. My parents took them to Princeton to the drive-in. They'll be gone all night," I said.

"Ah, very nice," he said smiling. "I see you've been out hot-rodding in your other car." He must have seen it in the garage when he went to park his cruiser.

"Not me, Officer," I teased. Then motioning to the clippings in my lap, I said, "I was clearing my head."

"What is all of this?" he asked as he picked up a few, looking at the headlines.

"These are all of the girls who have died under mysterious circumstances, like Anita Kent, in the last sixteen years."

"Where'd you get these? From that old crank at the newspaper?"

"I prefer to think of her as a hardened journalist, but yes. When you and Sully weren't having any luck, I took the initiative of finding out for myself."

"So, anything that might lead anywhere?"

I told him that from what I could gather from the newspaper clippings, not all of the deaths were suspected to be suicides, but all of the girls were seen acting erratically either right before they died or a few days before their death. Then I told him about my visit with Althea Kent and her assertion that Rhianna had given her belladonna, which Althea believes that Anita then took, resulting in her death. I also filled him in on my findings about belladonna, aconite, and Witch's Flying Ointment. I decided to save what Madeleine had told me for later; I was already handing him more information than he could hold.

"You went to see Althea Kent and questioned her about her daughter's death?"

"Don't be angry, Jack. You and your department have better

things to do than to go chasing my wild ideas, and if I hadn't followed my hunch and been meddlesome, I never would have found out the information I have." I said this all quickly. If I took a breath, he'd have time to think about the possible ramifications of my inquisitiveness. Then I'd be in for another lecture on sticking my nose where it didn't belong. "Besides, she seemed to know I was coming, which means I'm not the only one privy to what's been going on around here."

"What do you mean she knew you were coming?" he asked.

"She didn't seem surprised or put off when I started asking questions about Anita."

"That seems strange, but if you've been poking around as much as I suspect that you have," he said, shooting me a disapproving look, "it's going to get around."

"Anyway, all of this is beside the point," I said, getting up from the couch and going into the office with Jack close on my heels. I pulled out my research on belladonna and showed it to him, explaining that when mixed with aconite and a few other ingredients, the resulting ointment can be put on the hands and feet, giving the recipient the sensation that they are flying.

"I was thinking about what Jessy told me about George; that he had seduced a lot of girls, but that he wouldn't move on one until he had something to hold over her. When that failed, he'd bribe them with a scholarship from Midwestern Mutual. But what would happen if they wouldn't shut up? What if they were determined to tell what he was doing to them despite what dirty laundry or college scholarship he threw at them? What if he didn't seduce all of these girls? What if he attacked and raped some of them? These were all smart girls, college-track for the most part. Look, one of the headlines even refers to a girl as being a 'Midwestern Mutual Scholarship winner,'" I said, holding the article up for him to look at.

"Technically, even if he seduced them, it is still sexual assault because he was someone in a position of power and he was an adult. The majority of these girls were minors." He was quiet for a moment and then said, "I can see from your eyes that you have more."

"Rub a little flying ointment on them, put them in a dangerous situation, and let nature take its course—on the school roof, a bridge, behind the wheel of a car, on top of a Ferris wheel. But also, what would happen if you didn't mix the proportions correctly? What if you added too much aconite or too much belladonna and maybe some fentanyl for good measure?"

"Then you wouldn't just be flying; you'd be dead. . ."

". . . and you probably wouldn't even know it until you were suffocating, or your heart stopped pumping," I said, finishing his thought.

He sat down in the desk chair, rubbing his forehead, and I sat down across from him. We were both silent for several minutes. He was mulling over the information I'd given him, and I was waiting for his take on it all.

"Em, you've done some good investigative work here. Unfortunately, I don't understand how any of this ties to Rhianna or even helps clear her although it does cast quite a bit of suspicion on George, if he is behind any of this."

"Well, I don't really know either, but isn't there *something* here?"

"Yes, and I intend on taking all of this to the D.A. as soon as I've had a chance to look it all over. Tomorrow, I'm going to request that the M.E. check for the presence of belladonna and aconite in the blood samples taken from Jessy Becker. That will give me a place to start."

"But Rhianna's trial starts on Monday. Can't you take this information to the D.A. and ask for a continuance?"

"That's not my job, Emmy. Besides, you know Robert Price. If I tip my hand to him without the proper evidence, he'll shut me down from the beginning. Then three months from now, he'll hand it all over to Bradley and tell him to run with it," he said, commenting on the futility of the local system he had to work within. "Maybe if I can get the toxicology results back in enough time, I can take the information to the D.A., and he can give Rhianna some sort of plea agreement in exchange for information on the other deaths. Obviously, she couldn't have been involved in all of these deaths since a majority of them took place while she was living in Los Angeles.

"Damn! This all seems so far-fetched," he said, shaking his head. "I'll look into this next week and see if I can come up with something before Rhianna's trial. The likelihood that I'm going to find something worth reopening the investigation for is doubtful though. I hate to think that someone could get away with this if I can't fit it all together."

"You know we came back here because it seemed slow and safe and predictable, but the more I find out about people I've known most of my life, the more I'm beginning to think that you never really know anyone. Do I even really know you?" I speculated.

"Now, you're talking nonsense. Sometimes I think you know me better than I know myself. Sure this revelation is very upsetting, but nothing is going to persuade me that we didn't make the right decision by moving here. I realize you would have rather moved to the middle of Montana than moved back here, but you did it and you're making it work," he said.

"Now, I'm not so sure about *that*. If you're trying to butter me up so you can get lucky tonight, you don't have to. 'Cause, Baby, I'm a sure thing!" I said.

With that, we both left the subject of flying ointments, teenage suicide, and small towns behind us. We went upstairs to wash the outside world away from each other and create a world where Jack and Emily were the only inhabitants, even if it was for only a few hours.

Around midnight as I lay in bed snuggled up to Jack with my head on his chest and his arms encircling me, I wanted to feel peace and satisfaction, but only felt sad and guilty. I'd taken comfort in Jack's arms so many times without giving a thought as to what a gift it was to have this man who loved me, to have a family who cared. Tears stung my eyes as I thought about Madeleine laying alone in her bed a few blocks away in a house not so unlike mine with no one to call her own, no one to love her and help her feel like it all was going to be alright. Her selfless solitude was in glaring contrast to my petty differences with my mother and how I took for granted that Jack would always be there for me. I'd fought against the stereotype of the spoiled only child all my life, insisting that I wasn't selfish or self-absorbed, but I was a grown woman still focused on myself and how others had wronged me or treated me badly.

I thought Jack was asleep, but he must have felt my tears pooling on his chest and realized I was crying. He began stroking my hair, probably thinking I was upset about the investigation.

As my silent tears turned into deep sobs, he softly asked, "Emily, what's bothering you?"

I struggled to curb my crying as I sat up in bed, wiping my face. "Madeleine told me today that her parents were murdered by her younger sister."

"I know," he replied. "After I met her a few months ago and she had told me she was from Chicago, her name had stuck with me. It sounded familiar, but I couldn't remember why, so I searched her name on the Internet and found the newspaper reports of her parents' shooting and her sister's trial."

"Why didn't you tell me?"

"Knowing your compulsion for taking care of people and mothering them, I wanted you to get to know her on her own terms. I wanted you to like her for who she is and not out of some need to take care of her. Besides, I knew she'd tell you when she was ready."

I shook my head, amazed at how well he knew me. "You know what I told her after she finished her story?" I rhetorically asked him. "I told her we were her family now and that as long as I had a home and a business, she was always welcome."

He pulled me back onto his chest, and I settled my head into its familiar nest between his collarbone and his chest, thinking how my head fit there like a puzzle piece. I thought about how empty my heart had been before I met Jack, and how I'd been trying to fill that space with education and work, which only distanced me from other people. I thanked God that Jack had recognized in me a piece of himself that was missing because I'm not sure I would have come out of myself enough to see it.

I raised my head and looked into his eyes. I wasn't looking into them to see him but to see myself reflected in them. I liked looking at myself through Jack's eyes because he loved me more than I loved myself. His vision of me was blurred by love and was softer and kinder than my vision of myself, which was sharply focused by my own criticism and angst.

I lowered my head back into its nest and prayed that Madeleine would find someone who loved her like Jack loved me. Someone who would soften the pain of the past and would brighten her view of the future. Someone who would be her hope when she felt all hope was lost.

CHAPTER 25

The week went by so quickly that I felt like I was on one of those super trains in Japan. Everything was fast and foreign. Jack did his best to find some relationship between the cases. He brought home all the Sheriff's Department's files on each girl in the newspaper clippings, and we raked through them for pieces that we could puzzle together. But it seemed useless. The only similarities we could find were their ages, that they were all young women, and that they had been students at MHS. Toxicology results didn't show drugs that were found in Mara or Jessy. Unless the toxicologist knew to look for it, aconite and belladonna would not necessarily show up on a toxicology test. The victims had all been seen acting erratically before their deaths, but there was no mention of someone in common between them or any other information that would point to anything other than a suicide or an accident caused by teenage recklessness. However, there also hadn't been a lot of investigation into the deaths. The previous sheriff had taken them at face value. He had seen them as senseless tragedies that were the result of teen angst and nothing more.

On Thursday, Jack got the new toxicology report on Jessy Becker he'd requested from the Medical Examiner. Jack was always charming, and the M.E., Gloria Stanley, had put a rush on the testing. Jessy had tested positive for belladonna, so it was probably a correct assumption that she'd been under the influence of Witch's Flying Ointment when she died.

Everything seemed so achingly close but nothing clicked together. It was like an itch between your shoulder blades that you can't scratch without someone else's help.

Finally, Jack and I decided to do some personal interviews. I'd already talked to Althea Kent, so that took care of Anita Kent's family. Tammy Black's mother died shortly after her daughter's death, and her father had died several years before that. Alice Walker's parents divorced and they both moved away. We could have contacted them by phone, but we decided to focus on people we could talk to face-to-face. That left the parents of Julie Conners, Kim Beakman, Bitsy Byers, and Lori Landers. I wanted to talk to Lori Landers's parents because I'd been there for her spectacular leap from the Ferris wheel. I was also interested in Kim Beakman since the newspaper article had identified her as a Midwestern Mutual Scholarship winner. Jack said he'd talk to the parents of Julie Conners and Bitsy Byers.

The next day as I prepared to conduct my interviews, I couldn't come up with an angle with which to approach Lori Landers's parents, so I decided to walk the three blocks from my bookstore down to the public library where Kim Beakman's mother worked.

Kim's mother was a short, rumpled, oily-looking woman with dirty dishwater blonde hair and piercing blue eyes. She'd been a librarian since I was a child, and I remembered how her eyes had terrified me. Whenever a patron made too much noise, she'd stare the person down until the person felt the stab of her eyes and shut up. I decided to go right up to her and not put up a show of looking for some book. After I introduced myself and we exchanged pleasantries, I got right to the point.

"Mrs. Beakman, I'm doing a story for the *Daily Inquirer* about former Midwestern Mutual Scholarship winners, and your daughter had been awarded the scholarship."

"My daughter's dead. I don't know how I can help you."

"Yes, ma'am, I am aware that your daughter is deceased. The truth is: I'm looking into some improprieties that have been discovered since Mara Tierney's death. It seems some of the scholarships weren't awarded by academic merit but more on the whim of Mrs. Tierney herself."

"Well, my daughter had a 3.8 grade point average out of four points, was in the National Honor Society, and was salutatorian. She had recently started at Indiana University and was home for the weekend when she died. She wasn't a drug addict, like they said she was."

"It certainly sounds like she was qualified. How did she come about applying for the scholarship?"

"George Tierney. He knew we would be struggling to send her to college, and he suggested she apply for the scholarship."

"Was Mr. Tierney her teacher?"

"She never had his literature classes, but she was on the yearbook."
"I see. Yearbook was fun. I was on the yearbook when I was at MHS. Why did they say your daughter might have been on drugs when she had her accident?"

"She was seen weaving all over the road before she hit the bridge. She almost hit several cars head on before she crashed. But they never found a drop of drugs or alcohol in her blood. There must have been something wrong with her car. She was a very careful driver."

"Where had she been, and where was she going?"

"She'd been across the river at the movies and was on her way home."

"Was she with friends?"

"No. She'd gone alone. My daughter didn't have many friends. She was more interested in studying and going to college," Mrs. Beakman stated matter-of-factly.

"So as far as you know, she was alone that night?"

"Yes, but I don't see what that has to do with her winning a scholarship."

"I'm sorry, you're right. I was being plain nosy. . . So what sort of information did she have to submit to be considered for the scholarship?"

"I don't know. It's been so long ago, and frankly, she took care of all of the details. I remember her saying that Mr. Tierney was helping her. She stayed after school a few times to work on an essay or something with him."

Now that was some information I could use. "How many times did she stay after?"

"I don't know. Half a dozen."

"For a scholarship essay?" I asked, barely concealing the surprise in my voice. I didn't want to overstep and be called on it again.

"She was also interested in photography. I remember he was showing her some developing and photography techniques as well."

I bet he was, I thought to myself, and then said, "Well, this all seems normal. Thank you for your help."

"I thought you owned the bookstore up the street," she said, just as I thought I was going to get away without rousing her suspicions.

"Oh, I do. I'm doing some freelance work for Miss Bette at the newspaper," I said, hoping Miss Bette would back me up if Mrs. Beakman called to check up on my story.

As I walked back to the store, I mentally went over our conversation. Nothing seemed out of the ordinary besides George spending a lot of after-school time with a student. But who knows if they were alone. Damn, I should have asked Mrs.

Beakman that question.

"Amateur," I mumbled to myself.

I wasn't looking forward to my interview with Lori Landers's parents. I still didn't have a good angle, so I decided to be straight with her parents. Her family lived on Third Street, the poor end of town. When I pulled up in front of their house in my new minivan, I saw pretty much what I'd imagined I would: bare patches of dirt, instead of a nice, lush lawn; old bikes, an oil drum, and toys scattered in the yard; and a house in desperate need of painting and some repairs.

Mr. Landers answered the door. Unlike his house, Mr. Landers was a surprise. He was a clean shaven, tall, thin man who was nicely dressed in khaki pants and a plaid button down shirt. The inside of the house was well ordered and clean.

"Mr. Landers, I'm Emily Romano. I'm working with the Sheriff on some old cases and Lori's death is one of the cases he's looking into." I had nothing else to offer and seeing what a contrast Mr. Landers was to what I'd expected, I didn't have the heart to make up some story about why I was there. But my presence there might also open old wounds or give him false hope.

As he opened the screen door for me, he said, "Please keep your voice down; my granddaughter is taking a nap."

"How old is she?"

"Two. I watch her during the day while her mom is at work."

"That must be a lot of work."

"She's worth it. She and her momma are all I have left. About three years ago, my wife finally succeeded in drinking herself to death." He motioned for me to sit down on the couch, and then asked, "What do you want to know about Lori?"

"I was a classmate of Lori's. I remember her as being fun-loving and full of life. At the time, I couldn't understand why she did what she did."

"Lori was like her mother: wild and impulsive without a thought of what consequences her actions would have on those around her. I don't think Lori meant to kill herself. She struggled with drug use. I think she was high and didn't quite know what she was doing."

"The toxicology reports didn't mention drugs. Did the medical examiner say anything about drugs?"

"No, but Lori took a lot of herbal drugs before they became popular like they are now. She knew what could make you high or give you a thrill without showing up in a blood or urine test. I tried to be strict and keep a thumb on her, but it was hard to do when her mother was getting drunk with her while I was at work. My wife couldn't hold a job and someone had to pay the mortgage," he said.

"We can only do so much for others and the rest is up to them," I said, trying to be sympathetic. I liked Mr. Landers and felt sorry that his life had been so hard.

"True."

"Where did Lori learn about herbal drugs?"

"I don't know. She had always had an interest in the occult. I suppose that's where she learned about it."

"Did she practice witchcraft?"

"No. She seemed to be in it more for the effect. You know, rebellion against religion and authority. That sort of thing," he explained.

"Who were her friends?"

"Anyone who could get her alcohol or drugs. It really was a shame. She was a very smart and creative girl. She had a real talent for writing and drawing. That George Tierney tried to help her, but she wouldn't have any of it."

My ears perked up at the mention of George's name. "How was Mr. Tierney helping her?"

"He encouraged her to write. He kept her after school, trying to help her with her writing and encouraging her to enter contests. He even tried to get her to apply for that scholarship his wife's company offered. Said she'd be a shoe-in. He's such a nice man, always trying to help his students get out of this town. It's a shame about his wife although I hear she wasn't a very nice woman."

"Yes," I said, not realizing I was being ambiguous.

Mr. Landers looked at me, trying to figure out what I meant.

"Was Lori friends with Rhianna Reese?" I said, holding my breath while I waited for him to answer. I figured if they both had an interest in herbal drugs then perhaps they had been friends. I thought I had been friends with all the same people Rhianna had been friends with in high school. Obviously, there was a lot I didn't know about her.

He thought for a moment and then said, "I don't know. Maybe."

That wasn't much of an answer, but I'm not sure what I would have done if he'd said "yes."

"Thank you so much for your help, Mr. Landers. I appreciate you taking the time to talk to me," I said standing and extending my hand to him.

"It was nice having a little company. You're that woman that owns the bookstore, right?"

"Yes, I am."

"That was a nice addition to the town. I like the library," he said, motioning to the book on the end table, *Leaves of Grass* by Walt Whitman. "But I might stop by sometime."

"I don't have a lot of poetry, but I can order you anything you want. I'll give you a discount too."

I thanked him again for his help and quickly left. I wasn't sure why I was in such a hurry; maybe I was afraid of what I might uncover if I'd stayed and questioned him further. I couldn't quite decipher this new batch of feelings. I was desperate to find answers, but for the first time when I'd come close to really uncovering something about Rhianna's involvement with George and the deaths of these girls, I ran. Perhaps I was worried I'd find verification that Rhianna was a killer. It was safer to internally doubt her innocence than to find hard and fast facts to validate my doubts.

Suddenly, I found myself sitting in my new minivan behind my store. I didn't remember driving there. My hands were shaking, and my heart was pounding. I took some deep breaths, trying to calm myself. I had an appointment to meet Jack and go over what we'd each discovered during our interviews, but this rush of feelings had thrown me for a loop. Had I subconsciously deluded myself so much about my ability to detect a murderer in my presence that when reality came crashing in, I shut down?

"No, I'm stronger than that. Buck up, for God's sake," I said to myself. I closed my eyes and thought about everything I'd gone through in the past few months, trying to convince myself that if I could go on after being poisoned and clinically dead, losing a baby, and nearly being blown up in a car accident, I could go on if Rhianna was found guilty of murder. But then I thought about how I'd hidden in bed after the car accident, crippled by fear and reality.

But I wasn't home in bed. I was out investigating a string of deaths which could lead to Mara Tierney's murderer. I was dealing with reality. If it turned out that Rhianna did kill Mara and even if it turned out that she had something to do with these other deaths, I'd deal with that, too. My life didn't stop after all these other tragedies and it wouldn't stop now.

Then, in a flash, something came to me. One person whose life *had* seemed to stop was Joe Campbell. Where had Joe Campbell disappeared to? I hadn't heard anything about him since the night Madeleine called me relaying the fight between George and Rhianna. As George's best friend, Joe Campbell could be the key to my investigation. I couldn't believe I hadn't gone to talk to him sooner.

I backed the still-running minivan out of my parking spot and drove over to the high school football field. When I pulled up to the RV Joe was living in, I saw the curtains rustle and the RV shake a bit as someone inside it moved around. Joe Campbell was a big man, and I imagined the movement of his body would easily shake the mid-sized RV.

I knocked on the door, but no one answered.

"Joe, I know you're in there. Open the door."

Still no answer.

"Joe, I saw you looking out the window. Open up. I only want to ask you a few questions."

"No. You asked Jessy Becker a few questions and she ended up dead. Go away!" he shouted through the closed door.

"What are you afraid of Joe? If someone is threatening you, that's a crime. The sheriff could help protect you."

"Go away!"

Crossing my arms over my chest, I turned my back to the door and looked out over the football field and up to the high school. Could whoever Joe was afraid of be watching him from the high school? Could that person be George Tierney? Deciding that it was fruitless to try to force him to talk to me, I went to meet Jack at his office.

As we sat at his desk, eating chef salads from Wilma's, Jack told me he'd been able to talk to Julie Conners's father, but Bitsy Byers's mother said she wouldn't talk to Jack without her attorney. The Byers family was the third-wealthiest family in town, the Kregers (Madeleine's ex-in-laws) were the second, after John Fletcher, the farmer. Wealthy people are conditioned to cry for an attorney at the least sign of trouble, so her reaction to Jack's visit didn't surprise either of us.

When we compared our information, the girls all had one person in common: George Tierney. They'd all stayed after school with him for extra help. Mr. Conners, Julie's father, said Julie was dyslexic, and even though she had a high grade point average, she struggled for every "A" she earned. In George's American Literature class, she'd fallen behind on her reading, so she stayed after school to get additional help from George even though the school had a reading specialist who had helped her. At the time, Mr. Conners hadn't thought much about it; he'd been preoccupied with some trouble his farm was having (he'd defaulted on some debts to other farmers and was struggling to get his reputation back). He admitted that Julie pretty much took care of herself. He said she was a good kid who never got into trouble, which is why it was such a shock when she died and the coroner said she was pregnant. Jack said that Mr. Conners had broken down and told him that he and his wife would have helped Julie; they would have raised the baby. But when she died with no note or anything, they were left to fill in the blanks themselves. He said the only conclusion they could come up with was that she was worried about disappointing them. Mr. Conners even went so far as to point the finger at George Tierney. He and his wife suspected that George had taken advantage of Julie and that she hadn't known how to handle it or where to turn.

So that was it. Of the three people we'd talked to, the common link was George Tierney.

"But is it enough to arrest him?" I asked Jack.

"No. I need to interview more people and do some background work on George and Mara, which I can do, but it's going to take some time. More time than we have," he sighed. "I'm sorry, Em. I'm not giving up on this, but there is no way we're going to have any new evidence to present to the D.A. or Rhianna's lawyer before the trial starts on Monday."

"We'll keep working. Maybe if she's convicted, we'll have some evidence for her appeal," I said, trying to sound hopeful.

"Have you talked to Rhianna lately?" Jack asked.

"No. She won't speak to me. I came by to see her last week, and Meg Kaiser said she refused to come out of her cell when she found out it was me. I haven't talked to her since she told me Reba was coming to get Andy."

"Do you know anything about Andy?"

"No. Reba wouldn't tell me where she was taking him—oh, and speaking of people who won't talk to me, I went by Joe Campbell's trailer because I wanted to ask him how much he knew about George's private life. After all, he had an affair with George's wife and has been his best friend for who knows how long. But he wouldn't let me in. At first, he acted like he wasn't home. When I said I knew he was home, he said he wouldn't talk to me because after I talked to Jessy Becker, she was murdered."

"Well that's odd, especially since Jessy's supposed murderer is locked up back there," he said, jerking a thumb toward the back of the building where the cell block was. "You're right. He could give us some valuable information, or at the very least, insight into George's personality."

I nodded my head. My chest ached with hopelessness. Jack must have seen it in my eyes.

"Hey, let's stop thinking about this for the weekend and enjoy the holiday. The trial starts Monday and we'll both have to testify," he said.

The next day was July Fourth, and we were planning an all day cookout for the Sheriff's Department and for my employees. Later that night, we would caravan across the river to the fireworks. The audience would sit in the grass of the George Rogers Clark Memorial on the Indiana side while the fireworks were shot off on the Illinois bank of the river. We were all looking forward to taking a break from all the chaos of everyday life and relax and enjoy ourselves, even if for only one day.

CHAPTER 26

O ur Fourth of July barbecue was what every small town American celebration of Independence Day should be. Tables of potato salad, cole slaw, Jell-O salad with carrots and raisins, Jell-O salad with pears, a Jell-O mold with whipped cream, green bean casserole, an unending supply of hot dogs and hamburgers, and American cheese as far as the eye could see. Besides the Sheriff's Department employees (minus Bradley who didn't honor us with his presence, but also offered no regrets), my parents and Madeleine spent the majority of the day in our backyard. Unfortunately, Sully had gone on vacation and wasn't there either. Janney and her brother, Brian, came as well. I had never met Brian, and I was impressed at how well-mannered and social he was for a sixteen-year-old boy. He even played tag with the little kids. I told Janney how lucky he was to have her watching out for him.

It was a happy day for Jack and me. Everywhere we looked there was someone we loved sitting in a lawn chair or lounging on a blanket on the grass. Children were running around the yard, playing hide-and-seek or swinging on the swing set. Tubs of beer and soda dotted the lawn, and in one corner of the backyard, a congregation of men was asleep on chaise lounges, having succumbed to too much food and beer. Father Bob stopped by, and I even spied Harry standing across the street. I couldn't persuade him to come into the yard, so I took him a hot dog and a hamburger, and he walked down the street eating double-fisted.

That night, we sat on a blanket in the cool grass on the river bank watching the fireworks. Jack held Bella in his lap and I held Elly, feeling the boom of the fireworks' explosions reverberating in her chest as well as my own. As if we hadn't had enough to eat all day, we gobbled popcorn and drank cold soda pop as we "oohed" and "aahed" over the fireworks' display and tried to identify our favorite burst of color. I felt sleepy and satisfied as I carried Elly to bed. Her face and hands covered in stickiness, and her body filthy from the joy of playing all day without having an adult's agenda impressed upon her.

It was one of the few times since we'd moved back to Middletown that I'd felt happy to be there. I'd enjoyed the day, being around people I wanted to be with and knowing that the majority of those people were there because they wanted to be with us and not only because of the free beer and food. I was thankful for our large home and our big yard. We'd had big parties in Chicago but had always felt cramped in our brownstone. I went to bed happy that we'd decided to come home and that we had made a success of living here.

Bang, bang, bang. I sat up in bed not sure if I'd actually heard someone knocking or if I'd dreamt it. It was the middle of the night, Sunday night. I looked at the alarm clock; technically, it was early Monday morning.

Bang, bang, bang.

I jumped as Jack reached out for my hand in the dark. I wasn't dreaming.

"Who the hell could that be at two in the morning?" he growled.

"I'll go see," I said, standing up to put on my robe.

"I'm coming with you. There's no way I'm letting you

answer the door alone at two A.M."

He went down the front steps to the front door, and I went down the back kitchen steps to the kitchen door, unable to decide at which door our early morning guest was knocking. I flipped on the kitchen light, and my heart jumped into my throat as I saw a face in the window of the back door. I called out to Jack that it was the backdoor, and I went to answer it. As I got closer, I could see it was Joe Campbell.

I let him in. He was apologetic for the late hour.

"I wanted to talk to you about why I wouldn't open the door for you Friday afternoon," he said. When he saw Jack, he clammed up. "Sheriff."

"Jack, this is Joe Campbell," I said.

"Yes, I remember you from the high school football games I've been at and of course, from that thing a few weeks ago at Rhianna Reese's," he said, shaking Joe's reluctant hand. "What can we do for you at two in the morning?"

"Well, I wanted to talk to Emily, but now I'm having second thoughts."

"Really, Joe. You come to my house at two in the morning for a chat, yet you don't think my husband will be here?" I said, realizing he wanted to talk about George but not in front of the Sheriff. He was here for a friendly chat, not a formal statement.

"Well, I . . ."

"You want to talk about George?" I prompted.

"Yes."

"But you don't want to make any sort of official statement?"

"Yes."

"I'll tell you what," Jack said, picking up where I left off. "You talk to us off the record with the understanding that if a formal statement is needed at any time as evidence against George that you will come down to the station and make one?"

Joe thought about it for a few seconds, and then agreed.

Joe and Jack sat down at the kitchen table while I shuffled around the kitchen making coffee.

It turned out that Joe was a treasure trove of information and had good reason to be wary of seeing the sheriff in an official capacity. He said the reason he wouldn't talk to me on Friday and the reason he came to the house in the middle of the night was that George had been watching him and had been calling Joe on his cellphone, threatening to kill him if he didn't keep quiet about George's affairs.

"I have never been afraid of George, even though I know enough about his life to put him behind bars for a long time. But I first started to worry after that scene in front of his house with Rhianna. I had never seen him act like that before. You have to understand that George held Rhianna in great esteem. It sounds corny, but in George's mind, Rhianna is the love of his life. Mara was more like George's beard, his cover that his life was normal. So to see him so angry with Rhianna and to treat her in such a threatening way was shocking. Then after Jessy Becker was killed, I started taking George's threats to heart. Jessy's death was a message to anyone who was thinking about unburdening his or her conscience to the police."

"Do you know for certain that George killed Jessy?" Jack asked.

"No, but I knew that George and Jessy had an ongoing relationship and that Jessy had recently defied George by talking to Emily," Joe said, motioning to me.

More importantly, he said that she had not only talked to me but had revealed important information about how George had controlled the girls he had seduced. Joe didn't know how George found out about my conversation with Jessy. He speculated that Jessy's rebellious streak had gotten the best of her, and when cornered by George, she'd told him everything just to spite him.

"How did you find all of this out?" I asked.

"At five o'clock the day that Jessy hit you," Joe explained, looking at me, "George called me and told me to turn on the T.V. to channel twelve. The local evening news' top story was about the car accident and Jessy's death. Then George said, 'Maybe people shouldn't go around telling the sheriff's wife about my love affairs and how I maintain them. Maybe everyone should keep their mouths shut.'"

My blood ran cold. Had I gotten Jessy killed? But as I started to blame myself, I stopped. Jessy made her own choices. I didn't force her to do anything. I felt suddenly angry that Joe was insinuating that I had something to do with Jessy's death.

I quickly turned that anger on him and asked, "So, what did George have on you? What role did you play in this twisted little group?"

Jack shot me a warning glance; I'm sure he was afraid my anger and judgmental tone would make Joe shut up. So I decided to sit back and watch a professional detective in action.

"My affair with Mara," he confessed, "but of course, that's no secret anymore. George and I both started teaching at Middletown High School on the same day. We had had a lot in common; we were both newly married and both fresh college graduates, starting our first teaching positions. It was only natural that we quickly became friends. I taught science and was also an assistant coach on the football team. Like George and Mara, Sandy and I had liked Middletown and decided to stay. The four of us used to do a lot together, but after we had our two kids and George and Mara remained childless, Sandy and Mara started drifting apart. Eventually, Sandy refused to socialize with George and Mara anymore because George continually made sexual advances toward her. George became obsessed with wife swapping," Joe paused for a moment, staring off past me into our darkened living room. He shook his head, and then continued, "Over time, I realized it wasn't so much that George wanted to be a swinger as much as he wanted to fulfill a sexual fantasy of watching Mara have sex with another man.

"After a while, Sandy forbad me to see George outside of school, but George found reasons for me to come over, such as needing my help with a home improvement project or with a car problem. Out of politeness and a sense of obligation to our friendship, I would come over and give him a hand. But when I would get there, Mara would be scantily clad and would make awkward sexual advances toward me.

"But the weird thing was, she was uncomfortable with it. I could tell by the way she moved and her wording. She wasn't attracted to me anymore than I was attracted to her. She was doing what George wanted her to." He rubbed his eyes. "I should have listened to Sandy and stayed away from them. But I didn't. I'd lie to her and say I was going to Gary's Bar to watch the game or some other such nonsense. I don't think Sandy was ever fooled. She didn't want to know."

Eventually, George wore him down. One evening after the two of them had spent the day drywalling in the Tierney's basement, Joe and George were relaxing with a beer. George pushed Joe to drink more and more until Joe was drunk beyond reason. Somehow, George finally convinced Joe to sleep with Mara.

"I must have blacked out because I don't even remember doing it, but I've seen the video several times, so I know I did," Joe said, hanging his head in his hands. "I felt sorry for her. I could tell from the recording that she didn't want to do it."

George had Joe right where he wanted him. He had proof that Joe had been unfaithful and threatened to show the video to Sandy if Joe didn't cooperate with George's demands. When George was interested in a girl at school, he would make it Joe's job to dig up the valuable dirt on the girl that would make her pliant to his seduction.

"I never slept with any of the girls. And I never saw George with them outside of anything that couldn't be explained as normal student-teacher contact, but when they started dying. . . At first, I told myself it was a coincidence that George had asked me to get information about Lori Landers, and six months later she jumped off a Ferris wheel, killing herself. Or that Bitsy Byers was missing and then turned up dead. But after a while, I couldn't delude myself any longer."

"Why didn't you come forward if you thought he was killing these girls?" Jack asked casually, careful not to push.

"I was covering my own ass. I felt culpable because I had given him information to entrap or seduce the girls. And I had my family to think of. If he was capable of killing these girls and making it look like suicide or an accident, what could he do to my children or to Sandy?"

"And by now you were in love with Mara Tierney; weren't you?" Jack prompted. I stared at him in disbelief. His honed police instincts had picked up on something that I had completely missed.

"Yes," Joe admitted. "When I would travel with the football team, she'd tell George she had out-of-town business for the insurance company. We'd meet at a motel. At first, we just talked. Later, we saw one another as a refuge against George's control."

"But you weren't really out of George's control," Jack offered.

"No. We did exactly what he wanted us to do. He had talked so much about watching Mara have sex with another man, but once it really happened, he became obsessed with how much time we spent together. He threatened us, and he began to beat Mara. I don't know for sure, but I think he was also forcing her to have sex with other women."

"How does Rhianna fit into all of this," I blurted.

"Rhianna and Jessy were George's favorites. Unlike the others, when the initial thrill of doing something forbidden, like sleeping with their teacher, was over and the true weirdness that was George became evident, the other girls wanted to stop seeing him. Some of the girls realized that they couldn't stop seeing George until *he* wanted the relationship to end. These girls eventually left town or went away to college. For one reason or another, shame or some bit of blackmail that he still held over them kept them silent. But some girls wanted to end their relationship with George and expose him for the predator he was, so he killed them. It's only speculation. I don't have any evidence. But Rhianna and Jessy both came from controlling backgrounds and were eager to rebel against their families. George was sort of a father figure to them at first, providing the affection and approval that they craved at home but weren't getting.

"At one point though, George's demands became even too twisted for Rhianna and she ran away. George hired a private investigator and was fixated on finding her. She had too much information and was too valuable to him. To her credit, it took the private eye two years to find her. Granted, the private eye was no Sam Spade, but when he did find her, George was charming and understanding—the father figure whom Rhianna had initially been attracted to. He told her she could stay in L.A. as long as she promised to keep their secret. However, the whole time he was trying to convince her that it was forgive-and-forget time, he was undermining her. I don't know the specifics of it, but he got her pregnant on purpose. After she found out she was pregnant, he wrote her charming letters promising to divorce Mara and marry her, but, of course, once she came back to Middletown, he never followed through. And then he had Andy to use against her."

"Do you know who killed Mara?" Jack asked.

"No. But I don't think Rhianna knew the fentanyl was in that bottle. If she were a killer, she wouldn't have stayed under George's control this long. I guess that's true for any one of us."

"Why would George tell Sandy about your affair with Mara?" I asked.

"To show me how much pain he could inflict on my life. That was only the tip of the iceberg. Again, it was all about control."

It was four A.M. when Joe left. I felt dizzy from lack of sleep and too much coffee too early in the morning. Jack and I both had to attend Rhianna's trial in four hours. Sleep was not going to come easily with what Joe had told us. It was incomprehensible to me how much control one person could exert over so many others. But in my mind, the people George controlled, with exception of the young, impressionable girls he'd seduced, were responsible for their own downfall. If Joe had listened to Sandy, he wouldn't have continued his relationship with George and never would have slept with Mara. To me, Joe was as sick as George. He had to have been getting some kind of thrill out of George's overtures, or he would have broken off their friendship like Sandy wanted.

"You're right," Jack said, when I brought this suggestion up to him. "I agree with you. Each person played a part in putting themselves under George's control."

"I'm surprised that George would even be interested in Sandy. It's not like she's a beauty. She is a good, kind woman, but what most people would describe as mousy. Come to think of it, Mara was sort of a plain Jane as well," I said.

"Think about it, Emmy. What would George's motives be for choosing women who weren't beautiful?"

"They'd be more likely to have poor self-esteem and be easier to control."

"Yes. People who seek to control other people don't choose victims who are strong and confident. George chose people he could easily intimidate; people he could easily break down to control, and build up to make them do what he wanted. It's typical abuser/codependent behavior."

I stared up at the ceiling above our bed and still couldn't understand how someone could allow another person to have that much control over them. Then I remembered a guy I had briefly dated during my sophomore year of college. It was during a time when I was feeling very alone, vulnerable, and unsure of myself. One night, he had too much to drink and wanted to have sex. We hadn't been dating that long, so I said no. When I refused, he punched me in the face. I ran away from him as fast as I could. My roommate urged me to have him arrested for assault. When he called to apologize and I refused to come crawling back, he threatened to kill me. His threat scared me, but I didn't think he would follow through. All the same, I hid out in my dorm room for several weeks until I heard through a mutual acquaintance that he'd flunked out and gone home. I should have gone to the police, which might have prevented some other woman from being hit, or worse, raped. I was just happy to have escaped.

But what if my vulnerability hadn't been a passing phase, and when challenged, I hadn't had a well of strength to draw from? Would I have complied like Mara, Rhianna, and Jessy had? I closed my eyes. *Who was I to pass judgment?*

CHAPTER 27

onday morning dawned on a town that was quite different from what it had been on Independence Day. It was as if the fireworks had blown the protective shell off the town, and now all the cockroaches were crawling in—the media. I'd never seen a media circus before, and the sleazy artistry of the news crews turned my stomach. I had been summoned to testify as a witness for the prosecution and was expected to be in court that morning. Jack and I rode together in his cruiser to the courthouse. He'd warned me before getting out of the car not to make any sort of statement. I figured the media hounds would go crazy for a statement from the sheriff, so I wasn't surprised when he had several microphones shoved into his face and reporters screaming questions at him. What shocked me were the amount of microphones pushed at me with questions like:

"Is it true that you and the accused are lovers?"

"Are you still taking care of her son?"

"Will you leave your husband?"

"Have you been misleading the Sheriff in his investigation in an effort to free your lover?"

The last question set me on fire. I kept a placid exterior and did what Jack had told me to do and kept my mouth shut—for once.

"Where do they get these questions?" I asked, incensed,

when we were safely inside the courthouse and away from the reporters.

"They come to town early and talk to the people in the coffee shops and stores. They look for any kind of gossip they can use to exploit a story."

"Obviously, my behavior hasn't been above reproach."

"Emily, all you did was stand by a friend in need. You can't be responsible for what others say and do. Don't start letting the gossip get to you now; this may be a long, drawn out trial."

"I can't believe this is such a big story. People are murdered everyday in big cities. There were stations from as far away as Chicago and Indianapolis out there."

"It's a big story because it happened in a small town. It's the *Sleepy Burg Touched by Murder* angle."

As a witness, I was sequestered in a small room adjacent to the courtroom with the other witnesses, Ruby Collins and Janney, until called to testify. We had been warned not to talk to one another, the thought being that we could taint one another's testimony, resulting in a false account of what happened. We were also being sequestered until after our testimony, so we wouldn't be swayed by something we heard in court or in the testimony someone else gave. Jack didn't have to be sequestered because his testimony was based on police facts, not an eyewitness account. I felt groggy due to our late-night visit from Joe Campbell and my eyes hurt. The glare from the fluorescent lights was merciless. I looked around at Ruby and Janney. Ruby looked her usual sallow, washed-out self, her unnatural red hair clashing with her bright fuchsia suit, a bad Chanel imitation. Janney's long brown hair was pulled back in a plaid headband that matched her blue and green Tartan plaid skirt. With her navy blue jacket and white blouse, she looked like a Catholic school girl. Her outfit and hair emphasized how young she was, but her brown eyes were old, like someone who'd already seen a lifetime's worth of pain.

Jack said that he figured Robert Price would save my testimony until after the other eyewitnesses. As Rhianna's friend, I was considered hostile. He also figured Price would use me to introduce other issues, such as motive and Rhianna's relationship with George. Price hadn't called me to go over my testimony like he had Janney and Ruby, probably because he did consider me hostile and wanted to see if he could trip me up on the stand. Therefore, I was startled when the bailiff called me as the first witness to testify. Immediately, I judged this as a tactical error on Price's part and felt a wash of relief rush over me as I considered for the first time that Robert Price's skills as a prosecutor may be as inept as his skills as a person.

When I entered the courtroom, I was suddenly nervous. The courtroom was standing-room-only with onlookers. Trying to calm myself, I looked for Jack in the place where he had sat during the arraignment. We made eye contact, and I felt my confidence recovering. When I took my oath to tell the truth and sat down in the witness chair, I looked across the short distance to the defendant's table at Rhianna. She looked uncomfortable in her well-tailored business suit. The suit must have been her lawyer's idea. Rhianna always wore bright purples and yellows, and never would have chosen the drab gray suit she now wore. I willed her to look up at me, but she sat resolutely staring at the blank legal pad in front of her.

I was so involved in my own thoughts that I was startled when Robert Price asked me to state my name and address. He began by asking me routine questions about what I did the day of the murder and what I saw. I matter-of-factly told him my version of the events up until I lost consciousness.

"Now, Mrs. Romano, you've testified that Miss Reese is your friend and fellow business owner, is that correct?" Robert Price asked.

"Yes."

"Isn't it true that your relationship is a bit more than just friends?"

"I've known Rhianna since we were kids. I took care of her son for a few weeks."

"Isn't it true that you and Miss Reese are lovers and that you intended to leave your husband for her?"

Before I could answer, Judge Lawrence banged his gavel so violently that I jumped in the witness seat. "The jury will disregard Mr. Price's last question, and it will be stricken from the record. Mr. Price, please approach the bench."

The Judge was so angry his face was an unhealthy reddish-purple. When Robert Price stepped over to the bench, the Judge spoke in a slightly lower voice than he'd used to strike the D.A.'s comments from the record. "Mr. Price, this is my courtroom and as long as I'm in charge here, you will not use it to get across your personal agenda. This is a place for facts and not for rumors, petty jealousies, and innuendo. Mrs. Romano is a good Christian woman. I'm not going to let you use my courtroom to malign the reputation of one of this town's more prominent and productive citizens. Now, you step over to the witness stand and apologize to Mrs. Romano or you will be in contempt."

Begrudgingly, Robert Price stepped in front of me and quietly apologized, so that I was the only one to hear. Then he bellowed out another question.

"Well, if you and Miss Reese were such good friends, did you know of any conflicts that she may have had with Mara Tierney?"

"No."

"Nothing between her and Mrs. Tierney's husband?"

"No."

"You mean to tell me that you and Miss Reese were such good friends that you mothered her child while she was in jail and while she was out on bond, but you didn't know of the trouble between her and the Tierney's regarding that child?"

"No, not until after she was arrested. And I did not mother Andy. I cared for him. Rhianna is his mother."

"So your *good* friend didn't confide in you?"

"Not until after Mara died. That is very personal information, and I don't hold it against her that she didn't tell me." With that comment, Rhianna looked up at me for the first time since I'd taken the witness stand.

"Answer 'yes' or 'no'," he instructed.

"No," I said. This was the part Jack had told me about, the part where Price brought in Rhianna's possible motives for killing Mara.

"So you know of no reason why Miss Reese would want to murder Mara Tierney?"

I looked at Rhianna's lawyer, thinking he should be objecting to this line of questioning since it called for me to speculate about Rhianna's possible motives, but he remained silent.

"No," I answered.

"Why do you think Miss Reese killed Mrs. Tierney?"

Again Mr. Jennings remained silent. Price was trying to trick me into revealing my doubt in her, so I said, "I don't think Rhianna killed Mara. Besides, if she wanted revenge, Rhianna could have done something far worse than give her an overdose."

"Oh," he said, intrigued that I could be revealing something valuable. "What could she have done that was worse than that?"

I looked around the room and could see that everyone was waiting for the juicy information I was about to dish. Jack looked worried, like I could be exacting my own revenge on Rhianna for being betrayed. Rhianna sat looking at the defense table. Mr. Jennings was thumbing through his notes.

"Well, Mr. Price, she could have given Mara a bad haircut. To some women, that's worse than death." The courtroom erupted in chuckles.

Suddenly, as if startled by the laughter, Mr. Jennings was on his feet and shouting, "Objection!" which made the gallery full of people laugh even harder.

The Judge let the gallery enjoy my joke at Mr. Price's expense. My comment so chagrined Robert Price that he said he had no more questions for me.

When the Judge asked him, Mr. Jennings declined cross-examination.

I sat down behind the defense table where Rhianna's parents should have been, but one look behind the prosecution's table told me they thought their daughter was guilty. I wondered what was up with Jennings; perhaps he wasn't as sharp as I had first thought he was.

I craned my neck looking around the courtroom for George, but he was nowhere to be seen. Jack had said George was scheduled to testify that afternoon about his relationship with Rhianna, so he might have been sequestered like the other witnesses had been. As I scanned the gallery, I saw the usual onlookers and gossips: Mrs. Carlson and her buddy Eileen Johnson as well as Althea Kent. In the back of the room, Joe Campbell caught my eye and gave me a small wave. I nodded and turned my attention back to Robert Price, who was now calling Ruby Collins as his next witness.

Ruby's version of the events was much like mine. It was pretty cut and dry—they were all talking, and then Rhianna was calling out Mara's name with no response. The part that held my interest was what Ruby said happened after I collapsed. She got tearful when she retold how Jack tried to resuscitate me and needed to give me several doses of narcan.

"The sheriff was determined to save his wife's life. He is a kind and generous man who truly loves his wife," she told the jury, whereupon Price asked the Judge to strike the witness's "sentimental comments" from the record since they did not pertain to the facts of the case. I looked over at Jack and winked. I could have sworn he was blushing, but with his dark complexion, it was difficult to tell.

Since Ruby had no further testimony and Jennings wasn't interested in questioning her either, she was dismissed from the stand and Janney was called. Again, Janney gave a similar account of the events that day.

"I had just cut Mrs. Collins's hair and was preparing to dye it when Rhianna lifted the dryer from Mara's head," Janney said. From somewhere behind me, I heard Ruby Collins let out a small gasp as Janney revealed her secret—that she dyes her hair. I turned to see her dabbing her forehead with a fuchsia hankie that matched her suit. "Rhianna was calling her name, but Mara was slumped in the chair with her head lulled back," Janney recounted.

"And then what happened?" Price asked.

"Rhianna backed away from her, knocking over the curler caddy again."

"Yes, what next?" he prodded.

"That's when Emily came out of the back room and began attending to her."

"And what was everyone else doing?"

"We were standing there watching. I think we were all in shock. Then Emily said she wasn't breathing and to call an ambulance."

"Anything else?"

"Emily asked for a towel. She said that there was something on Mara's head that was burning her hand. After a few minutes, the paramedics arrived. They gave her several doses of narcan and shocked her, but there was no response. The paramedics loaded her onto the gurney and took her to the ambulance, but it was pretty clear she was dead. And then, Emily collapsed and the sheriff began trying to revive her."

"And was he successful?" Price asked.

"Well, she's sitting right over there isn't she?" Janney said. The courtroom again broke out in laughter at Robert Price's expense.

"Let me rephrase the question," he said after the laughter had died out. "Was Sheriff Romano able to revive his wife at the scene?"

"No. She had to be taken to the hospital. I understand that they had to give her a shot to the heart to revive her."

"Objection, hearsay," Mr. Jennings said. Maybe his coffee had finally kicked in, I thought.

"Sustained. Miss Dickens, please keep your comments to events that you witnessed," Judge Lawrence told her.

"I have no further questions, Your Honor," Price said.

Jennings asked Janney a few questions about how long she had worked for Rhianna and about routine practices around the beauty shop, but nothing that I felt added to her testimony in any significant way.

After Janney's testimony, the Judge called a two hour recess for lunch. Jack had to take Rhianna back to the jail for lunch although I doubted she would eat anything. I tried to sneak past the reporters, but they were waiting at every exit. As I made my way through the crowd, wondering if they would follow me to the store, Jack brought Rhianna out to the patrol car and the reporters left me like yesterday's news. I walked across the street to the store and filled Madeleine and Harry in on the testimony. Something was bothering me about the testimony that I'd heard. I couldn't identify what was out of place, but something was. I had that feeling again, that itch I couldn't scratch.

Madeleine volunteered to go across the square and get us a pizza at Dancing Dave's. As soon as she'd left, I sat next to Harry on the sofa and began to ruminate about what was bothering me.

"Harry, something's not right. Someone said something today at the trial that didn't mesh with my memory of the events." I thought maybe if I talked out loud long enough that I'd figure it out. "Ruby Collins said pretty much the same thing I did. That one minute they were all talking and the next minute Mara was dead.

"Janney had the same recollection. They were all talking, and then Rhianna was backing away from Mara . . . knocking over her curler caddy." I sat next to Harry, silently going over the testimony. "Wait, she didn't just say that Rhianna knocked over the curler caddy; she said Rhianna knocked it over *again*. The curler caddy must have been knocked over the first time when Janney and Mara were scuffling.

"I can see why that stuck in her mind. Whenever something hits the floor, they have to rewash it because of health codes. I remember hearing water running right before Mara collapsed. Rhianna must have been rewashing the curlers from when it was knocked over during Janney's scuffle with Mara."

But then my excitement faded. So what? The curler caddy got knocked over twice. There had to be more to it than that. I stood up and began pacing back and forth. I felt like Sherlock Holmes on the mental trail of the conclusion to a mystery. I remembered how Holmes would pace in his Baker Street apartment, puffing on his pipe as if stoking his brain.

"You got a cigarette, Harry?" I asked in desperation. "No, you don't smoke; do you?"

He shook his head.

"Wait. I still have some hidden in the backroom," I said, going to retrieve them. As I did so, I heard Harry go into the bathroom off the main part of the store.

I found the cigarettes in the bottom of a roll of paper towels. As I was lighting the cigarette, I got lost in my own thoughts and let the match burn down too far, singeing my fingers. I dropped the match and the cigarette onto the vinyl floor, making a burn hole.

"That's it," I yelled as I stamped them both out.

Janney said in her testimony that I had asked for a towel because the solution on Mara's head was burning my hand. I didn't say that at all. I only asked for a towel. I didn't take the time to explain why I wanted it; a woman's life was at stake. I had never shared with anyone but Jack and Brett Bradley, when he took my statement about Mara's death, the details of my attempt to resuscitate Mara. Sure, I'd questioned everyone else, but I'd never shared my side of the story.

So, how did Janney know that the solution was burning my hand? She wouldn't have known unless she knew what was in the bottle and what its effects were. The analysis of the perm solution revealed that the bottle contained mostly rubbing alcohol, water, and enough fentanyl to kill a horse. The last part might be a slight exaggeration but only a slight one. Everything clicked together so fast that I thought I physically felt the tumblers in my brain fall into place. Click, click, click. I plunked down in my desk chair and dialed the landline phone, calling Jack's cellphone. I swiveled around, facing the wall and perused the bulletin board where I kept important information tacked up while I waited for Jack to answer.

"Romano."

"Jack, get over to the bookstore right away."

"What's wrong?"

"I know who killed . . ." The phone went dead. I swiveled

back around to check out the phone and came face-to-face with the barrel of a gun. On the other end was Janney.

"That was stupid. You know he's going to come over here," I said.

"Shut up! You couldn't keep your nose out of things. You couldn't let Rhianna take the fall," Janney said.

"Why should I let an innocent person go to jail?"

"She's not so innocent."

"Shut up and get out here," another woman yelled from the front of the store.

Who was with her? I wondered. The voice was familiar, but I couldn't place it. Janney waved the gun in the direction of the store, and I followed the wave.

"Mrs. Kent," I said, when I saw the owner of the voice. "What is this all about? Did you two plan this together?" I was terrified, but my curiosity was piqued. Perhaps Janney was right, and I couldn't keep my nose out of things.

"Well, it was my idea," Althea Kent said, "but I knew Janney would help me after what those people have put her through."

"What people? Rhianna? Mara Tierney?"

"Yeah, among others," she said.

"So, your motive for killing Mara was that she wouldn't pay the death benefits on your daughter's life insurance, and you, Janney, murdered Mara because she fired your mother, taking away her health coverage?"

"Those are small time reasons compared to what they really did to us, to our families," Althea explained. "George Tierney killed Anita. He gave her that stuff that made her feel like she was flying. Then he put her on the roof of the school because she was going to go to the police and tell them about how he liked to seduce his female students."

My stomach clenched. All the evidence that I'd found had

pointed to this, but to hear it confirmed made it even more sickening. To think of all those years he fooled everyone; I thought I was going to vomit.

I gulped hard, and asked, "How do you know what you're saying is true?"

"Because he told me," Janney said, "When George tried to seduce me, I threatened to tell. He told me what he'd done to Anita because he knew she was my second cousin. Then to show me how much power he had over my life, he made Mara fire my mother. You know what happened after that. After my mother died, I went to Althea. *Together,* we came up with the plan to kill Mara and make it look like Rhianna did it."

"But what does Rhianna have to do with this?"

"She's been helping George seduce and blackmail girls since she was in high school," Althea said. "She's as evil as he is."

"Why didn't you go to the police if you knew all this about George?"

"What proof did we have? It was our word against his. This was much simpler," Althea explained.

Murder was the simplest option? I wondered. I didn't understand the twisted logic the two of them had used to justify murdering another human being. But I did know that grief could drive people to do all kinds of destructive and unhealthy things, even murder.

"We knew that if we killed Mara we'd be taking care of two birds with one stone," Janney added. "We knew that either he or Rhianna would be accused of the murder, and we made the evidence against Rhianna so convincing we were certain she'd be convicted. But we also knew that once the spotlight was focused on Rhianna and George that someone would rat them out, which Jessy Becker did when she talked to you that day. And the next day, she was dead."

"George killed her," I said.

"Bingo," chimed in Althea.

"So that day at the beauty shop, Janney started a fight with Mara and knocked over the curler caddy. While you," I said to Althea, "Rhianna, and Mara were picking up curlers, Janney switched the perm solutions. There were no fingerprints because Janney was already wearing latex gloves since she was preparing the dye for Ruby Collins's hair."

"See, I told you she'd figure it out," Althea said, reproaching Janney. "I saw your face when Janney was on the witness stand. I knew you'd heard something that didn't fit. That day you came poking around the dairy I tried to give you clues that would lead you to Tierney, but you kept on trying to prove Rhianna was innocent."

"I'm stubborn," I said. Then I remembered something, and said to Janney, "You took my notebook."

"Yeah. I saw the way you were always writing in it and then hiding it whenever someone came around, so I figured it had something important in it. All your theories about the murder were written in it. I was surprised that you had considered me and Althea as suspects. We thought we'd be the least likely suspects."

"It's always the least likely suspects you have to look out for," I said. Turning to Althea, I said, "You must be the brains of the operation, and Janney, here, is the brawn, since she switched the perm solutions and now she's the one holding the gun. Tell me, how do you think you're going to get away with shooting me? Are you planning to make it look like a robbery? Janney, you know my husband will be here any minute." Just then, the front door rattled. Apparently, they had locked it behind them and put up the closed sign. It was Madeleine, holding the pizza.

"You better let her in. She has a key anyway, and I'd hate to see her drop the pizza and ruin it," I said. I was trying to remain calm, but my insides felt like Santa's belly—they were shaking like a bowl full of jelly.

Janney opened the door for Madeleine.

"Why'd you close the store?" Madeleine asked as Janney was sticking the gun in her face. "Oh."

"Guess what? I figured out who killed Mara Tierney," I quipped. "You're just in time to help Althea and Janney here figure out how they're going to get away with shooting me —and now you." As I said this, Harry stepped out of the bathroom and stood next to me. He didn't seem surprised by the scene he'd stepped into, so I guessed that he'd been listening at the door. I'd forgotten he was in there. Funny how having a gun pointed at you affects your short term memory. "And now Harry." I said, adding his name to the list of possible victims. "You might as well give up. Jack will be here soon with back up, too."

"She's right," said Jack, as he stepped out of the backroom, aiming his gun at Janney. Janney started to move her gun toward him.

"I wouldn't do that if I were you," I advised her. "You point a gun at a police officer and he'll shoot you." I looked at Janney in her Catholic schoolgirl outfit and thought of the waste of potential. Now, she was going to spend the rest of her life in prison.

She must have realized what I was thinking. I saw something flashy in her eyes, a moment of recognition, of desperation. It was only a flicker that lasted no longer than half a second but felt like it lasted forever. I felt myself falling as I heard two nearly simultaneous gun shots. I fell to the floor in what seemed like slow motion. Then, I scampered behind a chair near the mystery section.

"Emily? Are you all right?" I heard Jack yell from across the room.

I sat up in my spot on the floor and patted my body, no holes. "Yes," I responded, peering over the top of the chair and looking around. Jack and Althea were the only people I saw standing. There were only two shots fired. *Where was everyone else?* Then I saw the pool of blood on the floor. I followed the blood to where Harry laid a few feet away.

Suddenly, recollection came rushing back at me. After that flash in Janney's eyes, she had shot at me and Jack had shot at her. Harry pushed me to the floor and had taken the bullet that Janney had intended for me. He had seen the look in her eyes, too, and he'd pushed me out of harm's way.

"Jack! Harry's been shot," I screamed. I crawled over to his body and pressed my hand over his upper left chest where blood was spurting out in intervals: an artery. "Harry, oh Harry. What have you done?"

His eyes were glassy as he looked up at me. He put a hand on my cheek, smearing it with blood, and pulled me toward him.

"Someone," he whispered, "someone . . . watching."

And then the surging blood slowed.

"Emily, he's gone," Jack said quietly.

"No, no, no, no," I wailed, taking Harry into my arms.

CHAPTER 28

A fter the paramedics took away Harry's and Janney's bodies, I put together what had happened. Jack and Harry had both seen the look in Janney's eyes and recognized the desperation there. Jack shot to kill and Harry leapt to save. Althea didn't even put up a fight when she saw that Jack hadn't hesitated to shoot a nineteen-year-old girl who was pointing a gun at his wife. Jack found Madeleine curled in the fetal position behind a table of books; the ruined pizza face down on the floor next to her. The paramedics took her to the hospital to be treated for shock. I couldn't help but wonder if she thought about her parents. I also wondered what effect her past would have on her after witnessing first-hand two people being shot dead.

The gun shots drew the media to the bookstore, and there were pictures of Jack escorting me out of the store to his police cruiser plastered all over the news that evening. Every picture was the same: Jack with both arms encircling me, trying to protect me from the prying media, and me, walking next to him, stone-faced and stunned. My white cotton shirt was so saturated with blood that it looked like it was a rusty-brown. Over the following weeks, that picture of my bloodstained shirt and stone-still face would be used to demonize me and turn me into the meddlesome gossip who had interfered with a police investigation to bring myself notoriety, or so an unnamed Sheriff's Department source said. It wasn't too hard to figure out who the "unnamed source" might be. Though

Jack could never prove it, Robert Price and Brett Bradley clued the media on to how I had insinuated myself into the investigation into Mara's murder. They used me as a political tool to cast doubts on Jack's abilities as a sheriff—just as Jack had tried to warn me that they would do.

The store was closed for a week while the police collected evidence, and all of the blood was cleaned up. I was relieved to have the time off; I wasn't sure if I could ever go back into the store that I loved so much because now it held such painful memories. I hoped I wouldn't lose Madeleine as an employee and as a friend. She'd been through so much with her parents' murder that I wasn't sure she could take what had happened. I felt like trouble had been following me, but maybe it was trouble I had created for myself.

The murder charges against Rhianna were dropped, but once Althea Kent began her confession, new charges were filed against Rhianna for concealing a crime and for corrupting minors, among others. However, the charges against her were pled down to a lesser charge for her testimony against George. She was given five years probation, which she immediately violated after George's trial when she disappeared from the state. I never heard from her or Andy again. I can only assume that wherever she is she's with Andy and Reba. George was arrested for murder, statutory rape, aggravated sexual assault, fraud, distributing drugs to minors, corrupting minors, and child pornography, to name a few.

After I found everything out about the circumstances Rhianna was living under, I could no longer judge her and feel self-righteous about the fact that I'd been a true friend to her and she hadn't reciprocated. She had been under George's thumb since she was sixteen years old. By the time of Mara's murder, he'd convinced her that if she ever left him (again) or betrayed him, he'd kill her and Andy. She'd gone from being controlled by her family to being controlled by George. When George had tracked her down in Los Angeles, he told her that if she didn't come back to Middletown, he'd kill Reba, who was a student of his at the time. Getting her pregnant was just extra insurance to make sure she came back. When I returned to town and she learned that Jack was in law enforcement, she had reignited our childhood friendship to keep George wary of following through with his threats, which was also why she chose me as Andy's guardian. She knew George would never try to hurt or take Andy if he was living in the sheriff's house. I also realized that Rhianna, Annie, had protected me from George when I was in high school. George had shown an interest in me, but Rhianna had convinced him that I was not a good target. I suppose protecting Andy from George was some small payment for Rhianna's sacrifice on my behalf.

George had not acted alone all those years, but his other accomplices were all dead. Joe confirmed that in his official statement, which he made as he'd promised Jack he would (and which got him eighteen months behind bars for failure to report a crime and helping to corrupt minors). Mara had been as much under George's control as all the others. She had succeeded in her position at Midwestern Mutual because George wanted her to. The more power she obtained at work and the more confidence she gained in that realm the harder George had to work to keep her pliant at home.

Perhaps George used herbal drugs to keep her under his control like he did with the girls whom he seduced and brought into their sick circle. George knew that if he had hooked the girls on illegal drugs that would have drawn attention, more parental questions, and police investigations. Because of all the dirt he had on them, some of the girls, like Bitsy Byers and Julie Conners, had actually died by suicide.

Jessy had been one of the girls he'd liked and had kept under his control, like Rhianna, for several years. After Jessy returned home from college, which she'd attended with the help of a scholarship from you-know-who, she helped George and Mara in their twisted games.

As for Mara, I never found out why she stayed with George and helped him all of those years. Maybe she liked it. Maybe that was how she got her kicks. Or maybe it was like Jessy and Joe had said: Mara was in so deep that she figured this was her life and there was nothing she could do about it. After all, Jessy had been right about Mara's murder unraveling George's carefully constructed web of deceit.

One of the many sad stories that came out of Jack's investigation into George and Mara's background was that Mara's family didn't know anything about her death. George lied when he told me they hadn't cared. They had cared very much. Mara's two brothers hadn't heard from or seen Mara in ten years because George had isolated her from them so he could maintain control over her. Mara's family made arrangements for her body to be moved to Iowa, where they all lived. She was buried next to her mother, who had died five years earlier, never knowing or understanding why her only daughter had cut ties with her family.

Two days after the incident at the bookstore, a tall, proud woman in her mid-sixties with kind blue eyes came to see me at home. It was Harry's daughter, Isabella. She told me her mother, who had died eight years ago, had told her Harry was dead, so she'd never gone looking for him. A few months before Harry died, he had given Father Bob a letter to be opened upon his death. In the letter, he told Father Bob where to find his daughter and also gave instructions for his funeral. Isabella said she found a letter addressed to me on his bedside table, which he was probably planning to send me. Father Bob told her who I was and how I'd befriended her father in the last months of his life.

I felt sorry for Isabella. She was a nice woman, and it wasn't right that her mother had stolen Isabella's chance to get to know her father. Isabella told me the funeral would be the next day and that she wanted me to give the eulogy for her father since I'd known him best in his last days. She hoped it wouldn't be too short of notice. I told her I would, although I had no idea what I was going to say. Harry had spoken to me twice and both times were as he was saving my life. When he rescued me from the car accident he said, "You have to get out." The next time were his dying words—"someone watching." I still don't know what he was trying to tell me.

After she left, I went to the window seat in my bedroom and read Harry's letter to me:

Dearest Emily,

As you have figured out by now, I am a man of few words. A long time ago, I found it unessential to talk to people. I first stopped talking to my wife because she didn't understand, couldn't understand, what I'd gone through in Korea. Whenever I wanted to talk about the horror I had seen there and the friends I had held in my arms as they died, she would turn away and tell me that was all in the past. After a while, I figured if she didn't want to talk about what had been the most important event of my life, I didn't want to talk to her at all. As a result, she left me and took my daughter with her. Isabella was about the age of your little Arabella the last time I saw her. Now, she thinks I'm dead. I guess after all these years it's best that it stays that way.

After my wife left, I stopped talking to everyone. The only time I speak now is during confession. Eventually, I found that most people weren't worthy of the breath it took to speak to them anyway. If you didn't look or act a certain way, they assumed you were a bum or not right in the head. They treated me like I was invisible. I let them continue to think that because it made my life easier. I wasn't inclined to talk to anyone—until I met you. When you opened your bookstore, I knew you were different. You were trying to bring something new and useful to this dead and useless community. I would see you in church with your husband and your daughters, and I could tell that your heart was good and earnest. When you came over to me and gave me a cup of coffee, that was the first time someone who wasn't a priest had spoken kindly to me in thirty-five years. And what you had to say, that the people in this town were more of a threat to you than I was, was the way I'd felt for all these years. I knew you were someone I should get to know.

But the reason I'm writing to you now and why I sit in your store everyday and on the bench across from it isn't because I wanted to meet you but because you are in danger. Someone is watching you. I've seen them watching your house and watching your store. I think I've even seen them following your car. I don't know who they are or if it is more than one person because they are often disguised, but I wanted to warn you to be careful. Be on the lookout. You are precious and you need to take care of yourself, so you can continue to be the only bright spot in my life. You also need to take care of those wonderful girls of yours. Be there for them like I never could be for Isabella.

You are like a daughter to me even though I've only known you for a few months. I have to tell you that your words to me about laying down the burden I've been carrying has done more healing in my life than any priest ever did during absolution. They have only forgiven me in the name of God, whereas you told me to forgive myself, for me.

Devotedly yours,

Harry

An hour later, Jack found me still sobbing in the same spot I'd sat down to read Harry's letter. After I let him read the letter, a few tears slid down his cheeks as well.

"Jack, he saved my life twice. Now, he's gone, and I can't repay him."

"Emily, he did what he wanted to do. He died in the most honorable way possible. 'There's no greater love than to lay down one's life for a friend,'" he said, paraphrasing a New Testament verse. "Maybe saving your life helped him put to rest some guilt he may have felt over living through Korea when so many of his friends hadn't."

"He was watching over me. I bet it was him that I saw that night out the window as I sat here. Remember? If he was looking out for me at work, why wouldn't he watch over the house at night? What do you make of the warning he gave me?"

"He probably noticed George and some of the others snooping around and was afraid for you. Turns out he was right to be worried."

Thinking back over the past couple of months, I said, "Jack, I still can't understand why Janney pulled the trigger."

"I've seen it happen before. Someone finds themselves in a situation they can't get out of with consequences they can't face, so they decide to commit suicide by cop. It happens all the time, especially in stand-offs. Someone waves a gun around or shoots a hostage so the police are forced to shoot to kill," he explained.

Suddenly, Jack's face crumpled with pain as he said, "I don't know what I would have done if Harry hadn't pushed you out of the way. We'd be going to your funeral tomorrow instead of his."

I held him in my arms, trying to comfort us both. "I sure have needed a lot of rescuing in my life," I said in his ear. "But if I hadn't, we may have never met since you rescued me from that mugger."

Still holding on to me, he replied, "He was the one who needed rescuing. You gave him a pretty good beating. Don't sell yourself short. You can take care of yourself."

"Jack," I whispered, "would you have still married me if you'd known how much trouble I was going to be?"

He pulled away from me studying my face, trying to figure out if this was another one of my lame attempts at humor to elevate an all too serious mood. When he saw that I was sincere, he cupped my face in both of his hands and said, "In a minute. I'd do it all again, without a thought."

I went to my desk in the den to put together some thoughts about Harry. Miss Bette wrote a very nice story for the front page of the paper lauding Harry as a hero. She detailed the medals he'd received as a Marine in Korea and recounted how he'd saved my life twice. She'd also revealed something no one else knew but her: Harry was a published author. I even had some of his books in my store. He'd written a series of books about a group of Marine Corps buddies and their exploits during the Korean War entitled *Green was Their Blood*. His nom de plume had been Jake Isabell; even then he'd been thinking about his daughter. I wondered if they were autobiographical. I looked forward to reading his books, but I couldn't bring myself to go back to the store yet and get one.

As I wrote my notes for the eulogy and thought about how Harry had died protecting me, I still felt that he was looking after me in some way. Then I knew the best way to honor him.

St. Michael's Catholic Church was filled to capacity the next morning. Miss Bette's article had drawn in a lot of people. Some were there as curious onlookers. Others felt they'd missed a chance to get to know a fine member of their community by passing Harry every day on the street and never acknowledging his presence, which is exactly the bent that Father Bob put on his homily for Harry's funeral Mass. He said the people of Middletown not only missed getting to know Harry, but also missed the face of Christ in their fellow human beings. The community had shunned him because he was different, just as Jesus had been shunned by non-believers. He told them that if any of them had taken the time to get to know

Harry, as I had (he named me as Harry's only friend), they would have found a deeply sensitive man who had separated himself from the rest of the community out of pain. He reminded them that they could have eased his pain if any one of them had reached out to him like I had.

After Father Bob finished speaking, a guilty silence hung in the air. As I stepped up to the lectern, no one but my family, Madeleine, and Harry's daughter, Isabella, made eye contact with me.

"Father Bob gives me too much credit. Harry made his choices in life; they were hard choices that cost him dearly. They cost him his daughter, and eventually, they cost him his life. I am grateful beyond any words I could ever express that Harry made the choices he did because his choices saved my life not once but twice. His choices gave me the chance to see my daughters grow up, to live my life with my wonderful husband, to be a better daughter to my parents, and to enjoy the friendship of those who reach out to me. I hope I can earn the gift Harry has given me and that I can live a good life that will be a tribute to his gift.

"Isabella asked me to speak today about her father. But there isn't much I can tell you about Harry. He only spoke to me twice and both times were as he was saving my life. I'm sorry that I will never get to know what an extraordinary person he must have been and that I will never get to talk to him about his books. The only thing I know for sure about Harry is that he was my guardian angel; he watched over me. The only appropriate tribute I can think to give him is to ask each of you to look on your loved ones, your friends, and your fellow townspeople with kindness and compassion. God touches us in the unlikeliest of ways, and if we cut ourselves off from someone because we judge them to be different or flawed, we are cutting ourselves off from God himself. While we are judging others for their flaws, we should look carefully at ourselves because the traits we hate in others are the same traits we hate in ourselves. We never know what struggles others are dealing with in their lives. You never know when the person you are shunning could be the very person who saves you."

Later that night, I was lying in bed next to Jack, thanking God for the privilege of being there. I had meant what I'd said in my eulogy about trying to live my life to honor the gift Harry had given me: my life in exchange for his. I was thinking about what people had been saying about me: that I'd interfered with the murder investigation and put myself in danger for attention. At some level, I felt guilty and wondered if they were right. *How had my involvement in investigating Mara's murder affected the chain of events that unfolded?* If I hadn't gotten involved, then maybe Janney wouldn't be dead and her brother would still have her to take care of him instead of being sent to Kansas to live with an aunt he barely knew. But then I thought about how Janney chose the path that led her to my bookstore holding a gun—pointed at my head no less. How could she do that to someone who had tried to help her? At any moment, she could have chosen a different path. I had nothing to do with the choices she made.

Then I thought how if I hadn't been involved in this mess then Harry wouldn't be dead right now. But I might have never gotten to know him if I hadn't been involved in the investigation. If I had sat back and let the events fall like so many leaves from a tree, would George ever have been brought to justice? Would Rhianna have gone to prison for the rest of her life for a crime she didn't commit? Either way I flipped the coin, something negative would have happened because every action has a consequence. Only chaos had come from these events, and no matter what had happened and in whatever order they happened, things were always going to end badly. Even though these events had brought chaos, order and normality would eventually be restored. To have order, there must also be chaos. There was no point in second guessing how it all had turned out.

I had left Middletown because I wanted to be the narrator of my own story. Live my life on my terms. Harry showed me that I didn't have to leave to live the way I wanted to live. He'd been telling his own story for years simply by *not* telling it. So my story was actually that I'm like everyone else in this town—I was more than what you saw on the surface and not everything that you thought I was. I wasn't better than the rest of them—just different, just me.

One thing I knew for certain was that I hadn't had a craving for cigarettes since I burned my fingers on that match. That's something else I could thank Harry for. I had finally quit smoking. . . Smoking.

I sat up in bed and shook Jack awake.

"Jack!"

"What? I was sleeping. What's wrong?" he said. He was finally getting back to feeling like he could be annoyed with me again.

"Jack, the night I saw someone standing under the blue spruce tree in the Jensen's front yard. . ."

"Yeah. What about it?"

"It couldn't have been Harry. Harry didn't smoke."

ACKNOWLEDGEMENTS

When I read a book, I always read the acknowledgements because the author alone did not accomplish the work. There are always people in the background making the final product possible. Like all who came before me, I did not write this book in a vacuum. The journey to publishing this book has literally taken my middle daughter Katy's lifetime. I started writing this book when she was about three years old. I would sit down to write while she napped and her older sister, Madeleine, was at school. Her younger sister, Trinity, was not born yet. Katy is now twenty-five and is a writer too. Like any journey, there were twists and turns in the road that slowed my progress. There were stops along the way where I was not working on the book or writing at all. Finally, I decided to stop letting others hold me back so that, like Emily, I could take control of where the journey ended.

There are many people who encouraged me along the way. First, I have to thank my sixth grade teacher, Mrs. Mattox, who first recognized I had a talent for writing. Another teacher I have to thank is Mr. Larry Pulleyblank, my high school English teacher, and definitely <u>NOT</u> the inspiration for George Tierney. Pulley encouraged me to follow my dreams, and he always seemed to appreciate my humor. Rachel Smith was one of my first readers when we were young mothers together. Holly Deiaco-Smith has always been my champion. Over the years,

Holly has checked in to see where I am in getting my novel published. I send her random texts asking her opinion about the title or an update on what I am doing with the book. Carol and Paul Cutjar also read an early draft way back when. Marc Faulk helped me put together my first website and blog, spending his lunch hours at my house discussing how to best display my work. We encouraged one another for many years. Marc is a talented artist and comic book writer. Thank you to Jennah Bryant who designed my beautiful cover, and Toni Dengel who took my author's photograph.

I have to thank Mikhail Smith and Erin Rice for giving me the push I needed to establish a daily writing habit that helped me speed to the finish line. Heather Cantrell, Ginny Young, Wendi Bennett, and Julie Buckler, my cheering section. Janet Stewart, one of my many librarian friends, read the final draft and gave her stamp of approval. A librarian's approval is gold, in my opinion. Of course, I have to thank my parents, Glenn and Pam Heckler. I wish daddy was here to see the finished product.

Finally, my husband, Matthew Todt, who has been my partner in crime for the past thirty-six years. His has been the steady hand on my back gently pushing me forward, always believing in me. Thank you for spending your life with me. Thank you to Madeleine, Katy, and Trinity, my amazing daughters and the accomplishments I am most proud of, your support means everything to me.

ABOUT THE AUTHOR

Glenna Heckler-Todt

Glenna Heckler-Todt wrote her first book in the third grade and has dreamed of being a novelist since she was twelve years old. Famous among her friends and family for her wit, wisdom, and red hair, Glenna, an Illinois native, currently lives in Southern Ohio with her husband of over thirty years, one of her Trinity of magnificent daughters, and her two dogs. A blogger for many years on topics ranging from motherhood to politics, Permanent Death is Glenna's first published novel. A sequel to Permanent Death is on the horizon.

www.ingramcontent.com/pod-product-compliance
Lightning Source LLC
Chambersburg PA
CBHW030155200626
46812CB00017B/2068